Necromancer Falling

Nat Russo

AUTHOR OF #1 AMAZON BESTSELLER NECROMANCER AWAKENING

Praise for *Necromancer Awakening*

"Mind-blowingly good."

Nicholas Rossis, #1 Bestselling Author of the epic fantasy series *Pearseus*.

"Best book I've read this year. Nat Russo could turn into my favorite author."

Phillip Ferriera, Owner of ReviewBoard.Com

"Necromancer Awakening by Nat Russo is one of the finest examples of fantasy genre fiction I have ever seen. I started to say, "seen in a long time," but the qualifier isn't applicable, since Russo is well able to hold his own among such lights as Martin, Gaiman and Gabaldon."

C. L. Roman, Editor, Brass Rag Press

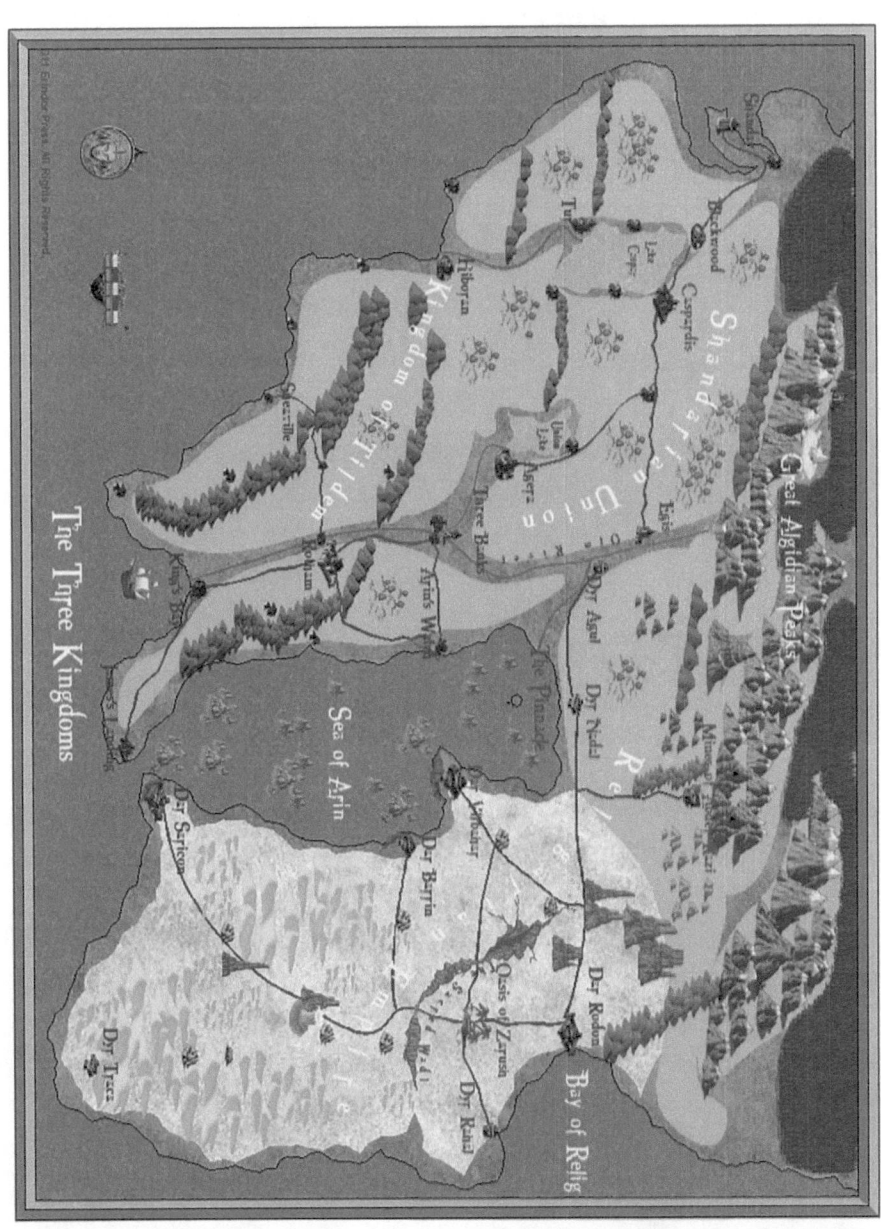

The Three Kingdoms

Copyright © 2016 by Nat Russo
All rights reserved.

Published by Erindor Press
www.erindorpress.com

ISBN: 0-9960059-2-7
ISBN-13: 978-0-9960059-2-0

Cover Art and Design:
Atanas Stoykov

ACKNOWLEDGMENTS

Book 2 of a trilogy is always a tough one. It's the middle section of a larger, overarching story, yet it has to be a story unto itself. Necromancer Falling was no different. It wouldn't have been possible without an army of people.

I have to point the first finger at Joan Reginaldo and say "Thank you for making me a better writer." I can always count on her honesty and objectivity, and it remains an ingredient of incalculable value in the spell I weave to create Erindor and its inhabitants.

My colleagues in software engineering, John Boyd, Ian Mitchell, and Adam Takvam. Thank you for humoring me and allowing me to spend time talking about my crazy stories when I (we all) should be working.

I'd like to offer a special thank you to David Steiniger, another colleague of mine, who also happens to be a subject matter expert in firearms of all shapes and sizes. No, you don't understand. David travels to historical reenactments all over the place with a collection of antique firearms you wouldn't believe! David spent a lot of time chatting with me about matchlocks, flintlocks, and others I can't even pronounce, all in the name of getting the details right. Those details brought many scenes to life that otherwise would have been missing that special *something*.

Erindor wouldn't have the depth it has today without the input of my good friend and fellow necromancer, Joe Smithey. Not only is he responsible for Nuuan, he also taught me a thing or two about *shrillers*. I'll keep bugging him to write that shriller-centric novel he keeps talking about.

I would be remiss if I didn't mention my lifelong friend and "brother from another mother", Mike D'Onofrio. Mike and I have known each other since elementary school. He created the original *Aelron* character in EverQuest (full name: Aelron Addonis). He was a vital member of our *Enchanted Circle* guild, and I gleefully bastardized his character for my own purposes.

My beta readers; Julia Byers, Raymond Clarke, Michelle Dalson, Katie Drake, Ken Hughes, JC Steel, Ian Tennant, and Thomas Weaver. Thank you all so much for time and input.

Lastly, I simply cannot do this without the support of my family. This may come as a surprise, but most writers have day jobs to pay the bills. My family happily allows me to spend my "off" time writing crazy stories and swearing at my laptop.

For Casi, Nic, Toby, and Bowie.

CHAPTER ONE

¹*In the days before the Foundation; in the days before days...*

²*The Power emerged from the darkness and gave life to the multiverse.* ³*But life was not in its proper place, and chaos reigned.* ⁴*Chaos created a seed of wickedness and planted it next to the Tree of Life.* ⁵*The seed took root and grew alongside life, becoming one with The Power's gift.*
- *The Mukhtaar Chronicles, attributed to the prophet Habakku*
Origines Multiversi, Emergentiae 1:1-5

Chaos is mentioned several times in the Origines as a being separate from The Power, and seemingly equal in divinity. Ancient theologians put forth the notion of two creator gods. I am more inclined to view Chaos as one half of a dual nature within The Power itself. Lord Fahad is in full agreement with me on this matter.
- *Coteon of the Steppes, "Coteonic Commentaries on the Origines Multiversi" (circa 520 RL)*

The reference here is to Fahad Lord Mukhtaar Morcos, a contemporary and close confidant of Coteon who appears in more detail later in the Chronicles.
- *Mujahid Mukhtaar, Private Commentaries, 45 CE*

Nicolas Murray tumbled through the void. It had been nice to be back in Texas, even if only for a few minutes, but he couldn't stay. Erindor was going to need him now more than it had when his birth father, Kagan, had been archmage.

And that was saying something. Kagan had been one evil bastard. He'd started a war among the Three Kingdoms to keep eyes focused away from his use of *life* magic—a magic whose true purpose was to aid in childbirth. Kagan had found a way to channel the magic through the Orb of Arin to construct his perverse *Great Barrier*; an impenetrable dome over the continent that kept a formidable enemy at bay, but slowly drained life from the Three Kingdoms over the course of four decades.

Nicolas had destroyed the Orb of Arin, which brought the gods of Erindor back to their rightful place. But when the orb shattered, it brought down Kagan's *Great Barrier* as well.

Kagan built that dome for a reason, and I went and tore the thing down. What's waiting outside it?

Though Kagan had been misguided, an army of Barathosians had been about to invade when the barrier went up. And Nicolas had no way of knowing if they were still out there.

Whatever was out there, worrying wasn't going to change anything.

Nicolas focused on another presence tumbling through the void with him. He needed to take his mind off problems he didn't have solutions for.

Kaitlyn.

Her presence was comforting, and though they had no form, he could feel her and Toby as if they were touching him.

He had so much to tell her. So much to show.

And there'd be a lot of work to do when they arrived. The Pinnacle sanctuary was in ruins, largely because he'd blown out an entire wall when he destroyed the orb. He'd need some rest before getting started. And people were going to have questions.

He had questions of his own, though.

What was he supposed to do now that he was the religious leader of Erindor? He was basically the pope of another world.

Speaking of which, how the hell did this *new* religion jive with his *old* one? If he told the nuns about this, they'd strangle him with a rosary! How could he go around acting like the pope and take himself seriously?

Aw hell. They're gonna make me wear some kind of funny hat, aren't they?

Kaitlyn had said he looked like Jesus when he arrived back in Texas. Hopefully they had razors in Erindor.

He didn't want to look like Jesus.

No offense, Lord. You're not a bad lookin' guy, it's just...the beard don't work for me.

He felt himself slowing, but there were no visual landmarks in the void. Only blackness.

The blackness soon changed to a dull gray, then white, then disappeared entirely, leaving them standing on a marble floor, surrounded by columns, in the middle of the most sacred room of the Pinnacle; the sanctuary.

They were in Erindor.

A presence tingled in the back of his mind, like someone gently touching his scalp, as the necromantic link he shared with Kagan reasserted itself. When the gods had returned, the God Arin took Kagan's life and bound him to Nicolas as an undead penitent in punishment for his atrocities.

"I think I'm gonna be sick," Kaitlyn said.

Nicolas rubbed her back. "That's normal. Take it slow."

Toby dropped his *gatorpickle* toy—named so because it looked like a cross between an alligator and pickle—let out a whining yawn, and wagged his tail as he stretched on the marble floor.

Kaitlyn grabbed her stomach and doubled over.

"It'll pass, once you eat."

He looked around, wondering why they were alone.

Something wasn't right.

The sanctuary floor had been swept clean. All shards of the broken Orb of Arin—destroyed less than an hour ago in the battle for the Pinnacle—were gone. An uncomfortable-looking stone chair, wide enough for two people to sit side by side, sat in front of a panoramic window on the opposite wall. A wall that shouldn't be there.

But that wasn't the most unexpected thing he saw.

Floating several feet off the ground was a complete, unbroken, orb of power. The orb's multi-hued light cascaded over its surface like liquid, divided in places by swirls of energy that drifted away from the orb in misty vortices.

Nicolas flinched as a peal of thunder broke somewhere above. He looked through the window at the voluminous gray clouds gathering on the horizon

"What the hell is going on?" Nicolas said.

"Holy one!" Tithian said as he entered the sanctuary.

Tithian looked different. The mother of all battles had just taken place, and Tithian decided to change clothes? What about the wounded? What about the dead cichlos and Three Kingdoms soldiers? What about the families of the Council magi who lived here at the Pinnacle?

"Where were you?" Tithian said. "You never sent a message. We've been frantic! The Council is in a shambles. They need their archmage."

"Their *what*?" Kaitlyn said.

"Long story," Nicolas said. "Magic was learned, bad guys were beat down, I became the pope—"

"You what?"

An expression of disbelief crossed Tithian's face as he looked at Kaitlyn.

Toby picked up his toy, ran over to Tithian, and jumped up on the man's thighs. Tithian's expression changed to one of sympathy, and he bent to scratch behind Toby's ears.

"What happened to your dog?" Tithian asked.

"How the hell did this happen so fast?" Nicolas asked. "I'm gone ten minutes and you rebuild the place?"

"Ten minutes? Holy one, I haven't seen you in six months."

"Two things," Nicolas said. "First, I told you less than an hour ago to knock it off with the *Holy One* business. And secondly, *what the hell*?"

"Listen to me, Holy…*Archmage*," Tithian said. "If we don't present you to the Council soon, there will be problems. I cannot hold them together any longer. They're demanding to see you."

"But we *destroyed* the Council," Nicolas said. "You were there."

"I told you! It's been—"

"Tithian, slow the hell down and tell me what you're talking about. What's going on?"

Tithian rubbed his forehead. "In your absence, the Barathosian Armada appeared off the coast of Dar Rodon."

"Remind me. Dar *what*?"

"Dar *Rodon*. Capital of the Religarian Empire. Far to the east. Nearly a hundred and fifty leagues."

"So it's true?" Nicolas asked. "Kagan was right?"

Nicolas thought he'd saved the world by bringing Kagan's barrier down. Had he eliminated one threat only to expose the Three Kingdoms to an even deadlier one?

"The Barathosians were waiting all that time?" Nicolas asked.

The necromantic link that tied Nicolas to Kagan became stronger when he mentioned Kagan's name. Kagan was close.

"You did what needed to be done," Tithian said, tapping Nicolas on the chest. "What none of us were capable of doing. And no, they weren't waiting. They *materialized* off the coast. No sailing, no slow build up of forces. Just an…*appearance*. The entire armada, as far as we can tell."

"Six months," Nicolas said. "How is that possible?"

"I suppose it shouldn't come as a surprise," Tithian said.

"Why not?" Nicolas said.

"For a start, you were born forty years ago but aged no more than twenty. I'd say time misbehaves around you far more than it misbehaves around others."

Kaitlyn put her hand on Nicolas's arm. She looked like she was about to throw up. "If he was born forty years ago, but only aged twenty, then why did time *speed up* when he came back here? When he left me, he was back within a few seconds. But when he left *you*, he was gone six months. It doesn't make sense."

"No," Tithian said. "It doesn't."

"What are we going to do if they invade?" Nicolas said. "Kagan raised that damned barrier because he didn't think the Three Kingdoms would survive an attack."

"There have already been minor skirmishes in southern Religar," Tithian said. "I think they've been testing the Empire's defenses."

Kagan entered the sanctuary, gripping the wooden handle of a straw broom. He swept the floor as he moved from side to side, criss-crossing around the room. He wore the same black zucchetto-style skull cap that Nicolas remembered. A red scapular—trimmed with black—wrapped around his shoulders and covered his white robes. Though he was undead and pasty, his corpse hadn't decayed. He smelled only of incense and the dust his broom was pushing around. It must have something to do with how soon after his death he'd been raised. He swept the broom across Kaitlyn's path, hitting her shoes in the process.

"Excuse *you*," Kaitlyn said with a surprised expression.

"Don't mind him," Nicolas said. "He's a little…"

"Evil?" Tithian said.

"I was going to go with *assholish*, but that will work."

Kaitlyn turned and gazed at the orb.

"How did that thing get here?" Nicolas asked. "Did Arin return?"

Tithian bowed his head briefly when Nicolas named the god. "We waited for weeks before starting reconstruction on the sanctuary. We wanted your input. But when the weather started to turn, we could wait no longer. Shortly after the wall was complete, the orb simply appeared. A similar orb appeared at Pilgrim's Landing, and we've had reports from Aquonome that an orb materialized in the cichlos temple as well."

"Three orbs?" Nicolas asked. "Arin promised *two*."

Tithian had to jump backward as Kagan hit his boots with the broom.

Kaitlyn yelled as she drew close to the orb. She put her hands on her head and doubled over.

Nicolas and Tithian rushed to her side and helped her into the nearby stone chair.

"This is my fault," Nicolas said. "I should have told you to sit down as soon as we got here. The hunger is normal."

"The hunger I can deal with," Kaitlyn said. Her voice was strained. "It's the knives in my temples I'm worried about."

"Tithian," Nicolas said, "do I have a room here? Chambers or something like that?"

"You do."

"Can you help me with her?"

"I'll be okay," Kaitlyn said as she stood. "It's Tithian, right? I'm Kait."

She extended her hand to Tithian and doubled over once more. Tithian tried to help her back to the seat, but she stopped him.

"I shouldn't have stood so fast," Kaitlyn said.

Nicolas placed his arm around her waist to steady her balance.

"Can you have some food brought to…wherever we're going?" Nicolas asked.

"I'll take care of it," Tithian said. "You should change into something cleaner. Those Arinian robes look like they've been through a battle."

"They *have* been."

Tithian chuckled. "That's right. Ten minutes, you say. You'll find clothes in your chambers, including formal robes appropriate for the ritual tomorrow morning."

"What ritual? No, no, no. I don't need any ritual. I need rest. *Kait* needs rest. I met my birth father an hour ago and he tried to kill me. Give me a break over here!"

"Have you not heard anything I've said? The Council has demanded an installation ceremony. Now that you're back, I can prove you actually exist. They need leadership. We all do. Half of them think *I* usurped Kagan's throne, and the other half think *Lord Mujahid* did. We need to quell the rumors."

Nicolas groaned but nodded. "We're going to need something less...blue jeans and Converse for Kaitlyn to wear."

"I'll have a selection brought to your chambers for Lady Kaitlyn."

Kagan hit Tithian with the broom's handle as he swept past him.

"And can you please tell him to stop?" Tithian asked.

"Stop what?"

"He's been sweeping around the clock since you sent him for a broom six months ago!"

Nicolas shook his head and sent the order through the necromantic link. But part of him couldn't help thinking it served Kagan right.

"I don't know what to do if the Barathosians decide to attack for real," Nicolas said. "I hope you have some ideas."

"Perhaps," Tithian said. But he turned away without continuing.

"Perhaps what?" Nicolas asked.

Tithian faced Nicolas, but he seemed uncertain.

"Perhaps *what*?" Nicolas repeated.

"In your absence, we discovered what I believe may be the *protoforges*," Tithian said.

Nicolas waited several moments for an explanation that wasn't coming. "From now on, just assume I'm going to ask *what* whenever you talk."

"When you brought the Great Barrier down, there was one final upheaval of the land. A terrible one. It struck Tildem the worst. But that's not important. What's important is what we *found*...buried deep within the mountains of Tildem."

"I still don't know what a *protoforge* is."

Tithian furrowed his brow as if Nicolas had said he didn't know what a door was.

"Apologies," Tithian said. "I sometimes forget you..."

"Don't know jack about Erindor?"

Tithian frowned. "Jack who?"

"The protoforge things, Tithian."

"The protoforges are spoken of in the *Origines Multiversi*, a set of books written by the ancient prophet Habakku. Those books tell us how

Erindor was created. What life was like millennia ago. What the gods expect of people. And so much more. They even tell us of the first Mukhtaar Lords."

"We have a similar book back on Earth. A few, if I'm being honest. But you're saying you *found* them in Tildem?"

"We can't be *certain*, but..."

"But you're certain?"

"Certainly!"

"Well *what are they*?" Nicolas asked.

Tithian leaned forward. "Simply put, they were the molds in which the first Orbs of Power were formed."

"Why is this important? Don't get me wrong. I'm an archaeologist. I understand the importance of relics. But what's the connection to the Barathosians?"

"Oh my god, Nick," Kaitlyn said. "Tithian just told you they found the thing that makes *those* things." She pointed at the orb. "By the transitive property, those protoforges sound really powerful and important."

"Okay! You don't need to be all—"

"*Knives in my temples*, remember?"

Tithian made a placating gesture with his hand. "I'm going to have the fragments tested. If these *are* protoforge fragments, they may serve our purposes in Dar Rodon. If the *Origines* is correct, they can be unpredictable. And if *we* can't predict what they'll do, then neither can the Barathosians..."

"Now tell me the part you left out."

"Excuse me?"

"Dammit, Tithian," Nicolas said. "I'm not trying to interrogate you, but I don't understand why you're holding back. We've got a problem that needs solving, and I can't do this by myself."

"That's right," Tithian said. He glanced at Kagan, who stood silently next to the Orb of Power. "In your absence, I'd forgotten just how unlike your father you are."

"*Birth* father," Nicolas said.

Tithian nodded. "I meant no offense, Archmage."

"Dammit all!" Nicolas had had enough. He needed an adviser, not a subordinate. "You're not *offending* me. And if your idea about these protoforge fragments doesn't pan out, we'll try something else. I'm not going to get pissed off because you tried something that didn't work. Just tell me what you need to tell me. I'm not Kagan."

Tithian grinned. "You most certainly are not. Right, then. When I received word from my contacts in Tildem, they had no idea what they'd uncovered. But I suspected. So I attempted to use a translocation orb to teleport to Hiboran—that's a city in the far west of Tildem, close to the mountain range where the fragments were uncovered."

"Attempted?"

"It didn't work. Not...*exactly*. Instead of materializing outside of Hiboran, I felt a...*deflection*. I ended up some fifty leagues to the northwest of Hiboran, outside a city called *Tur*. Gave an onion farmer a pretty good fright when I materialized in his house. Every subsequent attempt to travel there met with the same result."

"How will these fragments help us?"

"They seem to disrupt magic. We don't know what the Barathosians have at their disposal, but it certainly can't hurt our efforts."

Nicolas helped Kaitlyn back up.

"She needs food *pronto*," Nicolas said.

"You both need rest. We'll regroup tomorrow before the ceremony."

Nicolas nodded and followed Tithian out of the sanctuary.

A elron grunted as the trailer rolled over a deep rut on the forest road.

Forty years ago he'd joined the Shandarian Rangers as an equal. Now he was in a cage on the back of a trailer being kicked out and taken back to his home. All because he couldn't *moor*—telepathically bond—with an adda-ki. Only rangers could tame and ride the massive feline mounts. So, if he couldn't moor, he wasn't worth keeping around, in their opinion.

That wasn't entirely fair. He *had* killed a fellow ranger as well. That might have played into their decision to evict him.

Letcher had it coming. But they don't see it that way.

He banged his head on the side of the cage as the wagon lurched over another deep rut.

"I'm not complaining," Aelron said, "but can we try to miss a few of those?"

"Someone forgot to gag him," a ranger said. The others erupted in laughter.

Aelron didn't catch which one had said it, but it was a reminder to keep his mouth shut. His escort hadn't bound his wrists or ankles—he was in a steel cage, so why bother?—and he wanted to keep it that way.

As he glanced around his rolling jail cell, it became clear the dense forest of towering pines was a prison unto itself. With the seasons turning, if he didn't die of exposure between here and Caspardis, which was two-hundred miles to the south, then a shriller or roaming crag spider would do what the frigid weather couldn't. And it would be no use trusting this unmaintained roadway they traveled. For four decades, the road dead-ended in an impenetrable yellow dome. No one knew whether anyone under it was still alive.

Aelron didn't know what the rangers had in mind for him, but he was certain riding into the area once covered by that dome was a bad idea. He'd lost friends to that dome when it was still up, and he didn't have many friends left to spare.

More accurately, he had *no* friends left. Forty years their brother, but now they treated him like a pariah.

If only I had more time!

It was no use lying to himself. Time would solve nothing. He was twenty years past the age most Shandarian Rangers had *moored* with an adda-ki, forming a bond that ended only when rider or mount died. But his ageless face was another difference they wouldn't let him forget.

And he couldn't give them a reason for it, because he didn't know *why* he'd stopped aging.

Killing Letcher was simply the final entry on a *long* list of items they didn't like about him. It mattered little to them he'd only done so in self-defense.

Freya, Captain Jacobson's *adda-ki*, roared for no reason Aelron could decipher. But then there was little about the giant feline mounts, with their bright-red fur, that he understood. Not only would they not *moor* with him, but the riderless ones became aggressive whenever he approached. They stampeded the last time, killing two rangers and injuring five others.

Another *infraction* they held him responsible for.

Captain Jacobson glanced over his shoulder at Aelron and glared through eyes made feline by the mooring process. Jacobson sat straight-backed atop Freya. He wore a brown leather jerkin pulled over a woolen shirt that had seen far too many fights. His beard had grown ragged from weeks without a shave.

Two paces, Aelron thought. *One jump over the rail and two paces to Jacobson. I can free that dagger he hides in his boot and...what am I saying? I'm not a murderer, despite what they think!*

Aelron glanced around, searching for an alternative.

Seven paces to the forest and I can disappear into the trees. They'll never find me in that dense foliage.

But that wouldn't work either, and he didn't need to flip the cursed silver coin he kept in his pocket to know it. Jacobson wasn't alone. Ten of the best Shandarian Rangers in the order followed him. Aelron's skills were impressive, but he wasn't immortal.

"Keep your eye on him, Brother Orvin," Jacobson said, nodding toward Aelron. "You too, Brother Simmons."

Aelron ran his fingers over the ranger medallion that hung from his neck.

Seven paces. That's all he had to survive and they'd never see him again.

There were plenty of game trails he could use, but he was right back to the same problem. Killing a ranger in single combat was tricky enough. Escaping from a group of them on high alert would be nigh on impossible.

He let go of the medallion and it fell to his chest. He was surprised they'd let him keep it. It identified him as a ranger, and that was one association he couldn't lay claim to anymore.

"I still can't get used to it," Orvin said. He shook his head and smiled. "I've never seen it *not* there. It's *always* been there, right over that hill!"

Though he appeared the same age as Aelron, Orvin was a boy. And unlike Aelron, Orvin had never known a world without a yellow dome.

Aelron looked up at Orvin without lifting his head. "Things change, kid. Domes come down. Friendships end."

Orvin lost his smile.

"That's enough," Jacobson said without taking his gaze from the road. "Open your mouth again and I'll have you bound and gagged. By Arin's helm."

The look on Jacobson's face made Aelron's spine tingle. Whatever he'd seen over that hill had made his face lose all color.

The wagon shuddered as the driver came to a stop, and Aelron took his first look at what Jacobson had seen.

The dense forest of northern Shandarian Union came to a precipitous end in a perfect line spanning untold miles to the east and west. The line wasn't only perfect in form. It was perfect in the path of destruction that lay in its wake. It formed a ridge in both directions, as if the land beyond had sunk a dozen or more feet and become devoid of life. Forest and grass gave way to dirt, dwarf trees, and sagebrush. Where the ground around the wagon was rich with dark topsoil, the dirt beyond the ridge was cracked and dry.

It was as if the gods themselves had drawn a line in the ground and destroyed everything on the other side of it.

What has that dome been hiding all this time?

"Brother Orvin," Jacobson said. "Unhitch the wagon and let the *unmoored* ride with you."

"But the ridge, Captain? Looks like a fifteen foot drop."

"You've a lot to learn about that new mount of yours, Brother Orvin," one of the other rangers said. Aelron couldn't see who.

Jacobson chuckled and patted his adda-ki on the head, running his hand through the black splotch on her otherwise bright red mane of hair.

"You can leap twice that far, isn't that right, Freya?" Jacobson said, ruffling Freya's mane.

"Captain," Aelron said.

"I said that's enough," Jacobson said.

"Please," Aelron said. "Hear me out. We don't know what we're riding into. That dome was up for forty years and we haven't heard from *anyone* trapped inside since it came down. That place looks like the gods destroyed it for a reason."

"Frightened?" Jacobson asked. "You should be. No, we don't know what we're going to find. But that doesn't change what you did. And it doesn't change our duty."

"I was defending myself."

"You killed Letcher because of a *coin toss*, you festering murderer!"

"As I told the tribunal, he was planning to—"

"I'll not hear any more of it! Your case was tried. I'm not your judge."

"No. You're my executioner."

Jacobson turned away.

"Easy to hide behind the decisions of others," Aelron said. "Isn't it?"

"You'll not die by my hand, *boy*."

"We're of the same age."

"Nor will you die by the hand of any man here. Be grateful we had an arrangement with your father."

"My father may not even be alive."

"That's your problem. Now, unless you want to be bound and dragged behind Freya, no more talking."

"Captain, we found something," Simmons said, carrying something in his fist. "In the ravine. It was just standing there."

Simmons tossed a white object in the air, which Captain Jacobson caught with ease.

Strange. Aelron could have sworn Simmons tossed it out of reach, but the object made an unnatural arc downward and landed in Jacobson's hand as if drawn to it. His eyes must have been playing tricks, because no one reacted to the odd movement.

Captain Jacobson flipped the object over in his hand. It was a tiny, white statue of some sort, depicting a smiling man with arms clasped behind his back.

Something about it made Aelron uneasy.

Captain Jacobson grinned a wicked grin. As he moved his adda toward Aelron, one slow step at a time, he shook his head and put the little statue in a saddle bag. When he looked back up from the bag, the grin was gone.

"What are you lot doing?" Jacobson said. "Let's get this over with!"

Aelron thought it best not to speak as they guided him across the ravine and into a land he no longer remembered.

CHAPTER TWO

Early scholars of the Origines invariably held the belief that Necromancy is the only true magic. My position is different, and perhaps would have been considered heretical five hundred years ago. We should not come to such a hasty conclusion. While it is true the only sacred writings we possess show the institution of Necromancy, that should not be taken to mean the other gods have not passed on magic of their own.
- Coteon of the Steppes, "Coteonic Commentaries on the Origines Multiversi" (circa 520 RL)

Zorian Osa gazed through the portal of his cabin on the Barathosian flagship *Vengeance*, toward the city called Dar Rodon, whose buildings reflected in the mirrored surface of the Bay of Relig.

Zorian would never admit it, but the stark contrast between the azure bay and the pale sands of the desert city was beautiful to behold. He'd heard about the deserts of the Three Kingdoms—vast expanses of sand

and dry ground, ever-changing dunes making it impossible to map certain regions accurately. Barathosia had nothing comparable.

Zorian had no experience of these Three Kingdoms people, yet somehow he doubted they were *cowards*, as his superiors would have him believe.

No coward could build that palace beyond the bay, with its multi-leveled terraces and spiraling towers. The Religarian palace glowed from whitewashed walls and cast a brilliant light on the pristine inner city that surrounded it. It rivaled the Palace of Ages, home of the Diamond Throne and the Glorious One—the empress herself.

It would be a shame for the armada to destroy it all. Zorian would do his best to avoid the outcome Admiral Unega was so set on achieving.

That might be difficult, though. The admiral tolerated Zorian's presence on the ship for one reason only. The Glorious One had given him no choice. As *Zhuma*, Zorian served as the Barathosian archmage's attache to the military, outside of the military command structure. It allowed him to ask questions without being subject to the whims of higher command. And there were questions he needed answered, if he were to fulfill his mission.

Admiral Unega had ordered the chimeramancers to *chimeraport* the armada here, and Zorian needed to know why. He had no idea what the admiral was planning, and that troubled him. He'd never met a man he couldn't read. Others often commented on how accurate Zorian's intuition was, sometimes accusing him of using magic to discover the secrets men held close to their hearts. That wasn't true, of course. Zorian could no more channel power than he could jump off the *Vengeance* and swim back to Barathosia. But it didn't require *magic* to understand the predictable nature of powerful men. They would do everything it took to *protect* that power.

"Tullias," Zorian said.

A young man standing in the corner of the room, wearing a simple brown tunic and trousers, stepped forward.

"Yes, *Zhuma*," Tullias said.

Zorian still wasn't used to the honorific. He'd never owned an indentured servant before.

"Prepare my things," Zorian said.

Tullias bowed his head and began gathering items from Zorian's wardrobe.

Zorian pulled his jacket tight as a cold gust blew through the portal, scattering the parchment on his desk and spreading the salty scent of seawater. What curse of the gods would cause the weather to be frigid at this time of year? Back home, the blossoms of the *zahngzee* tree were in full bloom, spreading their perfumed scent everywhere, but this place was on the verge of winter.

A knock at the cabin door startled Zorian. He had no friends here, and there was only one person on the ship who would summon him.

"Enter," Zorian said.

A sailor wearing a wide-brimmed hat with a crimson feather plume entered the cabin.

"Zhuma," the man said.

Zorian was confused. The sailor wore a tight leather vest, buckled bandolier, billowing pants, and knee-high boots as if he were a member of a landing party. But not just any landing party. The ornate, golden buckle around his waist identified him as a diplomatic escort. And the crossed anchors on his epaulets meant he was an officer. A lieutenant.

"Going somewhere, Lieutenant?" Zorian asked.

"Admiral Unega requests your presence."

The admiral had never treated Zorian poorly, but there was something dark about him. A malevolence that disturbed Zorian. A summons was unnerving.

"Let's be off, then," Zorian said. "Best not to keep him waiting. Tullias, continue. I expect this mess straightened out when I return."

"Yes, Zhuma," Tullias said.

Zorian pulled the cabin door shut behind him and followed the lieutenant into the wide hallway. Floral-scented slats of wood, carved from *zahngzee*, ran horizontally along the hallway, stopping at even intervals where cabin doors prevented them from continuing. There was nothing warm about the pale wood, which added to Zorian's discomfort in this wintry hell. It was times like these Zorian wished the ship was smaller.

The *Vengeance* was more a floating city than a ship, a wonder of Barathosian engineering. Hallways crossed at odd angles, and some spiraled up and down among the numerous decks, allowing sailors to move from one deck to another. They entered a spiral at the end of the hallway and climbed ten decks to the Admiral's Deck, where they emerged onto the outer walkway and its oppressive cold wind. Storm clouds told Zorian he'd have rain to deal with as well as the cold. Soon, judging by the sound of the distant thunder.

They walked more than a quarter mile along the outer walkway before they reached the entrance to the command chamber, a security measure designed by the ship's architects. Six towers lined the outer perimeter of the ship, and the three port-side towers were in clear view of the outer walk, providing elevated positions for archers to destroy any invading force that managed to make it this far. Kill holes were spaced at uneven intervals both above and below the outer walk, allowing the ship's massive security force to pick off any invaders that survived the archers' attack from the towers.

None of it would matter, though. No navy on Erindor could survive a frontal assault against the armada. A small ship might have a chance to go undetected during a large battle, but the boarding party wouldn't live long enough to set foot on the deck, much less make their way through the labyrinthine passageways and up to this outer walkway.

No, the admiral was safe in his command chamber. Safe from foreign enemies, at least. But more than a few Barathosians would like to see him dead.

Such was the reality of Barathosian politics. Those below wanted your power. Those above wanted to keep you from taking theirs.

The admiral had nothing to worry about from Zorian, though. Not directly. Zorian had greater ambitions than to command a few thousand ships, and the admiral might come in handy someday. First the Three Kingdoms had to be dealt with, though, and Zorian would do everything in his power to see it done. But he wouldn't do this for the admiral, or from some imperial sense of retribution for a murder that took place before he was born.

No, Zorian would do this for the only reward that mattered. The only *title* that mattered—*Sian'jo*. A title that hadn't been granted in centuries. It was given only to someone who fulfilled an *okotba*—a personal mission given by the Empress herself, upon which the very honor of Barathosia rested. Success would mean no one but the Glorious One could command him. He would rise above even the Great Houses. He would unify the temples for the Barathosian archmage against the *real* enemy— the growing chaos enveloping Barathosia, just as the god Arin had predicted.

Failure meant humiliation and a painful execution, of course. And that's if he survived the mission.

But he would not fail. The Glorious One's words echoed in his mind.

"Two of you I send," the Glorious One said. *"One I've sent to reclaim the honor of my family. But you, Zorian, always so proud of your cleverness. You I send to capture. If you're so clever, bring me their archmage. But bring him to me in shackles of his own making. Make him stand before me of his own free will. Do so and the world shall bow before you and call you Sian'jo."*

"I will not fail you, Glorious One," Zorian had said.

"It matters little to me which of you succeeds."

As the lieutenant slowed in front of him, Zorian focused on the task at hand.

The entrance to the command chamber was a simple wooden door with several sealable arrow slits and a tiny porthole. The porthole had been opened once the chimeramancers *chimeraported* the armada; it was a sign they were no longer in Barathosian waters.

As Zorian and the lieutenant approached the door, the walkway gave slightly under their weight.

The final defense.

There was nothing beneath Zorian for more than twenty decks, and with the single pull of a rope in the command chamber, the walkway would fall open, dropping an invading force to their deaths.

Or drop a rival to an untimely demise, Zorian thought.

That wouldn't be Zorian's end, though. At least not yet. The admiral needed him. Zorian would go along with whatever plan Admiral Unega hatched, so long as it aligned with his ultimate goal.

Zorian walked a fine line. He had to remain competent, yet non-threatening. Tenacious, yet respectful.

The chamber door opened, allowing Zorian and the lieutenant to enter.

The command chamber was forty feet across and thirty deep, with walls that could be opened into extended decks for the admiral to have a commanding view of his armada. The fore and starboard decks were opened, providing a view of more than a thousand *Predator*-class warships spanning from the horizon over the fore deck to the horizon over the starboard. And that was but half the armada under Unega's command.

Four signalers sat against the port wall, prepared to convey orders to the armada on the admiral's behalf. Four brightly colored flags, one for each of the four fleets of the Armada, along with dozens of white flags—

each painted with an elaborate symbol representing a command—rested against the aft wall.

Though the walls were open, no icy wind pierced the command chamber. The chimeramancers saw to that.

Admiral Unega sat on a simple stool in the far corner of the room, at the column between the fore and starboard decks. He hunched over a parchment on the small table in front of him, tapping the document with the bottom of an ivory figurine.

The admiral was out of uniform, which was strange, and his gray hair was mussed, as if he had been roused from bed and given no time to comb it. His sunken eyes and weary expression seconded that supposition. This must be an emergency meeting.

Vincen, an old chimeramancer, was present, as was Lucian, a *vivamancer*—something the Three Kingdoms magi called a *life magus*. Zorian understood Vincen's presence, but Lucian had no purpose here. There were no pregnant women on board—a vivamancer's stock in trade—and it was inconceivable that Admiral Unega would be trying to fulfill the empress's original mission of cultural exchange.

But what if he was?

Zorian's mind raced. If the admiral managed to succeed in not only bringing vengeance upon the Three Kingdoms by killing the archmage, but *also* fulfilling the empress's decades-old mission—a mission said to originate with Arin himself—then the admiral might be the adversary the Glorious One warned Zorian about.

What is your purpose here, Lucian?

Zorian would have to keep his eyes on that one. Vivamancers were revered as holy in the Barathosian empire. If Lucian took it upon himself to declare Zorian an enemy, it would put an end to Zorian's ambitions.

It might put an end to Zorian, for that matter.

"Mester Vincen," Admiral Unega said. "I want the Fourth Navy off the coast of Religar by this evening, including the Fourth's command ship. Can you and your brethren achieve this *and* maintain our current operations?"

"It won't take all four of us, Admiral. One chimeramancer should suffice to keep our operatives moving. The rest of us will handle the Fourth."

"Good," Admiral Unega said. "I shouldn't have to remind you how crucial our timing is, but I will anyway. You can resume your cartographic operations at the harbor when you return."

"Understood."

Admiral Unega stared at Zorian, but he remained as inscrutable as always.

"The Mester has...seen things in his dreams," Admiral Unega said, picking the parchment up from the table as he stood. "He believes it's time, and I agree."

"As do I, Admiral," Lucian said. "I couldn't agree more."

Zorian might not be able to read the admiral. But Lucian, on the other hand, was an open book. His presence on the Vengeance was by luck of the draw. There was nothing special about Lucian, and he knew it...and it ate away at him. Zorian could tell by the way he flaunted that cheap golden bracelet of office, and by how he reacted whenever someone mentioned his last assignment, which was a small temple in Barathos. There'd be a moment—an ever-so-fleeting reaction of embarrassment and shame. A humble temple priest would never amount to much. But a vivamancer who brought the true faith to the cowards? Now *that* was currency Lucian would be able to leverage at the court of the Diamond Throne.

It was all beginning to fall into place for Zorian. Perhaps this *was* about fulfilling the empress's original mission. It might be difficult for the admiral to convince a high ranking vivamancer to risk his status on a gamble, but a priest with no future would jump at the chance to change his destiny.

"I've ordered a landing party formed," Admiral Unega said. He thrust the document he was holding toward Zorian. "Read it."

> *Emperor Relig*
> *The time has come to fulfill your oath.*
> *Dobros Unega*
> *Admiral of the Diamond Navy and Scourge of Yantoo*

"Short and to the point, Admiral," Zorian said. Yantoo...now *that* was a battle for the chroniclers. As a boy, Zorian was taught how the *fearless Captain Unega*, in a final push to overcome the Talerion invasion, ordered his powder ships run aground and set alight. Stories said the resulting explosion was greater than ten orbs of power being destroyed at once. He enslaved the survivors of Yantoo, forced them to rebuild the city—complete with a statue of himself—and slaughtered the family of any woman who refused to come to his bed.

Unega could make a horrible enemy.

"Deliver it to the emperor," Admiral Unega said. "If he refuses in any way, report back immediately."

"If I may ask," Zorian said. "What is the nature of his oath?"

Admiral Unega remained expressionless. How did the man do it? How was he the only person Zorian couldn't read?

"The Emperor of Religar isn't their archmage's most devout follower for nothing," Admiral Unega said. "Exploit that relationship. And when the opportunity presents itself, kill him."

"The emperor?"

"The archmage! You think I've waited forty years to assassinate a backward potentate of a poverty stricken nation?"

Of course. Vengeance.

It was the very name of this ship. A name Admiral Unega had chosen himself.

And it was the very thing he swore to be an instrument of for the Glorious One.

"Of course not," Zorian said. "When do I leave? I'll need to gather some things."

"Immediately. And one more thing."

Something told Zorian he wasn't going to like this.

"Lucian is going with you," Admiral Unega said. "As is Lieutenant Belding. When you've dealt with the archmage, report back. Lucian will remain behind. He has *other* work to do."

Lucian smiled at Zorian.

Zorian suppressed a small surge of anger. This confirmed his suspicions. The admiral intended to fulfill the empress's old mission. He was Zorian's adversary for the coveted title of Sian'jo.

"If I may, Admiral," Zorian said. "Would it not be better to send a Mester with me? Perhaps Mester Vincen could employ his art to bring this mission some success?"

"The emperor employs the service of a *cognitomancer*," Admiral Unega said.

"I'd rather bed down in a viper's nest than go anywhere near one of those blue-robed demons," Vincen said. His tone was incredulous.

A chimeramancer would never take that risk. The danger of a cognitomancer taking control of a chimeramancer was too great. Chimeramancers had the power to turn their dreams into reality, albeit temporarily. But a cognitomancer controlled a person directly. If the person being controlled was a chimeramancer...

"Of course," Zorian said. He faced Lucian. "I'll enjoy the conversation." Zorian was tempted to mention Lucian's *inconsequential* temple just to watch the man squirm, but he refrained. It would be childish and petty. And besides, he needed to keep Lucian on his side for now.

For now.

"Gather your things," Admiral Unega said. "You may take your manservant with you. It wouldn't do to have Lucian folding your clothes."

Zorian nodded.

"And don't return until the archmage is dead."

Sorry, Admiral. But that is one thing I will not do. I have...other plans for him. If the Glorious One wants the archmage in shackles of his own creation, then I shall give him the tools he needs to forge them.

Zorian began the long trek back to his quarters.

CHAPTER THREE

[1]The Power, seeing his gift tainted by Chaos, cast his breath into the multiverse and created the great realms of Air, Ground, Fire, and Water. [2]His breath formed the air, his substance formed the ground, his spirit formed the fire, and his blood formed the water.

- The Mukhtaar Chronicles, attributed to the prophet Habakku
Origines Multiversi, Emergentiae 2:1-2

Nicolas woke to the sound of Kaitlyn crying out.

Moonlight poured in through the large window at the foot of the bed, casting everything in shades of blue. The gems in the wall-sized map of the Three Kingdoms shimmered like stars on the wall next to him.

Nicolas sat up, but Kaitlyn was still asleep.

"Kait," Nicolas said, putting a hand on her cheek. She was bathed in sweat.

Kaitlyn groaned and turned away.

"Kait," Nicolas said. "Wake up. It's just a dream."

"Archmage, are you all right?" a deep voice said from the other side of his chamber doors.

"Kait!"

Kaitlyn stirred and grabbed Nicolas's hand.

The chamber door burst open, sweeping the dark room with golden torch light.

"Archmage!" a large man with a sword said from the doorway. His voice sounded like it reverberated in a fifty-gallon drum.

"I'm okay," Nicolas said.

"Forgive me, Archmage," The man said. "When you didn't answer, I...I didn't—"

"It's fine. She was dreaming."

"Cool ren faire," Kaitlyn said. "I want a henna tattoo." She rolled over and laid her head back down.

"We're okay," Nicolas said. "What's your name?"

The towering man drew back. "Archmage?"

"Gonna be confusing if we're both called *Archmage*, don't you think?"

"Uh...Diggins, Archmage. Hartwood Diggins, sergeant-at-Diggins. I mean *arms*! Sergeant-at-arms! I'm Diggins, not arms." Diggins took a deep breath. "Hartwood sergeant—"

"Yeah, we covered that, Sergeant Diggins. You can be...as you *were*?"

"Archmage?"

"At ease?"

"But I'm not at attention."

"Look, I have some things to learn around here. What I'm trying to say is, would you mind if I went back to sleep for now?"

"Oh! Certainly." Diggins turned to leave, but stopped. "Dismissed, Archmage."

"Excuse me?"

"The word you were looking for. *Dismissed*. Say that and we'll get the point."

"I prefer to ask politely. Will that work too?"

Diggins shrugged. "I suppose it will, Archmage."

Diggins closed the door behind him, casting the room into moonlight once more.

"*What* do you have to ask politely?" Kaitlyn asked.

"You're awake? You scared me for a minute."

"How?"

"Well...it's nothing," Nicolas said.

"What aren't you telling me?"

"It's nothing. Just—"

"Nicolas Murray."

Nicolas grabbed the back of his neck. He was sure it was nothing. Hell, she'd stepped through a portal to a different world earlier today. But there was no way she was going to go back to sleep now.

Not when she'd called him *Nicolas Murray*.

Nicolas picked up the *Shrillers and Adda* board from the nightstand and carefully placed it on the mattress between them, standing three of the adda pieces up when they toppled over. Whenever Kait felt anxious or sick, board games always seemed to cheer her up. He'd spent an hour or so teaching her the basics earlier in the evening.

Kaitlyn sat up and glanced at the board.

"You screamed," Nicolas said. "You've never done that before. I'm not gonna lie. You scared the bejeezus out of me. Your turn, I think."

Kaitlyn placed two shriller pieces on the board and counted to five, then removed them.

Nicolas pursed his lips.

"I remember having some kind of dream," Kaitlyn said. "It was odd, but every time I remember something specific about it, it slips away."

"Well, I'm sure everything's fine."

Nicolas moved the larger adda pieces until they formed circles around the smaller ones, careful to avoid the crag spider nests and hunters.

"I don't know," Kaitlyn said. "What was Tithian saying about you being born forty years ago?"

"I know you need answers, Kait. I just didn't want to overwhelm you. I had the mother of all freak outs when that *thing* pulled me through the portal. I just assumed you'd be doing the same. I guess you're a lot stronger than I am."

"You *were* all alone."

"True."

"I understand you're trying to be thoughtful, but that's not how it's coming across. Can you just tell me everything tomorrow? I'm okay with playing tourist tonight. But you need to start talking tomorrow morning." She moved one of her pieces on the board. "Oh, and *checkmate*. Or…whatever you're supposed to say when you win."

Nicolas stared at the board with wide eyes. "That's not possible."

"You play this like you play chess. You can't save all of your pieces all of the time."

"Is that your professional opinion, *chess master Kaitlyn*?" He smiled. "Tithian would say—oh crap. I forgot."

Nicolas remembered the installation service he had to be a part of in the morning. He'd forgotten to tell Kaitlyn.

"Tomorrow morning there's some kind of ceremony I have to go through," Nicolas said. "No one but Council magi are allowed in the Council chambers, so you can't be there with me. It's a stupid rule, but I can't do anything about it until *after* the ceremony. You could check out some of the shrines. I think you'd love the architecture here. Maybe let Toby meet some of the locals. As soon as the ceremony is over, we can have that conversation. How's that for a plan?"

The moonlight provided ample light to see she didn't think much of his *plan*.

"I swear I'm not forty years old."

"Why do they keep calling you *Archmage*?"

"Because that's who I am here. I'm the archmage. My birth father was the old archmage, but he was an evil bastard and I forced him into early retirement. So they gave me the job."

"Safe to assume you're not going to introduce me?"

"No need to. You already met him."

"Tithian?"

Nicolas laughed. "No. The dead dude with the broom."

"The *what*?"

He hadn't meant for it to slip out that way, but there was no way to put that particular cat back in the bag.

"I told you you're safe here, remember?" Nicolas said.

"Stop talking to me like I'm five. I don't need you to keep telling me I'm safe, ass!"

"It's going to be okay."

"Oh...my...god! Tell me it's going to be okay one more time. I *dare* you!"

"I don't know what you want from me!"

"I want to know about this secret world of yours. I want to know about this life you've lived away from me for...however long you were here. I want to know you're the same person that left me in that apartment. For God's sake, Nicolas, your father, Doctor Murray, just died, and you haven't even mentioned him."

Nicolas shut his eyes and lowered his head. "A *year* ago, Kait. Dad died a *year* ago. I can't explain why because I don't understand it myself. It was a *year* for me."

"You were a scared college student who couldn't tie a neck tie last time I saw you. And now you live in a palace? You have guards? People serve you? You think it's normal to be surrounded by dead things?"

Nicolas shook his head. He had no idea where to begin.

"And what does all this mean?" Kaitlyn asked. "Are we ever going home? What about school? What about finals? Are we ever...ow!"

Kaitlyn grabbed her temples.

Nicolas put his arm around her and settled her back down on the bed. At least he could do that much.

Kaitlyn wiped beads of sweat from her forehead and rested her hand over her eyes.

"It's going to be okay," Nicolas said.

"I swear to god, if I didn't have a marching band in my head I would *knee you in the nuts.*"

"I'm sorry, I just...I'll leave for a bit."

Nicolas swung his legs over the side of the bed, but as he began to stand, Kaitlyn tugged him back down.

"Tomorrow," Kaitlyn said. "You tell me *everything.*"

"I will. And I'll introduce you to Mujahid, if he's around here. You'll like him...well...if he's not being all crotchety like he can be sometimes. But I'm sort of his boss now. No, wait...he said I'm his postulant. So is he my boss? How can anyone be the archmage's boss? What the hell does the archmage do, anyway? Oh God, I'm so screwed."

"Nick."

"What?"

"It's going to be okay."

He sighed. Sometimes she knew exactly the right thing to say.

Aelron's fate had been decided by *The Moot*, the court of elders at the ranger mother house, and there was nothing he could say to Captain Jacobson to change it. Still, there was a growing anger inside. His pulse thrummed at his temples. There was nothing he could do except stew in an impotent rage that would only get him killed if he didn't get it under control.

He took a deep breath and looked out at the desolate countryside.

It was as if they'd ridden into one of the hells. The fragrant pine forests of the north ended abruptly, giving way to a dead land, devoid of even a blade of grass. The rangers traveled light, only packing water. Food was something they could hunt for with ease. But the lack of game trails worried even Simmons, their best hunter.

The terrain of the northern region of the Shandarian Union grew flat as the rangers made their way inland through a torrential downpour. They'd stopped and donned Arinwool, making sure to cover their adda-ki as well, rendering them invisible to all but each other.

Aelron couldn't see them, though. Being *unmoored* meant he didn't share a mystical bond with an adda-ki, and so he didn't have the creature's heightened agility or keen eyesight.

Aelron donned his as well, but when he asked why they were traveling with stealth, all Jacobson said was "We're not ready to meet with our southern brothers just yet. Best we give that some time."

Several hours into their journey, soaked from rains that slowed but never stopped, they emerged from the near-barren fields onto a muddy road that, according to Jacobson, ran between the capital city of Shandar and the city of Caspardis.

Aelron recognized the names. He'd even been to Caspardis once. But he was five when his father sent him to live with the rangers. After forty years under the dome, he doubted those cities existed as anything other than ruins anyway.

His opinion changed when he spotted crops growing a few hundred paces up the road. A herd of domestic adda grazed there—shorter versions of the adda-ki. Muscular, hooved, less agile. More a source of food and transportation than a weapon of war. Could there be survivors? Someone must have tended those fields and shepherded those adda.

And there was smoke rising from nearby thatch-roofed buildings.

Aelron thumbed the silver ring Master Nigel, his blademaster, had awarded him. It was set with a stone resembling the cat's eye symbol of the Shandarian Rangers, and was only supposed to go to a moored ranger. But Nigel had made an exception.

"Whoa, men," Jacobson said, pulling his mount to halt at the head of the group.

Aelron could see Jacobson's outline, but only because he knew what to look for.

The rangers formed up around him.

"This is as far as we take you," Jacobson said.

"But Captain," Orvin said. "Our agreement was to take him to his father."

Jacobson struck Orvin with the back of his hand, and Orvin grabbed the pommel of his saddle to steady himself.

Striking a subordinate without cause was forbidden, and from the looks on the faces of two of the other rangers, they intended to do something about it.

They urged their adda-ki forward. But before they reached Jacobson, Simmons rode between them and waved for them to stop. He whispered something Aelron couldn't hear.

"Simmons!" Jacobson yelled and nodded toward Aelron.

Simmons spun his adda-ki and shoved Aelron off the back of Orvin's mount.

Aelron landed hard on his side, splashing mud and water up around him. Rough hands tore at his Arinwool until he was visible.

"Don't forget the medallion," Jacobson said. "We don't want people getting the wrong idea."

Aelron cursed. He'd hoped they'd forgotten about it. Without the medallion it would be difficult, maybe even impossible, to convince people he was a ranger. And without that, he was nothing more than a vagrant. A drifter.

And *that* violated the Shandarian Justice Protocols. Was that what Jacobson wanted? For Aelron to get arrested by a local ranger patrol and tossed in jail before he reached his father?

The medallion lifted off his chest and disappeared into the pocket of whichever ranger was doing Jacobson's bidding. They hadn't removed their Arinwool, so he couldn't see who had taken it.

Whoever it was hadn't thought to check Aelron's cloak, or he would have discovered a small piece of Arinwool tucked away for safety. Aelron thanked the gods he'd had the presence of mind to hide some earlier. It wouldn't be enough to render him invisible, but it *would* render him immune to magic. Any spell cast against him would either reflect back toward the caster, or else be absorbed by the Arinwool itself.

"Captain," Simmons said. "What about the ring?"

"Maybe you should check with Master Nigel first," Aelron said. Nigel and Jacobson weren't on friendly terms, and Nigel outranked him.

Aelron couldn't see Jacobson, but an awkward silence stretched on for several moments.

"Keep it," Jacobson said. "Just make sure you don't go identifying yourself as a ranger."

The truth was Aelron didn't care about the festering ring. He treasured Nigel's friendship, but sentiment wasted on an object was a weakness an observant enemy could exploit. Nigel *himself* had taught Aelron as much. But right now, the ring gave him power over Jacobson. And he liked *that*.

Jacobson pulled the Arinwool hood from his head and stared at Aelron through feline eyes.

"Now that the dome's down, you can go back to your festering family," Jacobson said.

The downpour grew stronger, making it difficult to hear Jacobson's voice.

"We did our part," Jacobson said. "But hear me well when I say this, Aelron *unmoored*." He spoke the last with disgust. "Our duty ends here. When we turn and leave you'll be governed by the Shandarian Justice Protocols, like everyone else. Violate them and you'll suffer the fate you *deserve*, rather than the one that's been *negotiated* for you."

So that *was* what Jacobson was after.

"You're just going to leave me here?" Aelron asked. "No food? Water? Not even *you* would survive in a land without animals."

"You have everything you were sent with," Jacobson said. "Even the money your father gave you. Provisions weren't part of the negotiation."

Aelron couldn't see the other rangers, but he heard their laughter.

"Neither was a map, I take it," Aelron said as he climbed to his feet.

Jacobson's hand appeared from under his Arinwool, pointing toward the small village ahead.

"That's east," Jacobson said. "Make for Dyr Agul. You're welcome."

"What village is that up ahead?"

"Don't know. Wasn't here forty years ago."

As Jacobson and the rangers left in the direction they'd come from, Aelron had a decision to make.

East or west?

Aelron regretted what he had done the moment he formed the question in his mind. The familiar dread, which often faded but never vanished, washed over him in waves, covering him like dirty water.

He retrieved a silver coin he kept in a special pocket hidden in his cloak. It wasn't just any coin. It was the only thing that kept the dread at bay when certain questions needed answers. He hated that coin, but he needed it all the same. And he'd learned to never disobey its command.

The coin had told him to kill Letcher sooner, while the man was asleep, but he disobeyed it. And doing so nearly cost him his life. He'd won in the end, using Letcher's own dagger against him in a fist fight. But how much simpler it would have been had he done what the coin had told him to do sooner.

And there were other times. Times rangers and civilians could have been saved, if only Aelron had obeyed the coin. There must be at least a dozen people dead who should be alive, and a dozen people alive who should be dead.

He wasn't going to make those same mistakes again.

Aelron turned the coin over in his hand, alternating between the side stamped with an adda, and the side stamped with an adda-ki. He pushed the dread away, telling himself he'd get around to flipping it in a moment. Besides, it wasn't all that bad. What was it Master Nigel had told him after he'd beaten Aelron at a game of *Shrillers and Adda*? "You can't plan some things," Nigel had said. "Oftentimes chance rewards us better than strategy."

Chance it is, then. If it comes up adda, I go east, toward Dyr Agul. Adda-ki, I go west.

He flipped the coin into the air with his right hand. As it descended toward his waiting palm, the tension in his neck eased with every inch it fell. When it landed, the euphoria was pure relief, like he'd taken a good piss after holding it a half-hour longer than prudent.

He flipped the coin onto the back of his left hand.

Adda. East it is.

He put the coin back in its special pocket and headed off toward the village as the sun set behind him.

CHAPTER FOUR

¹The Power looked upon his creation and found it incomplete. ²The beasts of the air shared his freedom, but they were not like him. ³The beasts of the ground shared his strength, but they were not like him. ⁴The beasts of the fire shared his warmth, but they were not like him. ⁵The beasts of the water shared his speed, but they were not like him.
- The Mukhtaar Chronicles, attributed to the prophet Habakku
Origines Multiversi, Emergentiae 3:1-5

Sun had set, plunging the roadway into darkness. It was the first time Aelron had felt safe since the rangers left him. His black cloak and dark trousers would keep him hidden from prying eyes.

Heavy rains pelted him as he followed the muddy road into the village. He pulled his black hood over his head to keep the water out of his eyes.

As he got closer to the village, his stomach grumbled.

The scent of roasting meet threaded its way through the smell of rain and damp earth.

As hungry as he was, he'd have to be careful. It didn't take much to get small-town folk suspicious, and the last thing he needed was a fight.

The scent was a good sign, though. He needed provisions if he was going to survive out here. Whatever had happened under the dome made game and vegetation scarce. It didn't matter how good the hunter if there was nothing to hunt.

He should find a place to gather his thoughts, away from the road leading into the village.

A partial building on his right—uneven bricks and no roof—would provide no shelter from the downpour. The brickwork looked sturdy, though. It would have taken something powerful to cause its collapse.

No. On second look, it was under construction. Judging by the parapets and gated yard, it was a military barracks. The Union wanted a garrison here for some reason.

And, if custom hadn't changed, Union soldiers built their *own* barracks.

A sobering thought. He put his attention back on the road in front of him.

Two tile-roofed buildings, each with an awning, formed an entrance to the village proper. There was no gate, but a muddy road ran between the two buildings into the village center.

He patted the pocket containing his special coin to satisfy his paranoia. A nervous habit, like the way he always rinsed a cup before filling it, even it had just been washed—there might be dust in it. Or the way he lined his daggers up before going to sleep—he might need to retrieve one in a hurry. Though he wondered, sometimes, if the absence of the coin would be any worse than its presence.

I could make my way around the northern building. Then they wouldn't see me coming.

The fewer people he encountered, the safer the village would be. All it would take is someone asking the wrong question, and it could set off a chain of events that demanded the coin's intercession. That's the way it always worked. If anyone—himself included—asked a question with only two possible answers, the coin's malevolent compulsion would take hold, squeezing him in its grip until it drove all other thoughts from his mind.

Better to take some food and vanish than to confront a bunch of inbred farmers who felt invincible around strangers.

But which way would be safer, taking the road, or using stealth around the building?

As soon as he formed the question, the compulsion returned in the form of tension in his neck and shoulders. It was mild at the moment, but if he didn't didn't consult the *coin,* panic would follow.

He took the coin out of its pocket.

Adda, I follow the road. Adda-ki, I sneak around the building.

He tossed the coin and caught it on the back of his left hand. The tension evaporated even before he glanced at the result.

Adda. Road it is.

As the wind shifted, driving the rain into his face, sounds of merriment and song came from the village center. What would people be doing out in a storm like this?

Celebrations meant foreign merchants and craftsmen. Perhaps this town would be less suspicious of strangers than other hamlets he'd visited in the northern country.

He stopped at the corner of the building on the north side of the road and listened.

Too many conversations to pick one out. There must be at least twenty people.

The music swelled and with it the crowd's laughter.

At least twenty more dancing. Musicians. Cooks. Serving people.

A familiar dull *crack* told him someone was on the losing end of a punch to the jaw.

He reached for his daggers and swore when he remembered they'd been taken.

But he couldn't stop now. The only way was forward.

He leaned around the corner to get his first look at the village center.

The village was little more than a ring of buildings circling an area one hundred yards in diameter. The glow of torches lit an expansive, rectangular cloth canopy that spanned the village center, held aloft by tall poles decorated with corn stalks and gourds. Beneath the canopy, people danced in time to festive music played by a troupe of bards at the far end of the makeshift pavilion. Smaller tents lined the outer ring between the canopy and the buildings, and people stumbled in and out carrying tankards.

Harvest festival. I could go for one of those tankards about now.

"Oy!"

An aging, high-pitched voice startled Aelron from behind.

"Who are you, skulking about then?" the voice asked.

Malvol's festering stones! If I'd been listening, I'd have known he was coming.

"No skulking," Aelron said as he turned. "I promise."

Standing before him was an older man in his late fifties, wearing a tall hat, a hide cloak, and a chain of office around his neck. It was too dark for Aelron to make out which office it represented, though.

I'll have the advantage of speed. I can tangle him in his own cloak. His arms are folded under it, so he's probably not very good with a blade. And he's favoring his left knee.

"And what do you call it, then?" the man said. "Looks a lot like *skulking* to me."

Aelron straightened up and held his hand out. "Aelron. You are?"

"The bleedin' constable, that's who."

Wonderful.

"Well met, sir," Aelron said. "You have a name, Constable?"

"Constable. Now what are you about?"

"Look, I'm just passing through. I've never been here before and wanted to see what I was getting myself into. That's all. I swear it."

"That's all?"

"That's all. I'm going to walk straight into that crowd, buy a drink and a meal, and be on my way. I'll be out of your hair before you know it."

Just let me walk into the crowd, old man.

"Well you keep in mind, *ale rod*—"

"Aelron—"

"...that I'll tolerate no chicanery, subterfuge, or churlish behavior. I was appointed by the local ranger captain *hisself*. If I catch wind of any furtiveness, skullduggery, or devious machinations, I'll bring the full force of the Shandarian Justice Protocols down on you like a blacksmith's anvil!"

"I think you mean *hammer*, friend."

"I said no chicanery!"

Damned inbred farmer.

"I do apologize," Aelron said. "It'll never happen again. Tell me, though. What village is this?"

The constable squinted as if he didn't understand the question.

"Where am I?" Aelron asked.

"You okay, mate? This is Blackwood." A note of pride entered the constable's voice, and he straightened his back. "Twenty-seventh largest village in the Shandarian Union. Says so right on the sign."

"You have a sign?" Aelron must have missed it. He was getting sloppy. First, an old man crept up on him, and now he was missing signs.

"Did one of those quakes shake your brain loose, man? Of course we have a sign! In case you weren't listening, we're the twenty-seventh largest village in the Union. It's a *wooden* sign. We even have wooden buildings, for Arin's sake! Wouldn't be much of a village without a sign, now would it?"

Why is he going on about wood ?

"How far outside of Dyr Agul are we?" Aelron asked.

"That's a different festering country."

"How far?"

The constable looked toward the east, through the village center.

"Well, I don't know," the constable said. "Nearest city is Caspardis. About seventy miles southeast, along the road you skulked in on. Now get your meal and skulk on out the other side of Blackwood."

"I'll do that."

"And you just remember —"

"No *chicanery*. I know."

"Or devious machinations! One whiff of duplicity or surreptitiousness and I'll—"

"Bring down the anvil. I remember."

"I'm watching you, *ale rod!*"

Aelron shook his head and went over to an outer tent. He memorized the layout of the village center as he went, the same way a *Shrillers and Adda* player memorizes the position of pieces on the board before his opponent's turn to hide them.

Three paces between tents. Four paces to the canopy. Fifty paces and I can be out of the village.

A drunk stumbled out of a long tent next to Aelron, spilling his tankard on the muddy ground.

Aelron pulled the tent flap aside and stepped inside.

The ground under the tent was mostly dry, save for footprints, so they must have pitched it before the storms. Four rough-hewn wooden tables and benches ran parallel along the length of the tent, ending near several kegs of ale beneath the bar at the far side. Patrons sat shoulder to shoulder on the benches, eating roasted meats and drinking ale. The one exception was a bench on the far left side of the tent. Only a skinny drunk and a dwarf in patchwork robes sat at that bench.

The atmosphere was noisy, filled with laughter and song, and the smoke from a large cooking grill created a layer of haze at the ceiling of the tent that escaped through screened vents along the pitched center. Water collected in muddy pools under the vents, however, as the pelting rain gained entry. Men exited with haste through a flap in the right side of the tent, then returned at a relaxed pace. The ground near that flap was muddy. It must lead outside to a privy.

Five paces to the barkeep. That skinny drunk next to the dwarf in patchwork robes is hiding a dagger at his back. Not very well, either. I can take it easily if I need it.

Aelron made the short journey to the bar, trying to stay aware of the skinny drunk, in case he decided to leave or change positions. A portly barkeep, dressed in a dirty apron, pulled a tankard from a cupboard as Aelron stepped up to the bar.

"Two crowns for the tankard and two more for what goes in it," the barkeep said without looking up. "Two crowns a fill thereafter, any stall. Five crowns for a meal. Doesn't include a tankard, though."

"Surprised all that dancing and singing is going on out there," Aelron said. "It's really pouring down."

"Canopy out there is keeping 'em dry. No one's going to miss the harvest festival because of some rain."

Aelron retrieved his coin pouch. Fifty Shandarian marks. That's all his father had given him all those years ago.

"Five marks for the meal," Aelron said, getting hungrier with every coin he counted out. "And four for a full tankard." He slid them over to the bartender.

"You deaf?" the barkeep asked. "I said *crowns*. We don't take those relics here."

Aelron examined the coppery coins in confusion. He had no idea what a *crown* was.

"Come on," Aelron said. "They must be worth *something*. The metal alone is—"

"Isn't worth the shite you took this morning. Turn around and leave the way you came. Come back with Pinnacle crowns. Whether they're yours or someone else's, I don't give a shriller's bunghole."

Why would the Pinnacle have its own currency? And why in the hells would everyone else be using it?

Aelron's ring—the one Master Nigel had given him—clanked against the counter as he scraped the coins back into their pouch. He'd been hoping to hang on to it longer. Maybe use it to barter for a mount. But it was the only thing of value he had. And food trumped transportation.

Aelron slid the ring off his little finger and slapped it onto the counter.

"What's this worth?" Aelron asked.

The bartender whistled. But rather than examining the ring, he stared into Aelron's eyes, as if examining *them* instead.

"Where'd you get this?" the bartender asked. "You're no ranger. Don't have the eyes."

"Gift."

The bartender brought the ring to within a few inches of his face and spun it around. "This is real."

"I know."

"You get it off that patrol that rode through earlier?"

Aelron caught his breath. If there were rangers nearby, this may not end well.

"Didn't know there was one," Aelron said. "Did a ranger a favor once. He gave me a ring in return."

A tipsy woman with long brown hair pushed Aelron aside and slammed an empty tankard on the counter, along with two silver coins. She wore a black dress that revealed more than it hid, and her acrid perfume rose above the roasting meats to stab Aelron right in the nose.

"Crowns!" The woman said. "Now give me my crowns' worth!"

"Sounds like a gift you should keep, friend," the barkeep said to Aelron, as he filled the woman's tankard and took her crowns. He slid the ring back across the bar toward Aelron.

"I look like the sort who wears jewelry to you?" Aelron asked. He slid the ring back to the bartender.

The woman nudged Aelron and smiled. "You're a handsome one. Come keep me company." She indicated a bench near the side entrance.

He looked her up and down, and her smile grew wider.

"Like what you see?" she asked.

Probably no weapons, but I can't tell. She's too far gone to make use of them anyway. And not enough muscle tone for a trained fighter.

"Love every inch," Aelron said. *You win the prize tonight, madam. You picked a seat near an exit.*

As she shifted her weight, a glint of light reflected off something near her armpit. Aelron took the woman's hand and brought it up to his lips, lifting her arm to see a metal clasp on her dress.

Nothing dangerous.

"Ooh, a charmer, you are," the woman said. She stared at his lips for a moment that lingered longer than decency allowed, then walked back to her seat.

"I'll give you a meal and a full tankard," the barkeep said.

"That's all?" Aelron asked. "That ring is worth far more than that."

"Be thankful I'm interested. Can't sell it anywhere. I'm stuck with it once I take it."

"I have a long road ahead. Was hoping to buy some provisions for the trip. Maybe a mount too."

"Keep that woman's hand near your mouth a while longer, and she'll buy everything you need."

Aelron considered. The money his father had given him was worthless. He could hold out, hoping to sell the ring for a higher price to another buyer, but that was a long shot. And it was doubtful anyone in Blackwood would feel different from the barkeep.

And the last thing he'd eaten was a small rodent two days ago.

"Take it," Aelron said. "But at least give me an extra helping of mutton."

The barkeep nodded and filled the tankard.

"You're not going to wash that out first?" Aelron asked.

The barkeep gave Aelron an incredulous look. "It's clean."

"It's been sitting out there for—" Now wasn't the time or place.

When the barkeep finished filling it, Aelron took his dust-infused tankard of ale to a seat on the bench next to the drunk woman. The barkeep followed with a heaping plate of mutton, cabbage, and potatoes.

The woman draped a shapely leg over Aelron's thigh and placed a hand in his lap as he ate.

Aelron stared at her exposed cleavage, trying to detect the distinctive marks of a concealed weapon.

"Interested in what I've got under this dress, are you?" she asked.

"More than you realize," Aelron said.

"Play your cards right and you'll see."

Mention of cards reminded him of the coin he carried. He pulled it out of its pocket and stared at it. What was he doing here? His instinct had told him to go in the opposite direction, but the coin never lied. When the rangers left him, it told him to follow the path in the direction Jacobson wanted him to go. And that decision had led him here. To Blackwood.

He lifted his tankard and took a drink.

A man brushed past, in a hurry toward the exit. Either he'd been putting off a trip to the privy longer than he should have, or there was something important through the side exit. He kept looking over his shoulder, back toward the dwarf in patchwork robes, but by the time Aelron turned to get a better look at the dwarf, he was gone.

How'd he manage that? No way he could have gotten to the front exit that quickly.

"Why'd you bother arguing with the barkeep if you've got that?" the woman asked.

It took Aelron a moment to realize she was talking about the coin.

"This?" Aelron asked. He rolled the coin between his fingers, making it travel from thumb to little finger and back again. "This isn't money. It tells the future."

The woman laughed. "And what does it have to say about me? Will I—"

Aelron pressed a finger to her lips before she could start something he'd end up regretting.

"It's best not to ask any questions you don't want a truthful answer to," Aelron said.

The muffled sounds of men arguing entered the tent through the side exit.

Anger in close proximity to alcohol won't end well.

Aelron focused on the conversation as best he could. The music and revelry made it difficult to concentrate, but the men repeated the same words several times. *New archmage.*

"Excuse me a moment," Aelron said. "I need to use the privy."

If there was a new archmage, something was very wrong.

"I'll be here, sweetie," the woman said, giving his thigh a firm squeeze as he stood.

The rain had slowed to a sprinkle, but the ground was a sheet of mud. The stench of human waste overpowered everything else. He turned to the left where several men relieved themselves into a trench dug in the dirt.

There was a strange sensation as he turned, like someone was watching him. He glanced around and saw no one, so he shrugged the feeling off.

"I'm telling you, now's the time," a voice said. It was one of the voices Aelron had heard earlier, and its source was behind the tent, hidden from view beyond the privy trench. "The new archmage is—"

"That dwarf knows more than I'm comfortable with," another voice said. "It's never good when he shows up."

Aelron approached, pressing his back against the tent wall as he crept toward the trench. He pulled his hood over his head. Between the darkness of the night and the tent's shadow, he'd be hidden once he rounded the corner.

"The new archmage is a great unknown," the voice said. "If that dwarf knows what the master is planning—"

"The dwarf can't know that, you fool. He's just a necromancer."

Aelron glanced around the corner. If his memory of such things was correct, the second man wore the robes of a Council magus; white alb with a black scapular reaching to mid-chest. But this scapular was trimmed in red. The ones Aelron remembered had no trim.

Aelron checked his cloak for the tiny scrap of Arinwool. With a Council magus involved, it may come in handy sooner than Aelron wanted. He was certain he could take the other man, if it came to a fight. But it was always best to let a magus kill *themselves* when possible.

That sensation again. Someone watching. Waiting in the shadow, just as he would do. But every time he checked, there was no one.

Must be nerves. It was time to act.

Aelron stepped out from the shadow toward the man speaking with the Council magus.

"I couldn't help overhearing," Aelron said. "New archmage, you say?"

"Take him!" the Council magus said. "No one can know I'm here!"

The other man pulled a dagger from his cloak and rushed at Aelron.

Aelron arced his fist up into the man's throat with a single knuckle extended. The man grabbed at his neck and collapsed onto the muddy ground, unable to breathe or make a sound.

A wave of power passed over Aelron and funneled into the patch of Arinwool before reflecting outward. The Council magus must have tried to use magic against him.

Aelron knelt next to the choking man. "Don't worry. You'll be dead soon." He looked toward the magus, who had collapsed on the ground. "And from the looks of those boils on your face, so will you. Though that's on *you*, not *me*."

The Council magus narrowed his eyes, as if about to weep. "How?"

"Arinwool. Is that spell you cast fatal?"

The magus nodded.

Aelron shrugged. "That's the risk you take when you try to kill somebody. Sometimes they kill you back."

A black blur moved through the shadow Aelron had emerged from, then disappeared. Aelron tried to follow the image with his eyes, but it disappeared as quickly as it appeared.

The choking man gave a final kick and grew still. Aelron grabbed the man's dagger, then turned to the Council magus.

"Your friend's dead," Aelron said. "So what do you say you make it all mean something and answer my questions?"

The magus didn't answer.

"Someday a necromancer will raise you," Aelron said. "I'm no magus, but I think it might go better if you had fewer secrets."

The magus squeezed his eyes shut.

"Tell me what you know about this new archmage," Aelron said. "Perhaps I'll light a candle for you at the next temple I pass."

"His name is Nicolas Murray. But no one's seen him since—" The magus coughed, and another boil formed on his forehead. " —since he killed Kagan. Many in the Council question whether he actually exists or whether the Mukhtaar Lords rule the Pinnacle in secret, fulfilling the ancient ambition of Tycon Mukhtaar."

"Murray?" Aelron asked. "You must have misheard. Only an Ardirian can be archmage."

The magus's face went from pale to light green.

"Why are you so interested?" the magus asked.

"Because *I'm* an Ardirian."

The magus choked and coughed up blood.

"Garrison," the magus said.

"What?"

"Garrison. Co...commander."

The magus went limp, his eyes devoid of life.

A mix of uncomfortable emotions spun through Aelron's mind. If someone had killed his father, then where did that leave Aelron? Where did that leave his infant brother…the one he hadn't seen since he was five? He'd expected to be welcomed back by his family at the Pinnacle. Now he had nowhere to turn. Maybe the Mukhtaar Lords could help? He was told one of them was his father's Prime Warlock. But this magus seemed to think the Mukhtaar Lords had usurped the Obsidian Throne.

The more he thought about it, the more he had no idea what he was getting himself into. Only one thing was certain. He wasn't going to let any usurper—be they Mukhtaar Lord or some stranger named Murray—go unpunished. If he had to walk from here to the Pinnacle, then so be it.

But what had the magus meant about the garrison commander? Did this commander know something about his father?

Aelron stood and walked back into the tent. Having someone to hunt didn't mean he couldn't finish his meal first.

K aitlyn smiled politely as Sergeant Diggins showed her the Pinnacle gardens. Gorgeous place. Flowers she'd never seen before grew in all shapes and sizes. Their exotic scents intermingled with the saltwater breeze blowing in from the ocean. But it was getting increasingly difficult to hide the pit she felt in her stomach.

She lifted her tiny crucifix necklace off her chest and rolled it between her fingers.

Nick said he'd been gone a year. She wanted so much to believe him. He'd never lied to her before. But when he disappeared from the apartment, he reappeared a second or two later. He *had* to be hiding something. Or, maybe he was just mistaken.

That wasn't fair, though. Nick had gotten pulled through that swirling *thing* dressed for a funeral. Two seconds later he looked like a homeless person wearing a bed sheet.

Then, he raised Mr. Landing from the dead. She'd seen it herself.

Moreover, these people *knew* him. At least that *Tithian* guy did.

And she was walking around on an alien planet!

But the truth didn't make this any easier. This was all well and good for Nick, but he seemed to have forgotten about *her* Five-Year Plan. What about graduation? Grad school? She'd finished her bachelor's in

Psychology, but she wanted her master's as well. What about planning the wedding?

And what about the nightmares she'd been having that featured a decapitated head.

She wasn't prepared to tell Nick about that yet. He'd freak out. He'd had the same dreams before that *portal* opened in his living room and brought him here.

Sergeant Diggins had been talking about something, and she'd missed it. Something about a rose bush that only bloomed when some goddess or other showed up.

She couldn't do this right now. There was too much on her mind.

"Sergeant Diggins?" Kaitlyn said. "Would you mind giving me some time to myself? I know the way back."

"Of course, my lady. If you need anything at all, there will be two guards at the door we came out of."

Diggins bowed and set off toward the Pinnacle, though Kaitlyn wasn't sure of the correct terminology. Some people spoke about the *building* as if it were the Pinnacle, and others spoke as if it were the entire island.

Not that it mattered. From what she could tell, the building *covered* the island.

A flash of red crossed her peripheral vision, farther down the path, and she faced it.

A woman with long red hair, in a floor-length red dress, walked along the path toward a distant hill. The woman glanced over her shoulder, and something about her face felt familiar.

Thoughts of Nick, the mystical portal, college degrees, and dreams with decapitated heads, drained away and left her with one purpose; follow the woman.

As she crested a hill, the path continued downward toward a shrine and the deep azure ocean in the distance.

Kaitlyn followed the woman, who walked a hundred yards ahead of her, down the path, past the mysterious flowerless rose bushes, toward a statue on a tall base set within an enclosure. The enclosure was concave, like the inside of a clam shell.

Kaitlyn entered the enclosure and hesitated when she saw the woman waiting for her.

The woman had the deepest blue eyes, and her smile filled Kaitlyn with a warmth that was equal parts love and pride. The woman stepped toward the front of the statue and disappeared behind the base.

As the saltwater breeze intensified, it carried a different scent with it this time. The strong scent of roses.

Kaitlyn followed in the woman's steps, but when she rounded the corner of the statue's base, the woman was gone.

The flowerless rose bushes had seemed dormant, but now they bore the most gorgeous roses Kaitlyn had ever seen. Perfectly formed, the deepest red, enormous—at least the size of her head—and fragrant beyond any flower she'd smelled before.

Kaitlyn glanced up at the statue and gaped.

Though the figure in the statue wore different clothes, and had brown hair instead of red, there was no mistaking the face.

It was the face of the woman who had led her here.

The nameplate on the statue read "The Goddess Shealynd".

She glanced down at a stray rose at the base of the statue and bent to pick it up. It must have blown off of the shrub.

Footsteps on the path told her she wasn't alone.

A man with long dark hair smiled at her. He wore a midnight blue robe. He raised his left hand, touched his thumb to his chin, and extended his little finger. As he pulled his hand away from his face, something materialized next to him.

But what she was seeing made no sense. Standing before her was a giant, walking fish. It had enormous eyes that turned independently of each other, and they focused on her, examining her from head to toe.

There was something non-threatening about both of them, though. The man, though he didn't seem familiar like the woman, exuded an aura of care and protection.

"Hello," Kaitlyn said. She took a few steps to get closer to the man, but she stopped and jumped back.

The decapitated head from her dreams appeared between her and the man. It was the head of a woman with auburn hair, and she wore a scowl.

In her dreams, the head stayed still, and it didn't appear angry. But this time, she glided toward Kaitlyn quickly, like a predator swooping in to attack.

Pain erupted at her temples as the dizziness took her.

She fell next to the roses, and her vision went black.

Nicolas stood before the massive double doors that opened into the Council Chamber. His nerves were getting the better of him. Tithian was by his side, going over details of the installation ceremony with several other council magi. Nicolas wished Kaitlyn could be here, but the rules were strict. No non-council personnel allowed. He hoped she was enjoying her walk. Tithian had assured him that she would be safe on the Pinnacle grounds. These were different times than when he had left.

Still…how was he supposed to calm his nerves by embracing his cet if his cet was off strolling through the tulips on a nature hike?

And where the hell was Mujahid? He'd hoped to introduce Kaitlyn this morning. But as usual, the man was off on some mysterious chore. He wouldn't be surprised to learn Mujahid kept secrets from *himself*.

Nicolas took a deep breath and peeked into the Council chamber.

It was every bit as impressive as he expected it to be. The room was like a miniature colosseum, oblong with stadium seats. A marble banister, split in places to allow people to enter the stadium, separated the seats from the large open area in the middle. It was as if the room and everything in it, except the banister, were carved from sandstone.

In the center of the chamber, a series of steps led up to a raised platform on the far end of the room. Nicolas's eyes followed the steps, up past a wooden podium, to the blackest of black objects. The Obsidian Throne. It wasn't much more than a black chair. Sure, it was a *big* black chair, but there wasn't anything fancy about it. Just a seat, two arm rests, and a tall back.

Next to the Obsidian Throne was a small table with two objects; a chain of office and a zucchetto—the form-fitting skullcap worn by higher-ranking Catholic clergy. Well, he was sure they didn't call it a zucchetto here, but that's what it was nevertheless. And he didn't like it one bit.

Two liveried pages distributed a pamphlet of some sort as council magi entered the chamber. Were those *programs*?

"You're making that face again, Archmage," Tithian said.

At least Tithian had stopped calling him *Holy One*.

"Do the robes fit well?" Tithian asked.

Nick held out his arms and examined himself.

"I look like Kagan," Nicolas said. "Same damned robe."

"One, it's only a uniform," Tithian said. "A symbol that everyone understands and respects. And two, it's not the *same damned robe*. Dead Kagan is wearing the *same damned robe*, remember? That's something you need to change, by the way. We can't have him running around wearing official robes anymore."

Nicolas agreed and sent the command through the necromantic link.

"Done," Nicolas said.

"And three," Tithian held a finger in Nicolas's face in an uncharacteristic display of assertiveness. "It's not the robes that make the man. It's the man who makes the robes."

"Well, I appreciate your—"

Sergeant Diggins, the guard who checked on Nicolas the night before, ran up behind them, panting.

"Archmage," Diggins said. "I came as quickly as I could. Just like you asked."

"Ahh," Tithian said. "I see you've already met Sergeant-at-Diggins."

Diggins blushed.

"It's okay, Diggins," Tithian said with a smile. "We all get flustered now and again."

"Thank you, Prime—"

"But for future reference," Tithian said, "if you're going to interrupt someone, it is me and *not* the archmage you should interrupt. Protocol, Diggins. You address *me* if the archmage and I are together, and preferably *not* while the archmage is speaking."

"Understood, Prime Warlock."

"Now, what is it you would like to say?"

"Archmage, I found Lord Mukhtaar."

"Mujahid?" Nicolas asked.

Diggins nodded. "I told him you were upset that you didn't get a chance to introduce the Lady Kaitlyn to him, and he promised to seek her out on the grounds."

"So he won't be attending the ceremony?" Nicolas asked.

"Lord Mukhtaar said you'd be better served by Prime Warlock Tithian and the Council magi."

Nicolas looked down. It was difficult to conceal the disappointment.

"Thank you, Diggins," Tithian said. "If there's nothing else, that will be all."

Diggins saluted and walked away.

"I understand why you feel close to Lord Mujahid," Tithian said. His voice had softened. "But I promise I'll help you through this."

"It's not that," Nicolas said, placing a hand on Tithian's soldier. "Trust me. You're the bee's knees of Prime Warlocks."

"I'm...not sure how I feel about that."

"It's a good thing. Means you're a decent dude and I have a great deal of respect for you."

"Well...thank you, Archmage."

"I'm worried about him, that's all. He was a man with a single purpose for forty years, and now that's just...gone."

"Ahh, I see," Tithian said. "I've known Lord Mujahid for many years, and believe me when I tell you he's a man who finds purpose where most of us wouldn't recognize it. He'll never tell you this, but he has a heart the size of the Pinnacle. And it's that heart that keeps him away from your installation ceremony."

"I don't understand."

"Consider this. He's a *Mukhtaar Lord*. As much as I *know* he wants to attend, if he enters those chambers, all eyes will be on him from beginning to end. He wants this to be *your* day. And, in some ways, mine as well."

"See?" Nicolas said. "Like I said. The bee's knees of Prime Warlocks. I feel better already. But can we get this show on the road?"

"There are times I feel as if I need a translator," Tithian said.

Nicolas stared into the chamber, nerves threatening to get the better of him again.

"You're going to do fine," Tithian said. "I'll precede you and make my way up the dais. When I announce you, you enter the chamber, climb the dais, and stand beside me. You're not *officially* the archmage yet, so I'll seal the chamber without your permission and begin the ceremony myself. And that will be the *last* time in our relationship that happens. Ready?"

Nicolas nodded. "But just so you know, I'm not wearing that funny hat outside of that room."

Tithian smirked and entered the Council chamber.

A voice yelled "Tithian Bel-Enrog, once and future Prime Warlock."

The hundred or more magi in attendance stood in unison and the room grew quiet.

Tithian faced them when he reached the top of the dais.

"Magi of the Council," Tithian said. "I present to you Nicolas Murray, formerly Ardirian, heir apparent to the Obsidian Throne."

This was it. Nicolas entered the chamber and kept his eyes on Tithian. The place smelled sweet from the incense, like a mixture of frankincense and sandalwood.

A loud thud told him the Pinnacle Guard had closed the heavy stone doors behind him.

For the love of god, don't let me trip over these robes.

The climb up the dais set his nerves on edge with every step. The higher he climbed, the sharper the stares of the Council's eyes on his back became.

"Magi of the Council," Tithian said. "We have come here today to perform a ceremony according to Arin's law. Let the chamber be sealed!"

"May it be as you command," the Council responded in unison. Nicolas hadn't been expecting that, and he jumped at the chorus of voices.

A wave of necropotency emanated from Tithian, giving Nicolas mental goose bumps, as if someone had tickled his mind. The giant stone doors sealing the chamber took on a yellow glow that grew in intensity then vanished, leaving a yellow echo in Nicolas's vision.

With the amount of power Tithian had used, Nicolas was pretty sure it would take an army to bust down those doors.

"The chamber is sealed," Tithian said. "Nicolas Murray, before you lie two symbols of the office you seek. The chain, by which you bind us to Arin's holy words. And the *qiyaaht*, by which you protect and safeguard our knowledge of the faith."

Key-yacht sure is a funny word for zucchetto.

"These are symbols that cannot be given," Tithian said. "You must take them upon yourself, free of compulsion, free of doubt. And so we ask you, Nicolas Murray, heir apparent, to spend the next few moments in prayer with us before you take them up."

Everyone kneeled and Nicolas followed along. It was odd, being asked to pray to Arin. And it was another offense that would make him worthy of a catechism uppercut from one of the nuns back home.

Nicolas, a voice said in his mind.

Nicolas held his breath. He remembered that voice. It was Arin.

You embark on this journey during perilous times, Arin said. *I warned you of this the last time we spoke.*

But what should I do? I don't know how to be an archmage! I don't know how to fight a war!

Be the person we chose, Arin said. *Take your rightful place in the world, the place few think possible, and the fog will lift.*

And with that, Arin's presence vanished from Nicolas's mind.

But something had remained behind.

A sharp burning sensation struck his mind, and he turned inward. Fiery text emblazoned itself inside his well of power, beneath the symbols of the skull and the arrow—the keys to unlocking his necromantic power. When the fire dimmed, and the letters turned black, he recognized the text. It was the last thing Arin had told him. *Take your rightful place in the world, the place few think possible, and the fog will lift.*

Nicolas didn't understand what had happened, but as the black letters faded away, he knew one thing with certainty; he couldn't forget those words if he tried. Just thinking about them made them reappear.

"Rise," Tithian said. When he looked at Nicolas he raised an eyebrow.

Nicolas kept his eyes forward. He had no idea how to tell Tithian what had happened.

Tithian continued. "If you accept the responsibility placed on you by Arin, if you choose to be the one who binds us to his holy will, then take up your chain of office."

Nicolas studied it for the first time. It wasn't elaborate or jeweled like he had expected. It was a gold chain, with large links, terminating in a medallion that had a bas-relief of Arin's Helm carved into it.

Funny hat and a big ass medallion. Great. Now I'm gonna look like Flavor Flav in choir robes.

There was no turning back now. He picked up the chain and placed it around his neck. When he released the chain, the Helm of Arin glowed yellow for a moment, then faded.

And from the expression on Tithian's face, that wasn't expected.

Several Religarian magi dropped to their knees, and others prostrated themselves wherever they could find room.

"Brothers and sisters," Tithian said. From the tone of his voice, and the way he stumbled over the words, it was clear he had gone off script. "Arin's holy presence has blessed us this day. Please. Rise. The ceremony is not over."

The magi hesitated, but one by one they stood. Their facial expressions were different. No longer were they struggling to get through a tedious ceremony. Now it was clear they were witnessing something mystical, and their demeanor had changed accordingly.

Tithian faced Nicolas. "If you accept the responsibility placed on you by Arin, if you choose to be the protector of our ancient faith, then take up the qiyaaht and place it on your head."

The qiyaaht was black, broader than a zucchetto, and it didn't have a stem on the top. It also extended farther down around the head.

Nicolas placed the qiyaaht on his head and let go, expecting it to glow, or hum, or do something else that no good hat should do. But nothing happened.

Tithian nodded toward the throne and Nicolas sat.

"Magi of the Council," Tithian said. "Let it be known throughout the Three Kingdoms that Nicolas Murray, formerly Ardirian, first of the Murray dynasty, has taken upon himself the symbols of office and now sits on the Obsidian Throne as our archmage."

The Council chamber erupted in applause, and the sudden outburst startled Nicolas enough to make him smile. He wasn't sure what to do, so he waved at everyone.

As the applause settled down, Tithian continued.

"Magi of the Council, let it be known…what is…"

"Tithian?" Nicolas asked.

"My seal," Tithian said. "It's been…*banished.*"

"I don't care who's wearing what, push that door open!" Mujahid yelled.

Nicolas stood as the giant chamber doors swung open.

Mujahid entered, and all eyes turned to him. His face was different. Nicolas had never seen him this concerned.

"Archmage," Mujahid said. "You must come quickly."

"What is it?" Nicolas asked.

"It's the Lady Kaitlyn. Something's happened."

Nicolas ran down from the dais and followed Mujahid through the doors.

CHAPTER FIVE

¹*The Power reached into his being and pulled the gods from within.* ²*The first he named Arin, for Arin was his exalted firstborn.* ³*The second he named Shealynd, for Shealynd emerged from his Love.* ⁴*The last he named Zubuxo, for Zubuxo was last in all things.*
- *The Mukhtaar Chronicles, attributed to the prophet Habakku*
Origines Multiversi, Emergentiae 4:1-4

It should remain ever at the forefront of the student's mind that the Origines was not written by the gods.
- *Coteon of the Steppes, "Coteonic Commentaries on the Origines Multiversi" (circa 520 RL)*

Nicolas was frantic. He had no idea where to go, so he followed Mujahid and Tithian as they ran through twisting passages to one of the many infirmaries in the vast palace-city.

The layers of ceremonial clothes did nothing to ease his chill.

"What do we know?" Nicolas asked. "What happened?"

"She was found unconscious by a Pinnacle guardswoman and taken to safety," Mujahid said. "I was on my way to find her at the time."

"This is my fault," Nicolas said. "I should have never left her alone!"

"We don't know anything yet," Mujahid said.

"She's probably exhausted from the journey," Tithian said.

"You weren't exactly the model of stability when you first arrived," Mujahid said. "I seem to recall you complaining about headaches…between rounds of vomiting all over yourself."

"Can you help her?" Nicolas asked.

Mujahid glanced at him. His eyes held a seriousness Nicolas hadn't seen since they were captured by the Shandarian Rangers.

"You know I'll do what I can," Mujahid said. "But we don't know anything yet."

"Turn left here," Tithian said.

Nicolas had gotten ahead of them and had to backtrack to make the turn. Passersby acted as if they didn't know whether to bow, kneel, or salute.

It was strange, moving around the Pinnacle like this. The last time he was here he had to disguise himself as an Arinian priest and sneak around.

"It's fine, everyone," Tithian said to the crowd.

"You have some teaching to do," Mujahid said.

"Sure you don't want that job?" Tithian asked. "You walked in these boots once."

"Kagan required no instruction on how to be pompous and arrogant."

"You can teach me anything you want after Kaitlyn's okay," Nicolas said. "Let's worry about one thing at a time."

Tithian pointed at a door across the wide hallway, and Nicolas went first.

The entrance to the infirmary was no wider than any other door in the hallway. That is to say, it was narrow. Whoever had built the room had something other than an infirmary in mind. Stacks of furniture leaned precariously along the walls, and a table turned on its side was the only thing keeping them from toppling.

"Odd place for a hospital," Nicolas said.

"Forty years of quakes and disease made us improvise," Tithian said.

The rectangular room was the size of three or four old classrooms smooshed together, and three rows of beds provided little walking space between them.

Kaitlyn was the only patient. She rested on a bed near one of the windows. Someone must have brought flowers, because she held an enormous rose in her hand.

An attendant stood next to her with the back of his hand on her forehead.

Nicolas drew necropotency into his well of power. He wanted to be as prepared as possible, in case some use of magic could help her.

Mujahid pushed the attendant aside, but he drew back when the attendant's hand came away from Kaitlyn's face. It was subtle, and Nicolas wouldn't have noticed the reaction if not for his necropotency-enhanced senses. What had Mujahid seen?

With a fair helping of composure, Mujahid recovered and began casting necropotency forward.

Kaitlyn stirred and Mujahid touched the rose in her hand.

"This isn't just any rose," Mujahid said. "It's a Rose of Shealynd. It's…magical. What happened?" he asked the attendant.

"A guard found her at the Shrine of Shealynd, my lord."

Mujahid looked away as if considering something.

"Nick?" Kaitlyn said. Her voice was raspy.

"Right here," Nicolas said.

"Where am I?" Kaitlyn said. When her gaze landed on Mujahid, she jumped. "He was there! He was there with the woman!"

Mujahid shook his head as if to say *no*. But there was no mistaking the look in his eyes. There was only one other person on Erindor Kaitlyn could have confused Mujahid with.

"Nuuan?" Nicolas asked.

"New what?" Kaitlin asked.

"Did the man you see look identical to me, dear one?" Mujahid asked.

Kaitlyn narrowed her eyes, but she nodded.

"This is the man I told you about," Nicolas said. "This is Mujahid. *Lord* Mujahid, I should say."

"That's all right," Mujahid said, smiling at Kaitlyn. "There's no need for her to call me Lord."

Something was off about him, and Nicolas couldn't figure out what it was.

More importantly, Nuuan must still be alive.

"Mujahid has an identical twin brother," Nicolas said. "It was him you saw. That's true, right Mujahid?"

The look on Mujahid's face expressed the shock Nicolas felt.

"I can tell you I was nowhere near the Shrine of Shealynd today," Mujahid said. "As to whether it was my brother, the evidence certainly suggests it."

Kaitlyn pursed her lips and shrugged.

Nicolas leaned closer to her and put his hand on her head, brushing her auburn hair away from her eyes.

"Can you tell us what happened?" Nicolas asked.

"Don't leave anything out," Tithian said. "No matter how small you think the detail is."

"I was curious about the architecture you mentioned," Kaitlyn said. "So I took a walk around the grounds. Sergeant Diggins was kind enough to show me the way to the gardens."

"Were you feeling out of sorts when you embarked on your constitutional?" Mujahid asked.

"Embarked on my constitutional?"

Mujahid smiled and laughed.

Smiled and laughed!

Something was odd about him today.

"I felt fine," Kaitlyn said, "until I saw a woman in a red dress."

Mujahid leaned closer.

"I was…I don't know…*drawn* to her. I wanted to get a closer look, and she was farther down the path, but every time I'd get close to her, she'd take another turn and disappear. I caught up to her eventually. She was checking out some building at the center of the garden. You'd love it, Nick. Looks like an old Roman temple. There's a beautiful statue there in a clam-shell enclosure."

"The Shrine of Shealynd," Mujahid said.

"But when I went inside, she was gone," Kaitlyn said. "I know I wasn't seeing things. There was only one way out, and she was just *gone*. That's when I noticed the statue I told you about."

Nicolas gave Mujahid a questioning look.

"The statue of Shealynd," Mujahid said. "Go on."

"It was just weird, you know?" Kaitlyn said. "I could swear that woman *modeled* for the statue or something. Her face was almost identical."

Mujahid's face had issues of its own. It had lost all color in the last few seconds.

"Then what happened?" Nicolas asked.

"I went to get a closer look and smelled the most beautiful roses. Like *this* one." Kaitlyn held up the rose she was carrying.

The rose was the size of Nicolas's head.

"I saw this one laying at the foot of the statue," Kaitlyn said. "So I went over to pick it up. When I leaned against the statue…that's when I saw them."

"Saw who, dear one?" Mujahid asked.

"You," Kaitlyn said. "Or…your brother…the man who looks like you. He did something odd with his hand."

That grabbed Mujahid's attention. "What did he do?"

Kaitlyn put her thumb on her chin and extended her little finger.

"Like this," Kaitlyn said.

Mujahid nodded. "That's Nuuan."

"Something you're not telling me?" Nicolas asked.

"He wasn't alone," Kaitlyn said. "There was something else with him."

"Some *thing* else?" Nicolas asked.

"The man who looks like Mujahid was standing next to a…a *giant fish*. But the fish had legs."

"A cichlos?" Nicolas asked Mujahid.

Mujahid shrugged. "Nuuan is as familiar with them as I. Who's to say?"

"But that's not the worst part," Kaitlyn said. "The decapitated head from my dreams was there too."

"The what?" Nicolas and Mujahid said in unison.

"You never said anything about a floating head!" Nicolas said.

"I've been…trying to find a time to tell you about those," Kaitlyn said.

"Arin be praised," Mujahid said with a wide smile on his face.

"Oh don't you start!" Nicolas said.

"It's too soon to tell anyway," Mujahid said.

"Tell what?" Kaitlyn asked.

Nicolas rubbed his temples. "Whether or not you're a necromancer. Like us."

Kaitlyn gave Nicolas an incredulous stare.

Nicolas rubbed her arm. "I...need a minute. Is there anything I can get you? Something to drink?"

Kaitlyn shook her head. "I'm fine."

Nicolas walked toward the infirmary entrance. This was a lot to absorb. First, being told that something had happened to Kaitlyn, then learning Nuuan was somehow involved. *Then* discovering Kaitlyn might be a necromancer, with all the risk and trouble that brought with it.

The weight of everything that had happened over the past year pushed down on his shoulders. It was too much for one person.

I just wanted us to start our lives together. Now this. And somehow I have to figure out what to do about the Barathosians, too?

Nicolas needed more than a minute. He needed a week on a beach with some drinks...the kind with those little umbrellas.

When Nicolas stepped into the hallway, people scattered out of the way, trying their best...but failing...to not look at him.

There's no reason for these people to be afraid of me. I'm not Kagan.

Mujahid stepped out behind him. "I suppose you'll want to know about the hand gesture."

"I want to know about *everything*," Nicolas said. "Yes, I'd like to know what the hand jive was about, but I'd *also* like to know why a Mukhtaar Lord is acting like a little girl at a dog shelter."

"Excuse me?"

"You're practically fawning over her!"

"Come now, lad, I didn't take you for the jealous sort."

"That's not it," Nicolas said. "That's not it at all. You're...not *you*. And that *bothers* me. You and Tithian are the only solid ground I have on Erindor right now. I can't have you flaking out on me. Not now of all times."

Mujahid put his hand behind his neck and massaged it.

"Did I ever tell you of my mentor?" Mujahid asked.

"You did," Nicolas said. "Not much, though."

"Her name was Mordryn. And she meant more to me than anyone I've ever known."

"*Remarkable* was the word you used, if I recall."

"Then I understated things. She was more than just remarkable. She was *everything*. And when she disappeared, all I had to remember her by was a broken blade and one of those roses the lady Kaitlyn is holding."

"The rose set you off then," Nicolas said. "I can understand that."

"Not the rose. Her face."

"I don't follow."

"As surely as I know I'm standing here, I know I was looking into Mordryn's eyes when I saw your lady Kaitlyn. The resemblance is uncanny."

"I grew up with her, Mujahid. She's not Mordryn."

"And here you stand."

"Mujahid, she's not—"

"I *know* she's not Mordryn, boy," Mujahid said, holding up his hand. "But you have to admit something is afoot here."

"So what do we do?" Nicolas asked. "I can't just let her lay in bed while I *hope* everything turns out for the best. Is she *Awakening*? Is that what this is?"

"You know as well as I it's too soon to tell. All we have is her description of a dream. Take any person on Erindor and give them a bit of bad cheese, and they'll be dreaming about decapitated heads too. Let's give it some time."

"I don't like this."

"I'll help her any way I can."

Fear bubbled up inside Nicolas, and he took a deep breath to stave off the panic. He remembered his own Awakening. The thought of Kaitlyn going through the same thing made him shudder. Why didn't she *tell* him about the dreams? He could have helped sooner!

If this is an Awakening, we can handle it. She's smarter than I am, and I managed to make it through okay.

Mujahid was right. There was nothing they could do except wait and see.

"Please stay close by," Nicolas said. "I won't know what to do if she gets worse."

Mujahid put his hand on Nicolas's shoulder. "Oh I doubt that. In fact, I suspect you'll know precisely what to do."

Nicolas wished he could believe him. "I'm serious, Mujahid."

Mujahid patted his shoulder. "I'll be out on the grounds for a while. We need to at least *try* to find this mystery woman in the red dress. And my brother. *And* this seemingly lost cichlos."

"You really think you're going to find them?"

Mujahid shook his head. "Not likely. But it will give me a chance to reflect. Sometimes we get so busy looking for answers in the world, we discount the answers within."

"You never did tell me about that hand gesture."

Mujahid chuckled and shook his head. "Nuuan's invention. From when we were boys. It was a way for us to make a humorous connection in an otherwise serious situation, as twins are often wont to do. We had but one rule; it had to be the left hand."

Nicolas smiled. "Like making faces at a friend in church."

"In Nuuan's case, it typically involved breaking wind."

"But why the *left* hand?"

Mujahid smiled. "So we could make fun of our friends who copied us with their *right* hands, of course!"

Mujahid gave Nicolas's shoulder one last pat and walked away.

N icolas had Kaitlyn taken to his private chambers, where she slept throughout the day. It wasn't home, but she'd be more comfortable without a bunch of attendants buzzing around her.

There was nothing they could do anyway, not if her problem was mystical. And all signs pointed in that direction. The dreams, the headaches, what more could there be? She'd have to face the Halls of Power soon.

And once she stepped through that black door, there was nothing he could do to help her.

The sun had set an hour earlier, casting the room in bluish hues of moonlight. Once again, the gems representing cities on the giant map of the Three Kingdoms shimmered.

Kagan brought a tray of food from one of the many cafeterias at the Pinnacle and placed it on the buffet next to a wooden weapon rack across from the king-sized bed.

Nicolas was sure they weren't *called* cafeterias, but he had no idea what the word for it was here. Cafeteria would have to do.

Kaitlyn never woke to eat, and Nicolas didn't want to disturb her, so he sent Kagan away and left the food on the wooden buffet.

He'd come to understand how invaluable wood had become over the last forty years, and it sickened him how much of it surrounded him in these opulent chambers. A wooden four-post bed with a canopy, wooden dresser and wooden wardrobe, wooden nightstands, ornate wooden frame around a panoramic mirror, two wooden chairs, a wooden writing desk with a wooden chair of its own, wooden weapon rack, and yes, the wooden buffet. And as he lifted his head, he saw the wooden crown molding as well.

Nicolas was tempted to strip the room, sell it all, and have the proceeds distributed among the poor. But something told him Tithian and Mujahid would object.

The Council politicians wouldn't be too happy about it either. If the archmage sold all the wood in *his* chambers, it wouldn't reflect well on them if they didn't follow suit.

All these thoughts and more rattled around his mind as he was trying to doze off next to Kaitlyn. Earlier he couldn't think at all. Now that he wanted to sleep, thinking was all he could do. He spent a few moments focusing his concentration and embracing his cet—clearing his mind and imagining that room with many doors at the center of his Halls of Power. When he managed to let go, he drifted off to sleep.

He opened his eyes to a disturbing sensation several hours later.

A force outside of himself, yet also within, made him sit up and get out of bed.

What's happening? What is this?

He wasn't in control. Something had taken over his muscles…and that *something* was inside him.

As beads of sweat formed on his forehead, he took slow steps toward the weapon rack.

No! Fight it!

Even in the midst of panic he couldn't stop moving forward, one foot after another, until soon he was standing in front of the rack.

He watched in terror as his hand took hold of a dagger, pulled it from its clasp, and turned the point toward himself.

Fight this!

He began to summon a penitent to snatch the dagger away, but he couldn't channel necropotency. His mind wouldn't allow it.

He tried to scream, hoping Diggins or another guard was nearby, but he couldn't move his jaw. He was completely under the control of this new power.

No. Not completely.

He let go of the fear and embraced his cet once more. In the periphery of his mind, he could still sense his arm bringing the dagger closer to his stomach, but the more he let go—the more in control of his cet he became—the slower the dagger approached.

When he reached the center of his cet, where the image of Kaitlyn dwelled, she screamed and woke.

Nicolas was in complete control of himself once more. As he ran to her side, he sent a command through the necromantic link to Kagan, telling him to find Mujahid as quickly as possible.

"It was horrible!" Kaitlyn yelled. "Just…floating there!"

"What was floating? What was it?"

"The head! And it's getting closer! Like you said before…oh my god, Nick!"

"That's *not* going to happen to you."

"How do you know?"

"Because there's no place else for you to go, that's why. If you're a necromancer, *this* is your place. No invisible hand is going to take you anywhere."

The door burst open and Mujahid ran to the bedside.

"What happened?" Mujahid asked. "Your penitent wouldn't tell me."

"It's happening like it happened to me," Nicolas said. "Dreams…the skull…the whole nine yards."

"You never told me there was a distance element to your Awakening," Mujahid said. "I would have found that fascinating."

"What?"

"You said something about nine yards."

"It's just a saying," Nicolas said. "Like the *whole enchilada*. You know? The whole kit and caboodle?"

"The whole…enchiboodle?"

"Never mind that," Nicolas said. "She's *Awakening*."

Mujahid touched the back of his hand to her head.

"Lady Kaitlyn," Mujahid said. "This is important. How long have you been having the dreams?"

"They started a few days ago," Kaitlyn said.

"Wait," Nicolas said. "A few days ago for *you* means…you were having them while I was having mine! You never told me!"

"Oh, and you were a model of information sharing?" Kaitlyn said. "I didn't get the whole story until you got sucked through a black hole in front of the TV!"

"Please, dear one, just answer my questions," Mujahid said.

Kaitlyn exhaled a deep breath and nodded.

"Have you had violent attacks of nausea?" Mujahid asked.

Kaitlyn shook her head. "No."

"Visions of skeletons?"

She shook her head again, but this time she furrowed her brow as if she didn't understand why he was asking her these things. "*No*."

"Scenes of unimaginable atrocities and violence?"

"What the hell? No! Just a floating head."

"So you *have* seen the skull?" Nicolas asked.

"I never said it was a skull! I said it was a *floating head!*"

Nicolas looked at Mujahid. What could Kaitlyn be talking about?

"One man's grotesque rotting skull is another man's floating head, what can I say?" Mujahid said.

"What about the room with two doors?" Nicolas asked.

"Yes!" Kaitlyn said. "I've seen that!"

"Now we're gettin' somewhere," Nicolas said.

"How close was this severed head to you in your last dream?" Mujahid asked.

"I could touch it if I tried, and it was getting closer."

"Then there's no time to lose," Mujahid said. "I wish I had time to prepare you like I did with Nicolas."

"You didn't miss much except a lot of yelling and insults, trust me," Nicolas said.

Mujahid frowned. "Follow my voice, and do everything I say. Clear your mind and remember the room with two doors."

"I can see it."

"Good," Mujahid said. "Now, don't go anywhere near the white door, do you understand?"

She seemed confused, but she nodded. "Um...okay. No white door."

"I want you to focus on the black door," Mujahid said. "That's where you want to go. Look at it and tell me what you see."

She shook her head.

"It's okay," Mujahid said. "Focus on the black door. Ignore the white door and turn toward the black."

"That's what I'm trying to tell you," Kaitlyn said. "There *is* no black door. Just a red door and a blue door."

Mujahid turned away. His expression terrified Nicolas. It was clear he had no idea what Kaitlyn was talking about. And Nicolas sure as hell didn't have any idea either.

After several moments, Mujahid whispered.

"Chimeramancy? How can this be?"

"What's that?" Kaitlyn asked.

"Wait," Nicolas said. "What was that word you just used?"

"Chimeramancy," Mujahid and Kaitlyn said in unison.

"Yeah, that one," Nicolas said. "I'd forgotten all about it until you said it. I had a close friend in Aquonome—"

"Where?" Kaitlin asked.

"The cichlos...Toridyn?" Mujahid asked.

"Yeah, Tor," Nicolas said. "When we met, he told me he never wanted to be a necromancer in the first place. He wanted to be a *chimeramancer*, but they told him he couldn't. Then later, after the battle here at the Pinnacle, when Arin spoke to Siek Lamil, he told him the cichlos *chimeramancers* wouldn't have to make the *great sacrifice*, whatever that is. The cichlos must know something about this. But...and don't take this the wrong way, Mujahid...what in the name of Malvol's butt crack is chimeramancy?"

Mujahid winced. "Surely you didn't spend *that* much time with Nuuan?"

Nicolas held his hands out as if to say *well, answer the question*.

"Chimeramancy is a form of dream magic," Mujahid said. "And it hasn't been seen in the Three Kingdoms since long before the Great Barrier, notwithstanding the cichlos. In fact, long before Nuuan and I ascended."

"Can it make people do things they don't wanna do?" Nicolas asked.

"Oh, it's much more than that. Chimeramancers have complete control over their dream state. And whatever they dream they have the power to manifest in the waking world...but only so long as they maintain the dream. If they are woken or disturbed in any way, the dream collapses, and with it whatever reality their magic manifested."

"I can do *what*?" Kaitlyn asked.

"That's gotta be what this is," Nicolas said. "Before she woke up, she'd taken complete control of me. She made me stand up, walk over to the weapon rack, and damn-near kill myself."

"Oh my god, Nick!"

Mujahid squinted. "A strange manifestation. But then she hasn't Awakened, so perhaps she's creating realities from a dream state she doesn't completely control. If she doesn't Awaken soon—"

"How much time do we have?" Nicolas asked.

"Days? A week? It's impossible to determine with any accuracy. Had she been born and raised here, her parents would have taught her of the Halls of Power, and she would have recognized the signs herself."

"I'm going to send for the cichlos," Nicolas said. "But there has to be something we can do until they get here."

Mujahid nodded. "You may not recall your first day on Erindor as clearly as I do. You were under great stress. But I slowed your Awakening long enough to provide you with some basic knowledge. I can teach you to do the same for Kaitlyn. But there's no time to wait for them."

"Aquonome is hundreds of miles away," Nicolas said. "It would take more than a week to get there."

Mujahid shook his head. "Tithian can provide you with a translocation orb that will take you close to Caspardis. From there...you know the way."

"Wait," Nicolas said. "You're not coming with me?"

"It's clear to me Nuuan plays some greater role in this, and I think it's time for me to know what that is. I'm going to find him. I've waited long enough for his return."

"But I need you here!"

"There is...a *power* at play here that I don't understand," Mujahid said. "I fear what may happen if it is left unchecked. I *must* find Nuuan and figure this out."

Nicolas commanded Kagan to find Tithian. If he needed to bring Kaitlyn to Aquonome, he wanted to leave as soon as possible.

Mujahid spent several minutes teaching Nicolas the simple flow of necropotency that could slow the Awakening process of another. The method involved placing a shield around the other person's well of power so it wouldn't fill with ambient energy.

"I'll go first," Mujahid said. "Watch what I do. When I remove the shield, you try."

A wave of necropotency left Mujahid and swept past Nicolas. But when the power entered Kaitlyn, Mujahid shrunk away and stopped channeling.

"This...this isn't..."

"What is it?" Kaitlyn asked.

Mujahid smiled at her. It was the smile of a man who wasn't sure how to tell someone a huge spider was crawling on their head.

"Well?" Nicolas asked.

"She has no well of power," Mujahid said.

Nicolas's chest tightened and Mujahid put a hand on his shoulder.

"Chimeramancy is very rare," Mujahid said. "I've never had the opportunity to study it in depth. It seems they don't require a power source in the same sense that you and I do. So…"

"So you don't know how to slow her Awakening?"

"I have an idea. But neither of you are going to like it. And it's not going to be easy."

"Lay it on us."

"You must *not* sleep, young lady. Not for long, at least. Chimeramancers use dreams, and so you must stay out of a dream state. It will be difficult. The headaches will be excruciating, but I can teach Nicolas to help you with those."

Nicolas closed his eyes and lowered his head. "I can't do this alone."

"You must, and you will," Mujahid said. "Pack what you need, but do it quickly. Get Kaitlyn to Aquonome as soon as you can."

"I will."

"Now let's teach you how to deal with those headaches."

"Wait," Nicolas said. "There's…"

"What is it?"

"You've seen war," Nicolas said.

Mujahid gave him a questioning look. "I've seen more than any man should."

"I haven't. Not really."

"You fought one battle after another to bring the barrier down."

"Not the same thing. I'm talking about generals and armies and navies and…*everything* that goes into a war. The Barathosians are *out there. Right now.* And just when this place needs an archmage the most, I can't be here. I can't. And even if I were…what do *I* know? What would I *do* that could make any difference?"

Mujahid nodded and glanced at Kaitlyn. "I know what this is about."

"I need your skills," Nicolas said. "As a warrior. As a general. As a leader."

"You underestimate Tithian. And you underestimate the Three Kingdoms."

"I don't *know* Tithian. Not like I know you."

Mujahid harrumphed. "He's far more than he lets on half the time. But you can rest assured he has your interests at heart."

"It's not *my* interests I'm concerned about right now. Everyone looks at me with…expectation. Like I'm supposed to have a handle on everything. And I don't even know what an archmage *does* yet. How am I supposed to fight a war?"

"We've had precious little time to talk about what your new duties entail. But the Three Kingdoms doesn't need you to be a *general*. They need you to be an *archmage*." Mujahid shook his head. "If you confuse the two, we may as well hand the Three Kingdoms over to the Barathosians."

"But what does that *mean*?"

"It means don't be Kagan. It means be the bright, inquisitive—often infuriating—young man I know you to be. Arin didn't ask you to be archmage because he expected something *new* from you. He asked because he wanted the Nicolas he'd come to know. The Nicolas that stood up to an archmage when few others would. The Nicolas that brought down the barrier and rescued the gods themselves. *That's* what it means. Now, let's learn to deal with Lady Kaitlyn's headaches before they worsen beyond our ability to control."

Nicolas nodded and did his best to follow along.

A knock on the chamber doors told Nicolas Tithian had arrived, but it came as no surprise. Kagan was standing outside the room and warned Nicolas through the necromantic link moments earlier.

Toby had started whining long before Kagan's warning, though.

Beagle nose trumps undead spidey sense, I guess.

"Come on in," Nicolas said.

Tithian entered the room, and Nicolas could tell he wasn't happy.

Toby grabbed his gatorpickle and jumped up on Tithian's leg, for which he was rewarded with a scratch behind the ears. It seemed Toby had won him over.

"I don't have time to hear it right now," Nicolas said. "I love ya, man, but this is important."

"Just hear me out for a moment," Tithian said, closing the door behind him. His eyes turned toward Kaitlyn, who was sitting on the edge of the bed. He bowed his head in her direction. "Lady Kaitlyn. Please pardon my interruption."

Kaitlyn waved her hand. "You weren't interrupting."

Tithian faced Nicolas once more. "I understand. Truly, I do. And I'm not going to try to stop you. But you're our archmage now, and there are things you need to know. Not the least of which are the potential consequences of your chosen course of action. You are not yet a politician. But you need to be. And it's my duty to help you become one."

"What am I supposed to do?" Nicolas asked. "I can't just let her die."

"I really wish you'd stop saying that," Kaitlyn said.

Toby jumped up into her lap when she spoke.

"Of course you can't," Tithian said, waving Nicolas's comment away. "I'd never suggest it. But when you return to the Pinnacle...and you *will* return...you're going to find the Council difficult to tame. They've had months to consolidate their power without you."

"They have you," Nicolas said.

Tithian shook his head. "I'm expendable, Archmage, and they know it. You have a divine calling. I was *hired*."

"You did well without me."

"Barely. You have no idea what things were like when you were gone. Forty years of quakes, starvation, and disease, gone like *that*." Tithian snapped both fingers. "Loved ones thought dead returned to families who refused to believe they were real...families who had already disposed of property and other inheritances. Nations on the precipice of war because of an assassination—committed by your predecessor, I might add. And a people coming to grips with the knowledge that what they once thought sacrosanct—the Book of Life itself—could be forged by a madman. It was chaos, and it's a testament to Arin's power the Three Kingdoms didn't destroy one another in the six months you were away.

"And if all of that isn't enough, there's still the Barathosian problem to consider. They're sitting off the coast of Dar Rodon as we speak. They're not going anywhere, Archmage. Are you prepared to deal with them? Do you have any plan for how the Council should approach this situation? Because when you return, I fear for what may happen if you don't take definitive control."

Nicolas lowered his head. Kaitlyn was days away from death. He couldn't deal with all of this right now. But Tithian was right. He had a responsibility to the people of the Three Kingdoms. And in some way he had a responsibility to the Council of Magi. But there was someone Tithian left out. Arin.

Nicolas had sworn an oath to Arin at great personal sacrifice. At the time, he thought he'd never see Kaitlyn or Earth again. But having her back didn't change his obligation. It didn't change his duty to this new world. Well…new to *him,* at least. He'd fight off an army to save Kaitlyn if he had to. But he couldn't ever forget that he was the archmage.

"I'm not going to be able to do this by myself," Nicolas said.

"No one is expecting you to. But you *will* have to play your part. The part of an archmage. You can start by dressing like a Council magus. Remember, no one is going to recognize you on sight. You may think that a blessing, but trust me when I tell you it can be a curse."

"What about these?" Nicolas asked, tugging at the archmage robes he was wearing.

"No," Tithian said. "I'll not have you taking a risk like that without me. You don't go traipsing around dressed like the archmage without protection. Especially now."

Tithian opened the wardrobe and examined the contents. He rifled through several of the robes, shirts, and trousers until he came to a white robe with a black scapular. He took the robe and trousers off a hanger and laid them on Nicolas's bed.

"There's pants?" Nicolas asked.

Tithian raised an eyebrow. "You're not wearing pants?"

"No one told me about pants!" Nicolas held the pants at his side. Perfect length. "Wait. These aren't girl pants, are they?"

"You'll need this," Tithian said.

Tithian handed him a small, black sphere. Larger than a marble, but small enough to fit in the palm of his hand. It was cool to the touch. Nicolas examined it for markings, but the sphere was seamless.

"That's a translocation orb," Tithian said. "It's attuned to the Caspardis area. The city gate should be in view of your arrival point, as I recall. I'm…aware you've been there."

Nicolas sniffed.

Been there? That was an understatement. The last time he'd *been there,* he was tossed into a dungeon, found guilty of heresy, flogged to within an inch of his life, and tossed into Lake Caspardis to drown.

Yeah…he'd *been there.*

"How does it work?" Nicolas asked.

"When you want to travel, channel a small amount of power into it. It will do the rest. Just make sure you're touching whoever you want to travel with. The more people you take, the more power it will use. It *should* bring you back to the sanctuary here."

"Should?"

Tithian blinked. "It's best you don't get involved in some things."

"Tithian."

"There are objects of power at the Pinnacle that sometimes disrupt the flow of magic," Tithian said. "But they won't be here long."

Nicolas gave him a suspicious look.

"Please," Tithian said. "Trust me."

"I can't help but wonder about something," Nicolas said.

"What?" Tithian asked.

"I wonder what Kagan would do in my place. I mean, with the Council the way it is and the Barathosians invading?"

"I can't say for certain, mind you. But I'm willing to lay good odds on him assassinating a diplomat, imprisoning his own people under a magical dome that slowly destroys the world, and eradicating anyone who disagrees with him. But what do I know?"

"Point taken."

"When you're tempted to ask yourself what *Kagan* would do...stop," Tithian said. "Erindor has known a *Kagan* already. It's time for the world to know a *Nicolas*."

Nicolas nodded. "I will get Kaitlyn to the cichlos. And I will come back and set things straight here. You have my word."

"There is something I must do in your absence," Tithian said. "I have loyal contacts in Tildem. They work for me...in a sense."

"What does that mean? Spy stuff?"

Tithian waved his hand as if to tell Nicolas to speak quietly.

"I trust you to sort it out," Nicolas said.

"Lady Kaitlyn," Tithian said as he bowed.

When the door closed behind him, Nicolas put his arm around Kaitlyn.

"I know this is all crazy," Nicolas said. "But we'll get through this together. The people I'm taking you to, they'll know what to do."

"I hope so," Kaitlin said.

CHAPTER SIX

¹*The Divine Plan*
²*The Tree of Life grew to a wondrous height, drawing the gaze of The Power.*
³*But the Power looked upon the Tree and was repulsed, for chaos and wickedness had engulfed it.* ⁴*The Power drew the gods unto himself, and Arin spake:*
⁵*"Why have these great and terrible powers manifested themselves within us?"*
⁶*"We shall bring beauty to the Tree, children," The Power said.* ⁷*"We shall embrace the chaos and wickedness and call it Good.* ⁸*And in so doing, the Tree shall become beautiful in our eyes."*
⁹*"Your plan is wise, Father," Arin said.* ¹⁰*"Bestow all of your power unto me and I will do your will."* ¹¹*And so The Power extended his hands and planted his essence into Arin.*
- *The Mukhtaar Chronicles, attributed to the prophet Habakku*
Origines Multiversi, Emergentiae 5:1-11

The Ancient Religarian word for "to plant" (tabad'ul) is synonymous with "to transfer". Are we, then, to interpret this to mean The Power became powerless? Hardly. The Power retained enough essence to split the Tree of Life into two halves, as we see in a subsequent chapter of the Origines. It would be *unwise to think The Power transferred all of himself into Arin. But the question remains, just how much of The Power resides within Arin?*

- Coteon of the Steppes, "Coteonic Commentaries on the Origines Multiversi" (circa 520 RL)

Aelron couldn't be anywhere near this festival when *Constable Chicanery* discovered the corpses of that Council magus and his companion. That meant getting out of this village. Undetected if possible.

Wagon wheels churned mud on the west end of the village, slowed by the growing downpour. Four adda pulled a large wagon that towed a flat trailer covered with a canvas tarp.

Odd. One adda should have been enough to handle that load.

Aelron merely had to make his way across the village center, under the festival awning, and out onto the eastern road.

But he couldn't. The words of the dead magus were too specific to ignore.

Garrison commander.

The wagon train was having a tough time of it. Whatever was in the last wagon sank the cart into the mud up to its axle when it entered the village center.

Aelron glanced around the circle of buildings.

Across the festival grounds, thirty or forty paces away, was a sturdy building with a tiled roof.

That must be it. The building serving as the current garrison headquarters.

He lingered, uncertain whether he would draw more attention walking in the open or ducking from tent to tent. He'd lost track of the constable and didn't want any surprises.

One of the adda roared as the team heaved the wagon train out of the mud. Someone wearing a tall hat and thick chain of office ran from a festival tent to the wagon.

Constable Chicanery. There you are.

This changed things. With the constable hassling the wagon driver — probably warning the adda about *churlishness* — Aelron should have no problem heading straight for the building.

He strode under the festival canopy in the village center. Now was the time to move.

Music started up as the rain beyond the awning intensified, but a nearby lightning strike and thunderclap caused some in the crowd to scream and jump, including a musician. When the other band members stopped yelling at the startled man, they started playing again, and once more Aelron threaded his way through the crowd of dancing villagers.

Fifteen paces to the end of the awning.

Aelron drew his hood over his head, pulling it down over his forehead as far as it would go. When he dropped his arms, a woman in an orange dress grabbed him and spun him around, dancing in time to the music. He went along with it for a couple of spins before releasing her into the arms of another dancer.

Judging from the periodic waterfalls draining into buckets, the villagers had made collection points for the torrential rain. But they hadn't been efficient about it. The awning still sagged in the center.

Cold metal touched his right hand. A singing man was trying to hand him a tankard. Aelron nodded and took the proffered drink, which made the man happy enough to bother someone else.

Ten more paces.

Twenty or so people stood between him and the awning's end. The undulating crowd moved back and forth across his path, dancing this way and that to the rising music. Another singing man worked his way through the crowd, handing out tankards. Must be some kind of tradition. Aelron wished he'd known about it before he'd given up his ring. Hunger could make a person make bad decisions.

He put it out of his mind and picked up his pace.

Not too fast. You're just another reveler.

Aelron cursed as the woman in the black dress from the ale tent marched up to him. The look on her face told him she wanted to make a scene.

"So that's how you play, is it?" she said, slurring her words. "Steal a kiss, get a few quick feels, and run off to find more soft skin to fondle?"

All eyes were on her, and that meant all eyes were on Aelron by association. He couldn't risk being the center of attention for long. He had to get her away from the crowd and make sure she *stayed* away.

"There you are, my gorgeous girl," Aelron said. "Why didn't you follow me? I found the perfect place for us."

"You...what?"

"Beyond that tent," he said, nodding toward the sturdy building.

"The temporary barracks?"

So I was right. That's the garrison building.

"I don't understand," the woman said. "Why don't we just go back to my—"

"Think of how exciting it will be! Just yards from the crowd, and they'll have no idea what's going on."

She smiled. "Look at what a freak you are! Let's be on about it then. I'm Jayne, by the way."

He grabbed her hand and started walking toward the temporary barracks at a quick pace.

"Just promise me one thing," Aelron said. "Can you do that?"

Jayne smirked. "There's a *lot* I can do if you ask me."

"Don't ask me any questions. Any at all. Do you understand?"

"But what—"

"That sounds like a question."

A cold bead of sweat ran down his back. If she asked him the wrong thing at the wrong time, it could jeopardize everything.

People started reacting to how fast they were moving, so he slowed down.

You belong here, Aelron. You're just another face in the crowd. Just another inbred farmer like that moron constable.

The constable.

Aelron glanced at the wagon train and a nervous chill shuddered through him. He couldn't see the man's tall hat. But after a moment, the constable walked back into view, looking under the canvas tarp and yelling at the wagon driver. The driver was giving as well as he was getting, though—he kept waving his arms and pointing at the cabin wagon. The constable put his hand up to his chin.

At least someone figured out how to shut that old man up.

When they reached the back of the tent, which was covered by the barracks awning, Aelron spun Jayne around, threaded his arms up through hers, and pressed his forearm against the artery in her neck. She struggled for a moment, but soon she was limp in his arms. He laid her down in the shadows and stood.

"Sorry, Jayne. You'll have one hell of a headache, but you'll live."

He took one last look around the corner of the tent.

The constable was arguing with the wagon driver, holding onto the man's arm. The adda had pulled the wagon free of the mud, but the constable had a tighter grip than the soft ground. He wasn't letting that driver go anywhere.

Aelron turned toward the barracks and had to suppress the urge to jump back.

The constable stood three feet away, gaping.

Aelron stole a quick glance toward the wagon and cursed as the man in the tall hat, who he'd thought was Constable Chicanery, faced the village.

Malvol's stones, he must be a deputy!

"Ale rod!" the constable yelled through the pouring rain, staring at the limp form of Jayne at his feet. "What have you done?"

Aelron backhanded the constable across the jaw with one hand while grabbing his chain of office with the other.

The constable tried to cry out, but Aelron slipped behind him and shoved the large medallion at the end of the chain into his mouth, muffling any sound.

Aelron swept the constable's legs out from under him and planted him face-first into the dirt, raising his left hand to strike the back of the constable's neck with enough force to kill.

But as he drew back, he stopped. Was there no way out of this town without leaving a path of destruction behind him? Constable Chicanery might be an idiot, but he didn't deserve this.

The constable spit the medallion out of his mouth and inhaled.

Aelron pulled the medallion off the constable's neck and struck as a bright flash of lightning lit the village and surrounding landscape.

The constable lay unconscious on the ground. But in that split second of light, Aelron had seen guards leaving the barracks entrance.

He slipped around the corner of the building and leaned out to take a better look from a concealed position.

Jayne and the constable were less than ten feet from the guards, but the guards walked right past them into the village center.

As the last guard emerged and ran down the wooden steps into the village, Aelron jogged around the side of the building, taking advantage of the noise produced by the intensifying storm. Strolling through the front door wouldn't be a good idea.

The more he studied the building the more he realized it was an old farmhouse that must have been repurposed. There should be a root cellar entrance nearby.

He ran past a row of hoes and rakes leaning against the wall. As he rounded the corner to the back of the farmhouse, a sloped door came into view.

There you are.

The door was latched, but he could change that. He ran back and grabbed one of the hoes from the side of the building. He slipped one end of the hoe through the latch on the cellar door and lifted up from the other. The latch wasn't strong—security wouldn't be a big concern in a village like this—and it snapped in half with little effort. He pulled the latch away from the locking anchors and opened the door.

It was dark inside, and the smell of mold and mildew was overpowering, but this was the best way into the building without drawing attention.

He pulled the door shut above him and climbed down a rickety ladder, thankful it held his weight.

A sliver of light toward the ceiling in the far wall revealed where he needed to go.

His eyes adjusted to the darkness with ease, having come in from the dark stormy night, so it didn't take long for him to pick a path across the room. Creaks and groans from the ceiling told him people were moving around above him, and every so often a shadow would cross the sliver of light. His instinct had been right. Had he broken a window, or made the stupid decision to come in through the front door, he would have been caught.

From the sounds of the movement and muffled conversations, he estimated four people in the room above and two in the hallway.

He found the ladder leading up into the house, but something was strange about it. There were mounting brackets and holes for a much larger structure—something akin to a staircase. What had happened to it?

A shadow lingered in front of the sliver of light. When it vanished somewhere into the hallway, Aelron climbed the ladder and cracked the door open.

The door led into the building's main hall. Aelron could see the front entrance at the far end, and no guards were in sight. But the door hid the other side of the hall from view.

There was only one way he was going to find out if he was alone or not. Only one way that sounded good, at least.

He pushed the door open and ducked below the doorway, clinging to the ladder. When no one reacted to the swinging door, he climbed out into the hallway and stood up, taking a quick inventory of everything in view.

Five paces to the front door. Two side halls. Four rooms on this level. Stairs climb one level higher.

If the Shandarian army did things the way the rangers did, the garrison commander's office would be near the front entrance, at the end of the hall.

It'll be one of the first two rooms.

Aelron closed the door slowly, cringing when the hinges creaked, and started off down the hall.

There were voices coming from the nearest room on the right, and the door was wide open.

Probably not the commander's office.

He needed to get past that doorway to the one beyond.

The closed door across from it swung open and a soldier stepped out into the hallway, buttoning his pants.

Privy chamber. The farmer who built this place must have been rich.

Aelron pressed himself flat against the wall, still as a snake before it strikes.

Two rooms left. The commander's office has to be one of them.

The soldier walked across the hall into the open doorway.

Two choices remained, and neither was good, but one had the advantage. If he tried the door across from the open room, anyone inside would be able to see what he was doing. His best chance would be to try the door on the *same side* as the open room.

But I have to get past that open door first.

Footsteps on the stairs behind made him curse his luck. If he didn't get out of this hallway fast, whoever was on those stairs would see him. They'd bring whatever was left of the garrison down on him.

He pressed his back against the wall next to the open door and leaned around. Four soldiers sat at a dining table.

Those footsteps were getting closer. A few steps farther and they'd see him.

He lowered his hood and stepped across the doorway without slowing until he stood before the closed door.

The grinding noise of a bench sliding away from a table came from the open room he'd passed.

"Warren?" a soldier shouted. "Get your adda-smelling arse in here."

Aelron was out of options and time. He pushed the door open, hoping no soldiers were on the other side, and stepped into the room.

"I'm right here," a voice responded. It was the soldier on the stairs.

"Thought that was you," the first voice said.

Aelron closed the door behind him and turned around.

A writing desk was pushed up against the wall of what appeared to be an old kitchen pantry. A seal of office leaned precariously against an inkwell, and parchments were scattered around, including a sizable stack on the floor. If Aelron didn't know any better, he'd say someone had thrown them.

But the most interesting thing on the desk gave Aelron a chill.

A small white statuette, depicting a grinning man with his hands clasped behind his back. It was the same figure the rangers had found days ago.

But is it the same object, or merely a copy? Is this what the Council magus wanted me to find?

He stepped toward the desk and the wooden floor creaked and groaned.

"You hear that?" a soldier asked.

Malvol's festering arse.

Whatever secret the magus thought the garrison commander harbored, Aelron wouldn't decipher it now.

Aelron darted out into the hall...straight into a soldier.

"Who the hell are you?" the soldier asked.

Aelron struck a point between the soldier's ribs with a single knuckle, and all air escaped the man's lungs. The soldier collapsed as four others ran out into the hallway.

"Feels scary, I know," Aelron said, as the soldier gasped for air. "You'll be able to breathe again in a minute."

There'd be no way to fight all four of these soldiers in such tight quarters, but that worked as much to his advantage as his disadvantage. What was difficult for him would be difficult for them. He had to get out of the building. Between the storm and the revelry, there was a chance he could evade them.

Aelron bolted toward the front entrance and pulled the door open.

As he ran down the stairs into the mud, the adda-drawn wagon train rode toward the east entrance of the town. It was promising, but if he made his way straight to the wagon, it wouldn't do him much good. He'd only succeed if he could lose the soldiers in the crowd.

A bartender bent over to pick up a rain collection bucket under the canopy.

That's it! I'll lead them under the canopy and into the crowd.

He hesitated to make sure the guards saw him disappear into the crowd. When he was satisfied they were following, he raised his hood and kept as many people between him and them as possible.

He circled around the crowd to the southern side of the canopy. The soldiers had grown frantic, checking every person who wore a dark cloak.

They weren't very smart. That was a sure way to get themselves killed if he *had* been one of the people they'd checked.

The soldier he'd struck in the house was back on his feet and running for the canopy. When he reached it, Aelron pulled a dagger from his cloak and ran for the eastern support poles. It was time for that sagging canopy to work in his favor.

As Aelron ran past the first pole, he sliced through the canopy's lashings. He repeated the process on each support until he reached the northeast pole. With as much force as he could muster, he threw his shoulder into the pole and ran out from under the canopy.

The villagers' muffled cries were all the indication of success Aelron needed. The canopy had come down on everyone.

The adda-drawn wagon train had reached the eastern entrance. This was his only chance.

Aelron sprinted for the tarp-covered flat wagon at the end of the train. With dagger in hand, he severed a tie holding the canvas tarp down and crawled in, pulling the tarp back down over himself.

When the wagon train had pulled out into the darkness of the country road, he peeked through the gap between the tarp and the wagon.

The guards had made their way out of the collapsed awning and were starting a building-to-building search.

Aelron wasn't sure where this wagon was going, but he hoped it was better than where he'd been.

Zorian stepped onto the marble stairs that led up to the palace entrance. The walk from the harbor had been a long one, and he wanted to sit somewhere. But Admiral Unega's order that Lucian—the ambitious temple priest—accompany him was complicating matters. Zorian couldn't afford that clerical upstart getting the emperor's ear first. Lucian's presence frustrated Zorian. Countering Unega was going to be difficult as it was without having one of his lackeys interfering.

The entrance to the imperial palace in Dar Rodon reminded Zorian of the grand temples of Barathos. It had the look of new construction to it, though it was unclear whether it was indeed new or simply whitewashed. The palace may be a royal residence, but it exuded piety. Not the piety of a humble pilgrim performing a ritual at the end of a long pilgrimage, nor the piety of a hermit who spent his day in prayer. This was the piety of a wealthy noble who wanted the world to see how religious he was.

The palace spanned more than five-hundred feet across and four-hundred tall. Its white stone reflected the orange afternoon sun to such a degree that Zorian had to shield his eyes. He, Lucian, and Tullias—Zorian's manservant—climbed the marble steps behind Lieutenant Belding and several palace guards, who had joined them at the docks once their landing craft was secured. Not even Belding's voluminous hat was enough to block the palace's radiant glow.

Lucian stumbled on an uneven step, but he regained his balance with a well-placed hand on Tullias's back.

Zorian's frustration peaked.

"You will not speak to the emperor unless I am present and you are directly addressed," Zorian said. "Is that clear?"

"I serve at the Glorious One's behest," Lucian said. He folded his arms and rolled back his right sleeve, so his golden bracelet of office was visible.

"As do I. And I assure you a low-ranking priest from a small temple will not be missed by the court, regardless of your association with the admiral."

"I trust you will not interfere with my mission here."

"Have you ever seen battle on foreign soil?" Zorian said. "You'd have no reason to know this, but before becoming Zhuma, I was a naval commander. I've lost many good men to accidents along the way."

"I'm not the sort of man who—"

"Don't be one of them."

Zorian continued climbing the stairs as Lucian stopped.

Among other things, the palace was an impressive display of military power. Guards stood along both sides of the wide entrance hall. They dressed like desert nomads, in billowing white robes that could be swept over their heads to provide shade, but there was no mistaking their true purpose here. Two short and curved scimitars hung at their waist from a belt that partially concealed two daggers and a pouch. Scouts reported those pouches carried small, circular blades used as throwing weapons.

No, these weren't desert nomads. They were warriors, pure and simple.

The arched roof above the hallway was plated in gold mosaic. Oval windows along the sides of the arch allowed natural light to flood the hallway with an amber glow, accentuating the gold trim that ran along the walls and baseboards, and spotlighting the portraits along the way.

Pristine for a nation that suffered from decades of ground quakes.

When they arrived at the intersection at the end of the hall, their guard escort stopped. The wall across from them was a masterwork of ostentatiousness. Two latticeworks of gold filigree worked their way in from the edges of the wall in thick lines until they converged at the center and spread out, up and down, surrounding a portrait of a man that was thirty feet from floor to ceiling. The man was younger, in his twenties or thirties, with jet hair that hung below his shoulders. A bushy black mustache covered his upper lip, ran down both sides of his mouth, and hung to the center of his chest. His head was topped with a delicate gold crown laced with an ivy design that matched the gold chains hanging from his neck and waist. Precious stones decorated a chain that draped over his chest and swept over his back. His robe was form-fitting, emphasizing the muscled chest and arms resting at his sides. He held a rod in one hand and an orb in the other. He stood upon a map of the Three Kingdoms, with one foot in the Bay of Relig, and the other foot off the west coast of the Shandarian Union.

A golden plaque at the foot of the portrait read *The Destiny of Toren Relig.*

Cavernous hallways ran from left to right in front of the portrait, and a quick glance revealed similar portraits and gold filigree in each direction, on both sides of the hall.

The attempt at opulence was laughable compared to the Palace of Ages, within which sat the Diamond Throne. The Builders themselves had created the Palace of Ages in a time before recorded history. Nothing could compare to the way in which crystals and precious gems were *grown* to form the passageways and rooms…and even the Diamond Throne itself. This place might be lavish by Three Kingdom standards, but many Barathos nobles lived this way.

A woman whose face was painted as gold as the filigree approached them. A yellow silk veil hid the lower half of her face. She wore no shoes, and her form-hugging blouse and sheer billowing pants would be considered scandalous even at the Palace of Ages. The woman exposed her naval, which was the mark of a courtesan in Barathosia.

Lucian must be thinking the same, the way he gazed at her bare midsection.

Strange. Zorian had been told prostitution was frowned upon here. Perhaps the reports were wrong. A society could change in many ways over the course of forty years.

"Arin's peace upon you," the woman said.

It was disconcerting when she blinked. Painted on her eyelids were exact replicas of her own ocean-blue eyes, creating the illusion of a perpetual stare.

Zorian nodded without responding. She'd offered no name or title, so protocol dictated it was safe to assume her beneath his station.

"The emperor will see you now," she said. "This way."

She began walking down the hallway to the left. Long black hair spilled from the back of the yellow veil and fell to her waist.

Lucian lowered his head, but Zorian could tell where his eyes were staring.

The furniture between the giant portraits caught Zorian's eye. They didn't have much dark wood in Barathosia, and the deep browns and reds of the buffets and cabinets struck him as unnatural. But like everything else in this pompous monstrosity, they too were trimmed in gold.

He thought he'd seen the worst of it, but he was proven wrong when they turned a corner. Two golden doors that ran thirty-odd feet from floor to ceiling, and spanned thirty feet in width, gave the appearance of a giant golden square on the wall in front of them.

Zorian wanted to laugh. Emperor Relig was nothing more than a petty man who flaunted wealth and religion to control his people.

Or, Zorian could be underestimating this emperor. Emperor Relig may, in fact, flaunt wealth. But he *had* managed to conquer half a continent in the last forty years. And Zorian doubted he'd *purchased* it.

A little less arrogance from now on.

Arrogance could blind him to a truth that would otherwise be apparent. He couldn't afford that kind of mistake. Not here…not now.

He *would* outmaneuver Admiral Unega, and he needed to keep his wits about him to do so.

A small door cut into the larger golden monstrosity of a portal swung open, and the woman stopped.

"Only one may enter," she said.

Lucian took a step forward and Zorian stopped him with a stiff arm.

"You have a short memory," Zorian said. He faced the woman. "I am Zorian Osa. I have been sent by Admiral Unega to speak with your emperor."

"As you say," the woman said and stepped aside, allowing Zorian to walk past her.

Zorian entered the Religarian throne room and the woman followed. The door swung shut behind them, sending a deep echo through the vast chamber.

Guards stood around the throne room as they did in the hallway outside. A lone assassin might manage to make their way in here...but they wouldn't leave.

The throne room's central ceiling was a dome with an inner walkway running around the rim. Archers with longbows stood at intervals around a banister on the walkway's edge. Above them, a mural depicting the ascension of Arin into the heavens spanned the dome ceiling.

Did the Religarians believe the gods were once human? He'd have to make it a point to study their local superstitions. Such knowledge could be useful in the hands of the right person.

As Zorian's eyes drifted back down beneath the dome, his gaze fell upon a platform on the other side of the room. Polished stone stairs led to a golden throne, upon which sat Emperor Toren Relig, expressionless.

Another man stood to the emperor's left in a simple blue robe; he was old, with a hooked nose that had seen the end of a fist or two, and eyebrows that could attract nesting birds.

The emperor's lack of expression troubled Zorian. What most people considered *expressionless* was a myriad of subtle movements that, when examined by one such as he, could reveal the most well-concealed feelings. But Zorian saw nothing.

The woman stopped at the base of the platform, bowed, then climbed until she stood next to the throne. Her pose was...*casual*.

"I do not know *who* you are, though I know whence you came," Emperor Relig said. His was the voice of an old man. An old man who would have little trouble winning a sword fight.

The uniform Emperor Relig wore was identical to the one in his portrait. But hair that was once jet black was white as spider silk on the man who sat the throne.

Zorian bowed at the waist and remained staring at the marble floor. No need to break protocol just yet.

"Rise," Emperor Relig said.

"Your Imperial Majesty," Zorian said as he stood. "Allow me to introduce myself and make your knowledge whole. I am Zorian Osa, and I represent the Glorious One, Grand Empress of the Barathosian Empire, Servant of the Gods, Mother of Yantoo."

Zorian waited for the emperor to speak the traditional response, *long live the Glorious One*, but the response never came.

So much for protocol.

"Need I remind you, Emperor, that the Glorious One is also the Mother of Yotto?"

"How dare you address the emperor in such a tone?" the blue-robed man said.

"Forty years may be long enough for you to have forgotten your oath, Emperor, but I assure you the empress has not forgotten."

The blue-robed man took a step forward. "You will—"

Emperor Relig waved his left hand and the man grew silent. The emperor stood and began climbing down the raised platform, his steps emphasizing every word as he said, "This is *my* empire."

"The Diamond Throne is not interested in your *empire*, Emperor Relig. Only your obedience."

"You'll find my army has grown considerably since your predecessor last visited."

"Yes," Zorian said. "I understand you've expanded to the Great Orm river. A glorious military accomplishment. It takes the combined might of two kingdoms to hold your empire at bay. And now that your so-called...Treaty of Three Banks is it?...is null and void, I suppose there's nothing stopping you from picking them off one by one. Your *manifest destiny* will finally be complete, and that portrait of yours out in the hall will become reality."

The upward turn of the corner of Emperor Relig's mouth was subtle. *So he* can *display emotion. Time to remind him of reality.*

"I trust you've expanded your *navy* in the intervening years as well?" Zorian asked. A rhetorical question, of course. Zorian had his answer before he'd set foot on land. The only ships operating in the Religarian Empire were fishing vessels and merchant transports. "They must be hiding. Not one of the two thousand ships I arrived with reported any resistance."

The emperor's subtle smile faded.

"You swore a holy oath to Yotto, Emperor Relig. And in return, the Armada allowed your city to remain standing. Do you think your oath was somehow invalidated because of that...*shield* you concocted?"

"That was Archmage Kagan's doing, not mine," Emperor Relig said.

"Yes, Kagan has *much* to answer for," Zorian said.

The emperor narrowed his eyes in an expression of confusion.

"Now you threaten the holy archmage?" the blue-robed man said.

Zorian glared at the hook-nosed man and spoke slowly. "Who is this *inconsequential* man who keeps interrupting us?"

"Silence yourself, Saleem," Emperor Relig said in the tone of a father to an unruly child.

"Saleem, is it?" Zorian said.

"Saleem Abdul Bishara," Saleem said.

"I've learned something of your language," Zorian said. "Peaceful servant of the gods, is it?"

Saleem nodded.

Realization struck Zorian.

This is the cognitomancer. This is one of those blue-robed demons *our chimeramancers are so afraid of.*

"Well, *servant*," Zorian said. "You and I are going to have a productive relationship."

"I've heard enough," Emperor Relig said. "You will return to—"

"I speak with the authority of the Glorious One," Zorian said. "I *and the armada* will leave when her purpose has been fulfilled. Not a moment sooner."

Emperor Relig stepped forward until one foot was on a lower step.

"Speak to me in that tone once more, and you will no longer be Zorian Osa," Emperor Relig said. "You will be whomever my imagination sees fit to make of you. Won't he, Saleem?"

"As your Imperial Majesty commands," Saleem said. He bowed.

Zorian retrieved Admiral Unega's letter from his overcoat and handed it up to the emperor.

When the emperor read what Unega had written, he crumpled the letter and threw it back. It struck Zorian's chest and fell to the marble floor.

It irked Zorian that it had come to this. The emperor's decision was all but made. He could tell by the awkward silence. He'd seen it time and again in other lands, across oceans this paltry potentate didn't know existed.

And each time it was like a slap in the face. He shouldn't need the hasty scribble of a naval officer to add weight to his command.

When I'm Sian'jo, my words will carry all the authority I need.

The emperor's shoulders sagged by an amount most people wouldn't perceive. Now he'd relent. It happened the same way every time Zorian had to deliver the message, and to rulers far more powerful than Toren Relig. No one stood against the Diamond Throne for long.

"What do you want of me?" Emperor Relig asked. "Give it voice so we might bring an end to this. Your empire has been a ghost in the shadows of my palace for *far* too many years, and I'd have you *exorcised*. Once and for all."

Zorian smiled. "Then this will be easy, and everyone will soon be happy."

"Speak it."

"Bring me your archmage," Zorian said.

The emperor's face lost some of its color.

"Turn Kagan over to the Glorious One," Zorian said, "so that he can answer for his crimes against the Diamond Throne. It's quite simple."

"Why not take him yourself, with the *two thousand ships* you arrived with?"

"And destroy ourselves while navigating the most inaccessible sea on Erindor?" Zorian asked.

Something changed in Emperor Relig's expression. Was he growing paler still?

"Yes," Zorian said. "We know of the challenges of your Sea of Arin. You will fulfill your oath and bring him to me. *Personally.*"

"This...*thing* you ask," Emperor Relig said. "It's not as *simple* as you think."

"You're a powerful man, Emperor."

"No one is *that* powerful."

"You have one day to devise a plan and inform me," Zorian said. "One day *only*. I trust you will have prepared sufficient quarters for my stay?"

Emperor Relig glanced at the woman who had led Zorian to the throne room. "Anisah, see to it."

"Yes, father," Anisah said.

His daughter, eh?

"You traveled with another," Emperor Relig said. "What of him?"

"Tullias, my manservant."

"The other one. With the gold bracelet."

Zorian's gaze came to rest on Anisah. "I doubt he'll be with us much longer."

Anisah climbed down from the platform and led Zorian from the throne room.

Lucian and Tullias sat right where Zorian had left them, the former fondling his bracelet, as he often did when making a show of his status. He seemed confused when Anisah and Zorian kept walking, and he struggled to catch up.

"Will he not see me?" Lucian asked.

"Afraid not," Zorian whispered. "Only one audience per day. He did, however, offer some small comfort for the inconvenience."

"What did he offer?"

Zorian glanced at Anisah. "One of his courtesans. She's yours for the night. He implied she enjoys it rough, though. Are you all right with that?"

Lucian smiled.

For once, Zorian couldn't help returning the smile.

CHAPTER SEVEN

¹*The Prison*

²*Arin called his siblings to him and told them of a new plan.* ³*"I will not embrace chaos.* ⁴*I will not embrace wickedness.* ⁵*All power in the heavens has been given to me.* ⁶*I will lock The Power in a great prison.*

⁷*Zubuxo stepped forward.* ⁸*"Mine is the dominion of last things, for I am the last as you are the first.* ⁹*I will be the one to create this hell, for it is to be our father's last home."*

¹⁰*Arin agreed and empowered Zubuxo.*

¹¹*"I will create six prisons for the six sins of humankind; the proud, the deceitful, the murderous, the wicked, the mischievous, and the lustful," Zubuxo said.* ¹²*He spread his arms and the Six Planes of Hell stretched out before him.*

¹³*"I will send my children into the prison to purge my charges," Zubuxo said.* ¹⁴*And he spread his arms and called his children unto him, casting them into the Six Planes of Hell.*

- The Mukhtaar Chronicles, attributed to the prophet Habakku
Origines Multiversi, Emergentiae 6:1-14

If the text seems disjointed, I can only reiterate that much of the Origines is presented as such. What strikes discord in the modern ear rang as pure harmony in the ancient. There is no explanation for who these "charges" of Zubuxo are,

nor how they came to be in the six planes moments after the planes were created.
It is clear that Zubuxo is referring to the souls of sinful departed, and we must
accept that some indefinite period of time passed between the events in verses
twelve and thirteen.

- Coteon of the Steppes, "Coteonic Commentaries on the Origines
Multiversi" (circa 520 RL)

T he sting of fear pierced Nicolas when the wall of Caspardis
materialized about three-hundred yards in front of him. He
hadn't been expecting that, though in hindsight it was foolish not
to; he'd nearly been killed behind that wall.

He, Kaitlyn, dead Kagan, and Toby appeared on the crest of a hill
overlooking the city and Lake Caspardis beyond.

The translocation orb brought them to within three hundred yards of
the eastern wall of Caspardis. The dilapidated edifice was much as he
remembered it; sandstone, crenelations crumbling in places, iron
portcullis blocking the road that snaked its way into the city, and red
flags with a cat's eye set in the center spaced evenly between the
crenelations that hadn't collapsed.

Toby jumped and clamped down on his gatorpickle when the world
reappeared, but it didn't take long for him to calm down, spit the toy
out, and hop up on Nicolas's leg.

"That was disorienting," Kaitlyn said. She turned around, scanning
the lake and surrounding countryside. "Crazy. It's like someone plopped
a medieval city down in the middle of Wyoming. You know what I
mean?"

"Trust me," Nicolas said.

Something about the scene before him was familiar. No, not familiar.
Identical to his memory of Caspardis. They were standing on the same
hill where the Shandarian Rangers had held him in the military camp.
The camp was gone, nothing more than a phantom of his memory, but
the trampled dirt and wagon tracks were evidence enough of the reality
of his recollection.

"Are we going into that city?" Kaitlyn asked.

The sting of fear returned and his pulse quickened as he turned away
from the wall. *What the hell?* What he'd gone through had been horrible,
but he'd made it! He was here! He'd won!

"That's the plan," Nicolas said. "There's a boat launch at the docks that should get us close. Well, not close, but…that's where I was thrown into the lake."

"You were what?"

"Long story. Just a…misunderstanding with the local authorities."

Get a grip, Nick.

He took a deep breath and faced the wall.

"Wait," Nicolas said. "Something's wrong."

Where were the soldiers?

"Isn't it odd that the gate isn't guarded?" Nicolas asked. "Why would they do that?"

Kagan stood expressionless.

"Hey!" Nicolas said. "Dead Kagan. Speak up."

"Release me and I'll tell you," Kagan said.

Even in death Kagan was an asshole.

Nicolas sent a stream of images through the necromantic link. Images of hellwraiths—monstrous shrouded specters with glowing eyes and whips of shadow—from the Plane of Death. Images of how those hellwraiths carried unfortunate souls through a darkened doorway, never to be seen again.

Kagan lowered his head. "Enough! I'll answer."

"Keep it up and I'll make you wish Mujahid had tossed you into Hell."

"Playing God with your dead father creeps me out a little," Kaitlyn said.

"He's *not* my father," Nicolas said.

"I thought you said he was."

"Yes, Kagan's my birth father. But he's not my *dad*. Now answer my question, Kagan."

"There are no guards because the city watch has probably been reassigned," Kagan said.

"Helpful."

"You asked," Kagan said. "Perhaps if your question were more intelligent, the answer would have equaled it."

"Listen, you…" Nicolas stopped himself. He hadn't spent much time with dead Kagan, but the old archmage was well versed in pushing his buttons. He needed to stay calm. "So what question *should* I ask?"

"Do you notice anything else about the wall?" Kagan asked.

Nicolas scanned the wall. Everything was the same as he remembered. Except...

Except the gate. The city gate is closed. The rangers took me right through an open gate. Why is it closed?

Nicolas didn't bother speaking. He sent the question through the necromantic link.

"There are only two reasons to seal a city," Kagan said. "They're either trying to keep something in or keep something out."

"Dead guy has a point," Kaitlyn said.

Kagan smiled a subtle smile.

"Don't encourage him," Nicolas said. "So which is it?"

"I'm afraid you'll have to ask them," Kagan said.

Nicolas needed to get to the lake. It would be easier to go through Caspardis, but he didn't have time to deal with whatever was going on there. He'd just have to go around.

"They'll have to worry about themselves," Nicolas said. "I have problems of my own right now."

"Spoken like my true son," Kagan said.

"The difference is, I'm trying to help people."

"As was I."

Nicolas sent a ball of necropotency into Kagan's mouth, making it impossible for Kagan to speak. Caspardis was making him tense as it was. He didn't need to listen to this too.

"What was that all about?" Kaitlyn asked.

"He's an evil asshole trying to justify his evil asshole existence by convincing himself everyone else is just as much of an evil asshole as he is."

"No, how do you really feel?"

Nicolas faced her, prepared for an argument. But she had a huge grin on her face.

His tension drained away.

"How do you do it?" he asked. "I was a basket case when I ended up here, but you're acting like you're on vacation."

She cocked her head to the side, smiled, and started walking down the hill with Toby's leash in hand. "That's the lake you're looking for, right?"

He shook his head and jogged to catch up with her.

"What do we do once we get there?" Kaitlyn asked.

Well, the original plan was to…he supposed he should…if he could just get…

"You have no idea, do you?" Kaitlyn said.

Hell's bells, do I seriously not know what I'm going to do?

"Give me a break here," Nicolas said. "I'm sort of covering new territory."

"That's not true."

"How so?"

"You said you're taking me to this…*fish city*…to talk to someone who can help me, right? So how did you get there the first time?"

"By nearly dying, for starters. Then hallucinating until I summoned…"

That's it!

But this time it would be different. This time he knew what to ask for.

"Now *that's* the face I wanted to see!" Kaitlyn said. "Like I said, you've done this before."

Large boulders peppered the sandy shore to the south of Caspardis. Nicolas led them a short distance away to a relatively flat, firm surface with an unobstructed view of the lake. He could have summoned a cichlos anywhere, but he still had no idea what was going on in Caspardis. He couldn't afford the delay of another run-in with authority.

"I don't know how to prepare you for this," Nicolas said. "But what I'm going to do next might seem a little scary."

"I've seen you dance. I think I can handle it."

The sensation of laughing emanated from the necromantic link.

"You shut your cake hole," Nicolas said to Kagan. "And what's wrong with my dancing?"

"Nothing…if *The Seizure* is a new line dance I haven't heard of."

"Nice. Just so you know—"

Kaitlyn doubled over and grabbed her head.

"Kait!" Nicolas said.

He released a tiny amount of necropotency and directed it into her head, hoping to see something obvious so he could slow her Awakening himself. But he may as well have been staring at the engine of his car; anything more complicated than filling the washer fluid required a mechanic.

He created the pattern of power Mujahid had shown him and surrounded her brain with it, allowing it to sink in like a mystical shrink wrap. There was nothing else he could do.

"I am *so* tired," Kaitlyn said. "Can we just rest a bit?"

"We can't. Remember what I told you...no sleep for you...for either of us...until we get this figured out."

"Then we better hurry. I don't know how much longer I can last."

Nicolas embraced his cet and let go of all the worry, pain, and stray thoughts that had been keeping him from focusing. He concentrated on an image of *Cisic*, the cichlos he had summoned when he was drowning in the lake.

When the power embraced the skull symbol hovering over his well of power, he cast it forward into the water. It struck an invisible wall and rebounded on him from the void. It didn't hurt, but it was disorienting.

If at first you don't succeed...

Nicolas tried again. This was the first time he'd tried to perform a *pure* summoning — the act of raising the dead without a physical body — on a person he'd summoned once before.

Again, the power struck the wall and rebounded, but Nicolas pushed back, trying to break it open.

A sensation of *wrongness* overcame him and he released the power. It was like the feeling he'd had when he went near the white door in his hall of power. He wasn't sure what he was trying to do, but whatever it was...it was *just plain wrong*.

He sent a question through the necromantic link. *Why?*

"The being you seek has passed beyond the Plane of Death," Kagan said.

Cisic *had* told him his time would be short. Well, Cisic was a cool dude. He deserved his spot in the Plane of Peace.

But Nicolas was running out of options. He had no idea how to make a bubble of air, like Cisic did to help Nicolas breathe underwater, and he sure as hell couldn't swim as fast as the undead cichlos. That fish dude could swim as fast as—

The Aquonome transport bubbles! Why didn't I think of that first?

He considered sending dead Kagan to ask the cichlos to send one, but thought better of it. The cichlos could be a little touchy about who walked through their barriers. And there were certain laws of physics to think about. As *enhanced* as a penitent could be, dead Kagan had a human body, and a human could only swim so fast.

Once again he created a channel of necropotency from his well of power to the skull symbol, wrapping the skull in power and casting it forward. But this time he didn't concentrate on an image of Cisic or any other person. This time he concentrated on what he *needed*.

A cichlos who can swim as fast as the day is long.

The power radiated away from him this time, and he prepared an image to cast forward that would give him control over his new penitent.

Within seconds a great splash and spray of water came from the lake as an undead cichlos shot out of the water and landed next to them.

Toby jumped back and started baying.

"It's okay, boy," Nicolas said, but Toby was having none of it.

Kaitlyn grabbed Nicolas's arm.

"No, seriously," Nicolas said. "It's okay."

"I'll take your word for it," Kaitlyn said.

Nick sent a stream of images through the necromantic link. He knew just who to contact in Aquonome for help.

The undead cichlos vanished back into the lake.

"It won't be long now," Nicolas said. "I have friends there."

"That looked like that strange *fish person* I saw at the shrine," Kaitlyn said.

"A cichlos," Nicolas said. "I spent time with them when I was here. A lot of time, actually. They taught me most of what I know about necromancy."

Kaitlyn shook her head. "And they're going to help me too?"

"If they can? Absolutely. No doubt."

"And what if they can't?"

Nicolas didn't want to think about that. The cichlos had to help. He had no other options.

"Let's not borrow trouble right now," Nicolas said. "The cichlos should be here soon, and then we'll see what we see."

A wave appeared on the lake's surface, several hundred yards out, and headed toward them at incredible speed. Water sprayed in every direction, obscuring whatever was causing it.

When the wave slowed, the spray lessened and scattered into a diffuse mist, revealing a cichlos transport bubble. Two figures stood in the bubble; Nicolas's penitent and a living, red-skinned cichlos. As the living cichlos faced the front of the bubble. Nicolas smiled at the familiar scar around his left eye.

Toridyn!

Nicolas would recognize that goofy fish anywhere. Toridyn had been the only cichlos student to risk befriending Nicolas when the others shunned him.

The bubble floated to a halt on the beach, and Toridyn stepped out. Something was different about him. He was sure of himself, less self-conscious. And that wasn't all. Toridyn was wearing a midnight-blue cowl.

"So they went and promoted you," Nicolas said through a wide smile. "Is the siek just giving those damned robes away now?"

"It's about time you came back," Toridyn said. "Siek Lamil was wondering if you'd be here for the new temple dedication, but you took his sweet time. Really pissed on him."

"Took *your* sweet time. And pissed him *off*, Tor. Jeez, how many times I gotta tell you?"

"Why'd you bring dead Kagan?" Toridyn asked. "He's not going to be very welcome in Aquonome."

Toby bayed and hopped on Toridyn's leg.

"Aw," Toridyn said. "What happened to your dog?"

"What do you mean? He's fine. Doesn't bite, either. He might *beagle hug* you to death, though."

Toridyn stooped and pet Toby with his massive, webbed hands.

"Poor disabled puppy," Toridyn said. "I'll look out for you. I'm not all here either." He pointed to his injured eye.

"Kait," Nicolas said. "I'd like you to meet my good friend, Toridyn."

"What?" Kaitlyn asked. She narrowed her eyes.

"Not a good time to be rude," Nicolas said, confused. He nodded toward Toridyn and beckoned her closer. "This guy and I, we've been through a lot."

Kaitlyn pointed at her mouth and said.
"I...don't...un...der...stand...you."

Nicolas felt silly when he realized what was happening. During his first trip to Aquonome, the Orb of Zubuxo had given him the ability to communicate with the cichlos.

"What language are we speaking right now?" Nicolas asked Toridyn.

Toridyn looked Nicolas up and down with his one remaining good eye. "Cichlossean."

"I'll be damned."

"I understood that!" Kaitlyn said.

How was he slipping between two languages without knowing it? The words he was speaking sounded English to him!

"What's her issue?" Toridyn asked.

"She says I'm talking funny," Nicolas said.

"I always said you talk funny."

"You're a real comedian. You gonna be here all week? Incoming handshake, by the way. Prepare yourself."

"Don't worry. I'm used to humankind's habit of touching people inappropriately."

"Nick," Kaitlyn said. She didn't look amused. "Mind sharing with the class?"

Nicolas tried to force his mind to shift languages. He imagined the words he spoke were English.

"Do you understand me now?" Nicolas asked.

"Yeah," Kaitlyn said.

Good. That works.

"This is Toridyn, my good friend from Aquonome. He's a large part of why I'm still alive. I was just trying to introduce you and somehow the language thing happened."

"You learned an entire language while you were here?"

"Not exactly," Nicolas said. "I've got these…*things* in my head. I think they're responsible for it."

She stepped toward Toridyn. Nicolas was expecting her to shake his hand, but she spread her arms to hug him instead.

"If you kept him alive, then I owe you a big one," Kaitlyn said.

Toridyn's eye spun. He must have been even more surprised than Nicolas.

When Kaitlyn put her arms around Toridyn, something pushed them apart, as if they'd been electrocuted. Kaitlyn was on the ground, but Toridyn stood holding his head.

"What the *hell* was that?" Kaitlyn asked. "Something…*happened*."

"Yeah," Toridyn said. "Which hell did that come from? It's like you poked my brain, lady."

"I'm sorry," Kaitlyn said. "I was just trying to give you a hug."

"That's one violent hug you've got there," Toridyn said.

"Um…guys?" Nicolas said. He looked back and forth between them with wide eyes.

"What?" Kaitlyn and Toridyn said in unison, each holding their head. They pointed at each other. "I understand you!"

"But what happened?" Toridyn asked.

"That's a question for later," Nicolas said.

"Your timing is good," Toridyn said. "You need to come to Aquonome as quickly as possible."

"Yeah, we need to talk to the chimeramancers about Kaitlyn."

"You pissed on them too, by the way, asking for this transport," Toridyn said. "But it's not that. It's the siek. Something's wrong with him. It's not good."

Nicolas had no idea what Toridyn meant by asking chimeramancers for the transport. All he'd done was send his penitent to find Toridyn. But thoughts of the siek in trouble was a greater concern.

"What happened?" Nicolas asked.

"A few days ago, he collapsed outside the temple," Toridyn said. "We don't know why, and he won't tell anyone. He just…. He's…. I'm worried. It's not good. Not good at all."

"A few days ago," Nicolas said. He turned to Kaitlyn. "I don't think this is a coincidence. Didn't you say you saw a cichlos in your vision?"

Kaitlyn nodded.

Nicolas helped Kaitlyn to her feet and started walking toward the transport bubble.

"Then it's time we left, don't you think?" Nicolas said.

A guttural scream drew Nicolas's attention to his cichlos penitent. Something was wrong. The skeleton was clutching at its head, and a confusing stream of images entered Nicolas's mind; a man with long red hair raised his arms over a small white object and his eyes glowed white. The man stood within a ring of fire…cold fire that swirled like a whirlwind leaving shards of ice behind it. As the whirlwind grew in power and surrounded the small object, a tear in the atmosphere formed in front of Nicolas's penitent.

Something pulled the penitent away by the necromantic link. Nicolas poured energy into the link, trying the first thing that came to mind—he'd make the link too slippery to grip.

But the penitent wasn't slowing. It floated steadily toward the tear in the atmosphere.

Nicolas embraced his cet and allowed more power to flow into the link.

A strange tension pushed against him, as if the link had reached its capacity to channel and would burst if any more power entered it.

Nicolas cut the flow of power off and the penitent vanished into the rip in the air leaving nothing behind…not even the necromantic link.

"What the hell just happened?" Kaitlyn asked.

"Yeah…what *she* said," Toridyn said.

Nicolas shook his head. "I wish I knew. I *really* wish I knew."

The cichlos transport was every bit as strange as Nicolas remembered it being. All six sides were translucent, which did nothing to conceal the incredible speed at which they were traveling.

Nicolas did his best to put the penitent out of his mind. He had enough to deal with. Maybe Mujahid would know more.

The familiar multicolored ribbons of light appeared in the distance. They were the many tubular hallways, formed from barrier magic, that comprised the city of Aquonome. And they approached far faster than they had when he'd traveled with Cisic.

The tubes and domed hubs gave Aquonome the appearance of a gargantuan underwater spider with a bulbous abdomen. The first time he'd seen the city from a distance, he had no idea what it was. Now, he could identify the small central dome that served as a primary hub, where the many *castes* in Cichlos society came together for commerce. He recognized the giant temple of Zubuxo with the small training halls jutting out from the side. He even recognized the student dormitories and the tiny dome that must be the High Priest's chamber.

But instead of heading for the outermost barrier tube where Cisic had first taken him, the transport bubble rushed toward the temple dome. Toridyn didn't seem upset by the trajectory, and instead was spending an awful lot of time petting the "poor deformed doggy," as he'd taken to calling Toby. It was starting to piss Nicolas off, but from all the licking and hugging going on, Toby didn't take any offense from it.

"Isn't this a problem?" Nicolas asked.

"Isn't what a problem?" Toridyn asked.

Nicolas nodded toward the front of the bubble.

"We're fixin' to smash into the temple," Nicolas said. "Isn't that going to hurt?"

"Don't look at me," Toridyn said. "The chimeramancers are driving."

"Excuse me?"

"You think these things drive themselves?" Toridyn said.

Nicolas had an idea. It was a long shot, but it was worth trying.

"Kait," Nicolas said. "Touch the wall of this thing and tell me if you feel anything."

She was hesitant, but she took a couple of steps toward the transparent side wall and brushed the backs of her fingers against it.

"Be careful, lady," Toridyn said. "You go too far and you'll be swimming. Can't turn this thing around."

"Her name's *Kaitlyn*," Nicolas said.

"It's okay," Kaitlyn said. "I *did* stab him in the brain, apparently. Not that he didn't stab me right back."

Nicolas took a deep breath. "The wall. Do you feel anything?"

Kaitlyn shook her head. "What were you expecting?"

"I'm not sure," Nicolas said. "I was hoping if it was made by chimeramancers, you might sense something. Something might get triggered or something."

Toridyn laughed.

"What's so funny, fish breath?" Nicolas asked.

"That's *Sab* fish breath to you," Toridyn said, pulling at his midnight-blue cowl. "The pod is *created* by chimeramancy, but it's not chimeramancy itself. It's not like necromancy, where you can sense necropotency. Chimeramancers don't use necropotency. They use *dreams*."

Nicolas rubbed his forehead. How could he have forgotten something that important? Mujahid had explained it to him, but he was so busy worrying about Kaitlyn that he'd put the entire conversation out of his mind.

"How does that work, exactly?" Nicolas asked.

Toridyn's eye spun around. "What would you say if someone asked 'so, how does necromancy work *exactly*?'"

"Good point."

"They sleep. They dream. They make stuff happen. That's about all I can tell you, because that's all I know. I got stuck with you and Siek *are-you-still-ignorant* instead, remember?" Toridyn lowered his head. "I shouldn't have said that. He's not doing very well."

"Will you take me to him?" Nicolas asked.

"Why do you think this pod is headed toward the temple?" Toridyn said. "That reminds me...brace for impact."

"What?" Nicolas and Kaitlyn said at the same time.

The transport bubble rushed toward the opaque temple dome like a crash-test car speeding toward a wall. Nicolas pulled Kaitlyn close and huddled against the floor. As the bubble made contact with the dome wall…

…Nothing happened.

Not even a bump.

Toridyn laughed. "Sorry. Couldn't resist."

"You bastard," Nicolas said.

"You're not a very nice fish," Kaitlyn said.

"Hey!" Toridyn said. "That's racist!"

"I've called you far worse," Nicolas said.

Toridyn's eye spun. "True. Remind me why I'm your friend again?"

Nicolas smiled and led Kaitlyn out into the temple, where she covered her nose and scrunched her face up. He'd forgotten how bad this place smelled when he'd first arrived; algae, decaying fish food and decomposing organic matter. It was worse than an unkempt aquarium.

As always, the temple was devoid of people, except for a wandering cichlos priest or two.

"It's beautiful," Kaitlyn said. "Smells like a lake, but the artwork is gorgeous. I love the star field on the floor! The detail on the individual stars is breathtaking! So sad in a way, though."

"Are you *kidding* me right now?" Nicolas asked. "You've been here a half a second and you see it?" It had taken him weeks of daily trips through the temple to understand the *bright sparkles* on the floor were stars in a spiral galaxy.

"This surprises you?" Kaitlyn said. "The person who's constantly asking me where his stuff is in his own apartment?"

Nicolas was too busy staring at the front of the temple to respond. The massive statue of Zubuxo, which had once dominated the temple, was no longer alone. The gray orb of Zubuxo and the statue had been moved dozens of feet to the left, and an equally massive statue of Arin stood next to it, with a multi-hued, multi-faceted orb of Arin hovering at its feet.

And that wasn't all. Between the two orbs rose a translucent monolith, rectangular, but with one side angled down at forty-five degrees. A large parchment—no, an *image* of a parchment—hovered within the top of the translucent monument like a hologram, and an *image* of an open book floated below it.

"What's that book thing?" Nicolas asked.

"If I were you," Toridyn said, "I wouldn't let anyone hear you say that. You're the archmage now, remember?"

"That doesn't answer my question."

"You're serious?" Toridyn asked.

Nicolas pursed his lips and narrowed his eyes.

"Okay, okay," Toridyn said. "It's the Book of Life that Arin promised before you left, remember? It just showed up one day. That's why the siek advised Sabba to dedicate the temple without you. They didn't want to upset the gods."

"I'll take a closer look later," Nicolas said. "I saw the new orb at the Pinnacle, but I didn't see anything like this."

"We should hurry," Toridyn said. He walked toward Lamil's quarters, which were beyond the orbs some one hundred yards away.

As they stepped away from the transportation pod, it evaporated without so much as a mist, replaced by the original mural on the dome wall.

A rhythmic pulsing came from the large training hall to their right. The familiar formations of student necromancers conjured balls of electric-blue light and levitated them between their hands. Nicolas had spent months in Aquonome—most of those months in that very room—and he still had no idea what those balls of light were for.

"I see it and I still can't believe it," Kaitlyn said. "Is this where you learned how to…I can't believe I'm saying this…*raise the dead*?"

"Not exactly," Nicolas said. "But this is where I got better at it. Siek Lamil was an amazing teacher."

"Better?" Toridyn said. "Near perfect, if you ask me. Managed to kill Jurn, and that was no easy fight."

"You killed someone?" Kaitlyn asked. Her face had lost some of its color.

If this is how she reacts to Jurn, imagine if I told her the whole body count.

A sensation of amusement entered Nicolas through the necromantic link. Dead Kagan found this funny.

We're a stone's throw from the orb of Zubuxo, buddy, Nicolas sent through the link. *If you'd like to share your sense of humor with the hellwraiths for a while, I can arrange it.*

The amusement vanished.

"Easy, Kait," Nicolas said. "I told you we have a lot to catch up on, remember?"

"Don't tell me to take it easy. You *killed* somebody?"

"It wasn't like that, lady," Toridyn said. "Nicolas didn't have a choice. It was a duel to the death. It was either Jurn or Nicolas. And trust me...even Jurn's *mother* was happy about it."

"He was a real piece of work, Kait," Nicolas said. "Sadistic like you wouldn't believe."

"And the others deserved it too!" Toridyn said. "It *was* a war after all."

"*Others*?" Kaitlyn asked. Her mouth was hanging open, and Nicolas didn't like the expression on her face. It was a mix of disbelief and disgust.

"Don't jump to conclusions before I have a chance to tell you everything," Nicolas said. He faced Toridyn. "And *you. Zip* it."

Toridyn shrugged.

They passed around the side of the statue of Arin, back toward the siek's chambers. He should prepare Kaitlyn for what was about to happen.

"Siek Lamil can take things a bit literal at times," Nicolas said. "But he's an amazing person. A very wise man. Just...mind the cultural gap for now, and try not to take anything personally."

"What you're about to see," Toridyn said. "It isn't going to be pretty."

Nicolas swallowed. "All right. Let's go."

Toridyn walked into Siek Lamil's chambers and Nicolas followed him.

The chambers were more spartan than Nicolas had expected. Each of the three walls facing outside the temple were opaque, producing an algae-green glow. And what few personal effects Lamil had were were either splayed out on the floor or propped up on a desk made from Aquonome's barrier energy.

Siek Lamil was sitting on a barrier-energy chair next to the desk.

And he was wearing a bathrobe.

A *human* bathrobe. Enormous, but human just the same.

Nicolas grabbed Toridyn's shoulder. "What the—"

"Sab Nicolas," Lamil said without looking up. "We've been waiting a long time for you."

Nicolas felt the familiar tendrils of Lamil's telepathic energy enter his mind.

When last we met, you were no longer ignorant. Have you regressed? Lamil's voice boomed in his mind.

Nicolas smiled. *I'm told I'm smarter than I look.*

"I don't get it," Nicolas said. He elbowed Toridyn in the ribs. "This one said you were practically dying."

Lamil's left eye focused on Toridyn.

"I said no such thing," Toridyn said. "I merely said this wouldn't be pretty. Look at him! Look at what he's wearing!"

"It would seem Sab Toridyn does not approve of my wardrobe," Lamil said.

"I'm not saying it's a bad look, Siek, but where did you get it?" Nicolas asked.

"A merchant in Caspardis," Lamil said. "The city has reopened to us in recent weeks, and many are more interested in making money than in reinforcing old hatreds. But it seems I'm not the only one with an addition to my wardrobe. Is that a chain of office I see hidden beneath your robe?"

Nicolas stuffed the chain farther into his robe and nodded.

"No need to hide that which you've rightfully earned," Lamil said. "You wear it well."

Lamil focused both eyes on Kaitlyn and stood from his chair, which appeared to melt back into the floor.

"And so she arrives," Lamil said.

Kaitlyn looked as if she wanted to back away, but Nicolas put his arm around her and took a step toward Lamil.

"I've been waiting for you since the vision I had several days ago," Lamil said. "I saw you walking through a garden near a shrine of Shealynd. And I was filled with the most perfect knowledge you would come here."

"That wasn't a vision, Siek," Nicolas said. "It actually happened. She saw—"

"I can tell him what I saw myself," Kaitlyn said.

Lamil shrugged his shoulders and rotating his eyes horizontally, the cichlos gesture for amusement.

"I saw a fish—a *cichlos* at the shrine," Kaitlyn said. "It was you."

Nicolas leaned closer to her. "Kait—"

"I'm sure of it," Kaitlyn said, drawing away from him and taking another step toward Lamil. "It was you. And you weren't alone. Mujahid's brother was with you, and there was a beautiful woman."

"The woman," Lamil said. "I saw this too. But I saw no Mukhtaar Lord. This will require some meditation. I prefer not to act without more wisdom on this matter. But I can assure you of this, Kaitlyn. Though you saw me in the flesh, I was not with you in the flesh. I was in this very room."

Kaitlyn pursed her lips to the side.

"You can trust him," Nicolas said. "I owe him—hell, this whole world owes him their lives."

Lamil harrumphed. "I thought you wiser than that, Nicolas."

"Well, you might not accept the credit for it, but I'm givin' it to you anyway."

"Regardless," Lamil said. "This may have something to do with that room of many doors in your hall of power."

Nicolas remembered the room when Lamil delved his mind the first time they met.

"There were a bunch of black doors," Nicolas said. "And multicolored hallways leading out of it in odd directions. But I don't remember—"

The memory of Kaitlyn standing in the center of that room returned to him. He had sensed a presence when Lamil took him there, and that presence had turned out to be Kaitlyn. It had surprised Lamil when it happened.

"You may be right," Nicolas said.

"And how do you come to speak our tongue?" Lamil asked Kaitlyn. "I know Nicolas didn't teach you, because he does not speak enough Cichlossean."

"I don't know," Kaitlyn said. "I went to give Toridyn a hug and felt a pain in my head."

"You're not the only one, lady," Toridyn said. "I still have a headache."

"And afterward, I understood everything he was saying to me," Kaitlyn said.

"Yes," Lamil said. "I'm beginning to believe this is very much related to your hall of power, Nicolas. When I examined your pathways, it was after the gift of Zubuxo had been bestowed on you. There may be others who have been changed as a result. Perhaps the gift was transmitted by contact."

"Gift of Zubuxo?" Kaitlyn asked.

"Big black bubble thing," Nicolas said. "Near the statue of Zubuxo out in the temple. Almost killed me. Long story. But this isn't why we came here, Siek. We need your help. We need the chimeramancers, actually."

Lamil's eyes spun, and he looked Nicolas up and down. "Why?"

Nicolas explained Kaitlyn's situation, starting with their mutual vision in the Pinnacle garden. When he finished telling the story, he felt haggard, like he'd been running a never-ending marathon.

"Something is troubling you, *Sab,* and it clouds your cet," Lamil said. "What is it that prevents you from letting go?"

Nicolas's gaze drifted toward Kaitlyn and Toridyn. He was beginning to feel self-conscious.

"Guys, can you give us a second?" Nicolas asked.

Kaitlyn narrowed her eyes, but she followed Toridyn out into the temple carrying Toby. When they were out of earshot, Nicolas faced Lamil.

"Are you kidding me?" Nicolas said. "You of all people know what I went through to get back home. After all that time, I finally succeed, and now...now *this!*"

Lamil harrumphed. "Your regard for Kaitlyn is not what restrains you. You no longer fear death. You've been to the other side and returned."

"How can you say that?"

"What is the Third Law of Necromancy?" Lamil asked.

"I can't believe this—"

"What is the Third Law of Necromancy?"

"The Third Law of Necromancy states *there is no death.*"

"Since even I know you are incapable of fearing that which does not exist, my conclusion stands. Something else clouds your judgment, keeping you from embracing your cet."

How did Lamil always do this to him?

"I should understand how to fix this," Nicolas said. And that's what he believed. He was a master necromancer. The archmage, no less. If Kaitlyn had a problem involving magic, he should be the one to be able to fix it. "How can I call myself a *master* if I can't even help her Awaken?"

"And this lack of wisdom upsets you to the point where you've lost focus on your responsibilities?"

"You promoted me. You gave me the robe of mastery. Shouldn't that mean something? I thought you taught me all I needed to know about magic? So why can't I help her the way you and Mujahid helped me?"

There was an awkward silence while Lamil eyed him up and down. But after several moments, Lamil waved his hand and an image of a necromancer's Robe of Mastery appeared in front of them.

"Do you know why the robes and cowls of mastery are the color of darkest, midnight blue?" Lamil asked as he sat on a newly formed stool.

Nicolas shook his head. "You once told me it's a reminder we're capable of great evil."

"At one end of the spectrum there is white. Many believe white is the color of innocence and perfection, yet white is an arrogant color, reflecting all others and absorbing none. White, in its pride, believes in its own perfection and accepts no change."

In all his time at Aquonome, Nicolas had never heard this explanation.

"On the other end of the spectrum is black," Lamil said. "Many cultures in the multiverse see black as the color of perfection. Black absorbs all other colors without reflection. It is the most receptive and accepting of the colors, yet black also believes in its own perfection. It accepts all in a display of humility, yet remains the same. Unchanged. Betraying its pride."

"So where does midnight blue fall into this? It's pretty close to black."

"The darkest blue is a remarkable color, Nicolas. It neither rejects nor accepts all. It chooses carefully...with a discriminating eye, accepting only those colors that bring it closer to perfection, and rejecting those that draw it farther away. It grows closer to perfection with every acceptance, yet never reaches it. It is a visual reminder that though we strive for perfection, our existence will never be perfect."

"I don't *feel* any closer to perfection," Nicolas said. "I feel like a fake. A fraud. I don't deserve that robe and title you gave me."

"Let me assure you, I *gave* you nothing," Lamil said. "The road to mastery doesn't end with the robe and cowl. It *begins* there. I gave you nothing except the knowledge of the fact you're ready to learn. You're ready to *begin* your journey."

"That doesn't help me fix Kaitlyn's problem."

"I worry about you."

That surprised Nicolas. Lamil had never spoken to him like that before.

"I see a man before me who has regressed," Lamil said. "Where once you were centered and knew your path and purpose, now you flounder like a hatchling. I saw this happen once before."

"What was the outcome?"

"You should know. You killed him."

Nicolas remembered the suffering he'd endured at Jurn's hand. And yes, he remembered their final encounter as if it happened yesterday. But this wasn't the same. It couldn't be.

Nicolas shook his head. "You don't understand. You've never understood how much I love her."

"I understand more than you know about Love. I understand that it compels you. That it simultaneously binds you and sets you free."

"Then why the worry?"

"Because I also know something else. I know that unless you're careful, you will become each other's weakness instead of strength. The very force that draws you together will tear you apart."

Nicolas didn't want to admit it, but Lamil was right. When he'd left Aquonome, he was stronger. More confident. But the moment he discovered Kaitlyn was in trouble, he lost it. All that strength seeped out of him, leaving confusion and anxiety in its place. He couldn't continue like this. Yes, he loved Kaitlyn and was worried about her. But none of that was going to get them out of this situation.

Nicolas stood and adjusted his robe.

"I need to speak to the chimeramancers," Nicolas said.

Lamil's eyes rotated.

"Whatever Kaitlyn is experiencing, Mujahid seemed to think she was a chimeramancer. If anyone will know how to help her Awaken, it's them."

One of Lamil's eyes came to rest on the opening to the temple, while the other came to rest on Nicolas.

"While I applaud your newfound confidence, what you ask is not so simple."

"What do you mean? Just take us to them and introduce us."

"Introductions must take place in a controlled way, or catastrophe can happen in Aquonome. Accounting Day is several weeks away. We cannot disturb the chimeramancers until then."

"Why was I never told about these guys?"

"It is for cichlos, not human. You required no introduction, because they are not required to catalog you."

"Catalog?"

"It is what they do."

"You're one of the highest ranking members of the highest caste in Aquonome," Nicolas said. "I'm sure they'll listen to you."

"You don't understand. Chimeramancers are above such things. They are not part of the caste system. They serve a greater purpose."

"Then we have that in common."

Nicolas left Lamil sitting on his stool as he walked out into the temple. Whether Lamil joined them or not, Nicholas was headed for the central dome. He'd wasted enough time already.

CHAPTER EIGHT

[1]*The Rule of Love*

[2]*Shealynd stepped forward and beseeched her brother.* [3]*"Mine is the dominion of Love, for my name is love as yours is exalted.* [4]*I shall imbue this hell with love, for it is to be our father's last home."*

[5]*Arin agreed and empowered Shealynd.*

[6]*And Shealynd went forth, down into the hells, and shed six tears, one for each Plane.* [7]*But the six tears had power over the prison and its bindings.*

- *The Mukhtaar Chronicles, attributed to the prophet Habakku*

Origines Multiversi, Emergentiae 7:1-7

Nicolas entered the smaller central dome, followed by Kaitlyn — who held Toby's leash. Toridyn and dead Kagan brought up the rear, the former like a man waiting for his own trial to begin, and the latter just taking up space.

The central dome was much as Nicolas remembered it. Several multi-hued columns of barrier material stretched from floor to ceiling and served as chutes for distributing food. Each column was attended by two cichlos priests who wore the strange, leather-like cichlos clothing with the midnight-blue cowl of mastery around their shoulders. Cichlos entered through the tubular hallways and transportation bubbles circling the dome's perimeter and lined up at the distribution columns, where the priests gave them trays of food.

Three tremendous floating bubbles dominated the dome's center. Each bubble morphed as they floated up and down, changing shape and color, but they never touched. Occasionally, the top bubble would change color and the others would follow suit. Beneath them were three barrier chairs—more like recliners—occupied by rotund, sleeping cichlos in gray cowls. Barrier energy rose from the floor and formed a waist-high wall surrounding the column of bubbles. Two young cichlos stooped over the wall, examining something on its flat, overhanging surface.

People moving through the dome gave the area a wide berth, like tourists at the Grand Canyon who didn't want to press their luck with the guard rails.

Lamil had joined them, though he seemed even more concerned than Toridyn. What was it with those two? Nicolas just wanted to ask the chimeramancers some questions, but they acted like he was planning to exhume their dead relatives!

"I have a bad feeling about this," Toridyn said.

"Why, exactly?" Nicolas asked.

"Nick," Kaitlyn said. "Maybe you should listen."

"You too, now?"

Kaitlyn shook her head and turned away. That wasn't a good sign. The last time she acted like that, she didn't speak to him for a while. What was wrong with these people? Couldn't they see…couldn't *she* see he was trying to save her life?

And what was Lamil's problem? He always had an explanation…long-winded and philosophical, perhaps, but an explanation nonetheless. But now he seemed *scared*.

"What aren't you telling me?" Nicolas asked, staring at Lamil.

Lamil's eyes made a complex series of turns, independent of one another, and came to rest with one staring at the floor and the other staring at the chimeramancers. Nicolas had never seen that gesture before.

"The last time a chimeramancer was disturbed outside of *Accounting Day* was the day my sister died," Lamil said.

On the day the siek taught him to use the arrow symbol, he also taught Nicolas about his sister Tamil.

Nicolas grasped for words that wouldn't come.

"I'm sorry," Nicolas said. "I didn't know. But what else aren't you telling me? What is this Accounting Day you keep talking about?"

"To understand that, you must understand the purpose of the chimeramancers within cichlos society," Lamil said. "That is not something I can simply explain to your satisfaction."

"You're good at *simply* dodging my questions, though."

Lamil harrumphed. "Accounting Day comes four times every year. It is a day on which new members of our community are introduced to the chimeramancers, one by one, so that they might…commit them to memory."

Lamil walked past Nicolas and approached a young cichlos at the barrier ring.

The young cichlos didn't so much as nod his bulbous head. What was it with these chimeramancers?

"Siek Lamil," the young cichlos said. He stepped in front of an opening in the wall, blocking Lamil's entrance.

"I must speak with one of the cherished," Lamil said.

Since when do the cichlos refer to people as cherished?

The young cichlos's eyes spun. One came to rest in the direction of the gray-cowled, sleeping cichlos, and the other came to rest on Nicolas.

"If there is anything you need, I can provide it," the young cichlos said.

"You are not a Conjurer," Lamil said. "You are an apprentice."

"Why do you ask the impossible of me?"

Nicolas stepped forward, his anger returning to the surface, but Siek Lamil stopped him with his enormous hand.

"What is the Prime Duty of a Chimeramancer?" Siek Lamil asked.

Nicolas hadn't considered it, but it stood to reason if Necromancy had a Prime Duty, another school of magic would as well. Whatever the reality, this poor bastard was going to be sorry he got the siek asking questions!

The young cichlos harrumphed. "You are not my—"

"What is the Prime Duty of a Chimeramancer?" Lamil asked again. "You will proceed at half ration until I get the answer I am looking for."

The young cichlos's eyes spun until his gaze came to rest on Lamil.

"You would not do that," the young cichlos said.

"I'm pretty sure he would," Nicolas said. "You should see what he does when you give him the *wrong* answer. Hope you have a lot of time on your hands."

The cichlos glanced down at his hands and back to Lamil with a questioning look on his face.

Nicolas shook his head. When *would* the cichlos understand his sense of humor?

"What is the Prime Duty of a Chimeramancer?" Lamil asked.

"The Prime Duty of a Chimeramancer is to protect all who call Aquonome home, and perform the Great Sacrifice when called upon."

"That is correct," Lamil said. "Sab Toridyn. The catalyst, please."

Toridyn swirled his arms and a pulse of static electricity passed over Nicolas in a wave that made his arm hair stand up.

Kaitlyn rubbed her left arm.

When Toridyn's arms came to rest, he spread his hands and an electric-blue ball of light formed between them, like the blue ball manipulated by the students in the training hall.

Lamil placed his hand on Nicolas's shoulder.

"Do you deny the citizenship of Sab Nicolas?" Lamil asked.

The young cichlos appeared flustered, rotating his eyes horizontally, back and forth. "Of course not, Siek!"

"Do you deny Sab Nicolas's right to take a mate?"

Kaitlyn's face reddened. Though she didn't say anything, he knew she'd have plenty to say later about being "taken" as anyone's "mate".

"I do not," the young cichlos said.

"Sab Nicolas's mate is in grave danger," Lamil said. "Would you turn her away and violate the Prime Duty?"

The young cichlos stiffened for a moment, then backed away from the opening in the barrier ring.

"Which one?" Lamil asked.

The young cichlos gazed up at the floating bubbles. "Conjurer Torgar," he said. "But please reconsider."

Lamil's eyes spun toward Kaitlyn.

You're not actually reconsidering, are you? Nicolas asked Lamil telepathically.

After a pause that dragged on longer than Nicolas would have liked, he sensed a response forming in his mind. It was an image of Kaitlyn standing at the center of his hall of power...the image he had seen when Lamil delved into his mind when he first arrived in Aquonome. It had shaken Lamil when it happened the first time, and if Nicolas didn't know better, he'd say the siek was still disturbed by it.

She is important for reasons I do not understand, the siek's voice rang in his head. *I will do everything I can. But the young one is correct. What we're about to do is reckless. There will be consequences beyond our ability to predict.*

"You must wait until the *guiding dream* permeates the others," the young cichlos said.

Nicolas had no idea what a *guiding dream* was, but he hoped it would hurry up and *permeate.*

When the topmost bubble changed color, and the others pulsed a matching hue, Lamil faced Toridyn.

"Now," Lamil said.

Toridyn spun his hands around the ball of light, and the ball shot toward the lowest bubble. When the ball of light struck the bubble, it penetrated it and began to expand, a sphere within a sphere, until the ball broke through the bubble and both evaporated.

A murmur of voices rose in the central dome. Groups of cichlos bunched up against the dome wall, pressed forward by the surging crowd behind them. What were they doing?

Then it dawned on him. The transportation bubbles were gone.

"Tor," Nicolas whispered. "What happened to the transport bubbles? And what the hell do you call those things, anyway? I'm tired of calling them transport bubbles."

"Aqua-pneumatic chimeraporters," Toridyn said.

Nicolas nodded. "Well, what the hell happened to the transport bubbles?"

A guttural growl raised the hairs on Nicolas's arm.

"Siek Lamil," the voice said in a bass that vibrated Nicolas's chest. "I saw you approach from within the guiding dream."

"Conjurer Torgar," Lamil said. "I trust all is well."

A corpulent cichlos sat up from a chair under the column of bubbles and waddled toward them.

"You trust all is *well*?" Torgar asked. "This time it is you who are ignorant, Lamil."

Lamil's shoulders drew back.

"Did you stop to think I may have been holding the lake at bay beyond a breach in the wall?" Torgar asked. "Did you speculate as to whether I was providing transport to the surface, or protection to pods traveling beneath the city? Did you consider I may have been Traveling?"

"I assure you, Conjurer, I considered all these things. I have brought—"

"I know well why you are here. Did I not say I saw you approach in the dream? I know of the human's problem."

Kaitlyn drew closer to Nicolas, who took it as a small sign she might speak to him again at some point.

"But that places me under no obligation to help," Torgar said. "Nor does the fact she is the human sab's mate."

Lamil took a step forward. "The Prime Duty of Chimeramancy—"

"Was used as a cheap philosopher's trick to manipulate a naive apprentice," Torgar said. He faced the young cichlos who had backed away from the barrier ring. "We will discuss your lack of critical thinking later."

The young cichlos apprentice lowered his gaze to the dome floor.

"This is a human problem, not cichlos," Torgar said. He started walking back toward his seat.

Anxiety bubbled to the surface of Nicolas's emotions. This conjurer, or whatever he was, had to help!

Nicolas took a step forward, but Lamil stopped him. The complex movement of Lamil's left eye sent a clear message. *Do not speak.*

"Aquonome is no place for bigotry, Conjurer," Lamil said.

Torgar stopped in mid step. He turned his massive head until he was looking back over his left shoulder.

"Refusing to help is not *bigotry*," Torgar said. "I refuse to help not because the human is different, but because doing so would stop me from fulfilling my higher calling. I would think you of all people should know this. You are a moral philosopher, are you not?"

"I am merely a reasonable man," Lamil said. "But since you mention it, would you agree if I said we live in a world where things frequently go against our best designs?"

Torgar faced Lamil and folded his arms. "I would agree with that statement."

"And would you agree that in times of great need, we often must seek the aid of others?"

"Obviously."

"Then you would also agree that you yourself may require such aid in the future?"

"Your point?"

"Would it not be in the best interests of all to provide aid when it is requested and within our ability to do so? If you would expect to receive aid, surely you must expect to offer it."

"Your argument is flawed," Torgar said. "By returning to my duty I *am* providing the very aid you accuse me of refusing. And to far more than this single human."

Lamil's voice echoed in Nicolas's mind. *I cannot dispute his logic. His higher calling is of great aid to the entire cichlos people.*

Nicolas couldn't let this drop. He wasn't going to leave without getting the help he came here for!

Siek, you and Mujahid both told me it was dangerous for a necromancer to remain untrained. A danger to all. Isn't that true of Chimeramancers too?

Lamil's eye rotated once, then shifted back and forth. He was amused.

"If you'll excuse me," Torgar said.

"If my moral argument falls flat, perhaps you'll consider a utilitarian line of reasoning?" Lamil asked.

Torgar's eyes rotated outward then back toward Lamil. He was interested.

"Consider the consequences of Kaitlyn coming into her power without understanding it," Lamil said. "What action would you take if you discovered an unawakened *cichlos* chimeramancer, Conjurer?"

Torgar's eyes made the same rotation and he stepped forward. "We would take that person into our training dome immediately."

"And why would you do this?" Lamil asked.

"The reasons are as many as there are stars between here and Terilya."

Torgar was approaching. Was this a good sign?

"Consider what could happen if she entered the trance and *imagined* the city," Lamil said. "Think of the consequences if she got a single detail wrong. Details such as the contents of the secret places. The containment chamber. The—"

Torgar held up his webbed hand. "Enough." He glanced at the young cichlos apprentice. "Rouse the others. The Siek is correct, and in my anger I refused to see it."

"Righteous indignation can be justified," Lamil said. "But sometimes it clouds our better judgment."

"Yes, well, correct or not, you took exceedingly great risk in waking me." Torgar faced the young apprentice once more. "Do it."

The young cichlos nodded and hunched over something on the surface of the barrier ring. One by one the large floating bubbles changed color and evaporated, followed by the grumbling of the other two rotund cichlos in the reclining barrier chairs.

The dome grew silent except for the occasional murmur among cichlos near the transport bubbles. Nicolas had never noticed until this moment that there had always been a faint hum in the background, all throughout the city. The humming stopped, and the remaining transport bubbles vanished, leaving many cichlos stranded in the central dome. For the cichlos who lived at the extreme ends of the barrier tubes, that meant several miles of walking. Those inside the transport bubbles were left swimming back toward the city wall.

"It is in their hands now," Lamil said as he faced Nicolas and Kaitlyn. "You must do as they instruct. To do otherwise will be to invite disaster."

Kaitlyn nodded. "Thank you, Siek."

Lamil glanced at Nicolas. "She's far more polite than you were when we first met."

"I seem to remember there were…extenuating circumstances, Siek."

"Yes, well it seems we have new circumstances," Lamil said as he faced the approaching chimeramancers. "It is not common for them all to be awake at once. This will put a great strain on the city. They will be…*agitated*."

"He wasn't agitated already?" Kaitlyn asked.

"Step forward," Torgar said.

They entered the central ring together.

The three chimeramancers gathered with Torgar at their center, glancing back and forth at one another. Two of the chimeramancers shook their head and rapidly moved their eyes from side to side — worry.

Torgar spoke.

"Then it is settled," Torgar said. "I will lead the Awakening and take her into my fold."

Kaitlyn raised an eyebrow at Nicolas.

"There's nothing to worry about," Nicolas said. "Right, Siek?"

For once, Lamil had nothing to say. In fact, he seemed to be purposely not looking at Nicolas.

"Let the candidate step forward," Torgar said.

Kaitlyn swallowed and took several steps forward.

"What is your name?" Torgar said.

"Kaitlyn."

The three chimeramancers surrounded her and were communicating again, judging from the way they stared at one another.

They spent several minutes going over Kaitlyn's account of everything she'd experienced since arriving on Erindor, paying particular attention to her sleeping patterns. When she described her last headache, the one that left her doubled over, they adjusted their positions until they stood in a line in front of her.

Torgar nodded to the chimeramancer at his right, who closed his eyes and lowered his head.

The barrier floor bubbled up behind them and formed a ring that floated bench-height in the air.

"Be seated," Torgar said.

Kaitlyn pressed down on the ring, as if testing it.

When she sat, Torgar kneeled beside her. It struck Nicolas as oddly nurturing for the otherwise angry cichlos.

"Conjure your hall of power," Torgar said.

"My what?" Kaitlin asked.

"The room with two doors," Nicolas said. "Imagine it."

Kaitlyn closed her eyes.

"Do you see your…room with two doors?" Torgar asked.

"Yeah. A red one and a blue one."

"Good. Perceive yourself moving toward the red door."

Nothing happened for several moments, but Kaitlyn started fidgeting in her seat. She broke into a sweat.

"I can't," Kaitlyn said.

"You must," Torgar said. "If you cannot, it is not for lack of ability. It is for lack of imagination."

"Nice bedside manner you got there," Nicolas said. "I bet we don't even get a lollipop when we leave."

Lamil's left eye spun toward Nicolas and rotated. *Be quiet.*

"The red door," Torgar said.

"No," Kaitlin said. "I told you, I can't. It's pushing me away. Toward the blue door."

Torgar stood and backed away, making a sound Nicolas had never heard a cichlos make before. It was the startled cry of fear and disgust a person might make if they reached into a box filled with spiders.

The bench beneath Kaitlyn vanished, and she crashed to the city floor. All three chimeramancers looked at her as if she were a poisonous snake; equal parts fear and a desire to kill or run.

Nicolas cast a chord of necropotency forward and lifted her to her feet. He stepped between her and the chimeramancers. If they were going to try anything, they'd have to go through him.

"What the hell did you do?" Nicolas said.

"Get her away!" Torgar yelled. "Don't let her touch anything, not even the floor!"

Something sharp pushed against the chord of necropotency. Whatever it was, it wasn't any good.

So Nicolas pushed back.

A chimeramancer fell backward and landed on the barrier next to his reclined seat.

"Did you seriously just try to kill her?" Nicolas said.

He embraced the anxiety that bubbled up inside, letting it turn into a torrent that flooded his mind, and he opened a pathway between his well of power and the skull symbol. His mind flooded with images.

"No, Nicolas!" Lamil shouted.

A shield materialized around Nicolas's well, cutting him off from his power.

Dead Kagan lunged for Torgar and five undead cichlos materialized around him and dragged him back toward Lamil.

"Enough!" Lamil yelled.

How the hell had Lamil summoned five penitents in such a short timespan without collapsing? They were pure summonings, too. Far more difficult than raising a corpse.

"Your cet, Nicolas," Lamil said.

Nicolas took a deep a breath and tried to calm down. His cet was there somewhere…hidden behind images of ripping Torgar's head off.

"What have you done, Lamil?" Torgar said. "The entire city may be imbued now. We have no way of knowing!"

"What are you talking about?" Nicolas asked. He faced Lamil. "What is he talking about?"

"He's right, I'm afraid," Lamil said. "If she cannot approach the red door—"

"How could you bring a cognitomancer into our midst?" Torgar said.

"A cog *what*?" Kaitlyn asked.

"Even her footsteps could be imbued," Torgar said. "What would happen if one of us touched them and she took control?"

Lamil's eyes made a complex circuit of independent rotations.

"She hasn't Awakened yet," Lamil said. "She could no more imbue her footsteps than you could."

"What is he talking about?" Kaitlyn said.

"This is worse than I feared," Lamil said. "I must seek Gormala's advice."

"The witch is under no obligation to her," Torgar said.

Lamil faced Nicolas. "That is for Gormala to decide, not you."

"We are finished here," Torgar said. "And if you had the best interests of Aquonome at heart, you'd allow Gormala to *make* no decisions."

Torgar returned to his reclined chair.

"You never mentioned any *Gormala* before, Siek," Nicolas said.

"The list of things I have not mentioned to you is larger than the list I *have*. Is there an obligation I am under of which I am currently unaware?"

"Can this *Gormala* help me?" Kaitlyn asked. "That's what you implied, isn't it? That's why Torgar is so upset?"

"A single cognitomancer killed tens of thousands of cichlos. That is why Torgar is *upset*, as you put it."

"How?" Kaitlyn asked.

"It was not the result of malicious intent," Lamil said. "It was the result of ignorance. Ignorance and an imbued bed sheet destroyed the city of Meculor."

"But what do you mean by *imbued*?" Kaitlyn asked. "Are you saying something was *added* to the bed sheet? Or the sheet was infused with something?

"That goes to the heart of what a cognitomancer does," Lamil said. "Humans call them *enchanters*, and for good reason. They enchant objects and people with nothing more than the power of their mind." Lamil walked past them toward one of the small barrier tubes leading away from the central dome. "Come. We can discuss matters while we walk. We don't have far to go."

The cichlos in the central dome had returned to their routines, but they parted around Lamil as he led the group into a small barrier tube. It was a different tube than Nicolas had entered when he'd first arrived in Aquonome a year ago. But so much about it was the same.

Columns of multi-hued barrier energy formed rooms—*apartments*, judging from the families who came and went from the circular, dilating doors. A small cichlos—a child, whose head had not yet grown sufficiently to accommodate his full-sized cichlos eyes—hopped from one side of a dilating door to another, until his father took him by the hand. Nicolas didn't recall dilating doors from his last trip, but much of Aquonome was transitory in nature. The cichlos chimeramancers used barrier energy to form chairs, tables, and even these rooms, on an as-needed basis.

"What, exactly, does an imbued object do?" Kaitlyn asked. She strode next to Lamil, as if daring someone to comment on her feet touching the city floor.

"Chimeramancy and Cognitomancy are two ends of a single spectrum," Lamil said.

"Like Necromancy and life magic," Nicolas said.

"Correct. Chimeramancy takes what is in the chimeramancer's mind—the chimeramancer's *dreams*—and manifests it as reality. Cognitomancy is similar, yet different. A cognitomancer projects an image into another person's mind, changing the other person's *perception* of reality."

"And *that* was enough to cause that massive freak out back there?"

"Do you see the tube ahead?" Lamil asked. "See how it curves ever-so-slightly in the distance?"

"Yeah," Kaitlyn said.

"Now imagine the tube exists only in your imagination. A trick of the mind that led you to believe you could leave the central dome in safety."

"We'd all be swimming right now."

"You and Nicolas would be *dead* right now, crushed under the weight of Lake Caspar. This is what cognitomancers can do to other people."

"I've felt it," Nicolas said, looking at Kaitlyn. "That first night back at the Pinnacle."

"You will have an unparalleled ability to connect with other living beings," Lamil said. "Through physical contact, you will understand things about people they do not understand themselves. And it will change you."

Nicolas looked from Kaitlyn to Toridyn and back. "Any chance this *unparalleled ability* can help them speak a foreign language?"

"I suppose it is possible."

"That city you mentioned," Kaitlyn said. "Meculor. You said it was destroyed because an enchanter imbued a bed sheet. I understand that enchanters can put some kind of image in another person's head. But where does the bed sheet come in?"

"Powerful cognitomancers—enchanters, as you call them—can store an image of an alternate reality in an object. Anyone who comes into contact with an imbued object receives the stored reality, and remains in that reality until the enchanter releases them."

"And so an enchanter stored an image of an *alternate* Meculor in a bed sheet?" Kaitlyn asked.

"It was not done with malicious intent," Lamil said. "A cognitomancer who wasn't aware of her own power allowed a dream to imbue her bed sheets while she slept. Those sheets found their way onto the command bed of one of the chief chimeramancers of Meculor. The surviving conjurer told us the dream depicted Meculor above the water. In realty, however, Meculor was *below* water. These images invaded the *guiding* dream."

There was that term again. *Guiding dream.* Nicolas hadn't heard anything about a *guiding* dream during his previous stay in Aquonome.

"But there's more than one chimeramancer," Kaitlyn said. "Wouldn't the others have noticed and done something about it?"

A group of cichlos priests emerged from the lake beyond the barrier wall. They carried fish in small nets and began sorting them on the city floor as Nicolas and the others passed by.

"Chimeramancers must work in tandem to maintain a city this size," Lamil said. "They exist on the border between the waking world and the dream world, flowing freely among each other's dreams. But there is always one in command. One *guiding* dream. When the guiding dream revealed an image of Meculor above water, the other dreams changed to match the guiding dream's reality. The chimeramancers dropped the city's primary environmental defenses that hold the waters at bay. Meculor imploded from the pressure, killing nearly everyone. Only two survived to tell the story. One is the most powerful chimeramancer our people have ever known. And you've met him."

"Torgar," Nicolas said.

"No wonder he acted like I was going to kill everyone," Kaitlyn said.

"*One* of the reasons, yes," Lamil said.

"And what's the other?"

Lamil stopped in front of a rectangular section of barrier energy that formed a room on the side of the tube. There was another iris-like door, approximately ten feet in diameter, at the center of the rectangle. He faced Kaitlyn.

"Gormala was the cognitomancer who destroyed Meculor," Lamil said. "She was the other survivor."

The door dilated without a sound, and Nicolas peered inside.

The rectangular room was the entrance to an elaborate system of barrier chambers extending into the lake. In some ways, it reminded Nicolas of his Hall of Power. Each room had two doors.

Nicolas focused on the room beyond the iris door. A bed was pushed against the wall on the left, and a structure that looked like a desk—a flat surface with a chair behind it—stood against the far wall. The walls periodically changed color, gradually cycling through the visible spectrum. Nicolas found it soothing.

"Welcome," a voice said. It was higher-pitched than Lamil's, but still deeper than a human's. Nicolas couldn't see where it had come from.

"Please, enter," the voice said.

"Thank you, Gormala," Lamil said. He entered the rectangular room and gestured for the others to follow. "It has been some time."

When Nicolas stepped across the iris's threshold, he saw Gormala rising from a large barrier chair on the right side of the room, opposite the bed.

"Siek," Gormala said. "You honor me."

She bowed toward Lamil as they entered, but her eyes, which didn't protrude as far from the sides of her head as Lamil's did, stayed perfectly still. In a culture of people who expressed emotion with eye movements, she must be impossible to read.

That or she was emotionless.

When she stood tall once more, she was shorter than Lamil. But not by much. And she wasn't as broad across the shoulders. But other than that, she looked much the same as Lamil. In fact, she had the same sagging orange skin as Lamil. But where Lamil had black striations, her skin was uniformly orange. She wore a blue cowl that extended to the middle of her chest, like a scapular.

"Honoring you was not my intention," Lamil said.

If Gormala was insulted by Lamil's remark, she didn't let on. Her eyes remained focused on the siek.

"I come to you because this young woman is in grave danger," Lamil said. "Perhaps we *all* are if you do not help."

"I am very sorry," Gormala said. "I hope you know that."

Lamil's eyes made two slow circular motions toward the front of his face. He was calming himself down.

"No apology is necessary," Lamil said. "Tamil would not have held you responsible for her death. And so, neither will I. But you above all know how important this is."

"Of course. And thank you."

"You can help me?" Kaitlyn asked.

"Siek, you'll want to leave her alone with me for this," Gormala said.

Lamil nodded. "Sab Toridyn, come."

Nicolas handed Toby's leash to Toridyn. "I need to stay. I mean, if that's okay."

"I have no objection," Gormala said.

Toby wagged his tail as he followed Lamil and Toridyn through the iris door.

Gormala waved her hand and an elaborate bench rose from Aquonome's floor like water pouring upward. It was the size of a small, padded sofa. When it reached a comfortable height, the liquid energy solidified.

Gormala touched one of the two padded armrests. "Please, take a seat. Both of you."

Kaitlyn sat and made a gasping sound.

When Nicolas touched the sofa, the room changed.

Gone was the iris door. In fact, gone were the doors leading to the multitude of other chambers.

Cool mountain air blew across his face as he and Kaitlyn stood on the precipice of a cliff overlooking a city.

Nicolas instinctively stepped back, but he tripped and fell.

Instead of landing on rocky ground, however, he landed on the cushioned barrier bench in Gormala's chambers.

He blinked and looked around. The iris door had returned, as had the bed, desk, and two other exits.

"What happened?" Nicolas asked.

"That was trippy," Kaitlyn said. "I could *feel* the mist from the ocean on my face."

"I was on a mountain," Nicolas said.

Kaitlyn ran her hand along the armrest and down onto the seat cushion. "This is imbued, isn't it."

Gormala ambled to her desk chair and sat. "I can help you."

"Forgive me if this is inappropriate," Nicolas said. "I hear a *but* on the end of that sentence."

"You are of a higher caste, Sab," Gormala said. "Your statement was not inappropriate. Nor was it false." She faced Kaitlyn. "I *can* help you. But there is a cost."

Nicolas raised an eyebrow. Was she seriously trying to *hussle* them?

"I'm...not sure I can pay," Kaitlyn stammered.

"You misunderstand. The magic will exact its cost. And you can rest assured it is both something we possess and something we would rather not lose."

"We?"

"The Hall of Power may demand *I* pay the price," Gormala said. "Perhaps *both* of us. There is no way to know until it is paid in full."

"What was the price you paid when you Awakened?" Kaitlyn asked.

"*That* is an inappropriate question."

Judging by her reaction, Nicolas got the feeling that was similar to one necromancer asking another how many symbols of power they had. A priest didn't talk about that unless they trusted the other person. A *lot*.

"Do you have an object you hold dear?" Gormala asked.

Kaitlyn looked at Nicolas, then pulled out a small cross hanging from a delicate gold chain under her shirt. The cross was gold as well. It was the one Nicolas had given her before they were engaged. They'd gotten into the habit of looking through the church's gift shop after mass, and she'd always spend a few minutes admiring it.

"The *cruciform*," Gormala said. "An ancient symbol of power, and a good choice."

That got Nicolas's attention. First the similarity in religious architecture between Erindor and Earth, and now *this*?

"You *know* that symbol?" Nicolas asked.

"For some it symbolizes life. For others, vengeance and death. It depends upon the culture and age in which you ask the question. Let's begin. Call to mind your Hall of Power."

Kaitlyn closed her eyes. "I see it. Two doors. Blue and Red."

"Given that Siek Lamil brought you to *me*, I assume you see the disembodied head floating beyond the blue door."

"Yes."

"Good. This will be your path from now on."

"Will I ever see what's beyond the red door?"

"Perhaps," Gormala said. "You may enter it in the future if you wish. If you *can*. But remember that any test beyond the red door is a test outside of your natural abilities. Therefore, the likelihood of failure is high."

"What happens if I fail?"

"A meaningless question. If you fail, you will not live long enough to perceive anything *happening*."

"Okay," Kaitlyn said. "No red door."

"I will take your hand," Gormala said. "When you step through the blue door, I will guide the disembodied head to dissolve into your mind. It will become the substratum in which you mold new realities."

"Wait," Nicolas said. "No attack? No confusion? No...bad acid trip that involves a stinking, fire-breathing skull?"

Gormala took Kaitlyn's hand in hers. "Step through the door when you are ready."

Kaitlyn leaned back slightly and Gormala smiled.

"That's it," Gormala said. "I will perform the Awakening now. You're going to feel light-headed as the symbol dissolves. When it passes, you will feel a new construct in your mind. That is when you may collapse the Hall of Power. And when you do, I want you to create an image of something that brings you great peace. Touch your cruciform symbol—it must come into contact with your skin—and send the image into it."

"Why?"

"It will provide focus for more complex tasks in the future. I'll teach you after the Awakening."

Kaitlyn reached out and grabbed the arm of the bench. It must have begun. A moment later, she winced, then smiled.

"It's...*strange*," Kaitlyn said. "It's like air rushing around my brain."

"It is nearly complete," Gormala said. "You are doing splendidly. Allow the energy to dissipate." She tilted her head to the side. "That's it. Now, I will tie off the flow of ethereal—"

Gormala gasped.

"I feel something in my mind," Kaitlyn said. "It's like a...you remember those *pin art* toys back home, Nick? The ones where you'd press your hand into them and it would leave a perfect impression? It feels like that, only...huge. And the pins are smaller, and closer together. It's like I could make an impression of an entire building in it."

Gormala stood, but she wobbled. Her eyes, which had remained pointing forward until now, spun backward in their sockets, and she collapsed to the floor.

"Gormala!" Nicolas yelled.

Nicolas knelt beside Gormala and tried to find her pulse. But he wasn't sure where to look. In all his time in Aquonome, they'd never taught him anything of cichlos anatomy. One thing was certain, though: he hadn't felt a rush of necropotency. Gormala must be alive.

"What happened?" Kait said.

"Siek!" Nicolas yelled. The outer door dilated and Lamil and Toridyn entered.

"One second she was there, in my mind," Kaitlyn said. "The next, she was gone! Faded!"

"They'll help her," Nicolas said.

As Lamil knelt next to Gormala, a powerful wave of energy struck Nicolas and funneled down into his well of power. He turned toward Gormala and found Lamil and Toridyn staring back at him.

"No," Nicolas said.

"Why are they stopping?" Kaitlyn asked. She stepped toward Gormala, but Nicolas took her hand gently in his.

"It's too late," Nicolas said. "She's gone."

"How do you know? They're not even..." Kaitlyn lowered her head. "What am I saying? Of course you know."

"Sab Toridyn," Lamil said. "Inform the others."

"Yes, Siek," Toridyn said. He spun and jogged from the room.

Nicolas led Kaitlyn back to the bench and sat.

Kaitlyn stared at the ground with a blank expression.

"Gormala told you to do something after the Awakening," Nicolas said. "With your cross. Remember?"

Kaitlyn nodded and clutched at the cross.

"She said she'd teach me after," Kaitlyn said.

"We'll figure it out," Nicolas said. "There have to be other enchanters."

Kaitlyn let go of the golden cross and it fell against her chest. "It's done."

Nicolas hadn't sensed anything. "You...*did something* with it?"

"Exactly what she told me to do. I imagined something peaceful and sent the image into the cross."

"You mean...just like *that*? No struggling, no almost killing yourself, no nothing?"

"You should know. You've been through an Awakening too. Why? Did you have problems at first?"

Nicolas pursed his lips. "Nope. Not a one."

Lamil harrumphed and stood.

Three cichlos priests Nicolas didn't know entered the room and carried Gormala away.

"That poor woman," Kaitlyn said. "She told us there'd be a price to pay. I never thought it would be *this*."

Kaitlyn crossed herself and rested her hand on Nicolas's wrist, but she drew back as if she'd been shocked by static electricity.

"No problems Awakening, huh?" Kaitlyn said. "How many times did you pass out, mister *not a one*? Mujahid was right to be upset. You didn't raise his friend properly." She scooted farther back in her seat. "Whoa, that was a big bug. Its arms were swords?"

Nicolas snapped his gaze toward Kaitlyn. Her eyes were as wide as his felt.

"How do you know all that?" Nicolas asked. When Mujahid led him through his Awakening, Nicolas had lost consciousness while raising a penitent. The penitent—a skeletal warrior—had been Mujahid's old friend. Mujahid had to summon a warrior of his own and destroy the uncontrolled skeleton, sending his own friend back to the Plane of Death. He'd gotten quite angry with Nicolas after that.

Kaitlyn blinked several times and her eyes came back into focus.

"I don't know," Kaitlyn said. "When I touched you, I saw a bunch of things. No, that's not exactly right. I *felt* a bunch of things. *Knew* a bunch of things. Can I try something? On you?"

Nicolas scratched the tip of his nose. "Sure."

The room fell away, and once again Nicolas stood face to face with Ensif, the argram he summoned when Paradise was under attack. Ensif stood with all six tarsal swords extended. Nicolas heard shouts behind him. Saw Mujahid melting the rock. He smelled the stench of—

The room returned.

"That's what I saw," Kaitlyn said. "Was I close?"

"Close? You were *precise*. That was *exactly* what I lived through!"

Toridyn ran into the room, out of breath.

"Siek," Toridyn said. He was breathing heavily. "The fishing pod out there saw an army on the southern shore. It wasn't Shandarian."

"Human matters," Lamil said.

"That's what I thought, Siek, but this army appeared from nowhere. The pod says they materialized outside of Tur along with their fortifications."

"*Materialized?*" Nicolas said. He recalled what Tithian had told him about the Barathosian armada *appearing* off the coast of Dar Rodon. "Barathosians."

"Whoever they are," Toridyn said, "they took the city. The pod says it wasn't much of a fight. They knocked down the city walls within an hour of appearing and Tur surrendered. Now half of that force is marching north toward Caspardis."

This wasn't good, and Nicolas couldn't just sit here and do nothing. He was the archmage. He had to help somehow.

Now that Kaitlyn was safe, his duty was clear. He recalled Arin's words: *Take your rightful place in this world.*

It was time to obey that command.

"How fast can we get to Caspardis?" Nicolas asked. "Faster than that army can?"

"Much faster than the marching ones," Toridyn said. "But if they have others who can appear out of the air, not even our transport system is that fast."

"You can drive those things, right?"

"The aqua-pneumatic chimeraporters?" Toridyn asked. "You bip your betty!"

Nicolas had no idea what he was trying to say.

"I think you mean *bet your bippy*," Kaitlyn said.

"I don't get it," Toridyn said. "What's a *bippy*? And why is it valuable enough to bet on a game of chance?"

"Never mind," Nicolas said. "I want to get close to Caspardis, but not so close that we end up in the Barathosian's laps."

"The observation promontory," Lamil said. "During your father's reign—"

"*Birth* father."

"Apologies," Lamil said. "During Kagan's reign, we used a promontory to conceal our access to the surface."

"Between Blackwood and Caspardis," Toridyn said. "About a day's ride west of Caspardis, by adda."

"But what is your purpose?" Lamil asked. "What do you hope to accomplish?"

Nicolas was afraid Lamil would ask him something like that.

Kaitlyn stood after an awkward silence. "I think it's a good idea."

"You do?" Nicolas said. He stood. "I mean, thank you." He leaned in close and whispered. "What the hell's my idea?"

Kaitlin faced Lamil. "If we get there before the Barathosians, we can warn them. Maybe if they know what to expect, they can defend themselves."

Not a bad idea.

"How soon can we leave?" Nicolas asked.

"You should speak with the fishing pod first," Lamil said. "Perhaps they have details a cichlos ear might think unimportant."

Nicolas nodded and Toridyn led the way out of the room.

As they stepped through the iris, Kaitlyn leaned her head against Nicolas's shoulder.

Nicolas put his arm around her waist. "I wish this would all settle down so we could just *talk*. It's been ages."

"Me too," Kaitlyn said. "Then you can tell me about the angel. You know...the one on the Plane of Death who was *almost* as pretty as I am?"

Kaitlyn smirked and stepped ahead of him.

Great. This new power of hers is going to be just great.

CHAPTER NINE

[1]*Zubuxo's Anger*

[2]*And Zubuxo discovered the tears of Shealynd in his prison and was angered.*

[3]*"Why have you done this, sister?" he asked.*

[4]*"Punishment without love is vengeance," she said.*

*- The Mukhtaar Chronicles, attributed to the prophet Habakku
Origines Multiversi, Emergentiae 8:1-4*

This chapter of the Origines is deceptively short. Deceptive in that it hides two key tenets of Mukhtaarian theology: Anger is not a sin, and mercy for one's penitent is to be considered the most important attribute of a Mukhtaarian priest. Though the Mukhtaar Lords have disagreed on many things throughout the ages, on one thing they agree: mistreat a penitent and you will know their wrath.

- Coteon of the Steppes, "Coteonic Commentaries on the Origines Multiversi" (circa 520 RL)

Mujahid glanced around the Great Hall of the Pinnacle. It hadn't changed much in the six months since the barrier came down. Stoneware had given way to more delicate glass, now that the quakes had stopped. And the general atmosphere was more positive. Less fearful.

All thanks to Nicolas.

Mujahid sat in a plush chair in the dining area waiting for Tithian. He looked at the stairs, half expecting to see the man taking the steps three at a time.

The ornate spiral staircase on the north side of the room wound up to the sanctuary and other important chambers. Some rubble remained in the stairwell, but the sconces which once littered the floor were back on the wall where they belonged. The last quake had taken place after the barrier vanished, and it had been a bad one. Another unintended consequence of Kagan's actions. Reports from the northern borders suggested the Three Kingdoms had sunk into the ground. Mujahid hadn't verified the reports. Six months of stable ground had lulled everyone into a sense of security.

Peace, however, was always short-lived in the Three Kingdoms.

Mujahid caught the eye of a nearby servant and waved him over. It would be nice to finally relax a little. Nicolas's problems and the Barathosian Armada—anchored off the coast of Dar Rodon hundreds of miles to the east—could wait an hour or two.

The sight of Tithian emerging from the stairwell lifted his spirits. They'd spent time renewing their friendship over the last few months, catching up on mutual friends, listening to the traveling bards that frequented the Pinnacle, and generally making merry when possible.

"Ale and bread," Mujahid said when the servant arrived.

"We have many ales, my lord," the servant said.

"Shandarian Black," Mujahid said.

The servant returned with an open bottle and a glass and set them on the table. Mujahid inhaled the musty caramel aroma and smiled. Shandarian Black had long been his favorite. It was one of the few amenities at the Pinnacle upon which he placed any value.

Mujahid heard Tithian long before the man arrived. Tithian wore a set of laceless boots with hard soles, similar in fashion to the ones Nicolas was fond of. Their steady *tap tap tap* on the marble floor echoed off the walls and ceiling.

Mujahid looked at the servant and held up two fingers.

"Right away, my lord," he said.

"Religarian?" Tithian asked as he sat down.

Mujahid rotated the bottle until the label was facing Tithian.

Tithian grimaced. "A little too stout for my liking."

"I can tell him to keep the second glass if you like."

Tithian smiled, grabbed the bottle and Mujahid's glass, poured a drink, then slid the glass across the table to Mujahid.

"Drink deeply, old friend," Tithian said, "for tomorrow...tomorrow...how does that go again?"

"For tomorrow we may not have anything to drink."

Tithian chuckled. "I think the original dripped with more poetry than that. Something about warriors and death, or some such."

"The only drip I'm interested in today, is this ale dripping into my glass," Mujahid said.

"Careful. You're beginning to sound like Lord Nuuan."

"There isn't enough ale in the kitchens to accomplish *that*."

"There's enough to make you a decent Council magus," Tithian said with a laugh. After a moment of silence, his face grew more serious. "You really *should* get more involved in politics, you know. A man of your stature and wisdom could—"

"Prime Warlock!" The shout came from a Council magus running into the Great Hall from the eastern hallway.

Mujahid wasn't familiar with the woman, but her stiff accent gave her away as a Tildeman. She shoved a servant out of her way as she approached.

"Forgive me, Lord Mukhtaar," she said. "I didn't recognize you from behind."

"I get that a lot."

"Why the haste, Magus Kelley?" Tithian asked.

She glanced at Mujahid.

"Speak," Tithian said.

"I tried to find the archmage," Magus Kelley said. "But his guard informed me he's away from the Pinnacle again."

"You did well to seek me out."

"An invading force has taken King's Bay and is sweeping north."

Mujahid nearly choked on his ale. "Barathosians?"

"They were neither Shandarian nor Religarian, Lord Mukhtaar. That is all I can say with certainty."

Mujahid glanced at Tithian. "Did the news come by translocation orb?" Tithian would be the only one beside Nicolas who could authorize the use of an orb.

Tithian shook his head.

Mujahid rose from his char. "This news could be a week old! Gods, they could have taken Rotham by now. What of the Religarian scouts off the southern coast?"

"By all accounts," Magus Kelley said, "the scout ships saw nothing. By the time they were alerted, King's Bay was on fire and the invaders were moving inland."

"What of the survivors?" Mujahid asked. "What are *they* reporting?"

Magus Kelley's eyes misted. After several failed attempts, she spoke. "There were no survivors."

It was as if all the heat had fled the room.

"Not possible," Mujahid said.

"If you'll excuse me, I have to meet with the council," Magus Kelley said. "Twenty-thousand of my countrymen are dead this day."

She bowed and left the way she had come.

"I don't care what she thinks, that's not possible," Mujahid said. "There's no way the Barathosians could *slip past* Religarian scout ships. Not a fleet large enough to take King's Bay *and* slaughter twenty-thousand people. The number of archers and swords they'd need to accomplish it...it's just not possible."

"If they control the bay, they control the Orm," Tithian said.

"Twenty-thousand people!"

"The supply routes," Tithian said, rubbing his temples.

Mujahid hadn't considered that. If the Barathosians controlled King's Bay, then the meager Religarian navy would be useless.

"With your permission, Warlock, I'd like to address the Council in the archmage's absence," Mujahid said.

Tithian nodded. He wasn't a stupid man. He'd realize what was necessary now. For the love of Shealynd, Mujahid prayed the Council would realize as well.

The thought of Shealynd together with the tragedy of such great loss of life, brought back a memory. A memory he'd buried in the sands of the Religarian desert on the road to Dar Rodon. There'd been a great tragedy then as well, and the weight of it had threatened to turn him into a monster. Only Shealynd's wisdom had stopped him. Perhaps he should seek the goddess's wisdom as he had on that day.

"I need some time to gather my thoughts," Mujahid said. "I'm going to visit the shrine."

"I'll have the main bell rung when the Council convenes. Be prepared, though. It won't be long. Not with the situation as it is."

Mujahid nodded and walked out into the courtyard, wishing he'd had the presence of mind to take the ale with him.

The shrine was a short walk from the building, on a secluded hilltop overlooking the sea to the north. Large paving stones guided Mujahid over the lush lawn to a twenty feet tall statue, which was nestled within an arched enclosure.

The statue of Shealynd had eroded from millennia of strong northern winds carrying saltwater mist, but the form remained; a shrouded woman with open arms, holding a rose in her left hand.

No sooner did Mujahid see the stone rose than the sweet scent of the real thing reached him. He glanced around for the telltale blossoms with hope. Roses of Shealynd were mystical in nature, blossoming only when the goddess herself was present. The last time the scent had been this powerful was at a sacred wadi in the Religarian desert, on the road to Dar Rodon.

Shealynd, you gave me great hope that day. You changed the course of my life, and in doing so saved thousands of people. Please. Grant me your wisdom. Help me save thousands once again.

The rose scent overpowered the smell of saltwater, though the wind remained. In fact, the wind had picked up considerably, and with it came a soft resonance in the air, as if a woman were humming a tune nearby but out of sight.

A burst of golden light, and with it a wave of heat, struck the bottom of his chin.

A Rose of Shealynd materialized at his feet. But something was wrong.

Mujahid covered his nose to shield himself from a foul odor of decay and human waste. The enormous blossom turned black and flaked away in the wind, taking the heat and light with it. When the last spec of black disappeared, a small ivory figurine stood where the rose had been.

Mujahid picked it up and spun it around, but he didn't need to see the figurine's face to know who it represented.

The figurine depicted Malvol—the god of hate—as a man with a sinister grin and hands clasped behind his back. It was the grin of pleasure in another's misfortune. The few who pledged themselves to Malvol followed a path of animosity, sowing discord wherever they traveled.

There had been a cult of Malvol for as long as Mujahid could remember, but he'd never heard of any *miracles* being associated with the group. The cult and its priests were capable of all the evil mortal man could wreak, but never anything mystical.

So why would Shealynd give him a figure of Malvol?

The workmanship impressed him. Such attention to detail. An object of this quality should be in a museum. He should get Tithian to convince the Council to display it in a prominent location. After all, it came from the goddess Shealynd herself.

The Council. On second thought, maybe he *should* become more active in the Council, as Tithian had suggested earlier. Perhaps he'd become an official Council Magus. Surely a Mukhtaar Lord would be a great representative of...

Of where? Council Magi were elected by local governments to have a voice in religious policies that could affect the administration of secular law. But with Mujahid's connections, it shouldn't be difficult to rig an election in his favor—

What am I saying? Rig an election?

His face grew cold as realization dawned. This figurine wasn't carved from ivory at all. But he had to be certain.

The more I think about it, the more I like the idea. I can convince King Donal to appoint me Ambassador to the Council. That would ensure— No!

He had to drop the figurine, but he couldn't take the chance someone else would stumble across it. If it could alter the character of a Mukhtaar Lord this quickly, another person wouldn't stand a chance.

But my ambitions aren't great enough. Tithian was right all those months ago. There is no better person to serve as Nicolas's Prime Warlock than a Mukhtaar Lord. Nicolas is a fledgling priest and archmage. He needs a strong hand by his side.

In a moment of clarity, Mujahid reached inward, past his symbols of power, past the diaphanous fog that surrounded them—the enigmatic, crackling fog that appeared the day he ascended—and seized the necropotency in his well. When he ignited the symbol of ascension—the symbol of the Mukhtaar Lords that existed at the center of his well of power—his thoughts were his own once more.

But for how long?

The statue of Shealynd stood several yards away, and the pedestal it rested on was blessed by a priest of Shealynd. But could he make it in time?

Each step he took was labored, as if the figurine equaled his weight.

What if this thing takes control while I'm holding the power? I can't allow that to happen!

He opened a channel from his well of power to the skull symbol, and more than eighty years passed in an instant while he relived his penitent's life. When the skeleton appeared, he leashed it with necropotency and sent an order through the necromantic link.

With enhanced strength, the penitent lifted Mujahid and threw him toward the statue of Shealynd.

Mujahid dropped the figurine on the pedestal as he flew past it and released his hold on the necropotency. When the figurine left his grasp, a wave of clarity rushed over him, and he landed on his back, staring up at the statue.

He stood, dusted himself off, and approached the figurine. He had to know for certain.

It reeked of innocence, resting on its side next to the Statue of Shealynd, almost as if a child had left a cherished toy behind as a sacrifice.

He leaned closer, embraced the power, and ignited the symbol of ascension. For what he was about to do, he'd need the help of his new friend.

Mujahid turned inward toward a thin sphere of energy surrounding his symbols of power. The mindless presence of the hellwraith—the being that had nearly taken control of him during his frightening transformation at the battle for the Pinnacle—remained in the recesses of his mind, waiting to serve.

Mujahid opened a channel from his well of power, but this time he didn't make it flow into a symbol. Instead, he channeled it into the sphere, imbuing the hellwraith with energy.

The figurine began to glow in Mujahid's mystical vision. As he poured more of his energy—and the hellwraith—into the figurine, telltale striations appeared. And they pulsed with a fiery orange light in time with the beating of Mujahid's heart.

His worst fear was confirmed.

Hellstone!

The figurine had come from the sixth plane of Hell.

But how?

Certainly the god of hate was not a real entity? Sure, people invoked his name. Mujahid was guilty of that from time to time, though it was usually under blasphemous circumstances. But in all his time serving Kagan as Prime Warlock, no such being ever came forward during the Rite of Manifestation—the day on which the gods manifested in human form in the sanctuary. There had never been so much as a mention of Malvol's name.

Whatever the state of Malvol's existence, Mujahid wouldn't solve the mystery here and now.

He cast the hellwraith's presence forward into the hellstone and a void opened, surrounding the figurine. As the figurine fell into the void—a channel that would lead it straight to the *seventh* plane of Hell— Mujahid stepped back when he sensed the presence of another entity in the void. A malevolent entity. And it was trying to get out.

Every time he tried to force the entity back, horrible images would flood his vision; Nuuan being disemboweled by animate blades, the Pinnacle overrun by hellwraiths he couldn't control. It was like an Awakening gone horribly wrong.

He released the necropotency and the void slammed shut with a thunderous *clap*.

Whatever this was, it wasn't good. Only a Mukhtaar Lord could open the seventh plane of Hell, and Mujahid was acquainted with every twisted intelligence on that plane. There weren't many, to the credit of Zubuxo's power and mercy. But this was something else. This wasn't a soul undergoing the ultimate purge. This was a being of power.

Something far more sinister than the Barathosian invasion was at play here. But *what*?

As he took a step toward the pedestal, the Council bell rang.

Mujahid glanced toward the doorway leading back to the Great Hall and dismissed his penitent.

It was time to remind those bureaucrats why they feared him.

T he Council magi barely noticed as Mujahid passed the double stone doors and strode across the oblong room to the raised black throne at its center. The shrill voices of men arguing rang throughout the stone room. Six months ago, he and Nicolas had personally all but destroyed the Council and deposed the archmage. Yet these newly elected jackals fought sanctimoniously over some petty political argument or another and didn't even show him the respect of a head bow.

Mujahid climbed onto the dais next to the Obsidian throne and faced the Council.

"Quiet," he said.

A couple of Religarian magi glanced up, but plunged right back into shouting at anyone who would listen.

This wouldn't do at all.

When Mujahid stepped onto the platform, he leaned close to Tithian and whispered "grab onto something."

Tithian had no idea what Mujahid was planning, but he had the sense to hold on to the Obsidian Throne.

Mujahid ignited the symbol of ascension and released a shock wave of necropotency into the atmosphere. As the necropotency passed through the hellwraith's consciousness, a demonic wail followed the wave into the crowd.

Well that was new.

The chamber fell silent, but Mujahid maintained his hold on the necropotency and turned in a circle so all could see his face. One by one, the magi raised their right hands to cover their eyes.

"Do I have your undivided attention now?" Mujahid asked.

The room remained silent. The gathered magi stood still, as if the necropotency Mujahid released had pinned them in place.

"Answer me!" Mujahid yelled.

"Yes, Lord Mukhtaar!" The magi responded in unison.

Mujahid released the necropotency, but he allowed a few moments to pass before speaking.

"The light has passed," Mujahid said.

"May it bless us in its passing," the magi responded, then uncovered their eyes.

"Sit," Mujahid said. "And listen."

When the magi had finished taking their seats, Mujahid continued.

"Our way of life, and perhaps our very lives, are in grave danger," Mujahid said. "Kagan was misguided, but the Great Barrier *did* serve one important purpose; it kept the Barathosians out."

"Perhaps the holy archmage was right," Magus Kaseem of Religar said.

"Holy?" Mujahid asked. "And how do you define *holy*, if I may ask?"

"He spoke with the gods, face to face."

"I know devils who have spoken to the gods face to face. Are they holy?"

Magus Kaseem lowered his gaze.

"Would anyone else like to comment on Kagan's holiness while we're on the subject?" Mujahid asked. "No? Good. Because if I hear one more magus refer to Kagan as *holy*, I'll take that person to every city in the Three Kingdoms and have them proclaim Kagan's *sanctity* to those who suffered most at his hand. I suspect it will be a short trip from which I ultimately return *alone*."

Tithian placed a hand on Mujahid's arm.

Perhaps he *was* being too harsh on them. Most of these magi grew up knowing nothing else except Kagan and his infernal barrier. A year ago, many in this room would have been disgusted by Mujahid's open practice of necromancy. And no doubt, some must still subscribe to the heresy Kagan taught them…that necromancy ran counter to Arin's will and should be punished by death.

Mujahid took a deep breath and nodded at Tithian, who withdrew his arm.

"As I was saying," Mujahid said. "Kagan got one thing right. The Barathosians are a threat. He conveniently left out the fact he was the cause of that threat, but it is what it is, and now we have to deal with it."

"And how do you propose *dealing* with a fleet the size of which we've never seen before, Lord Mukhtaar?" a Religarian magus said.

Mujahid recognized her as Magus Yasmine from Dyr Rahal. He'd been acquainted with her grandmother in Dar Saricon.

"I don't suppose you have any Mukhtaar *tricks* up your sleeve to handle a ship the size of a palace?" Magus Yasmine asked.

"What ship are you referring to? If you know something, give it voice."

"The Barathosian flagship was spotted in the Bay of Relig," Magus Yasmine said. "Even if we somehow manage to defeat *thousands* of armed naval vessels, that flagship is larger than the imperial palace itself."

Could such a thing be possible? How could an object the size of a palace float? These sorts of questions often came down to the properties of matter, but Mujahid wasn't a natural philosopher. And he certainly wasn't a shipbuilder.

He waved her question away. "I don't have an answer yet—"

The crowd erupted in derision and shouting. He was losing control.

"But I know this," Mujahid said. "If we engage that fleet in battle, then we've already lost. Worse, that fleet isn't the only threat the Three Kingdoms faces."

Judging by their looks, he had their attention.

"Magus Kelley," Mujahid said, facing the Tildem section. She was sitting in the front row. And by her expression, he gathered she bore the entire burden of the tragic news of King's Bay. But not for long. "May I convey the news you brought to me and Prime Warlock Tithian?"

Magus Kelley nodded.

"Magi," Mujahid said, sweeping his gaze around the room. "Credible reports indicate a terrible tragedy has occurred in Tildem. The Barathosians have destroyed King's Bay, slaughtered every soul who lived within its walls, and now move north toward Rotham. For all we know, Rotham has already fallen."

Mujahid's last words echoed off the chamber walls and faded into silence. No one moved or spoke.

A sob from the Tildem section caught Mujahid's attention. The strong facade that had kept Magus Kelley's emotion in check had fallen. Magi nearby comforted her as best they could, but Mujahid knew better than to think the inconsolable could be consoled.

"And so I ask you," Mujahid said. "Will you stand together, nation next to nation, and repel this threat from Tildem's lands?"

The Tildem magi were politicians, but they did little to conceal the hope on their faces.

"They killed tens of thousands of people," a Shandarian magus said.

"How do you repel a force that large?" Magus Kaseem asked.

"Lord Mukhtaar," Magus Yasmine said. "You ask us to commit resources to assist Tildem when we have the bulk of the Barathosian armada sitting within a catapult's reach of the emperor's home. Who will assist us?"

"You have the largest military in the Three Kingdoms!" A Tildem magus shouted.

"A fact you'd do well to remember," Magus Yasmine said.

"Now you threaten *us*?" the Shandarian magus said.

"*Us*, you say?" Magus Yasmine asked. "The Treaty of Three Banks is null and void. There is no *us*. Unless, of course, you have a secret alliance with Tildem of which we are unaware."

This was exactly what Mujahid had feared. He'd allowed himself to hope, but he should have known better.

Magus Kelley stood and faced the Religarian section.

"'From whom the gods give much, much shall be taken,'" Magus Kelley said.

"Try quoting the *Origines* to the Barathosians and see how much they *give*." Magus Yasmine said.

Shouts of "*Blasphemy!*" intermingled with racial slurs hurled at the Religarians.

"Concede Arin's Watch and East Bank to the emperor and we'll consider some military support," Magus Yasmine said.

Magus Kelley sank back into her chair.

"Maybe we'll consider taking Dyr Agul," a Shandarian magus said.

"You can try," Magus Yasmine said. "And we'll hold Agera within a fortnight. Caspardis within a month."

Mujahid couldn't believe what he was hearing. Not in his worst cynical imaginings did he expect this.

"Your doom approaches, yet none of you see it," Mujahid said.

"You have no power over the emperor, Lord Mukhtaar," Magus Yasmine said. "You'll not be able to force his hand."

"The emperor," Mujahid said. "A paper king in a field of fire."

A Shandarian magus cheered, and Mujahid rounded on him.

"*You're* backed against an ocean with an enemy approaching from two directions, and you cheer the defeat of your front line?" Mujahid asked. "Will Shandar defeat an enemy the combined forces of Tildem *and* Religar could not?"

"There are political realities you're refusing to consider," the Shandarian magus said.

It was more than Mujahid could take. If they refused to see their current reality, perhaps they'd respond to their *future* reality.

He called to the shadows scattered around the room, and they rushed toward him and cloaked him. With an expulsion of force that rocked

Tithian backward, Mujahid's body shifted and contorted, until he stood twice his previous height. His spectral form hovered over the Obsidian Throne. Liquid flame dripped down his back from his crown of fire, but the heat comforted rather than wounded, welling up from within like waves in an ocean of lava.

A silence came over the Council, and several Council magi bolted for the chamber doors. But Tithian's seal was too strong for any but Mujahid to break.

Mujahid extended a spectral hand toward the center of the chamber, and a black vortex, blacker than the obsidian throne itself, opened like a tear in the atmosphere with the sound of ripping metal.

A rush of heat erupted from the black portal, carrying with it the agonizing screams of the damned.

Some of the magi covered their faces and backed away, but others didn't move at all. The latter were too busy retching from the noxious odors.

"Destruction comes to the Three Kingdoms, and you tell me of *political realities*?" Mujahid shouted, his voice a choir of ten men combined. "*There* is your *political reality*! Look at it. Hear it. Smell it. For *many* in this room will see it again, and *soon*. The Barathosians show no mercy. And when you come into my realm, you will see me standing there pointing a spectral finger back to this moment in time. The moment when ants divided territory in front of an oncoming plow."

Mujahid willed himself forward, hovering over the steps of the dais toward the portal. By traveling to the sixth plane of hell first, he wouldn't need a translocation orb to reach Tildem.

The Three Kingdoms would fall. That much was clear. The only questions remaining were who could be saved and how quickly.

One thing was certain; he wouldn't leave Donal to fend for himself in Tildem. Mujahid didn't know what, if anything, could be done to turn the tide in Donal's favor, but he had to do *something*.

"I go to Rotham," Mujahid said as he reached the portal. "The rest of you, I'll see in *hell*."

Mujahid dove into the vortex, hoping he wasn't too late.

CHAPTER TEN

¹*The Cleansing of the Heavens*

²*And the gods gathered around The Power with Exaltation, Love, and Final Things, and cast him into the other place.* ³*The Power lashed out at them, and split the Tree of Life in twain.* ⁴*Arin planted the half without wickedness and chaos in the heavens, where it grew to wondrous heights and formed the Plane of Peace.*

⁵*Zubuxo took the other half, the wicked half, and cast it down from the heavens, where it grew barren and thirsty and formed the Plane of Humankind.*

- The Mukhtaar Chronicles, attributed to the prophet Habakku
Origines Multiversi, Emergentiae 9:1-5

There are two problematic translations with this passage that I will point out for the sake of consistency. The first is the translation of Jah'ham as "the other place", when it is translated as "hellplace" or "the hell place" in other passages. The second is the recurrence of tabad'ul translated as "planted". There is no clear explanation for the former, but I find the latter acceptable. After all, whether Arin's half of the Tree of Life was "planted" or "transferred" seems of little import.

- *Coteon of the Steppes, "Coteonic Commentaries on the Origines Multiversi" (circa 520 RL)*

Aelron lifted the tarp and stole a peek out the back of the wagon. The rain had slowed to a mist, obscuring Blackwood in the distance until it was no longer visible. If he could remain undetected until the wagon reached its destination, he'd be able to slip out the back and off the side of the road.

Easier said than done with all this junk laying around. He stretched his leg a fraction of an inch an hour earlier and managed to knock two cooking pans together and topple a block of knives. If it weren't for the heavy rain, the noise would have alerted whoever was in the closed carriage.

Aelron didn't know who was in that carriage, but the muffled snippets of conversation gave him the impression they were Shandarian soldiers. They spoke about a garrison in Caspardis and rations from Shandar. Civilians didn't utter the words *garrison* and *rations* in close proximity to one another.

Laughter came from the carriage, and Aelron strained to hear the voices more clearly.

A high-pitched tenor that sounds like a bird chattering. A cackle and snort. A bellow from a barrel-chested man. And an older voice talking over the others.

Five men, including the wagon driver. But something bothered Aelron. An army wouldn't transport four soldiers like this. Enlisted men or conscripts would bloody well *march* their way to their destination. They wouldn't travel by covered wagon.

Officers. Has to be. Four Shandarian army officers, one of them probably a senior officer. Going to Caspardis. But why?

"Ambush!" the wagon driver yelled.

The wagon lurched to a halt as shouts rose from all around. Aelron tried to see what caused the commotion, but whatever was happening must be confined to the front and sides, because nothing but muddy road and barren land lay behind him.

The Shandarians must have been doing a good job of defending themselves, because the voice of a man with a strange accent—definitely not Shandarian—started shouting something about a time limit, as if something bad would happen if they didn't defeat the Shandarians more quickly.

"How did you miss them?" the older Shandarian officer asked. His question must have been directed at the wagon driver. "There's no place they could have been hiding!"

Between the lack of a response and the muddy splash that followed, the wagon driver would have to answer that question from the afterlife.

The wagon rocked, sending a stew pot rolling into Aelron's head. He brushed the pain away and looked out through the tarp.

The four Shandarian officers were surrounded by twelve men in strange outfits; tight-fitting white trousers, white shirts with black vests — vests too small across the chest to button — and large wide-brimmed hats, each with a foot-long black feather protruding from the side.

One of the foreign men stepped forward.

"General Bradford, his executive officer, and close advisers," the foreign man said. "Now, which one of you is the General?"

"There's no time for this, Basilio," another foreigner said.

"Who shall I kill first?" Basilio asked.

"Leave them alone," the older Shandarian man said. "It's me you want."

"That's where you're wrong, General," Basilio said. "We want you all."

Basilio nodded and four deafening *booms* in rapid succession made Aelron duck behind the wagon's rear gate. Acrid smoke blew toward him, and his eyes watered.

Four foreign soldiers, standing behind the dead Shandarians, placed smoking metallic tubes into their vest pockets.

"Time?" Basilio asked.

"I lost the count, but soon," a foreign soldier said as he approached the wagon where Aelron was hiding.

Aelron weighed his options.

He could slip out of the wagon and run south, but the land was barren and there weren't many places to hide.

He could slip out of the wagon and attack. But what if they used those metal tubes on him? He wasn't sure what they were, but the Shandarians were dead all the same.

He could wait to be discovered. It should be obvious he's not a Shandarian soldier. Maybe he could convince them he was a stowaway. Maybe that would buy him time to escape.

No. They'd killed a senior military official in the middle of the day on a road between two cities. They weren't going to give a festering shite about the life of some wayward drifter.

"At least the job's done," Basilio said. "Be quick about it. I'd like to know what they were hauling."

A soldier tossed the tarp to the side, giving Aelron no place to hide. As the tarp fell to the ground, their eyes met, and the soldier's face paled.

"Captain!" he yelled. "There's a—"

The soldiers vanished. One moment twelve soldiers surrounded Aelron and the next they were gone.

Aelron climbed out of the wagon.

What in Malvol's festering name did I just witness?

He approached the four dead Shandarian soldiers. Each of them had large wounds in the back of their heads. Blood and brains oozed onto the ground, creating a ghoulish slime in the mud. If those metal tubes could cause this much damage, he didn't care to ever find himself on the receiving end.

He bent down and started rummaging through General Bradford's coat. Did he have one of those mystery tubes as well?

The drumming of adda hooves drew his attention west, toward Blackwood.

Three riders approached. Shandarian soldiers from the Blackwood garrison, if Aelron had to guess.

He shook his head.

Off of the spit and into the pit.

Once again he was trapped. They'd see him if he ran, and they'd see him if he stayed.

Which should he do?

His hand moved to his pocket where he kept the coin, but he stopped himself, testing his boundaries. It was getting harder to resist of late, as if the coin had a will of its own. He moved his hand away from the pocket, telling himself it was all in his head, but the farther his hand moved from the coin, the more certain he became it wouldn't end well if he didn't follow through.

His neck tensed up. The coin would soon be the only thing on his mind.

He sniffed and pulled the coin from his pocket.

If it comes up adda, I run. Adda-ki, I stay.

Flip.

Adda-ki. Of course.

The dagger in his cloak bounced against his side as he straightened.

Maybe I'll get out of this without killing someone with it.

His shoulders tensed, and he swore.

Why did I have to ask myself that?

He tried to convince himself it didn't count because it hadn't been phrased as a question. But he knew better. It was no use. The urgency and anxiety were proof the question had been asked, and it needed an answer.

Adda, I use daggers. Adda-ki, no daggers.

Flip.

Adda-ki.

Festering hells!

Some said he was crazy. But they didn't understand how *real* a force *chance* was. Aelron didn't dare trifle with it. He'd done that years ago and it came back to bite him. Literally. He was lucky he could still walk. The coin had told him not to approach the *rockhound*, but he just *had* to get a better look. The miners called him an idiot, and the rockhound had proved them right. Six long months of recovery had convinced him to never disobey the coin again.

That and the constant anxiety; the incessant nagging at the back of his head that told him something horrible would happen if he didn't heed the coin's call.

The soldiers dismounted and circled Aelron, who was leaning against the back of the wagon. One of the soldiers, an officer, knelt in front of the corpses several paces away from the wagon.

"What happened here?" the soldier asked.

Aelron cursed the coin toss, as he surreptitiously rummaged through the wagon behind his back.

"I said *what* happened?" the soldier said louder.

Aelron looked at the kneeling man, pointed at himself, and mouthed the word "Me?"

"No, I'm talking to the adda!"

"The driver's as dead as the General," one of the soldiers said.

"I was..." Aelron nearly told the officer the truth; that he'd been hiding in the covered trailer when fighting broke out. Only one problem;

stowing away on a military vessel was punishable by flogging and one year in a Shandarian prison. A year in which the Rangers could find him and execute him for killing Letcher. The Shandarian Justice Protocols weren't known for being merciful or forgiving. But then, neither was the Shandarian Army.

"You were *what*?"

They weren't going to leave him with many options. He was standing over a pile of corpses, and even the truth wasn't in his favor.

"Secure this man," the officer said.

Best case, he'd be publicly tortured and sent to prison. Worst case…he didn't want to think about worst case.

Two soldiers reached for Aelron's arms.

Aelron leaped onto the flat wagon, narrowly avoiding their grasp. He picked up the iron stew pot at his feet and grabbed a ladle. As the two soldiers closed, he jumped off the wagon, over the nearest soldier, and planted the stew pot on the soldier's head. His momentum pulled the man down into the bloody mud.

Aelron kicked him in the ribs, spun, then struck the other soldier in the jaw with the ladle, sending a tooth flying in the process.

As the soldier held his mouth and yelled, Aelron pivoted toward the one on the ground and struck the iron pot several times with the ladle. The ringing sound had the fallen soldier kicking his feet to get away.

Aelron pulled the stew pot off the man's head and swung it toward the other, striking him in the jaw and knocking several other teeth lose. When the soldier grabbed his face for the second time, Aelron swung the ladle upward, hitting the man between the legs.

The first soldier had recovered and was rising to his feet.

Aelron flipped backward over the rising man, placing the pot back on his head and driving him into the mud. With the soldier on the ground, Aelron removed the pot, lifted it over his head, and drove it straight down into the soldier's face, spraying blood outward onto Aelron's legs.

The soldier twitched a few times then went still.

Doesn't count. I didn't use a blade.

The officer, who was kneeling next to the dead general, stood and drew his sword.

The second soldier, having recovered from the blow to the groin, was back on his feet and charging at Aelron, sword also drawn.

Aelron yelled at the top of his lungs and ran straight for the second soldier, wielding his ladle and stew pot like a sword and shield.

The man hesitated for the briefest moment, then raised his sword and swung toward Aelron's chest.

Aelron dove, rolled under the swinging sword, flipped the ladle around to the cupped end, then drove the handle up into the man's chest. As Aelron came to his feet, the soldier fell lifeless to the muddy road.

Still doesn't count.

Aelron flipped the ladle back around to the bloody handle. He walked toward the officer, who stood gaping.

"Who in Arin's name are you?" the officer asked.

Aelron raised the pot and ladle. "The cook."

The officer raised his sword and charged.

Aelron flung the heavy ladle, striking the officer on the forehead. The officer fell.

When Aelron reached him, the officer was rubbing his head.

Aelron kneeled, placing his knee in the back of the officer's neck. Would this one make the right decision if given the chance?

"If I let you go, you're going to tell the whole garrison about me, aren't you?" Aelron asked.

The officer tried to move his head, but he was pinned.

"I swear," the officer said. "I'll tell no one. Please, just let me go."

Aelron considered it for a moment. If he sent the officer away without a mount, he'd be long gone before the Blackwood garrison was a problem again. And less blood on his hands would be a welcome change of events.

It's your lucky day.

"Please," the officer said. "Can't you just let me go?"

Anxiety. Paranoia.

Aelron's pulse raced, and a bead of sweat formed on his brow.

Oh no. No. You shouldn't have.

This couldn't count! The man didn't know what he was getting himself into when he asked the question!

Fear. Urgency.

The rules were clear. The question had only two possible answers. That meant the coin.

No. I can't. I won't! I don't need you. Rules? There are no rules. This is all in my head!

He eased his weight off the officer's neck, and for a moment the compulsion abated. But the familiar dread soon embraced him.

The coin always remembered. The coin always punished. Always.

Aelron's arms shook and tensed. His breathing grew ragged.

Malvol's festering cock!

Aelron pulled the coin from his pocket. His breath came under control almost immediately.

"Let's play a little game," Aelron said. "Do you like games?"

The officer whimpered and closed his eyes.

"I asked you a question," Aelron said. "I was polite. Wasn't I polite?"

Aelron pressed harder on the man's neck.

"Yes!" the man said. "You were polite!"

"Which animal do you prefer, the adda or the adda-ki?"

"What are you talking about?"

"Pick one."

"I don't under—"

"Pick one!"

"Adda-ki!"

Good choice, given how things have been going today.

Flip.

Adda.

Aelron set the stew pot down and returned the coin to its pocket.

The dread left him.

Euphoria. It wrapped around Aelron like a cozy blanket in a chilly room.

Aelron took a glorious deep breath and exhaled, allowing the relaxation to make everything in the world right again. The coin would leave him alone a while longer. He'd satisfied the multiverse for now.

"Did I pick the right one?" the officer asked.

Aelron shifted his weight, gripped the officer's head in both hands, then snapped his neck.

"No," Aelron said. "You didn't."

Aelron stood and walked back to the wagon. Maybe there was something useful in the junk.

Or maybe he'd take the festering pot and ladle and become a cook after all.

CHAPTER ELEVEN

The first thirteen priests chosen by the god Zubuxo (listed in Ordinationem 1 as "Habakku, Davith, Natan, Nehem, Zerubula, Mose, Jeremi, Ezeki, Zephani, Catiatum, Ardirian, Nuuan, and Mujahid"), are said to have come from an eclectic blend of primitive beliefs and religions. Though it may be difficult to accept within the context of modern orthodoxy, when one steps back from current paradigmatic theology, one sees a simple truth; the gods had not yet revealed themselves to the Creator's creation. One should exercise humility and charity, therefore, when one reads that Habakku referred to Zubuxo as an illegitimate son, and Ezeki once accused Ardirian of buggery with an adda.
- Coteon of the Steppes, "Coteonic Commentaries on the Origines Multiversi" (circa 520 RL)

The smell of burning wood and charred bodies permeated the cave where Mujahid materialized.

I'm too late.

Shouting and screaming reverberated off the small cave's walls.

Mujahid ran to the cave entrance, where he peered around a large boulder toward the city, several hundred yards away.

Rotham-on-Orm, the capital city of the Kingdom of Tildem, was ablaze and covered by a noxious black cloud, lit from within by orange tongues of fire dozens of feet in the air.

The city wall, repaired after the Battle of Rotham, had collapsed into a pile of rubble on the north side of the city. But something was odd about the lay of the bricks. They poked outward as if the wall had been demolished from the *inside*.

The landscape was a vision of chaos. People joined together in small groups and ran north, while others shouted for friends and loved ones. Others still ran screaming from the city. Two injured men, covered in blood from head to waist, ran for the wall. But they weren't fast enough. A blur of motion approached from behind, and when it reached the injured men, their bodies exploded in a fog of red mist.

Mujahid had no idea what could have caused it. He had sensed no power or other arcane force at work. He considered using the mindless hellwraith within to open another portal. That would allow him to get closer without the risk of his approach being seen. But he thought better of it. Every time he used the hellwraith, it weakened to the point of being useless. It could sometimes take days to gather its strength.

A wagon emerged from the city through what was left of the northern gate, its driver whipping two adda who were already in a frenzy. As the wagon passed through the gate, a plume of smoke and flame shot up from the wagon's rear, which exploded in shards of wood.

A loud *boom* left Mujahid feeling as if someone had punched him in the chest. People who had slowed their escape picked up pace and started running.

The wagon driver leaped down from what was left of the front of the wagon and ran north, leaving the adda hitched to the burning wreck.

Mujahid ran, intent on freeing the terrified animals before the fire incinerated them, but someone got there first. The man's face was hidden behind long, unkempt hair and an equally long beard. But there was no mistaking his regal bearing, or the haste with which nearby soldiers obeyed his commands.

Donal Tanmor, the King of Tildem, along with two of his soldiers, had the adda unhitched by the time Mujahid arrived. When Donal saw Mujahid, he looked around in confusion for a moment. But then he smiled.

A fake smile. Mujahid had spent enough time around powerful men to recognize one.

Something is wrong here.

"I'm afraid there's no time for pleasantries, Lord Mukhtaar," Donal said. "We'd do well to make haste away from here. I've ordered General Garon to establish a rally point on that ridge."

Mujahid glanced in the direction Donal was pointing. People and soldiers gathered around a small tent on a rise above the city.

"Then we'll talk as we walk," Mujahid said. "What of the coven?"

Mujahid had instructed Donal to rebuild the necromantic coven in Rotham after the battle with Kagan's forces several months earlier. Though the king was sovereign in Tildem, Mujahid and Nuuan were absolute rulers of Clan Mukhtaar. And Donal was a necromancer under their charge.

"Five priests came to me after the barrier came down, but no more," Donal said. "They've joined their brethren in the city."

"You didn't take them with you?"

That fake smile again.

"Ten priests in all of Tildem and you risk them like this?" Mujahid asked. "Was I mistaken when I placed you in charge of the coven?"

"With respect, Lord Mujahid, there are greater concerns."

"We'll have to agree to disagree."

This wasn't like Donal, but Mujahid couldn't blame the man for taking risks. His country was in a shambles. First Kagan, and now this.

Still. Something was *off* about the man. Mujahid was certain of it.

"The stories they're telling at the Pinnacle about this invasion sound like the feverish dreams of a mad man," Mujahid said. "I hardly know what to ask first."

"I'll make it easy for you," Donal said. "James's Landing is no more."

"I knew of King's Bay, but not James's Landing. This is worse than I feared."

"No," Donal said. "It's far *worse* than your worst fears, Lord Mukhtaar. James's Landing was destroyed without a single soldier setting foot upon the shore, by ships that belched fire."

"Surely you don't believe—"

"I don't. I'm not a superstitious man. But whatever weapon they're using…how do you defend a city against something you cannot see or touch?"

"How did they slip past the Religarian scout ships? They would have had to navigate the southern coast of Religar to strike at Tildem."

"I don't know," Donal said. "But I can tell you what I saw with my own eyes here in Rotham. This foe, whoever they are, simply *appeared* outside the southern wall without warning. One moment the field outside the southern gate was empty of all but merchant traffic. The next, an army several hundred strong destroyed the wall and marched into the city. Had I not watched it happen, I wouldn't have believed the reports."

Mujahid pondered it all as they climbed the hill to the rally point.

While it wasn't impossible to teleport people from one place to another—he'd traveled here himself by way of a portal—there was no way a fleet of ships could have been transported in the same manner. Not even by translocation orb, for that matter. Objects of power were rare, and they took great sacrifice to create in the first place. Kagan had transported siege weapons for the Battle of Rotham, but that was using a complex pattern of *life magic* that only Kagan understood. It wasn't until long after the battle Mujahid learned the sacrifice required by life magic was the lives of unborn children.

The Barathosians were masters of life magic, though.

No. This had to be something different. Something new. Something they hadn't used—or didn't possess—when last they visited the Three Kingdoms. Last time, it was like any other battle. They outnumbered the armies of the Three Kingdoms, but their weapons were no better.

Donal glanced down at his trousers and shoved his hand back into his pocket. There was a struggle on his face, as if he were trying to control a mighty penitent. When the struggle ended, his face grew calm.

A deafening *boom* rocked the north wall of Rotham. The northeast tower collapsed, bringing several archers down with it. When the dust settled, Mujahid saw a curious sight.

A dozen long metallic cylinders, with openings the diameter of a man's head, rested on top of flat wagons. An animal twice the size of an adda pushed each of the wagons from behind. The creature had four long, curved horns extending outward and forward from the sides of its head. A device, or set of devices, connected the creature's horns to a frame on back of the flat wagon.

The cylinder on the wagon closest to the fallen tower had smoke billowing out of it. Behind it stood a horned creature, but unlike the others, this one's horns extended back *away* from its head. As it approached the rear of the wagon, however, the massive, pointed horns turned forward and slid into the strange frame.

A strong surge of necropotency came from within the city. People must be dying at a disturbing rate.

An undead soldier, carrying a blood-drenched sword, ran out from behind the wall and attacked a Barathosian in a wide-brimmed hat. As the fight dragged on, a woman in midnight-blue robes stepped out from behind some debris.

Mujahid ignited the symbol of ascension, flashing his eyes to catch the necromancer's attention. She nodded and ran toward them.

"How many of you are left?" Mujahid asked.

The necromancer lowered her hood, revealing long, straight blond hair.

"All of us, Lord Mukhtaar," she said.

"Your name?"

"Jaelin, my lord."

"Well, Magus Jaelin, it's time we put a stop to this. Given the look of your penitent, it's obvious you have battle experience."

"Aye."

"Then you're in command of your brethren until I say otherwise."

"I already command them, my lord. I'm the most powerful here, second only to you, of course." Jaelin faced Donal. "I mean no offense, Majesty."

"No offense was given or taken," Donal said.

"We'll start by retaking the northern gate," Mujahid said. "We can use the gate's tower as a fortified base from which to push farther into the city."

"And the Barathosian weapons?" Donal asked.

"Magus Jaelin," Mujahid said. "Order your brethren north toward the wall. Have them attack any Barathosian weapon installation they come across. Capture the weapon if possible, but don't risk your lives to do so."

Jaelin bowed at the waist and turned.

Mujahid thought better of it. "Wait. You'll be seen."

Jaelin faced him once more.

"Dismiss your penitent," Mujahid said.

Her skeletal warrior dropped to the ground in a pile of bones. She must have summoned him from a grave. They'd have to return his remains to their resting place when this was over.

Mujahid ignited the symbol of ascension and threaded necropotency into the symbol of shadow—a spherical void hanging in the midst of his other symbols of power. The symbol was often used by priests to conceal particularly gruesome deaths from the eyes of bystanders. But enhanced by the symbol of ascension, the symbol could conceal the living.

Mujahid pushed the symbol forward, stretching it until it wrapped around Jaelin.

Pinpoints of blackness raced toward her from the surrounding shadows. Some shot out from under leaning rocks, while others emerged from darkened doorways and overgrown brush. The shadows themselves would cloak Jaelin.

When they converged on her, Donal gasped. "Where is she?"

Mujahid looked at Jaelin and smiled. He couldn't see her face or even her outline, but she stood before him as an amorphous black fog visible only to him. Not even another necromancer would be able to detect her.

"She stands before us still, Majesty," Mujahid said. "Jaelin, it's important you make haste. Touch nothing except the ground you walk on and your own body. Speak to no one. Cast no magic. Do any of those things and the illusion will shatter. Now, find your brethren."

Jaelin ran back into the city.

"You'll have to teach me that trick," Donal said.

"Survive a few dozen more Halls of Power and I'll have no choice."

Mujahid channeled necropotency into the skull symbol and cast it into a corpse wearing a wide-brimmed hat.

The images from the *namocea*—the process that forced a necromancer to relive the life of their penitent in the span of a moment—took hold of Mujahid and he rode the penitent's time line for more than thirty years.

A moment later, when the namocea ended and Mujahid reawakened to the situation at Rotham, he ordered the penitent forward, into the city.

The horned creatures had disappeared along with the wagons they pushed, leaving nothing except impressions in the dirt.

Curious. They had been standing there a moment ago.

The necromantic link vanished. The undead soldier must have been discovered and killed as he entered the city.

A shame. Judging from the namocea, his penitent had been a good man.

The namocea.

Mujahid dug back into his memories of the man's life for any information that could help.

The soldier—Ibashi—had grown up in a place overgrown with large, bending trees, similar to the palm trees of southern Religar. But there was too much vegetation. A memory of humid heat warmed him and made him want to open his robes to cool himself.

Flashes of a temple hidden in a jungle behind the gaping maw of a beast. Men razing his village and taking him from his family. Rigorous training as a soldier. An instantaneous journey across an endless sea. Two men in gray robes. One of those men dead because of the journey…voluntarily.

Fear. Uncertainty. Disbelief.

This wasn't enough. Mujahid needed information. And so he'd try the unthinkable.

Can I summon him again?

Nicolas had told him he'd succeeded in summoning both the argram and the cichlos by focusing on need.

Well, Mujahid needed Ibashi. But he'd never heard of a priest summoning a specific person without that person's corpse to receive the power. And judging by how faint the necromantic link had been when Ibashi died, he was too deep within the city to find.

Mujahid embraced the necropotency and allowed it to flow into the skull symbol. He focused on Ibashi; his life, his home, his fears, his aspirations. When he'd succeeded in blocking out everything except the need for Ibashi, he cast the symbol forward and waited for the namocea to take him.

Memories of a journey over land and a fierce battle ran through his mind. He focused on the battle, and when he saw the enemy, he sighed in disappointment. He had failed. He wasn't Ibashi. He was a woman. Three argram, tarsal swords exposed and slicing through humans as they leapt from wagon to wagon, converged on her and killed her. Memories of a life lived eons ago, before recorded time.

When the images stopped and the binding was secure, he examined the skeleton of a frail old woman that stood before him. She had clawed her way up through layers of dirt, leaving a sizable hole behind her.

No, it wasn't Ibashi, but Mujahid smiled anyway. The woman was so close to purification that he was certain he could release her on the spot.

But it was more than that.

A small part of Mujahid was happy to discover Nicolas could do something he couldn't.

With enough preparation, and a little wisdom, that boy could ascend.

He expelled the thought from his mind as being too absurd to consider. Ascension required decades of experience as a necromancer. An intuitive knowledge of necropotency few priests possessed.

No, it was time to concentrate on the here and now.

"I release you from your penance, sister," Mujahid said.

The skeletal woman transformed into pure light and disappeared.

"How do you stop an army when a single one of their soldiers can destroy a city wall with the strike of a flint?" Donal asked.

Mujahid had no idea. Now, more than ever, he wished Nuuan was here to help him sort through this mess.

Where in the seventh hell are you, Nuuan?

"Do you have a penitent?" Mujahid asked.

Donal shook his head. "I'll summon one."

"Save your strength. Raise one of those corpses by the wall instead. It will consume less power and take less of a toll on you. Let's take back that gate."

Donal nodded and within moments had raised a dead Tildem soldier.

Mujahid took his own advice and did the same.

"My lord!" Jaelin yelled. She was running toward him from the gate, about a hundred yards away. "It's no use! The penitents can't touch them!"

"What?" Mujahid ran forward to meet her. "What do you mean?"

She stopped in front of him and caught her breath.

"I made it deep into the city before breaking your illusion. But it was no use. Every time we attack the Barathosians, they either disappear or the penitent refuses to touch them."

"That's not possible," Mujahid said. "Your penitent cannot *refuse!*"

He glanced toward the northern gate, where three Barathosian soldiers emerged, and ordered his penitent to attack.

It refused.

"Majesty," Mujahid said. "Send your penitent!"

"I've tried! It won't obey!"

Never in his considerable years had Mujahid heard of such a thing.

"We can't stay here," Mujahid said. "Until I discover why this is happening, we have to assume they can use our power against us."

This was troubling to a degree Mujahid was only now understanding. It brought everything he knew about the relationship between a priest and a penitent into question.

Mujahid glanced around, trying to feel the wind on his face. When he was satisfied it wasn't blowing toward them from the city, he ignited the symbol of ascension and cast a cloud of disease toward the gate.

Power returned to his well as the three Barathosian soldiers choked to death.

"Now that I've seen some of their tactics," Donal said, "I can defend Arin's Watch."

Mujahid gave him an incredulous stare. "Moments ago you were asking how anyone could defend against their weapons, and now you're going to save a city?"

"I must try."

"Arin's Watch will fall, with or without you," Mujahid said. "If you refuse to return to the Pinnacle with me, I urge you to press on to the Shandarian Union. I can be in Shandar in minutes. Within the hour I can alert the Union government. Perhaps they'll...offer assistance."

Mujahid didn't know why he said that. He didn't believe a word of it. And from Donal's expression, neither did he. But what else could they do? Tildem's army wasn't capable of handling this threat. And from what Mujahid had seen of those metal cylinders, he doubted the combined might of the Shandarian Union *and* the Religarian Empire could turn the Barathosians back.

And now *necromancy* had failed.

A nearby explosion knocked Mujahid off his feet. When he realized there was no impending attack, he shook his head.

"If *they* don't kill me, I'll likely trip over an anthill and do the job for them," Mujahid said.

Donal extended his arm. "Take my hand and let's make for Arin's watch."

Mujahid nodded and let the king help him to his feet. He didn't agree with Donal's plan to defend Arin's Watch, but maybe he could convince him otherwise on the road. Or better, maybe he could convince General Garon. Donal was many things, but foolhardy wasn't one of them. He'd listen to a battle-hardened officer.

Shouts reached him from the direction of the gate as the other necromancers arrived.

"Keep your penitents at the ready, all of you," Mujahid said, dusting himself off. "I'll summon another and scout to the north. Protect the king."

The necromancers bowed and fanned out behind the retreating Tildem soldiers.

Mujahid ignited the symbol of ascension and allowed the necropotency to embrace the skull symbol.

How about someone a little more evil *this time? Someone who'll stick around a little longer.*

He cast the symbol forward and waited for the namocea to take him.

Two days passed without Mujahid spotting another Barathosian. A day earlier, Mujahid recommended turning east toward the coast, secretly hoping they would find a Religarian naval patrol in the Sea of Arin to escort them out of Tildem. Donal had agreed with the course change, though Mujahid kept his true purpose hidden. Donal was being hard-headed about saving Tildem.

He couldn't fault the man. Mujahid would pay a dear price to protect the safety of the Mukhtaar Estate and all its secrets.

But Mujahid had ways of protecting the estate that didn't involve a foolhardy attempt to defend a defenseless set of walls.

As they drew closer to the sea, Mujahid found it unnecessary to scout far ahead. He tried to tell himself the Barathosians couldn't navigate the treacherous waters of the Sea of Arin this far north of James's Gate—the narrow straight between Tildem and Religar. But the truth was if the Barathosians *did* appear on the horizon, there was nothing he or anyone else could do about it.

Mujahid stood at the top of tall, white cliffs that ran north and south along the Tildem coast. A hundred feet below, gentle waves lapped against the shore of white sand, bordering the sea in a rim of white froth. Billowing gray clouds formed a thunderhead to the east, and the winds from the desert plains of Religar drove it toward them.

But that thunderhead wasn't the only storm on the horizon.

Hundreds of ships anchored off the cost of Tildem, forming a series of concentric circles around a massive catamaran that had three decks above water. There was something strange about the catamaran's pontoons, though. A row of narrow, rectangular portholes ran fore and aft along each pontoon, encased in a wooden frame. Pontoons were normally a single piece, or several connected at seams, but they never had portholes.

There was no way this fleet could have *slipped past* the Religarian scouts.

The crags north of the fleet were daggers of rock reaching into the sky, and they were impossible to pass without intimate knowledge of the sea and seasons. But the Barathosians were launching smaller, more agile vessels capable of navigating the twisting pathways of water and rock. And those ships were heading north toward Pilgrim's Landing.

That would put the Barathosians within reach of the Pinnacle.

As the small ships entered the craggy, narrow waterways, several turquoise blurs shot out from the crags and over the ships, creating a mist from the beating of their wings, which spanned at least forty feet.

Shrillers. Odd for this time of year.

Several shrillers circled the small ships, craning feathery necks as long as their wings.

The ships began to veer off course. Some crashed into the crags, while others collided with each other.

Something's wrong. Shrillers hunt in pairs or alone. They never swarm.

As the leading ship steered into a rock face, a shriller flew through one of the sails and crashed into the cliff, falling to the water and narrowly missing the boat's upper deck.

What's stirring them up like this?

The main flock flew south, over the concentric rings of ships, straight toward the catamaran. Or rather, straight toward the catamaran's pontoons. Several shrillers flew into the side, crashing into the closed portals and falling into the sea, only to rise and crash again.

"It's worse than I'd imagined," Donal said as he approached Mujahid from behind. "You should back away in case they spot you."

Mujahid stepped away from the cliff, but Donal remained, staring at the enemy fleet.

"Shouldn't you?" Mujahid asked.

"The shrillers won't harm me."

Mujahid raised an eyebrow. Shrillers were many things, but *discerning* wasn't one of them. Donal's expression, however, was smug.

"You're hiding something from me," Mujahid said.

"I'm a king, Lord Mukhtaar. I hide *many* things. But you should see this. It defies explanation."

Mujahid approached the cliff.

Several Barathosian sailors had run out onto the deck of the catamaran, stripped to their waists, and knelt at the bow, facing the incoming shrillers.

"Are they insane?" Mujahid said.

A shriller diverted off its trajectory toward the pontoon and swooped up across the bow, grabbing a Barathosian sailor in its hind talons and disappearing behind the crags. The other sailors remained kneeling, as if nothing had happened.

Mujahid knew religious devotion when he saw it. Those sailors were *worshiping*.

Two shrillers diverted from their path, but they didn't attack the bow. Instead, they plunged into the icy water without a splash and disappeared from view. One emerged a moment later with a Ranthean shark caught in its hind talons. The shark was the size of two adda, with fins sharper than a Religarian scimitar.

Other shrillers soon followed, dropping fish of all sizes on the deck of the catamaran before veering off and diving for the pontoon.

"I...I don't have the words," Mujahid said.

Donal laughed as he watched the shrillers.

"Speak up, man," Mujahid said.

Donal walked away from the cliff, but Mujahid wasn't going to let him get away.

"As Clan chief—"

Donal spun. "As *King*, some things are more important than Clan Mukhtaar." He lowered his voice as he walked off. "Some things are even more important than kingdoms and kings."

What was he hiding that riled him so?

A soldier in loose-fitting hide armor stopped and saluted King Donal.

"Majesty, General Garon says we make camp north of here," the soldier said.

"Not good enough!" Donal said. "Bring Garon to me, now! We march until we reach Arin's Watch."

The soldier gaped as if Donal had slapped him.

Mujahid gestured for the soldier to give them some space and stepped closer to Donal.

"I know how badly you want to protect Arin's Watch," Mujahid said. "But you've seen that enemy fleet. Even with the shrillers and the crags, they'll get there before we do. There's no longer a chance to defend Arin's Watch, but—"

"I'll not—"

"But you might just have a chance to take it back if the men are rested and prepared. Let the General do what he thinks is best for his soldiers."

"They're *my* soldiers, and they'll go where I direct them to go."

Mujahid's heart pounded in his ears. This wasn't like Donal.

"You have more than just an army to lead!" Mujahid said. "You have a nation. If you don't trust Garon, then replace him. But don't give a man authority and then undermine it. You're the king. Start behaving like the man I know you are, instead of the child you seem to be."

Donal straightened his back. Mujahid worried he'd overstepped his bounds. But after a moment, Donal relaxed.

"For a man who prides himself on protocol and formality, you certainly know when to dispense with it," Donal said.

"When Tildem is secure, I'll turn myself in."

"Tell the general to prepare his camp as he sees fit."

The soldier saluted and ran back toward the mounted soldiers who had crested the rise overlooking the sea.

It took forty-five minutes to reach the camp site, but it was clear General Garon knew his craft. A granite outcropping, curved like a crescent moon, protected the command tents on three sides. Moreover, the outcropping was at the top of a rise with a commanding view of the surrounding plains. This would make a great site to fortify.

Donal may have agreed to camp for the night, but Mujahid wasn't sure he'd see the logic of staying here indefinitely.

Shouting arose from the command tent area.

"Forgive me, Majesty!" a voice yelled.

"I have this all wrong!" Donal shouted as Mujahid approached.

A cook's table lay on its side, with pots and knives scattered around the rocky ground. The shocked cook was backing away from the king as if Donal were pointing a sword at his throat.

"I shouldn't have listened to you," Donal said. He faced the cook. "I bet you agree with them, don't you? Don't you!"

The cook looked to Mujahid for help. Mujahid dismissed him with a nod.

"Donal," Mujahid said.

"I'm the king!" Donal said.

"Something's troubling you."

Donal's eyes were wide, never settling in one direction for longer than a moment. His hands shook as if he were in the midst of a violent rage. Mujahid had seen this behavior before…in people addicted to Shandarian powder.

Donal thrust his right hand into his trouser pocket and grew calm. To all appearances, he was his old self again.

This was something other than a drug addiction. And if Mujahid was right, the situation was far worse than he'd imagined.

"I've made the wrong decision," Donal said. "You were right to say defending Arin's Watch would be futile and costly."

"I'm glad you see—"

"But you were only half right." Donal faced a nearby soldier. "Bring me General Garon."

The soldier saluted and ran off.

"If you're proposing a military operation," Mujahid said, "I implore you to share it with me. It would be best if—"

"I *absolutely* propose a military solution, Lord Mukhtaar. It's high time I began doing what's *right*, instead of what everyone *wants*."

Donal kept squeezing something in his pocket, clenching his fist and relaxing it.

General Garon stepped past the overturned table and saluted King Donal. Donal returned the salute, but he did so with his off hand, leaving his right hand clasped around the object in his pocket. It was a horrible breach of protocol, but if Garon felt slighted, he did a good job of hiding it.

Garon emanated an aura of command. The two short swords hanging from his waist were combat-ready, not ceremonial. His uniform was tactical; trousers secured around laced boots to keep water out, and a heavy cotton shirt—buttoned from neck to waist—instead of a general's coat with gold medals. His belt was thick, black leather. Several daggers and containers were tied down against it for stealth operations. In short, Garon was a man of war.

"General," Donal said. "We'll camp for the night if we must, but tomorrow we strike camp and turn around."

"Majesty?" Garon said.

"I should never have allowed you or the Mukhtaar Lord to talk me out of taking Rotham back. I intend to do so."

Garon's jaw clenched.

Mujahid couldn't believe what he was hearing. Rotham was lost.

"This is a mistake," Garon said. "With an army twice the size of Tildem's...*maybe* I could take Rotham back. That would be pressing my luck further than a gambling man would."

"You'll have to make do," Donal said.

"This isn't about preference, Majesty," Garon said. "Our cavalry is at one-third strength. Our archers are at one-quarter strength. We don't yet know if Commander Yuli's three centuries made it out of Rotham alive. Our infantry may as well be non-existent, unless you're suggesting I hand out swords and pikes to the refugees."

"Calm your tone, General," Donal said.

Garon stammered for a moment. Mujahid could tell he hadn't been expecting that reaction from the king.

"Forgive me, Majesty," Garon said. "I simply wish to understand. My officers inform me necromancy is no longer a viable weapon here. How are we to defeat an invading army at our current fractional strength that we cannot defeat when at full force?"

"That's enough!" Donal yelled. He squeezed his hidden fist so hard, Mujahid thought it would rip through his trousers. Donal's eyes darkened, the whites turning black as pitch.

Mujahid knew those eyes. Any Lord of Hell would. They were the eyes of the demon-possessed.

Donal released a surge of necropotency that swept around Mujahid, and a skeleton materialized.

Garon stepped back, hands on his swords.

Mujahid had seen enough. He sent a blast of necropotency toward Donal, knocking him backward onto the rocky ground. As the skeleton reached Garon, Mujahid summoned a penitent of his own at the foot of the other. Donal's penitent was no match for one enhanced by the power of a Mukhtaar Lord.

Donal regained his balance and faced Mujahid with the darkness of unfettered evil in his eyes. Again he drove his hand into his pocket and clenched his fist.

Mujahid wrapped Donal in a rope of necropotency, lifting him several feet off the ground.

Donal's coal-black eyes went wide.

"Garon!" Donal yelled. The tenor of his voice had changed, as if several people were speaking in chorus. "Do something! I'm your king, man!"

"The king is not himself at the moment, General," Mujahid said.

Garon drew a sword and stepped toward Mujahid.

"I'm not the enemy here," Mujahid said. "This is a matter of *priesthood* now."

Garon glanced at Donal and his expression changed from aggression to confusion. He sheathed his sword and took several steps back.

Mujahid faced Donal. "You summon a penitent to kill an innocent man?"

"I've watched you do the same and more," Donal said.

"Be silent!"

"I…will…not—"

Mujahid ignited the symbol of ascension and sent it into the hellwraith in his mind. It was a guess, but an educated one.

"I command you to be silent!" Mujahid yelled. The hellwraith leapt from Mujahid's mind and entered Donal.

Donal's words choked off as if a gag had been placed in his mouth.

It was exactly as Mujahid had suspected. Worse. There was evil at play here. *True* evil.

"Who are you?" Mujahid asked.

Movement on Donal's right side caught Mujahid's attention. The clenching hand again.

King or no, Donal was going to turn out his pockets whether he liked it or not. Mujahid grabbed Donal's wrist and yanked his hand out of its pocket.

When Mujahid saw what Donal held, he stepped back as if dodging the sharp snap of a snake.

Donal clutched a small figurine depicting a smiling man with hands clasped behind his back.

Malvol!

Pulsing orange striations coursed through the Hellstone.

There was only one way to deal with this, but Donal had to give up the Hellstone by his own choice.

"Majesty," Mujahid said. "The object you hold is an object of hell that should not exist on this plane. How you came to have it is a mystery for another time. But you *must* drop it willingly."

Donal squirmed and Mujahid retracted the hellwraith to allow him, or whatever creature dwelt within, to speak.

"The Lord of Hell and his little minions," Donal said. "Up your arse with your hellwraith! Or maybe Mordryn's arse, eh? Your brother certainly enjoyed her. And with as many times as she let him, the feeling was mutual! You can't place the blame on *her*, though. You *are* identical twins."

The words stung, but it wasn't Donal who spoke them. Donal knew nothing of Mordryn.

"You can fight this, Donal," Mujahid said. "Drop the idol and the evil inside will have no power over you."

Donal's squirming grew pronounced. A battle was being waged between two forces; Donal's soul and *something else.*

"You have the strength of your father," Mujahid said. "No. You have far more. And your people need you...the *true* you."

Donal's sword levitated out of its scabbard, and the blade's point turned upward and faced Garon. Donal opened his mouth and a dozen demons laughed.

Mujahid couldn't allow this. Garon was too important. And so was Donal.

"By my dominion over the seven stones of Abaddon, I command you to leave him!" Mujahid yelled.

Again that disturbing laugh came from all directions.

"I'll give you one last chance to drop that idol," Mujahid said, never taking his eyes off the sword. "Please, Majesty. Just open your hand and let it fall. I'll do the rest."

Donal laughed and the sword shot toward Garon.

Mujahid cast the hellwraith forward into the idol in Donal's hand, hoping he hadn't just killed a king.

A void opened around the idol.

The flying sword dropped to the ground within a foot of Garon, and the general picked it up.

Donal's eyes returned to normal as he looked down at the void surrounding his hand. The idol began to flake away, the flakes falling backward into the void, and Donal cried out. As the last of the idol flaked into the hellish portal, Donal's hand flaked away with it. His skin sloughed from the muscle and bone, which was dry and cracked like baked clay. When the skin vanished into the void, the bone fragmented and joined it.

Mujahid's gaze was drawn to the void. He could sense it again, that entity staring back at him from a place only a Mukhtaar Lord could go. But this time, an emotion passed through the void.

Amusement.

A dark presence flew from Donal to the void, and a demonic wail rose and trailed off.

When the last flake of idol and hand disappeared, the void collapsed and Mujahid set Donal on the ground clasping his bloody stump.

The mindless hellwraith returned to Mujahid, but it was dormant. Powerless. Just as it was after he'd first transformed during the battle at the Pinnacle. Any long-distance traveling Mujahid did now would have to be done the old fashioned way.

"Lord Mukhtaar," Donal said. His voice was raspy.

"Try not to speak," Mujahid said. "You're badly injured and I need to tend to it."

"When I asked you to take my hand and follow me to Arin's watch, this wasn't what I had in mind."

"Sounds like you'll live."

"Is that your opinion as a necromancer?"

"It's my opinion as a man."

Donal grinned.

"But, as a necromancer, I'd just bring you back anyway."

Donal lost his grin.

Mujahid chuckled. "The gods know you'd finally start making good decisions."

"I'd be forced to obey you."

"That's what I said. Now stop talking and let me do something about this mess of a wound."

It didn't take long for Mujahid to cauterize Donal's wrist with ambient necropotency. That stump wasn't going to be pretty, but Donal's appearance was the least of their concerns right now. An army of Barathosians occupied southern Tildem and pressed north to Arin's Watch, drawing closer with every passing minute.

The more Mujahid thought about that statue of Malvol, the more it troubled him. A similar one had tried to take control of his mind back at the Pinnacle, and this one had succeeded with Donal.

It was demonic possession. And whichever demon had crawled out of the pit and into Donal's body had no fear of the Abaddonian power stones.

The Abaddonian stones were among several divine artifacts binding all in the seventh hell to the will of the Mukhtaar Lords. If the stones failed, it wouldn't be evil the world would have to fear. It would be chaos. Chaos in its purest form. No, the stones couldn't have failed. That couldn't happen.

Ever.

Mujahid needed more information.

"Majesty," Mujahid said. "How long did you have that idol?"

"Two days. Perhaps three."

It was unlikely Mujahid had seen the only two figurines in the Three Kingdoms. Whoever that entity was within the portal, he or she was responsible for sending those infernal things into the world. He didn't want to imagine what would happen to someone who held one longer than three days.

May the gods grant that no one finds another.

Donal tried to sit up, but Mujahid laid him back down.

"None of that, now," Mujahid said. "You've lost too much blood to be a *sitting* king. You'll have to rule from your back for a few days."

"I have to keep the group moving toward Arin's Watch."

"As much as I know you don't want to hear this, Majesty, I'm going to say it anyway. Tildem is lost. The best thing you can do for the Three Kingdoms is move what little force you have north into the Shandarian Union and make a combined stand there."

Donal glared. "My duty is to Tildem."

"There *is* no Tildem. Not anymore."

"As long as I *live* there is Tildem!"

Mujahid looked up as several shadows fell across the ground between him and Donal. Jaelin and her group of necromancers had arrived. Garon knelt at the King's side.

"General," Donal said. "I owe you an apology."

"Nonsense," Garon said. "From what I gather, it wasn't you doing the talking anyway."

"I can't follow you to Arin's Watch," Mujahid said. "It pains me to say this, but I should be where I can make a difference." He faced Jaelin. "I'll not force you and the others to join me. But there's something you should know before you make your decision. When the Barathosians anchor off the coast of Arin's Watch, they'll turn the city into a charnal house."

"Well that settles it, then," Jaelin said.

Mujahid nodded. He figured she'd do the sensible thing.

"We're going to be needed most in Arin's Watch," Jaelin said.

"What?" Mujahid asked. "Did you hear what I just said?"

"I heard clearly, Lord Mujahid," Jaelin said. "Who will purify the dead if not us? You should go, though. You're far more important to the Three Kingdoms than we are."

The realization was like a punch in the chest. Had he strayed so far from his vocation that he placed other concerns above the purification of the dead? Had he spent so long *leading* the clan that he'd forgotten what it meant to be a *member* of the clan?

Vocation or not, what Jaelin said was true. It saddened him, but it was true. He wasn't a simple necromancer anymore.

Mujahid nodded and stood.

"His wound will heal," Mujahid said. "But keep him still for a few days."

"Where will you go, Lord Mukhtaar?" Donal asked.

"The Shandarian Union. I'll find passage to Agera in Three Banks. It's time I found my brother. I'll do my best to send aid. General, can you spare an adda?"

"Aye," Goran said.

Mujahid headed toward the hastily erected stable area, uncertain if he'd ever see King Donal alive again.

For the second day in a row, Zorian Osa sat outside the emperor's audience hall waiting to be called. He wasn't upset. Merely waiting. Waiting for the emperor to come to his senses and hand over the archmage.

It took a lot to upset Zorian. More than an impotent emperor whose only weapon was lack of cooperation.

He didn't get upset when the Imperial Guard dragged Lucian naked from his quarters after the attempted rape of the emperor's daughter. He didn't get upset when an assassin tried to kill him in his bed chamber not long after. He didn't get upset when, despite Zorian's warning, the emperor didn't call on him the next morning.

And he didn't get upset when he had to order the complete annihilation of Dyr Rahal as a result of the emperor's insolence.

It's not that Zorian was a warmongering man. Quite the opposite, which is why he'd resigned his naval commission to begin with. But choices had consequences, and Emperor Relig had chosen poorly.

No, he wasn't upset. It would take more than brutality, attempted murder, and genocide to shake Zorian.

A drum-like tap of shoes against the marble floor came from the intersection near the giant portrait of Emperor Relig.

A page in red and white palace livery approached at a full run and stopped at the guard outside the audience chamber. The page raised a sealed envelope before him, and the guard opened the chamber to allow the running, sweating servant to enter.

Of course Zorian wasn't upset. How could he be? He didn't need to see inside that envelope to know the message it contained. Emperor Relig was about to give him the audience he'd been waiting for. He was about to finally bring his futile resistance to an end and fetch the archmage.

Several minutes passed in silence until the chamber doors opened. Saleem Abdul Bishara, in a different blue robe this time, stepped out and stood before Zorian.

"Zorian Osa," Saleem said. "The emperor will see you now."

Saleem walked back into the chamber.

Zorian followed, and his gaze set upon a cage at the foot of the dais on which the emperor's throne sat. For a moment he thought the emperor intended to arrest him, but as he drew closer to the cage he saw a man inside. Some poor, tortured soul was impaled against a standing frame in the cage. The spikes drove through flesh in his arms and legs. It kept him immobile, but also alive. Blood pooled at his feet from the vicious beating someone had given him. His face was swollen to the point of forcing his eyes shut, and patches of scalp hung from his head. His arms were flayed from shoulder to elbow, the skin and flesh carved away and hanging to the floor. Whoever had tortured him had tried to stop the bleeding with fire, because his wounds were charred as if burned by a torch. The man moaned incessantly, but something in his mouth muffled the sound.

The smell of burned flesh made Zorian want to cover his face, but he couldn't allow the emperor to see that weakness.

As Zorian rounded the cage to stand at the foot of the dais, he took one last glance into the cage. The caged man's genitals had been torn from his body, stuffed into his mouth, and seared in place with flame.

A golden glint reflected off a bracelet on the man's right wrist.

"As you can see," Emperor Relig said, "your compatriot and my daughter had a misunderstanding. I've taken the liberty of clearing things up."

Saleem stopped next to the cage.

"Yes," Zorian said, facing the emperor. "You and I had a misunderstanding of our own, two days ago. I've cleared that up as well."

"You destroyed a city!"

"Dyr Rahal was it?" Zorian made a waving gesture as if the name were inconsequential. "If I understand your language well enough, it was a small city. Not a great loss."

"Thousands of my subjects are dead," Emperor Relig said.

Zorian stepped onto the dais and Emperor Relig brought his hand up to his chest. Guards moved to stop Zorian, but the emperor waved them away.

"Yes," Zorian said. "And consider this, Emperor. We annihilated that city with two ships placed off shore. Two ships. *Two thousand* such ships fill the Bay of Relig as we speak. There is enough combined firepower to erase Dar Rodon as a scribe erases an errant droplet of ink. I'd tell you Dar Rodon would be reduced to rubble, but it will be far worse than that."

Emperor Relig stepped back as Zorian reached the top of the platform.

"Why do you want the archmage so badly?" Emperor Relig asked.

"The murder of Yotto isn't sufficient?"

"That was forty years ago. You think me stupid? You think I'll accept *vengeance* is all you seek?"

"Your honor might last a mere forty years, but I assure you ours is eternal." Zorian took a step closer. "I'll not have this conversation with you again, Emperor. You know what I want. And you know the price of failure."

Emperor Relig swallowed and his gaze darted toward Lucian. "Give me more time and I'll end his life quickly."

Zorian chuckled. "Lucian? Take your time with him. It's *me* for whom you should act with haste."

"He's your countryman," Saleem said.

"Imagine how much consideration I give those who *aren't*."

"Long live the Glorious One," Emperor Relig said.

"Emperor, no," Saleem said.

"Draft the message," Zorian said. "Today. I'll not hold you accountable for the speed at which Kagan arrives. But I *will* hold you accountable for everything *within* your control."

Lucian moaned as Zorian walked past him toward the chamber door. But that didn't upset Zorian either.

CHAPTER TWELVE

If anyone should encounter the Mukhtaar Estate, they should turn in the opposite direction and proceed as far away as possible. For only the Mukhtaar Lords know its secrets, and only the Mukhtaar Lords may pass through its doors unharmed.
- Coteon of the Steppes, "The Mukhtaar Chronicles: Coteonic Commentaries" (circa 680 BCE)

If the people of Erindor knew how little we know of the estate's secrets...
- M

Let's not ruin a good thing, now.
- Nuuan

Mujahid's journey up river from Three Banks was far less stressful now that quakes were a thing of the past. But approaching Agera set him on edge.

Last time, he'd been chased through the streets, come face-to-face with a sworn enemy, and forced to escape during one of the worst quakes he'd ever lived through.

There were more important matters to consider, however. Nuuan had been missing for more than six months, for starters. But there was one person beneath Agera—in the necromantic coven of *Catiatum*—who might be able to shed some light on things.

William. There might not be a prophecy that could shed light on this situation, but William was one of the wisest necromancers Mujahid knew. And right now, Mujahid needed wisdom.

But the Catiatum coven held grudges older than Mujahid's grandfather. What if William had failed at the task Mujahid had given him—to merge his coven with the old Catiatum coven? What if the Catiatum coven had fallen into schism again and sought to depose Mujahid and Nuuan? Mujahid could be walking into a trap.

The dull thud of the gangway striking the pier brought Mujahid out of his thoughts. Deckhands ran this way and that to secure the river boat. One of them trotted up to Mujahid.

"Sir," the deckhand said. "This is for you." He flipped through a handful of small cards and gave one to Mujahid. "For your adda."

Mujahid stared at the card in confusion.

"They won't let you take it into the city. Some new law or something. But you can turn the card in at the trade office for another."

"What's wrong with mine?"

The deckhand shrugged. "Something about foreign livestock being cursed. I don't make the rules."

"That *livestock* was given to me by the King of Tildem himself, boy."

The deckhand shrugged. "You want the card or not?"

Mujahid scowled, took the card and turned it over. There was nothing more than a number and a signature on the other side. What could have happened to make Agera restrict the passage of animals?

"This is an outrage!" a man shouted from behind Mujahid.

A brown-turbaned man with thick muttonchops shoved past Mujahid and threw a stack of cards in the deckhand's face. The man dressed like a Religarian, but his desert robes were dark. Religarians favored white robes to reflect the sun's oppressive heat. And his accent was muddled, as if he were putting it on.

"Do you have any idea how long they've been on this boat?" the man shouted, waving his arms about. "A week! Adda on a boat for a week!"

"The Commerce Office will offer replacements for your—"

"*These* are *my* adda! Do you know what happens to adda when they can't roam freely? I've already paid the caravansary fees!"

Something was odd about the man. He kept slipping out of a Religarian accent into something akin to a western Shandarian drawl.

"What's the problem here?" the ship's captain said. Mujahid hadn't seen him approach.

The Captain's long, angular goatee was gathered with a tie of some sort, and the end bounced as he spoke.

The turbaned man pointed at the deckhand. "This *festering*—"

"You insult my crew one more time and you'll find yourself on the pier without the courtesy of a gangway," the Captain said. "Do I make myself clear?"

The turbaned man nodded.

"Good," the Captain said. "Now what's the problem? And I expect your answer to be so pleasant, the Chancellor's wife herself would want you over for tea."

The turbaned man's face had turned crimson, but he obliged.

"Captain," the turbaned man said. "The length of this trip has pushed my adda to their limits. I have to get them on dry land and tend to them."

"They're not staying on the boat, if that's what you're worried about. They'll be taken to the stockyards and held for two weeks. If you're in a hurry, I suggest you pick up those cards and trade them for a new team."

"But those are *my* adda! *They* are the ones I must take to Caspardis!"

The Captain shrugged. "Then hang on to those cards and come back in two weeks."

"They must be delivered within the week! My customer was insistent on that regard."

"Then you have a *business* problem which is of no concern to me," the Captain said. "I make the rules on *this boat*, not the festering city of Agera."

"Captain, please—"

"Take your cards and make a decision. Either way, I'd better not hear you're causing trouble for my crew."

The Captain strode back toward the wheelhouse.

"Any idea what this is about?" Mujahid asked the turbaned man.

"I wish I knew."

"You chose a poor color for Religarian desert garb."

The man stroked his muttonchops.

"A word of advice," Mujahid said. "Let your men do the talking. The nomad accent is proving too difficult for you."

Mujahid faced his cabin, but a hand on his arm stopped him. When he turned back, the muttonchopped man's expression was inscrutable.

"Not many would speak to me as you do," the man said. His accent had vanished, and the tenor of his voice had changed to a deep baritone. He stared at Mujahid's robe for a moment. "Brave, even for these times."

"*Businessmen* have never worried me much."

"Not that. Your choice of clothing."

"My style of dress is a sign of bravery here?"

"Perhaps everywhere. You expect forty years of hatred to vanish by decree?"

The man had a point. Maybe wearing the midnight blue hadn't been a good decision.

"Vanni Yarwen," the man said, extending his hand.

Mujahid paused for a moment before taking it.

"Samael," Mujahid said. He stumbled over the alias he hadn't used for a while. "I take it those adda of yours are more than meets the eye?"

Vanni shrugged and signaled one of the men traveling with him, who ran over and collected the Commerce Office cards scattered at Vanni's feet.

There was no mistaking the sign language concealed in Vanni's hand signal. The Thieves' Cant of Hiboran, from the west coast of the Shandarian Union, used by a group of people so deadly most feared to name them; the Azure Dawn. The gesture would have been nothing more than a hand wave to anyone else. But Mujahid had spent enough time in the underbelly of the Three Kingdoms to recognize the subtle finger movements.

"Perhaps you could use your priestly influence to sway the Commerce Office in our favor?" Vanni asked.

"You expect forty years of hatred to vanish by decree?"

Vanni pursed his lips. "Any idea where this office is?"

Mujahid glanced toward the dock.

Piles of rubble that once gathered at the base of crumbling buildings had been replaced by hitching posts and water troughs beneath whitewashed walls gleaming in the sunlight. The plaza beyond the pier had changed little since his last visit. It had been rebuilt since the quake, but it looked much as it did before the catastrophe; the stone fountain at the plaza's center, the buildings enclosing the plaza on three sides.

Agera was alive once more. Dozens of people hurried through the plaza. Some carried boxes and other items onto docked ships, and others sauntered past the buildings circling the docks—window shopping at the stores along the boardwalk.

But it wouldn't stay that way for long. The Barathosians would see to that.

"There's great trouble to the south," Mujahid said.

"Why do you think I travel north?"

"You saw the invasion first hand?"

Vanni shook his head. "Some of my supply lines have vanished. Only something big could cause that. Invasion, you say?"

"Don't plan any trips to Tildem," Mujahid said. "These *supply lines* of yours…have they been disrupted anywhere else?"

Vanni stared at him with a blank expression.

Mujahid would have to tread with caution. The Azure Dawn were secretive, and if Vanni were a Dawnmaster, it wouldn't do to underestimate him.

"I care not for the whereabouts of your suppliers," Mujahid said. "I'm only interested in saving lives. If you know something, it could help."

Vanni's expression never changed.

"War is upon us, Vanni Yarwen," Mujahid said. "The crossbow bolt that finds you will not question your ideology or business practices. It will not ask if you wear a chain of office or…*sapphire mark*."

Vanni's eyes grew wide. Mujahid couldn't see if Vanni wore the mark, but his reaction told Mujahid everything. By mentioning the mark—the sacred tattoo worn by every member of the Dawn—Mujahid had all but called him out.

"These are the times that will define your character," Mujahid said. "You might consider putting those talents of yours to good use now."

"Perhaps later," Vanni said. "My fate takes me down a different path than yours, priest."

Mujahid closed his eyes, ignited the symbol of ascension, and released power into the skull symbol. After a moment that spanned seventy years, a skeletal penitent appeared at Mujahid's side.

"This," Mujahid said, pointing at the skeleton. "*This* is later. This is the fate of *all* men, be they King or Dawnmaster. When I call you from the grave, Vanni Yarwen, your will shall be mine. Choose the right path *now*, of your own free will, while free will is still yours."

Vanni smiled and stepped toward Mujahid. "I'm familiar with these." He tapped the penitent on its bony forehead. "You're not the first necromancer I've encountered. Now, if you don't mind, I have some adda to tend to."

Mujahid released the necromantic link and the penitent vanished.

Most men were as brave as Religarian Imperial Guard until they were forced to confront their own mortality. Vanni was…different. If Mujahid didn't know better, he'd say Vanni was *courting* death.

As Mujahid faced his cabin, he glanced over his shoulder and raised his hand. He moved his fingers in the language of the Hiboranian Thieves' Cant.

May the shadows favor your passage.

It was the traditional blessing of thieves and smugglers.

Vanni blinked several times, but he soon returned to his old deadpan expression. As Mujahid lowered his hand, Vanni nodded and backed away.

Mujahid hadn't intended the conversation to go that way. Truth be told, he hadn't intended to *have* a conversation in the first place. He didn't expect Vanni to do anything other than forget this happened and return to whatever shady business he was involved in.

But a small part of him hoped.

Mujahid pocketed the ticket given him by the deckhand as he entered the Agera plaza. He didn't have the patience for bureaucracy just yet.

Dockworkers pushed cargo trolleys onto barges and other vessels while deckhands led livestock toward the stockyards west of the plaza. Passengers lined up along the piers, waiting for the call to board their chosen ships. The boom of a thunderclap made them jump and turn their eyes to the inky belly of an impending storm. Three more booms followed in rapid succession. This was going to be a bad one, and there was no awning to take refuge under.

It was unlikely the Catiatum coven was underground anymore, and the cave entrance would be a long walk beyond the city gate, which itself was a long walk from the dock. It was time for Mujahid to take some calculated risks.

Several Ageran guards from the local militia stood watch at the entrance to a large street. One of them should know something about the coven.

The older guards ignored Mujahid, but the younger ones regarded him as they would a person pulling a crag spider on a leash.

He'd made the decision to wear the midnight blue, and now it was time to pay the price.

"I wonder if you could help me," Mujahid said to the closest guard.

The guard looked at his compatriot as if uncertain how to answer. He must be the junior of the two, so Mujahid stared at the senior guard to punctuate the need for a quick answer.

"With what?" the senior guard said.

It was a start. At least he'd responded with words and not steel.

"It's been a while since my last visit here," Mujahid said. "Given...recent changes in social policy, can you tell me where I might find my fellow priests?"

"Look under any rocks?" a guard said.

"Probably buggering each other at the public bath," another guard said. The others burst into raucous laughter.

All six guards regarded Mujahid with contempt. Would they obey the decree, or would they try to drag him off into an alley? They'd all be brave...until they weren't.

"Enough of that, the lot of you!" a guard said from behind the others. "What's he done to any of you?"

"Who made you Chancellor, Jameson?"

Jameson was a young guard, which surprised Mujahid. He wasn't in charge, but he had a measure of courage.

"You know what this man does for a living?" Jameson asked. "He helps you sorry lot shuffle off beyond the veil to meet your maker. So a little respect is in order, don't you think?"

"We'll outlive him by decades."

"Think so, do you?" Jameson said. "And what if I told you necromancers can't die?" He faced Mujahid. "Necromancers don't die, right sir? You're already dead, if I know my necromancy! Dead and given life by Zubuxo himself!"

Mujahid wasn't sure what made the blood drain from their faces faster, the implication he couldn't die, or the fact he smiled without denying it. Whichever it was, they couldn't seem to get far enough away from him.

"Now what can I help you with, sir?" Jameson asked.

"Kindness is a rare thing in the world these days," Mujahid said. "Keep it up and your time with one of my brethren will be short."

"What's it like, being a necromancer's pet?"

If the boy knew the truth he'd never sleep again.

"Penitent," Mujahid said. "And it's strange and different. Now, can you tell me where I might find the local coven?"

"What if I wanted to be one?"

"A penitent?"

"No, a necromancer! What do I gotta do? You take some kind of vow, right?"

Mujahid didn't have the heart to let him down. If this guard hadn't shown signs of an Awakening yet, he wasn't a necromancer and never would be. Maybe a few harmless lies would soften the blow.

"Let me ask you some questions," Mujahid said. "I'll apprentice you right now, if you think you have what it takes."

Jameson nodded with more enthusiasm than anyone deserved to have.

"Are you comfortable around demons?" Mujahid asked. "For your first test, you'll have to hunt one on the second plane of Hell—they don't start hunting *you* until later. The final test takes place on the sixth plane of Hell. I'll transport you there, and you'll have to find your way home—without being caught by the hellwraiths, of course. Gods…memories of that still make me shudder."

Another thunderclap exploded through the plaza, as if to punctuate Mujahid's statement.

Jameson swallowed.

"You end up partially possessed after the trials," Mujahid said. "But it's *mostly* worth it. So what do you say? Want to give necromancy a go?"

"They're building a new temple about a half-league up the road," Jameson said. He was having a hard time looking Mujahid in the eyes. "You can't miss it."

"You have my thanks," Mujahid said. "If you ever change your mind, you know where the temple is."

"Think I'll stick with guarding for a while."

Mujahid waved as he continued up the street. As much as he hated lying to the boy, telling him it was impossible to become a necromancer might spark his interest even more. Mujahid had seen it happen before.

But what was this about a new temple? Why hadn't Catiatum sent word? Aufidius—the Catiatum coven leader—should know better. Mujahid would have to remedy that lack of knowledge. Perhaps Aufidius needed reminding the Catiatum coven was part of Clan Mukhtaar now.

Agera was a city under construction, with wooden scaffolding lining a portion of the street and construction workers hammering away with mallets and sawing away with serrated blades.

Mujahid stared for a moment, trying to absorb it all.

Wooden scaffolding. More times than he cared to admit over the last forty years, he thought he'd never live to see the day when wood was used for such mundane purposes. But with the barrier gone, tradesmen could work the great forests to the north again. Wood was in supply, and that meant great changes.

It meant terrible changes as well. The Three Kingdoms wasn't adapting well from an economy based on a lack of wood to one glutted by it, and the tenuous relationship between east and west grew more unstable by the week. Religarian stone wasn't in high demand in the west anymore, excepting the rare large construction project.

Mujahid shook his head. Amazing how something as simple as wooden scaffolding could remind him of how delicate the balance of power was now that Kagan and his infernal barrier were gone.

The Barathosians likely didn't know or care about the hardships of the Three Kingdoms. Come to think of it, Mujahid didn't know much at all about what the Barathosians might care about.

Kagan had assassinated the Barathosian Empress's son. But Mujahid was convinced this invasion was about far more than a debt of honor. In his experience, the obvious explanation for most wars was the *excuse*, not the reason.

But if it's not about the death of Yotto, then what is it about?

As he crossed another intersection, he passed a statue of a dragon standing in front of a merchant's shop. The dragon's curled smile reminded Mujahid of Malvol and those cursed figurines. Objects of power were rare—Hellstone even more so—yet he'd encountered two such objects in as many weeks. One had threatened to take control of him, and the other *had* taken control of a king.

But there was no connection between the two events. Perhaps this was something else William could shed light on.

A drizzle of rain fell, peppering the dirt street with pockmarks of water, and freshening the otherwise stagnant air.

The sound of chisels biting into stone echoed across the street.

A vast construction area had been cleared of debris, and several ruined buildings had been demolished to make more room. A wooden frame rose from stone foundations, and several stonemasons were busy chiseling and separating rock.

A man dressed in a midnight-blue robe spoke with a mason and seemed upset about the wooden frame, given where he was pointing and how furious were his gestures.

If they *were* attempting to build a Temple of Zubuxo, they were going about it all wrong. The man was right to be upset. Anything other than natural stone would render the temple ritually impure.

Time for introductions.

He crossed the intersection and called to the man. When he turned, Mujahid kept his eyes open and ignited the symbol of ascension.

The man dropped to one knee and shielded his eyes. The stonemason seemed confused by the action, but a glance from Mujahid sent him back to work.

Mujahid despised the display of authority, but this was the old Catiatum coven. Every time he'd dealt with them without a firm hand, it ended poorly. He'd need to keep them off balance.

"The light has passed," Mujahid said as he released the power.

"May it bless us in its passing," the man said.

"Rise, child."

"My lord," the man said. "To what do we owe this honor?"

Time to muster some feigned outrage.

"I found out from a young guard…a boy…that you were constructing a new temple."

"Yes, my lord. It's going to be a grand —"

"From a boy!"

The man lowered his head.

"Did your coven leader not think to send word to the Pinnacle?" Mujahid said.

"Of course, Lord Mukhtaar —"

"How does he intend to dedicate this temple without me or Lord Nuuan present?"

"I cannot say—"

"This isn't going to be a temple. It's going to be a *sacrilege!*"

"I've discussed the wood with—"

"Take me to the coven."

"That won't be necessary...*Lord* Mujahid," Aufidius said, emphasizing *Lord* as if he were humoring Mujahid instead of honoring him. "Sorry to startle you, my lord. I was across the street and saw Magus Claudio drop to his knee."

Mujahid wanted to wipe the smile from Aufidius's hairless face. Something about that man had always bothered Mujahid. Maybe it was the sharpness of his cheekbones, or the hook of his nose that gave him the appearance of a predator. Perhaps it was the sunken eyes that hinted at a darkness waiting for the right moment to be unleashed. The tattoo covering the right side of his face in the ancient tribal pattern of Clan Catiatum didn't lend itself to trust. But whichever it was, that smile was more malevolent than pleasant.

Aufidius didn't have the honor—perhaps *courage*—to wear the midnight blue. The robe he wore was better suited for a government magistrate than a necromancer. Bright blue from head to foot, trimmed with silver along the cuffs and collar. In place of a simple cincture, he wore a hide belt with a jeweled buckle. And instead of sandals, he wore shriller-hide boots.

"You like them?" Aufidius said, holding a turquoise boot out for Mujahid's inspection.

Mujahid wasn't fooled by the foppish display. Aufidius was a powerful priest, which was the only reason Mujahid appointed him when the last coven leader died.

"Some say shrillers are intelligent," Mujahid said.

"Clearly not intelligent enough to evade the hunter."

"What was your reason for not informing me of this temple? Tell me that I may judge *your* intelligence."

Aufidius lowered his head, but his expression wasn't one of a reprimanded humble subordinate. It was anger.

"We've only begun laying the foundation, my lord," Aufidius said. "The framing was a mistake from an overzealous worker, nothing more. He wasn't aware of our customs. I would have informed you long before it was time to consecrate the structure."

"Am I and Lord Nuuan not to oversee the design? The placement? Have you discovered a sacred line crossing this property? Did you even think to check, for that matter?"

"I assure you, all of the necessary rites were followed."

"You purchased the land with clan funds, did you not?"

"With Catiatum funds, yes."

Mujahid stepped closer to Aufidius. "Catiatum hasn't been a clan since I performed the blessing at your grandfather's birth."

Aufidius smiled once more, but it was a nervous smile. Had he forgotten Mujahid was far older than he appeared?

"I misspoke, my lord. I merely meant to say Catiatum *coven* funds. But our haste was well-intentioned, I assure you."

"I assume you have a coven house?"

Aufidius nodded.

"Take me. You can tell me of these *intentions* while we walk."

Aufidius led Mujahid to a side street next to the temple foundation. When Mujahid rounded the corner, Aufidius walked beside him.

"Before we discuss the temple," Mujahid said. "Is William well? What of the refugees from New Caspardis?"

"I'm afraid I don't have those answers, my lord. William left little more than a month ago and took the refugees with him. He told me you'd asked him to rebuild the New Caspardis coven and wanted to begin as soon as possible."

Mujahid sighed. "Ahh William! Of all the festering times to get motivated."

"You didn't ask him to do this, my lord?"

"Oh, I asked, all right. And it's moments like these I hate getting what I ask for. I suppose I'll have to carry on to Caspardis, then. I'll stay here for the night and get started tomorrow."

"Of course! We have a place for you, and we'll make sure you're well fed and well provisioned."

I bet you will. The quicker I move on, the better for you.

"Now, back to the temple," Mujahid said. "Why the haste?"

"An invasion force is coming, and I know not when it will arrive."

Mujahid was surprised he knew. And Aufidius had implied the invasion had something to do with the construction of the new temple, so he must have known before they laid the foundation stones.

That wasn't possible.

"Given how quickly they took Rotham," Mujahid said, "and how quickly they're likely to take Arin's Watch, I'd say within a month. Maybe two, if Three Banks holds long enough."

Aufidius blinked and furrowed his brow. His surprise was no act.

"Rotham?" Aufidius asked. "Arin's Watch? Are you saying an invasion comes from the south as well?"

"What do you mean *as well*?"

"I was speaking of the invasion from the *west*. Shandar has fallen. An unknown army moves east to Caspardis as we speak! They may have already taken it!"

Mujahid's face grew cold.

"Tell me what you know of this invasion," Mujahid said. "Every detail you have!"

"The stories defy credibility, yet Shandarian Rangers swear they're true. The strangest ship appeared off the coast of Shandar. They described it as a floating ziggurat, like an ancient *builder* temple. It materialized on the water, as if placed there by the gods themselves. But before anyone could approach it, fire rained from the sky. They say not one stone remains standing upon another in Shandar."

Mujahid stopped and steadied himself against a wall.

"And there's more," Aufidius said. "There's a...*strangeness* happening here in Agera. Something with the adda. Some have simply appeared outside the city walls, while others have vanished. Some that appeared didn't look like adda at all. They were several times the normal size, with four giant horns. People are saying the adda are cursed. That maybe they're the mounts of the ghost soldiers."

"You should know better."

Aufidius waved his hand. "Of course. But I can understand why the uneducated would call them such. Soldiers *have* been appearing and disappearing outside the city walls. I haven't witnessed the phenomenon myself, but people I trust have reported it."

Mujahid placed a hand on Aufidius's shoulder.

"How many of you are there now?" Mujahid asked.

"Total?"

"Priests."

"Exactly thirteen."

Mujahid balled his other hand into a fist.

"Damn Kagan!" Mujahid said. "Damn him straight to the hells!"

"Something we can agree on."

"Go now. There's no time. Collect everyone and everything you hold dear and leave this place to its fate."

"My lord?"

"The invasion force you spoke of is the Barathosian army."

"But that was forty years ago."

"When they sweep through Agera, it will fare no better than Shandar or Rotham. And there is *nothing* you or the other priests will be able to do. Take the coven east. Make for the Pinnacle."

"What will you do?"

Mujahid had gone over every scenario, but he was left with only two choices. He could travel to Caspardis in the hope of warning William before it was too late, or he could make all haste north and secure the Mukhtaar Estate.

The Three Kingdoms was surrounded. The bulk of the armada sat off the coast of Dar Rodon, and there was no telling how long that city would survive. Tildem was already under Barathosian control. Donal could slow the advance, but in the end the Barathosians would win. And now Shandar, the biggest, most powerful city in the Shandarian Union lay in rubble.

William, I'm sorry. But I must *secure the estate. I can't take the chance of it falling into Barathosian hands.*

The estate was more than just property. It was, quite possibly, the oldest structure known to humankind. It was the single largest repository of objects of power in the world. It was a conduit of divine power. It was the entrance to the Rite of Testing, and so many other...places. If a malevolent force ever took control of it...

Mujahid couldn't bear to finish the thought. He *had* to move the portal to the Mukhtaar Estate out of the Algidian mountains. Out of the Shandarian Union.

But to *where*? He'd have to figure that out along the way.

"I travel north," Mujahid said. "There is something I must do before the Barathosians arrive. Go now. Do what you must to save the coven."

"But the temple!"

"It's just a building. It won't do you much good when you're dead. Kagan killed enough of us. Now we must survive. Go. If they've taken Caspardis already, they could be approaching the city gate as we speak."

Aufidius gave an unenthusiastic bow and continued down the street.

Mujahid retrieved the card from his pocket and flipped it over in his hand.

"It's time I took the Commerce Office up on their offer."
He swore as he headed back down toward the docks.

CHAPTER THIRTEEN

In the days of the Reestablishment of the Lords, when the Mukhtaar line had failed, Mujahid Halabi stepped over the threshold, becoming Mujahid Lord Mukhtaar Halabi. The people rejoiced to the heavens, proclaiming "The Mukhtaar line has not failed. For Zubuxo has provided another."
- The Mukhtaar Chronicles, attributed to the prophet Habakku Reestablishment of the Lords 7:12-14

While some scholars take the "failure" of the Mukhtaar line to mean the end of the blood line itself, it is more likely referencing failure of a socio-political nature. What cannot be denied, however, is that a priest outside of the sacred Mukhtaar blood line ascended and was henceforth known as a Mukhtaar Lord.

Of interest here, however, is that Lord Halabi is never referred to as "Lord Mukhtaar" in subsequent texts. Only "Lord Halabi" or "Lord Mujahid". This is likely the origin of the dual attributions of Mukhtaar Lords. Those who descend, by blood, from the ancient Mukhtaar line (in other words, a "blood Mukhtaar") are properly referred to as Lord Mukhtaar. Those who do not descend from that line retain their surname.
- Coteon of the Steppes, "The Mukhtaar Chronicles: Coteonic Commentaries" (circa 680 BCE)

Nicolas stepped onto dry ground as the transport bubble evaporated on the shore somewhere west of Caspardis. Kaitlyn, Toridyn, Toby, and dead Kagan followed him up a small hill away from the beach.

Gentle waves lapped the shore of the vast lake, but they weren't so gentle as to make Nicolas forget where he was.

The city of Caspardis was out there, like an uncomfortable conversation waiting to be had. That place had left Nicolas with nightmares. It came to symbolize a hatred, bigotry, and violence beyond anything he'd witnessed back on Earth.

He gazed out across the lake, trying to take his mind off bad memories. But it was as impossible to shake those thoughts as it was to see the opposite shore. If it weren't for the unimpressive waves and lack of saltwater in the air, he'd think he was staring out across an ocean. And somewhere on that body of water was the platform where he'd been chained, weighted down, and tossed into the lake to drown.

No, it was impossible to be anywhere near this place and not think about what they'd done to him. What they'd done to *many* in the guise of justice and orthodoxy, all because of his birth father.

"You're somewhere else again," Kaitlyn said. "What is it?"

She'd never let him get away without talking about it. Strange thing is that he both wanted and *didn't* want to talk about it. More like he *needed* to talk about it, but didn't *want* to.

"I can tell her," Toridyn said.

"No," Nicolas said. "This is my story to tell."

Nicolas started walking inland, and the others followed.

"There's *evil* in this world," Nicolas said.

"Is it that much worse than back home?" Kaitlyn asked. "You promised you'd tell me everything, remember?"

He told her everything then, and each word threatened to consume him. The only way he could do it was to detach himself from everything—from who he was, from the woman he once yearned for, and from the man standing next to him who was responsible for it all; Kagan. It was as if he weren't talking to Kaitlyn but the air around her instead. Erindor itself needed to hear the story. He held nothing back. The shriller. The crag spider. The earthquakes. He even told her about the four-legged turkey. And yes, he told her about Caspardis. He told her how they'd arrested and tortured him. How he'd prayed another man would die so he'd have power to escape. How they'd stripped the flesh from his back with a scourge and threw salt in the open wounds. How they'd so disfigured him because of Kagan's law that if it weren't for cichlos magic, the mere sight of him would make her puke.

And he told her about the cichlos. About when he finally thought he was safe, they'd arrested him, beat him, and disfigured him once more. And just when he thought it couldn't get any worse, he was forced to become a killer himself.

All because of Kagan.

"You killed all those people," Kaitlyn said, "and you blame your *father*? You didn't have *any* say in it?"

"Kait—"

"This is a lot to take in," Kaitlyn said.

"I just wanted to be honest with you."

"I appreciate that. And I'm happy you opened up to me. But you've had a year to process all of this. I've had ten seconds."

A cold breeze swept up off the lake. Kaitlyn hugged herself and looked down. When the breeze subsided, she unfolded her arms and wrapped them around him.

"I can't imagine how hard it was to live through those things," Kaitlyn said. "And if I know you as well as I think, it was even harder to talk about. We'll get through this. All of it." She stepped back until they were looking into each other's eyes. "Just don't think this is the only time you'll need to talk about it."

"You going to use that psychology degree on me?"

Kaitlyn smiled. "I'm here. Whenever you need to talk. Just me. No psychology. And, technically, neither of us *have* degrees yet, remember? This a pretty elaborate way to avoid graduation, by the way. I'm not saying it's avoidant personality disorder *exactly*…but I'm keeping my eye on you."

Nicolas pulled her close and rested his cheek against hers, absorbing her warmth.

After what seemed like not enough time, he took her hand and started walking up the hill again.

Several hundred yards from the lake shore, Nicolas spotted an adda-drawn wagon stopped on the road. It reminded him of an old west stagecoach; symmetrical in design, like a bowl resting on an axle assembly. A closed carriage for passengers, a rack for luggage on top, and a driver's seat outside, toward the front of the roof. It was pulling a trailer of some sort, but there wasn't any activity around it. Maybe the driver had pulled over and was napping inside. The adda—snouts and hooves like a cow, manes like lions—looked from side to side periodically, but other than that, they were calm.

Nicolas would never get used to them having extra legs.

Cows should not have six legs!

When he took another step, a strong wave of necropotency washed over him and trickled into his well.

"Maybe you should stay here a minute," Nicolas said.

"It's just a—oh my god," Kaitlyn said. Her face paled as she glanced toward the rear of the wagon. "Nick, stay back. You don't want to see this."

That's right. She thinks I'm still afraid of dead things.

Nicolas stepped ahead of her.

Several bodies were sprawled in the mud at the rear of the wagon.

Yeah. Figured as much.

He sent a command through the necromantic link for Kagan to check things out. Taking chances wasn't something he was willing to do at this point.

Better to be safe…

"Tor," Nicolas said. "Grab a penitent and get ready for the worst."

"You're not freaking out?" Kaitlyn said. "You *have* changed."

Nicolas smiled. "I've seen things."

A moment later an undead cichlos stood next to Toridyn. The flexible bones of its chest heaved as if from the breathing of invisible lungs.

When Kagan sent the "all clear", Nicolas led the others toward the wagon.

"Kagan says there are eight of them," Nicolas said. "All dead."

"Sure he's telling the truth?" Kaitlyn asked. It was a legitimate question for a non-necromancer.

"He can't lie unless I order him to."

There was something about the four bodies at the back of the wagon—the way they were laid out, as if they were kneeling and had fallen forward—that reminded Nicolas of every bad mafia movie he'd ever seen.

These men, whoever they were, had been executed. But that didn't upset Nicolas as much as the realization of *how* they'd been executed.

Each of the four men had a large wound at the back of his head.

"This isn't possible," Nicolas said. "They've been shot."

He wasn't a detective, but he didn't need to be to see charring around the wounds.

"Kagan," Nicolas said. "What do *you* think could do something like this to a person?"

"Necropotency can be woven into projectiles," Kagan said.

Nicolas had plenty of experience with *that* little trick.

"No," Nicolas said. "That would punch a hole straight through, and it wouldn't burn."

"Then I know not what sort of magic could achieve this."

"Why is this a problem?" Kaitlyn asked.

As much as Nicolas hated the idea of handling a corpse, he needed to be sure. He knelt next to a body and lifted the head to get a look at the face.

Whoever this was, his face wasn't injured. It was a little dirty, and his eyes were open. But there was no exit wound. The back of his head was a mess of hair matted with blood and charred skin surrounding a hole the size of a large marble. It was like someone had struck an overripe cantaloupe with a hammer. The rest was more gruesome than Nicolas had been expecting. Whatever brain tissue hadn't sprayed back toward the shooter was pressed up against the other side of the man's skull.

Kaitlyn approached from around the wagon and stood next to him, covering her mouth.

Nicolas shook his head. "There's no gunpowder in the Three Kingdoms, Kait, much less *guns*. Whoever did this…I can't begin to imagine. But I'll tell you this much. They're not from around here. What is it?"

Kaitlyn was staring at a corpse on the ground next to the wagon.

"I don't think *that* one was shot," Kaitlyn said.

Three more corpses lay next to the wagon on the opposite side from where they'd approached. One in particular had his face smashed in, and another had an obviously broken neck.

"Tor," Nicolas said.

Toridyn wandered around from the front of the wagon, his penitent in tow.

"There's another one up here," Toridyn said. "Doesn't look like a soldier, though. Looks more like the wagon driver. We could raise them and find out what happened?"

Nicolas considered it. But the extreme toll the namocea would take on him now wasn't worth it.

"At the risk of sounding uncharitable," Nicolas said, "we're not really here for this. We can't afford to be fatigued if and when the Barathosians show up. We need to get to Caspardis as soon as possible, if we're going to make any difference."

"That's probably for the best," Toridyn said. "We can always—"

A tall figure approached from the roadside. Nicolas hadn't seen anyone standing nearby, and there was no place for this person to have hidden.

The person—he or she, Nicolas couldn't tell—was wearing a black cloak with a voluminous hood, pulled low to hide his or her face.

The person lifted their hand, and Nicolas expected to see a gun. Instead, they pulled their hood back.

The man was about as tall as Nicolas, with brown hair. And if Nicolas had to guess, he'd say the man was older than him, though not by much. It was the way he moved that was unnerving. Feline. Graceful with a side helping of whoop ass.

Nicolas stood and sent a command to Kagan to be ready for anything.

Toby growled and backed away, and Toridyn walked over to calm him down.

"Poor dog," the man said. "Missing some legs. How in the hells does he keep himself up like that without breaking his own back?"

His voice wasn't gruff, as Nicolas had been expecting. There was something almost *noble* about it, and there wasn't anything malicious or sarcastic in his tone.

"There's nothing wrong with my—" Nicolas stopped himself. Turkey with four legs. Cow with six legs. By Erindor standards, Toby *was* missing two legs.

The man raised his hands and Toby growled louder. "Didn't mean to offend."

"Just stay where you are," Nicolas said.

"I don't mean you any harm," the man said. He took another step forward and Toridyn's penitent seized him.

"The man said *freeze*, punk," Toridyn said. He stepped toward the man. "One more move and you'll make my day."

"Easy, there, *Five-O*," Nicolas said. "We don't know anything yet."

"I found them like this," the man said.

"Which is exactly what *I'd* say if I killed a bunch of people and got caught a few minutes later," Kaitlyn said.

"It's a little too close to Blackwood to get robbed," Toridyn said.

Nicolas stood and faced the man. Toridyn had a good point.

"There's a few too many valuables left for it to be a robbery," the man said.

"You understand him?" Nicolas said.

"I've had cichlos acquaintances," the man said.

Nicolas looked down at the dead men, and for the first time he noticed their coin purses were still there. Curious, he pulled the tarp back from the top of the trailer.

Cooking supplies and bedding. And no room for anything else.

Whoever this guy was, he was right. Nothing had been taken. At least nothing obvious.

"There's an army headed this way," the man said, "and I don't think they're planning on taking prisoners. You're a Council Magus. You must know *something* about that."

It took Nicolas a moment to remember he was dressed in Council robes.

"Suppose I am," Nicolas said. "And you know more than you're telling me."

"I'm trying to help. We can't stay here. We *have* to get to Caspardis."

Nicolas nodded at Toridyn, and the undead cichlos released the man. "Keep an eye on him, Tor."

Nicolas drew more ambient necropotency into his well, just to be safe.

The man lowered his eyes and walked closer. An odd expression passed over his face, as if he were arguing with himself—he ground his teeth and pursed his lips. He pulled a small object out of his pocket and looked at it in disgust. He was anxious about something.

"You prefer adda, or adda-ki?" the man asked.

"That's an odd question," Nicolas said.

"It can tell you a lot about a person."

"Why not just ask?"

"I just did."

It was almost as bad as talking to Siek Lamil. Nicolas had a feeling this guy wasn't going to quit until he got his answer.

"You're making a great effort to get on our good side, here," Nicolas said.

"Please," the man said. "I asked politely. Wasn't I polite?"

Nicolas glanced at Kaitlyn, who pursed her lips and shrugged.

The last time Nicolas saw an adda-ki, it wasn't under the best of circumstances.

"Adda," Nicolas said. He shook his head, incredulous that not only had the question been asked, but that he took the time to answer it.

The man tossed the object in the air, and Nicolas could see it for the first time. A small, silver coin. When the coin fell, the man caught it, flipped it over, and slapped it onto his opposite wrist.

"Adda it is," the man said. He seemed relieved, as if a weight had been lifted.

The man strode past Kagan, nodding as if not to be rude. He either didn't know Kagan was dead, or he didn't care. And he smiled at Toridyn!

"Name's Aelron," the man said, extending his hand.

"Elrond?"

"*Ael*ron."

"Sorry," Nicolas said, taking the man's hand in a firm shake.

"Why is that so festering hard for people?" Aelron asked.

"Nicolas," Nicolas said, giving Aelron's hand one last shake.

"That's the second time I've heard that name in as many days. Suppose that makes your name more common than mine."

"I still haven't met another Nicolas here."

Aelron gave him a quizzical look. "I thought you were a Council magus. Isn't the new archmage's name *Nicolas*?"

Nicolas had two choices. He could tell this stranger who he was and hope he wasn't a whack job, or he could play it safe. It was moments like these he wished Mujahid had come along. Mujahid could be crotchety, but he could see around corners Nicolas didn't know existed.

Of one thing he was certain; Kagan would have lied. And that was reason enough to tell the truth.

"It is," Nicolas said. "I mean, I am. I mean...I'm him. Nicolas Murray."

Aelron lost his smile.

Aelron stepped forward until he was inches away from Nicolas.

Nicolas prepared a command for the necromantic link, but could Kagan cross the gap fast enough?

Aelron's lip trembled as he balled his hand into a fist.

Take him!

Kagan lunged.

Nicolas prepared a bolt of necropotency.

Aelron dropped to one knee and struck his chest with his balled fist.

"Archmage," Aelron said.

As comprehension dawned, Nicolas ordered Kagan back.

Sonofabitch! I almost killed the dude!

"Please," Nicolas said. "No need for that now. I'm just a guy with a fancy hat."

Aelron glanced up at Nicolas as if he were looking at an alien.

"Well, I don't have the hat with me," Nicolas said. "But you get the idea. Go on, now, stand up!"

Aelron stood and took a step back.

"We're headed to Caspardis as well," Nicolas said. "And I'd appreciate it if you didn't mention this to anyone. I...had a bad experience there."

Aelron took another step back and massaged one of his temples. He pulled the coin from a pocket in his cloak, flipped it, looked at Nicolas with something akin to sadness, then put it back in his cloak.

"Sure do like playing with your money, don't you," Nicolas said.

The blank expression again.

"Despise it," Aelron said. "I despise everything about it."

"Okay," Nicolas said. He shared a glance with Kaitlyn. *This guy's brisket ain't done smoking yet.*

"Would you mind some company?" Aelron asked.

"You seem like a nice guy and all," Nicolas said. "But this is sort of a...family trip."

"If I had to guess, I'd say this was your first trip away from the Pinnacle. I can't, in good conscience, let you make it alone."

Kaitlyn gave Nicolas a look that made it clear she wasn't happy with the idea.

What do you think? Nicolas asked through the necromantic link.

An image of a squad of soldiers growing stronger with each new member returned from the link.

Strength in numbers, huh?

Kagan seemed to think it was a good idea, and it bothered Nicolas that he agreed.

A clap of thunder gave Nicolas a jolt.

Aelron pantomimed catching a droplet of rain. "Rainy season. You could use more hands around camp."

"Look, Aelron," Nicolas said. "It's not that I don't trust you. It's just that I don't *trust* you."

"Let me take point. You can watch me the entire way."

Nicolas looked away for a moment. Kaitlyn wasn't going to like this.

"All right," Nicolas said.

Aelron walked back to the wagon. "There may be some provisions here. I suggest taking the tarp."

Another thunderclap emphasized how good an idea that was.

"Are you sure about this?" Kaitlin asked in a loud whisper. "I'm all for being good Samaritans, but back in Texas we had cell phones, cops, tow trucks. We're in a place where underwater cities can implode because of bedsheets. We don't know him."

"You saw how he acted when he found out who I am," Nicolas said. "He thinks I'm some kind of holy man. Doesn't hurt to have that kind of loyalty around when things go sideways."

"On second thought," Aelron shouted. "I think we can take the whole carriage if you don't mind moving bodies. You and your friends can stay inside, Archmage. I'll drive."

"See?" Nicolas whispered to Kaitlyn. "He's helping. Tor, can you give him a hand?"

Toridyn nodded and Toby followed him to the front of the wagon.

"Everything's gonna be fine," Nicolas said. "Trust me."

"Whatever you say...*Archmage*," Kaitlyn said. "Just remember this face I'm making when things don't go as well as you *hope* they will."

Ouch.

Nicolas followed her to the wagon, silently praying everything would go as well as he hoped.

CHAPTER FOURTEEN

Coteon's contemporaries point to the establishment of the necromantic clans as the first verifiable historic event, suggesting it took place some 3000 to 4000 years before the Common Era. They, of course, were not aware of the Scrolls of Tal'mon, nor that they would be unearthed in the Religarian desert three millennia later (120 BRL).

The scrolls indicate the two earliest verifiable events are as follows:

Leras Ardirian founds the Necromantic Council and takes the ancient Pinnacle by force in 150 BRL.

Zafir Mukhtaar ascends in 130 BRL to become Zafir Lord Mukhtaar.

- Grindan, "The Crucible of Religar: On the Patterns of Nomadic Migrations" (10 CE)

Mujahid, if you're going to include the writings of a pretentious tosser like Grindan, can you at least sort out the dates for the rest of us? I shouldn't need a counting frame and two pints of stout to read a calendar.

- Nuuan

Brother, I will collapse the ancient dates into two categories: the Common Era (CE) and Before the Common era (BCE). Will this help your alcohol-addled *brain to decipher the timeline? Be mindful that our birth date will change to 30 BCE on the new calendar.*

- M

Several hours into their trip, the rain transformed from a gentle spray to a torrential downpour, making it feel as if the adda were dragging it through the mud, rather than pulling it. Aelron would have rather been inside, but a little water wouldn't kill him.

And he needed to build some good will if he was going to get to the bottom of what happened to his father, Kagan Ardirian.

Who in the hells was this Nicolas Murray? How had his father died? What were the circumstances under which this usurper had taken the Obsidian Throne?

This wasn't about envy over another man sitting upon a throne Aelron felt *he* deserved. No. Aelron could never be archmage. But he could still have children. And *they* might have magic. *They* would be the rightful heirs to the Obsidian Throne.

The coin had already told him what to do.

Kill him.

But Aelron wouldn't do that just yet. The coin hadn't told him *when* to kill the usurper, just that he needed to do it.

Aelron had a little time. Caspardis was at least another day's ride away. It would give him the chance to figure out why Nicolas had seemed genuinely upset about the murdered Shandarian soldiers. What usurper to the Obsidian Throne would give a whit about a handful of Shandarian soldiers? And why would this new archmage—if he *had* stolen the throne—be concerned about the defense of Caspardis? It didn't matter to the archmage who ruled which nation. The archmage held *true* power. The only power that mattered. He controlled the temples and bound kings and peasants alike in shackles made from fear.

Fear for their souls.

But why would Nicolas ask him to keep his identity secret? Why would he want to give up that weapon of fear?

No. Aelron wouldn't kill him just yet. There were too many questions that needed answers.

A blinding lightning strike silhouetted a ruined building up ahead, and the loudest thunderclap yet shook the wagon. A growl from inside the carriage told Aelron the dog wasn't happy.

Aelron wiped the stinging rain out of his eyes. At this rate, they'd have to swim to Caspardis. He guided the adda off to the side of the road, drew the reins in, then wrapped his knuckles on the hatch behind him. It slid open.

"This is no good!" Aelron said. "We keep moving and we'll sink! I'm coming inside for a minute."

The wagon lurched to a halt, and Aelron climbed down from the driver's seat and entered the carriage. He settled in next to Kaitlyn, who with a single glance made it clear how she felt about the seating arrangement.

Aelron didn't know if she was bad at concealing her dislike for him, or if she just didn't care.

"It's really pissing it down out there," Aelron said. "Every yard I drive, the wagon slows even more. Better just stop until the worst of it passes. I pulled onto harder ground for now."

"How long do these things usually last?" Nicolas asked.

"Won't be much longer. But the rain isn't the problem. It's the mud that's going to stop us. I don't think we'll be making it to Caspardis."

"Tonight," Kaitlyn said.

"What?" Aelron asked.

"We won't be making it to Caspardis *tonight*," Kaitlyn said. "You made it sound like we won't be making it there at all."

"Sorry," Aelron said. "I took it as implied. Before long this wagon will be up to the doors in mud."

"Tight quarters, but we'll make it work," Nicolas said.

"There are ruins not far ahead," Aelron said. "Maybe half a league. When it calms a bit, I think we can make it at least that far. Might have to drive *next* to the road, though."

"Maybe dead Kagan can drive," Toridyn said.

Aelron's pulse raced. Had he heard the cichlos correctly? Was *this* his father? Certainly not.

But Aelron hadn't seen Kagan since he was five years old. Could it be?

"This…" Aelron couldn't seem to start a sentence, much less finish one.

"Yeah," Nicolas said. "*That* Kagan."

A torrent of emotion pulled Aelron along by his heart. He ground his teeth as an uncomfortable heat spread under his skin.

"I'm sure the whole world has questions," Nicolas said. "But—"

"He's dead?" Aelron asked.

"As a doornail."

Forty years of wondering if he'd ever see his family again, and *this* was the reunion? He couldn't say he *loved* Kagan. He never really knew him. But he'd always hoped they could forge some kind of relationship.

And here he was. Dead. With his murderer sitting right beside him.

He wanted to lash out. A quick slice of his dagger, and Nicolas would be just as dead. The big cichlos would get involved. Might even kill him. His own dead father would kill him to protect the very man that murdered him. But Aelron didn't care. Someone had to pay for this tragedy of a family history.

Mother, dead. Father, dead. The only one who might remain was his baby brother...the newborn he never got a chance to know. But how would he ever find him?

"You killed him?" Aelron asked.

"No," Nicolas said. "But it wasn't for lack of trying."

"Then who?"

"When the barrier came down, the gods came back. Arin killed him right in front of me. Toridyn was there too. Then, Arin raised him back up and gave him to me as a penitent."

"I—" Aelron took a deep breath and exhaled. He wasn't thinking straight. If he put off his vengeance a little longer, perhaps he could find a way to communicate with his father.

"I guess what they say about only an Ardirian being archmage is a load of shite, then," Aelron said.

Nicolas leaned forward in his seat and folded his hands in front of him.

"Who are you?" Nicolas asked.

"What do you mean?"

"Who are you?"

Festering hells! I'm better than this!

Aelron leaned back. His moment of emotion may have been enough to give up the lie. He had to diffuse the situation.

"I didn't mean to pry, Archmage," Aelron said. "I can't pretend to understand the world of politics, its arbitrary protocols and niceties of court. But what are the odds, right? I mean…*Kagan Ardirian* sitting right here in front of me. Dead, of all things."

Nicolas leaned back. He seemed less tense. Maybe he bought it.

"As odd as it is for you, imagine how it is for me," Nicolas said. "He's my birth father."

Aelron's chest tightened as his mind raced. Nicolas was his brother? Nicolas was the newborn?

But the coin wanted him dead! Why?

"You said your name was *Murray*?" Aelron asked.

Nicolas nodded. "It is…and it's a long story. But don't let the name fool you. Unfortunately, I'm an Ardirian by blood. Like I said…he's my birth father."

A bright flash of lightning lit the carriage interior, followed by a series of thunderclaps so loud, it was as if Arin and Zubuxo had become bowling partners.

"Why *unfortunately*?" Aelron asked.

"Sorry?" Nicolas asked.

"I'm just curious," Aelron said. "You implied being an Ardirian wasn't a good thing."

"You been living under a rock?"

"My life of late has been somewhat…*ascetic*."

"What do you see when you look at this guy?" Nicolas pointed a thumb at Kagan.

"Like I said, I wasn't trying to pry."

"Now *I'm* curious. Tell me what you see."

Aelron looked down for a moment, then turned his gaze toward Kagan.

"I see an old man living out a rather ignominious existence," Aelron said. "Why in the Hells would his own god kill him?"

"He lied to the world for decades, not giving a damn what or who he destroyed." Nicolas faced Kagan. "Tell him what you did, you smug bastard."

And Kagan told his story, from the murder of Yotto in an effort to protect his power, to the construction of the Great Barrier and all the evils it caused.

"You left out the part where you tried to murder your own son," Nicolas said. He faced Aelron. "Within ten minutes of meeting him, he tried to kill me."

"*Meeting* him?" Aelron said. "I don't understand."

"Like I said, it's a long story."

Had Aelron gotten it all wrong? Nicolas wasn't a usurper at all.

It grew quieter outside as the rain died down.

"Looks like it's slowed enough," Aelron said. "I'll take us to those ruins. Maybe we can find a dry spot where I can whip something up with those provisions."

"You cook?" Nicolas asked.

"I recently discovered I have some skill with a ladle and stew pot."

Nicolas nodded as Aelron opened the carriage door and climbed out. Aelron had gotten his answers.

But the number of *questions* had grown larger.

When the carriage door closed behind Aelron, Kaitlyn scooted a few inches away from Toridyn.

"Was it my deodorant?" Toridyn asked.

Kaitlyn gave Toridyn an incredulous stare, and Nicolas chuckled.

"Something Nicolas used to say," Toridyn said. He faced Nicolas. "You ever going to tell me what deodorant is?"

"You put it under your arms, you oaf," Nicolas said. "To stop the smell."

"Why would it smell under my arms? That's not where the smell comes from."

"We don't need the details," Nicolas said.

"I don't trust him," Kaitlyn said.

"He might not have smelly pits like we do, but—"

"Not *him*," Kaitlyn said. "*Him*." She pointed through the carriage wall toward the driver seat as the carriage lurched forward on the muddy road. "And what's with the OCD behavior with that coin of his?"

"I never said I *trusted* him."

"You just told him *everything*. How do you know what he's going to do with that information?"

"There's just something…" Nicolas stopped.

"What?" Kaitlyn asked.

"I don't know. I can't explain it. There's something about this guy that seems….I've known evil people, Kait. He's many things, I'm sure. But evil ain't one of them."

"Being murdered on a dark, muddy road leaves you just as dead no matter *how* nice your killer is," Kaitlyn said.

"I know necromancy is new to you, but I'm not foolin' around when I say Tor and I can take this guy easily. I mean, if it comes to that."

Toridyn made a sound that indicated he wasn't so sure.

"Siek Lamil would say *the day you underestimate your opponent is the day he defeats you*," Toridyn said, imitating the siek's deep voice.

"There's another Cichlos saying I love," Nicolas said.

"Oh yeah?" Toridyn asked. "Which one?"

"*Zip it.*"

Toridyn faced Kaitlyn. "That's not actually a thing."

The carriage stopped next to the walls of a ruined two-story building about a hundred yards off the northern side of the road. Mostly dilapidated, all that remained of the second floor was a semicircle of brick, creating an overhang. The ground was wet, but the rain had stopped.

"This should work," Aelron said from the driver's seat, just forward of the trapdoor in the roof. "One of the rooms has all four walls intact. Should be dry enough inside to get a fire started."

"You think the ceiling will stay up?" Kaitlyn asked.

Aelron nodded. "See those bright specks on the rock? Religarian granite. Nothing short of a quake will tear those walls down."

"All the same, I think I'll stay out here," Kaitlyn said.

"Don't recommend it," Aelron said. "Firebugs will eat you alive. That's if passing marauders don't spot you first."

Kaitlyn mouthed the word *firebugs* to Nicolas, who responded with a shrug.

"Tor," Nicolas said. "When I looked under the tarp earlier there was some bedding. Grab it and let's get set up."

Kaitlyn leaned close to Nicolas. "I didn't realize how hungry I was until you asked Aelron if he could cook."

Nicolas put his arm around her and led her into the ruins.

Two hours later, Nicolas began to question Aelron's cooking skills. The meal was edible, if a person didn't mind pulling hair and the occasional stone out of their bowl.

When they'd finished eating, Toridyn smothered the fire with mud and Nicolas went off behind the walls of the ruins to clean the pots and pans.

As he scrubbed his bowl with water from his drinking skin, he fumbled the bowl. When he reached for it, he dropped the water skin, spilling its contents on the ground. He stared at the water as the last of it trickled out of the skin. And though three people, two penitents, and a beagle were less than twenty feet away, he was utterly alone.

A despair he hadn't felt since he was chained to the posts in Caspardis overcame him, and he stumbled back until his hand found the cold stone wall.

Everyone was expecting him to have the answers, to find some way of defeating these Barathosians.

And he couldn't even manage to wash a bowl without spilling all of his water.

I can't do this. I'm not a general. Hell, I wasn't even a boy scout.

He rubbed his forehead.

No. Stop this! I survived being beaten, scourged, and drowned. I've traveled to the Plane of Death. I toppled a despotic ruler and saved a continent. I will find a way to stop them. I will!

He grabbed the water skin, straightened himself up, and walked back into the ruins. Maybe a couple of hours of sleep would do him some good.

Nicolas stared through the carriage window at the night sky of Erindor with Kaitlyn leaning against his shoulder. She adjusted her position, and he closed his eye, soaking in as much of her presence as he could. He put his arms around her and squeezed, and she kissed him on the neck.

They'd slept for three hours in the ruins, which was an hour longer than Nicolas had planned. He couldn't get to Caspardis soon enough. Stopping was no longer an option. Not if the Barathosians could appear at will whenever they wanted to.

He opened his eyes and gazed out the window. The clouds had gone with the rest of the storm, and the sky was every bit as surreal as the Field of Judgment had been. Mujahid hadn't been lying about Erindor having two moons. They were big. Much bigger than the full moon on Earth. The larger of the two had a yellow tint and the telltale pockmarks of meteor strikes. The smaller was reddish in color and reminded Nicolas of Mars. It hung beneath and to the left of the larger moon.

But the moons weren't the brightest objects in the sky.

A radiant spiral galaxy filled the sky behind the moons, all six of its spiral arms visible like a gargantuan pinwheel.

It gave Nicolas a strange sensation, as if it were drawing him in.

A somber thought crossed his mind. An entire generation of Erindorians had grown up beneath Kagan's barrier, having never seen what he was seeing right now. In many ways, they were probably as amazed by the sight as he was. How unfair was *that*? This was their world. Their birthright. *He* was the alien here. He *should* be amazed by the night sky of a strange world. But them? It should be as normal for them as a tree, an adda, or even a talking dead guy.

How could you do that to people? Nicolas asked through the necromantic link.

"I did what needed doing," Kagan said. "What no one else had the power or gumption to do. I led."

It was as Nicolas suspected. The answers didn't matter. Because what he needed—what he *truly* needed if he was to help Kagan atone for his sins—was the namocea. He needed to live Kagan's life. He needed to see through his eyes. He needed to know his true motivations. Motivations that Kagan would most certainly never reveal on his own.

"Power or gumption to do what?" Kaitlyn asked.

"You're being a touch on the dramatic side," Kagan said, ignoring her. "I protected the Three Kingdoms when no one else could. Nothing more."

"Zip it, zombie," Nicolas said.

"I am *not* a *zombie*," Kagan said. "Zombies are mindless automatons, I am—"

Nicolas silenced Kagan through the link.

"*You* are *quiet*, finally," Nicolas said.

Kaitlyn pulled away and faced Nicolas.

"I know you have some issues to work through with him," Kaitlyn said. "But what if he's right?"

"Kait, you don't understand. He—"

"Let's stop the *mansplaining* before it starts, okay? It doesn't matter what *we* think. It only matters what he thinks. If *he* felt justified…if he has a clear conscience…"

"Two things," Nicolas said. "One, you'd make one hell of a necromancer. But two, you're oversimplifying. Conscience is a great guide, sure. But lie to yourself long enough, and eventually you start believing your own lie, don't you?"

"And who's to say what's *truth* to begin with?"

"Now *that's* not something a good Catholic girl would ask."

"You're a pope on an alien planet who has a dead man as a personal valet. You could use a catechism refresher yourself."

Nicolas chuckled.

"Who tells these people what's right and wrong?" Kaitlyn asked. "Do they have a Ten Commandments?"

Nicolas sat quietly for a moment. He knew her well enough to know what she was *really* asking. Where was God with a capital-G in all of this? Jesus? Mary? The apostles? And didn't he have the same questions? His prayers had always been directed at Jesus. When he prayed, that is. But he never dreamed the first god who'd talk back would be someone else's.

"If you found out tomorrow there was no god, would you change the way you live?" Nicolas said. "The way you treat people? The way you decide whether or not to steal or kill? Would you suddenly become a shitty person because hell didn't exist?"

"Of course not," Kaitlyn said. "But don't you think you should get to know him a little better?"

"Does a genocidal despot get a free pass because he thought he was doing the right thing?"

"That's my point. Who are you to judge when you can't really know what's in his heart?"

"Necromancers can, most of the time."

"Then that's worse, isn't it? If you know he felt justified doing what he did, and you choose to ignore that because you have some personal beef with him, doesn't that make you worse? Doesn't that make you *willingly* blind instead of *accidentally* blind?"

Nicolas rubbed the back of his neck. Why couldn't he have experienced the namocea with Kagan like he did with everyone else he summoned? It would all be so much *easier* that way.

He rested his head against hers. "The one talent I have as a priest that allows me to see into the heart of another person...I can't use that on him, because I didn't summon him. Arin just...gave him to me. I assumed it'd be done the necromancer way—I'd live his life in a moment, see through his eyes, get to know him better than he knows himself."

"Maybe Arin has a reason for you to do it the old fashioned way—talking to him, asking questions. It's the way everyone *else* has to come to their conclusions about other people. Maybe *you're* the one who isn't getting the free pass this time."

Nicolas put his arms around her again.

"You and Siek Lamil really need to have a longer chat next time," Nicolas said.

Toby yelped as the carriage tipped toward the front, and Toridyn slid off the opposite bench.

"What the hell?" Nicolas said.

A string of swear words rose out of the night as Aelron climbed down from the driver's seat. Nicolas and Kaitlyn met him outside.

"Broke a festering axle!" Aelron yelled, pointing at the front of the wagon. "I'm sorry, Archmage. This carriage is finished."

"Dammit," Nicolas said.

He climbed out of the wagon and prayed this trip wouldn't get any worse.

Aelron swore once more. The carriage was finished. He wasn't sure how far they were from Caspardis, but he wasn't looking forward to walking there in any case.

"Can't we just...rig something up?" Nicolas said. "We could use parts from the trailer we're towing."

"No," Aelron said. "It's no good. Wheelbase is too narrow. Even if it wasn't, we don't have the right equipment.

"Let's not be hasty." Nicolas glanced around the sides of the road until his gaze fell on Kagan, who was looking through the carriage window. "There's our way. Dead Kagan, get over here."

Kagan climbed out of the wagon and sauntered to Nicolas's side.

"Can you lift the front of the wagon?" Nicolas asked.

Kagan took the wagon by the adda hitch, and lifted it like he was lifting a glass of water.

"There's your new axle," Nicolas said.

"Gonna be a bumpy ride," Aelron said.

"It's all we have."

"Is that...*appropriate*?" Kaitlyn asked.

Nicolas rubbed his neck again, but this time in frustration.

"You're just going to make him carry us because he *can*?" Kaitlyn said.

"He's the only tool we have right now."

"I suppose. It just doesn't...feel right."

Kaitlyn sat next to him on the edge of the carriage.

"He's been the center of my reality for the last year," Nicolas said. "Everything bad that happened to me—happened to the Three Kingdoms—is his fault. He did it. No one else. I know you think I'm just laying blame. But you can't imagine the suffering, Kait, and I'm not just talking about myself. Can you imagine if we tried to have a baby and..."

Aelron could tell it was a private conversation. But what better way to learn the truth of a person than to observe when they didn't know they should have their guard up?

He needed to know what this brother of his was truly made of. Aelron's instinct was to protect his family, no matter how rotten it had become. And for better or worse, Nicolas was *family*.

But the coin wanted him dead, and it was never a good idea to ignore the coin.

Kaitlyn rested a hand in Nicolas's lap.

"I understand," she said. "You're doing what you think is right. But I don't see much reflection going on. You don't talk to him. And when he speaks, you shut him up. If he's supposed to acknowledge the evil he did and grow from the experience, this isn't good for him. And I have a feeling this isn't good for you either. I know the axle thing is you solving a problem, but just consider it. You're a priest here, from what Toridyn tells me. So...act *priestly* toward him."

Nicolas smiled and some unspoken communication passed between them as they entered the carriage.

Kaitlyn cared for him. It was obvious. And she seemed strong. Savvy. But then it would take a strong, savvy person to stay with a man who usurped a throne.

The carriage ride was smoother than Aelron had expected. If he closed his eyes, he wouldn't be able to tell that Kagan had taken the place of the front wheels.

A group of people were blocking the road ahead, so Aelron drew the reins in.

"Help us, please!" one of them shouted.

The carriage stopped and Nicolas climbed out.

"Let us pass, please," Aelron said. "We've no help to offer."

Four people pulled hand-drawn wagons; a man in his thirties, a woman who wasn't much younger, and two children. They wore the desert dress of Religar. Mud covered them from top to bottom, and they shuffled rather than walked. They must have slept on the road in the torrential rain.

They were blocking the road. And from the looks of things, they were headed toward Caspardis as well.

Not a good idea to be Religarian in the Shandarian Union.

"I said let us pass—" Aelron began, but Nicolas gestured for him to stop.

"What do you need help with?" Nicolas asked.

"Please, sir," the man said. "We've no food. We haven't eaten in two days. They kicked us out of Shandar before the invasion started because of where we're from. We went to Blackwood, but we had to leave there too. There was no one left to help."

"What do you mean, *no one left*?" Aelron asked.

"The invaders destroyed the town," the man said. "And Shandar's a smoldering ruin now."

"Aelron," Nicolas said. "Let's get these people fed."

"Oh, thank you, sir!" the man said. "I'm Robert. This is my wife Philomena, and my children, little Robert and Mary."

"Not exactly *Religarian* names, are they?" Aelron said.

"They're *our* names, now, sir." He faced Nicolas. "And what may I call you?"

Aelron leaned in and whispered to Nicolas. "You can't trust these people. I don't know why they're *really* here, but it can't be for good."

Nicolas stepped forward with his hand out. "Nicolas."

As Nicolas extended his arm, Robert stumbled and Nicolas bent to help him. When he leaned forward, his chain of office slid out from beneath his scapular, and the large medallion in the shape of Arin's helm dangled back and forth.

"Holy one!" Robert said.

All four dropped to their knees on the muddy road.

"None of that, now," Nicolas said. "Please, stand up."

The refugees shared shocked expressions, but they did as he asked.

"Holy one, you have more important things to worry about than us," Robert said. "You must stop them!"

"I'm just Nicolas. I don't want to hear anyone call me *holy*, okay? Archmage is fine, if you need to use a title, but not *Holy One*."

"Of course, Archmage," Philomena said.

The rangers had taught Aelron of the unbroken line of Ardirian archmages at the Elysian Fortress, and how they lived lives of great privilege and power. And here was Nicolas asking to be called by his first name.

"Caspardis isn't far," Nicolas said. "Right, Tor?"

Toridyn nodded.

"You'll be safe there," Nicolas said. "We'll get you fed for the trip." He faced Aelron. "Can you start a fire?"

After an awkward pause, Aelron nodded and began unpacking the trailer.

It didn't take long to set up a cook pot on the roadside. Aelron used the wagon's tarp as a makeshift roof to keep the fire dry, and he cooked up a pot of beans they'd gotten off the Shandarian soldiers. Nicolas made sure the refugees ate their fill before anyone else took a bite.

Kaitlyn and Philomena were getting along as if they were old friends.

After the meal, Nicolas helped Robert and the others load their things onto the wagon. Philomena did more staring than loading, though whether she was pleasantly surprised or appalled, Aelron couldn't tell. Probably the latter. Just the thought of an archmage doing manual labor made Aelron feel strange. Either way, it didn't take long to get everyone settled in the carriage.

When they'd finished loading, Nicolas joined Aelron and Kaitlyn on the driver's rooftop seat, and Aelron got the carriage back on its way to Caspardis.

They traveled several miles before Aelron broke the silence.

"This isn't a good idea," Aelron said.

"They'll never make it to safety without us," Nicolas said.

"I understand the priestly charity. But that's not what I was talking about. Even if you look past the fact they're foreigners of questionable origin, we've broken an axle already. This carriage wasn't made for carrying this many people."

Kaitlyn had been chatting with Philomena through a small, sliding porthole on the carriage top. Nicolas leaned back and stared down into the cabin.

"Everyone okay down there?" Nicolas asked.

The dog let out a howl. It seemed happy enough. As happy as a dog missing two legs could be, at least.

"A cichlos," Robert said. "I'd heard tales, but I've never met one. Now I can say I have a cichlos friend."

"Roger that," Toridyn yelled. "Everything's ducky down here!"

"Seriously?" Kaitlyn asked, looking at Nicolas. "You spoke like Rambo trapped in a fifties sitcom when you were here? Do you even *know* any soldiers?"

Aelron didn't even understand some of the words, much less the order in which they were used.

Nicolas smiled and shrugged.

The carriage creaked, and before Aelron could steady himself, the world did a somersault.

Robert yelled.

Aelron landed next to Nicolas, missing his face by scant inches, placing him closer to the wagon than Nicolas. This wasn't good.

The Arinwool in Aelron's pocket heated up, and something rebounded off of it. Someone must have tried using magic on him.

The adda hitch snapped, and the adda scattered into the field to the north.

Nicolas spun and grabbed Aelron by the wrist. A moment later, Aelron felt himself being dragged out into the field with Nicolas behind the adda, leaving a wake of mud behind them.

After a few near misses between dwarf trees and Aelron's tail bone, the adda stopped.

Nicolas dusted himself off and stood.

Aelron glanced back at the carriage.

It was all but demolished, and the wagon had rolled over, dumping everything into the mud.

Nicolas ran to the carriage. "Kait!" he yelled. "Kait!"

"Here!"

"Is Toby with you?"

"Yeah. He's fine. A little scared."

"Toridyn and the others?"

Kaitlyn poked her head out through the side of the carriage, which was now the top. "Everyone's okay. I think Robert may have a broken leg, though."

It took them several minutes to climb out from the wreckage, and Aelron had to help Nicolas with Robert. When everyone was accounted for, Nicolas approached Aelron.

"What do you know about the Shandarian Rangers?" Nicolas asked.

Aelron did his best to suppress the surprise that wrapped around his spine and set his pulse racing.

"What's to know?" Aelron said. "They protect the union. They can't tell a falsehood."

"They can't *lie*. Huge difference."

"They have eyes like an adda-ki and ride the very same as mounts."

"And magi can't use magic on or against them."

Aelron looked away. This situation was complicated enough without his relationship to the rangers coming out.

Nicolas stepped closer. "What aren't you telling me?"

"About the rangers?"

"About *you*."

"We've only just met, Archmage."

"I'm not an idiot. I know the effect of Arinwool when I feel it."

Festering hells!

"What's Arinwool?" Aelron asked.

Nicolas rubbed his forehead. "My concern is to get these people *safely* to Caspardis. *All* of these people. If you do anything that runs counter to that purpose, I'll find the deepest, darkest pit at the Pinnacle and have them prepare a sleeping pallet for you."

That's the archmage I was waiting for.

Aelron raised his hands. "I'm just here to help."

"Nick," Kaitlyn said from the other side of the carriage. "I think you need to see this."

Nicolas and Aelron jogged around to Kaitlyn's side and found her kneeling next to a large hole in the dirt road. Dirt and rock were scattered away from the hole, as if something had burst its way out from underneath.

The hole was precisely were Kagan would have been standing at the time the carriage rolled.

"This is bizarre," Kaitlyn said. She pulled a small statue from the hole.

It was a statuette of a man. The man had a wicked grin on his face, and his arms were folded behind his back. It looked familiar...

Jacobson! It's the very same statue Jacobson had held!

"Why would someone bury this in the road?" Kaitlyn asked.

Nicolas took the statuette from her. His expression grew dark; eyes narrowing, mouth curling into a snarl. For a brief moment, he blinked and looked at Kaitlyn. "Do you want to..."

The expression returned.

"What?" Kaitlyn asked.

"Nothing," Nicolas said, his voice lower than before. "I have an idea for this wagon when Tor gets back with the adda."

"Are you okay?"

Nicolas nodded.

"Then you should check on Robert," Kaitlyn said.

"It's just a damned leg! He'll be okay!"

"Nicolas!" Kaitlyn stared at him with wide eyes.

Nicolas massaged his temples. Where the hell was this coming from?

"Sorry," Nicolas said. "Something's...I'm not sure what I was thinking. Must be the stress from everything."

Aelron followed Nicolas to where Robert was stretched out on a sleeping pallet next to the overturned wagon. He was grabbing his right ankle.

Nicolas knelt beside Robert. An expression of deep concentration formed on his face.

"It's not like me to say I told you so, but," Aelron said. "That carriage wasn't built for that much weight."

"I don't think the weight had anything to do with it," Nicolas said. He held the statuette up for Aelron to see.

"That's the second time I've seen one of those," Aelron said. "First one we found in a ditch."

"We?" Nicolas asked.

For the love of each and every one of the gods.

"Some people I used to travel with," Aelron said.

"Who's it supposed to be?" Nicolas asked as he turned the statue over in his hand.

"No idea. You thinking about using the wagon still?"

Nicolas nodded.

"I'll get Toridyn to help me flip it over," Aelron said.

The less talking I do...the less talking I'll do.

"No need," Nicolas said.

Kagan headed in the direction of the wagon. Nicolas must be sending him instead.

"How's my Robert?" Philomena asked.

"Pretty sure he has a busted ankle," Nicolas said.

"That poor man," Kaitlyn said. "Is there anything you can do?"

Nicolas shook his head. "I tried. I just don't know how. Mujahid's the healer, not me."

Mujahid. Aelron knew that name from somewhere. Though it *was* a common Religarian name, he supposed.

"We can put him on the wagon," Nicolas said.

"Was it the spirit warriors, Archmage?" Robert asked. "Like the army that took Blackwood? An army of the dead?"

"What did this army look like?" Nicolas asked. "Did you see them?"

"They looked like you and me," Robert said. "It's the way they came and went that gave up the lie. They appeared from out of the air, like the way a necromancer's penitent appears. Then they disappeared once the job was done."

A snap and loud crash came from the middle of the road. So much for the archmage's wagon idea. It was useless. And in the process of turning over, it had destroyed everything that wasn't made of metal. Except for a small hand cart at the rear.

"Looks like we're on foot," Aelron said. "Too bad for poor Robert. He was a decent guy."

"Was?" Nicolas asked. "He's sitting right here."

Aelron shrugged. "We can leave him some rations. Someone will probably be along before they run out."

"I know you're not suggesting we leave him behind because he can't walk," Kaitlyn said.

"Holy one, no!" Philomena yelled.

"That's not an option," Nicolas said.

"There's nothing for it," Aelron said. "You said yourself you can't heal him. He'll slow us down too much. You think that army is going to slow down because we've got a cripple along for the walk?"

"Hey now," Nicolas said. "You can't talk about people like that. He's a man, like you or me. A living, breathing man."

Aelron didn't understand. This wasn't a question of Robert's humanity. It was a question of getting to Caspardis as quickly as possible.

"But he's of absolutely no use to you," Aelron said. "None of these people are. We don't even know them."

"We don't know *you* either," Nicolas said. "And where I'm from, you don't abandon people because you don't find them *useful*. If I have to carry him all the way to Caspardis on my shoulders, that's exactly what I'll do."

Kaitlyn smiled.

Aelron was at a loss for words. On the one hand, he didn't understand how Nicolas couldn't see the foolishness of this decision. Sometimes you had to leave people behind...people you cared for, even...for the betterment of all. But on the other hand, he had yet another of those *answers* he was seeking.

An archmage who doesn't want power, accepts he doesn't know everything, and shows compassion when it isn't politically convenient.

But the coin wanted him dead.

Toridyn jogged over from the wreck.

"Slow down, amigo," Toridyn said. "Aelron may have the compassion of a feral crag spider—"

"Hey, now," Aelron said.

"But he's right about that army," Toridyn said. "Now sit tight, and don't let your bed bucks bite."

"That's *sleep* tight," Nicolas said. "And it doesn't even fit the...never mind. What's your idea?"

"How quickly we forget," Toridyn said.

A haunting melody filled the space around them with soothing notes as Toridyn's penitent began to sing.

When the song ended, Robert grabbed his leg. His eyes were wide.

"The pain's gone!" Robert said. "I think I can walk, if I tried!"

Robert began to push himself up, and Philomena and Kaitlyn each took an arm to help. But Robert shrugged them off. In a moment, he was standing on his own and walking in a circle.

"I can't believe it!" Robert said.

"I know that feeling," Nicolas said. "But Tor, why didn't you just heal him yourself?"

Toridyn's eyes spun in a circle as his chest heaved with laughter. "Me? I can't carry a tuna in a bucket!"

"*Tune,* you goof," Nicolas said.

Robert tried to gather his sleeping pallet and satchel, but Nicolas stopped him.

"You've been through enough," Nicolas said. "Just carry your *self* for now. I'll get the rest."

Robert smiled, though it was clear the arrangement made him uncomfortable.

"Kagan," Nicolas said. "Gather anything from the wagon that's still useful and put it in the hand cart. I've got a new job for you."

"You were serious," Aelron said. It wasn't a question. "You were going to carry that man all the way to the gates of Caspardis. Why?"

Nicolas placed his hand on Aelron's shoulder. "I told you. He's a human being. We're not worth more than him just because we outnumber him." Nicolas pulled his chain of office out from behind his scapular. "And I'm not worth any more because of this damned chain. If we don't take care of each other, what does that make us?"

Nicolas squeezed Aelron's shoulder. He leaned over to pick up Robert's belongings, but Aelron stopped him.

"No," Aelron said. "I've got that."

Nicolas smiled and nodded, then caught up with Kaitlyn and Philomena.

Aelron picked Robert's pack off the ground and followed.

But the coin wants him dead.

CHAPTER FIFTEEN

[16]In the days of the Reestablishment of the Lords, Zafir Mukhtaar looked into the Abyss of Nehem and stepped over the threshold, becoming Zafir Lord Mukhtaar. [17]The world trembled as he emerged, burying the nearby tribesmen in salt and sand. [18]When the light shone forth from his eyes, the priests bowed and gave thanks, for Zubuxo had not abandoned them.

[19]And it came to pass that Shealynd appeared to Lord Mukhtaar and marked him. [20]He built her shrine and ascended with her to the heavens.
  - The Mukhtaar Chronicles, attributed to the prophet Habakku
    Reestablishment of the Lords 5:16-20

The "Abyss of Nehem" is likely metaphorical in nature. Nehem, one of the first thirteen priests, preached a message of self-knowledge and reflection. From this, we can conclude that Zafir's ascension took place after achieving a certain degree of enlightenment.

As for the dates of Lord Mukhtaar's reign, the Scrolls of Tal'mon set the dates from 1330 BCE to 1221 BCE.
  - Coteon of the Steppes, "The Mukhtaar Chronicles: Coteonic
    Commentaries" (circa 680 BCE)

The abyss is quite real. Nuuan and I located it some three hundred miles *northeast of Dar Saricon. It took more than a dozen penitents longer than a month to unseal the ancient temple complex. But the real challenge was keeping curious nomads away. In our ascended state, I estimate the same task would have taken less than a week.*

- Mujahid Mukhtaar, Private Commentaries, 45 CE

I t had been a long day on the road, and Nicolas was grateful to finally stop.

Aelron had run out of drinking water, so Kaitlyn had given him her water skin to use. She had a dizzy spell when she handed it to him, but Nicolas chalked it up to being tired from the road.

She wasn't the only one who was tired. Toridyn and the refugees had fallen asleep not far from the cook fire, which was casting an amber glow on the ring of boulders surrounding their camp.

Aelron, however, had gone off somewhere to hunt the wild boar that roamed about. He said they were easier to sneak up on at night, and no one had any objections. Why should they? Aelron was doing a great job of keeping everyone fed.

Kagan was walking a patrol around the perimeter of the camp, several hundred yards away, and Kaitlyn had volunteered to clean the cooking supplies. A few minutes after she disappeared around a boulder with the cooking implements, a strange set of images emerged from the necromantic link.

They were confusing—a side effect of Arin having summoned Kagan for him—but he got the general idea. Someone was trying to have a conversation with dead Kagan. But Kagan wasn't responding to the person's questions because Nicolas hadn't given him permission to speak.

Nicolas quickly scanned the camp. Toridyn and the refugees were all asleep, and Toby's nose was poking out from inside Toridyn's sleeping pallet. Kaitlyn was cleaning pots on the other side of the boulder.

That left Aelron.

Stay quiet, Nicolas sent through the necromantic link. *Don't let him know I'm coming.*

What the hell was Aelron up to? One minute he was the most straight-shooting guy on the planet, and the next he was a mako shark in a kiddie pool. But there was something familiar about him. Something about his eyes.

Nicolas stood and Toby's nose flared a few times. He started crawling, but Nicolas held his hand out. Toby got the idea and crawled back in to Toridyn's sleeping pallet. He didn't look happy about it, though.

Nicholas used the necromantic link to find Kagan.

No matter how much cover Nicolas had, his footsteps would be loud on the dry ground. Aelron would hear him coming before he got close enough to hear the conversation.

Nicolas paused for a moment. Did Kagan have a way of relaying what Aelron was saying? Even if he did, though, the imagery returning from the link had grown confusing since the wagon rolled over. It would be better to hear it with his own ears.

Nicolas had used necropotency in the past to lift objects and other people. Could he use it to lift himself?

Only one way to find out.

Nicolas began weaving a rope of necropotency, but abandoned the attempt. What would he attach the other end to? Besides, he needed some measure of control over this. All he needed was to get his feet an inch or two off the ground and the noise problem would be solved.

He wrapped himself in a bubble of energy and heaved upwards.

The ground was hard in this part of the Shandarian Union. At least that's what his shoulder blades told him when he landed on his back after doing a complete somersault.

A high-pitched whine came from behind.

Toby had crawled out of the sleeping pallet and was staring at him.

Maybe I need to control each foot independently.

It would be tricky, but it was worth a shot.

Nicolas pushed himself to his feet, opened his mind, and laid a platform of necropotency under each foot. He couldn't help smiling as he rose off the ground. Now he needed to walk.

"See Toby?" Nicolas whispered. "I know what I'm doing."

Toby wagged his tail twice and stopped. He wasn't convinced.

Nicolas took a step forward with his left foot.

Step, however, would imply a far greater degree of control than what Nicolas exercised. It wasn't so much a *step* as it was an uncontrollable slide with ever-increasing momentum and no possibility of recovery. Worse, his right foot was stuck where he'd left it.

Shit! Shit! Shit!

This was going to get real painful real fast if he didn't do something. But all he could do was release his grip on the necropotency.

He landed in front splits and rolled over in pain holding his groin.

Toby whined and laid his head on his front paws.

"Yeah, get a good laugh," Nicolas whispered.

This wasn't going to work. He had no idea how to lift himself in a controlled way. It wasn't the same as lifting something else. The physics of it was all wrong, like he was violating some fundamental law or something. He'd have to do this the old-fashioned way.

He told Toby to stay and set out in Kagan's direction, using the sparse dwarf trees for as much cover as he could get. He'd need to be careful. Erindor's night sky provided substantial ambient light, and only Nicolas's scapular was dark. His robes were white. Covered in mud, but white just the same.

The images from the necromantic link were scattered and confusing, but Nicolas concentrated. He needed information before he walked into something he couldn't handle.

An image of a child in danger, followed by an overwhelming sense of abandonment, made Nicolas pause for a minute. The pain was visceral. But it didn't make sense. Why would Kagan feel *abandoned*? Was he in danger?

Nicolas shook it off and crouched on his way to the next dwarf tree. He was close. He couldn't see them, but Aelron's baritone voice, subdued to a hoarse whisper, was impossible to miss.

"Why?" Aelron asked. "Don't you have anything to say for yourself?"

Kagan came into view. He was scanning the horizon.

Ignore me, Nicolas told him.

Aelron was right behind Kagan, gesturing furiously.

"Damn you," Aelron said. "How could you do it? Nicolas wouldn't abandon a crippled old man, but you send me away? And what of my birthright, old man? Did you give me so much as a second thought after I left?"

Send him away? Who the hell is this guy?

Something glinted near Aelron's waist. Aelron was holding a dull, chipped dagger the size of a large hunting knife behind Kagan's back.

Nicolas prepared to summon another penitent. But as he reached for ambient necropotency, there was little of it around. Enough to pull off a few simple tricks, maybe, but summoning a penitent was out of the question. He'd have to grant Kagan permission to cast if he needed to. Neither of them would be able to accomplish much, but combined they may be able to incapacitate Aelron.

"It's telling me to kill him," Aelron said. "Do you know *that*? Does *that* loosen your dead tongue, old man?"

Who is he talking about?

Aelron was bouncing something in his other hand. That damned coin again.

A confusing series of images erupted from the necromantic link, but Nicolas couldn't make anything out of them. All they shared in common was an overall sense of urgency. But Kagan wouldn't be fearful of Aelron, even if he knew about the dagger at his back. The blade would mark him up a bit, sure, but it wouldn't destroy him.

Aelron tossed the coin and flipped it onto his left wrist, which was holding the dagger at the back of Kagan's neck.

"See?" Aelron said. "The same thing. Over and over and over. I can't fight this much longer!"

A wave of necropotency emanated from Kagan, and he flew up and forward as if a bomb had exploded behind him.

Why the hell did he do that?

Aelron flipped the dagger into his hand blade-first, then launched it over his shoulder without looking.

The dagger dug into the dwarf tree next to Nicolas's face, pinning the hood of his robe, until the guard let it burrow no farther. Nicolas tried to step forward, but his robe was cut from thick cloth, and the dagger was firmly planted.

"You sneak like an adda carrying a desert nomad's belongings," Aelron said. "You'll be tempted to use magic. A word of advice...*don't*."

There wasn't a lot of time. Nicolas had to do something before Aelron closed the distance between them. A physical confrontation was out of the question. It was clear Aelron was a fighter. And a good one at that.

Nicolas caught himself weaving a net of necropotency until he remembered the incident with the wagon. If he cast the net at Aelron, it would rebound back onto him. He'd accomplish nothing.

There was nothing he could do but try to talk Aelron down.

"I don't know what's going on with you," Nicolas said, "but I know it doesn't have to be like this."

Aelron flipped the coin.

"Festering adda-ki!" Aelron yelled. "Twenty-seven tosses in a row!"

Aelron closed the coin in a tight fist and pounded it against his forehead several times, scrunching his face as if he were in pain. He opened his eyes and flipped it again.

When he slapped the coin onto his left wrist, his breath was ragged. A moment later, Aelron chuckled.

"I tried, friend," Aelron said. "I really did. I swear it on my honor. But the multiverse wants you dead for some reason. Any idea why?"

"All I know is there's some grade-A freaky shit going on here as usual. It wouldn't surprise me to find out something is manipulating that coin of yours."

Sweat beaded on Aelron's forehead. He paced. When he spoke, his voice broke, choking back a sob.

"You were going to carry that old man back there," Aelron said. "Why'd you have to do that? Why couldn't you be the man I'd envisioned? A man like Kagan, or worse."

Aelron pulled the dagger from the tree and held the blade to Nicolas's throat. His arm trembled, and Nicolas felt a drop of moisture form where the dagger touched.

"It doesn't have to be like this," Nicolas said.

As the blade's pressure increased against Nicolas's throat, Aelron yelled a guttural cry and pulled away.

"No," Aelron said. "Damn it all!"

Kaitlyn walked out from among the dwarf trees and Nicolas's stomach did a somersault.

"It's okay, Aelron," Kaitlyn said. "You don't need it."

"I don't *want* to," Aelron said. "I *have* to."

"I know. I've...seen."

"Something worse will happen."

Kaitlyn shrugged. "Maybe. But if it does, it has nothing to do with that coin."

What was she talking about? How could she know what Aelron wanted or didn't want to do?

"I've gone against it in the past," Aelron says. "It never ends well. Something bad always happens."

"And how many times have you listened only to have something bad happen anyway?" Kaitlyn asked.

Aelron turned his gaze from the balled fist holding the coin to Kaitlyn.

"Yes, I've seen," Kaitlyn said. "That coin doesn't control anything. Whatever is going to happen is going to happen."

Aelron shook his fist.

"This coin has saved my life in ways you wouldn't believe," Aelron said. "It kept me from entering a building that collapsed less than five minutes later. It told me to set a trap at my door that killed a man who was sent to assassinate me that same night. It led me to *you*, Nicolas. And in no uncertain terms, it's told me one singular thing about you from the moment we met. Kill him! Don't let him get any farther! And if you don't believe me, I'll show you."

Aelron opened his fist and tossed the coin. When he saw the result, he laughed.

"Adda-ki," Aelron said. "For the twenty-ninth time. Let me translate that for you. *Adda-ki* means *kill the archmage*. Tell me, how is it possible for a fair coin to land the same way twenty-nine times in a row? It isn't. That's how."

Aelron raised the dagger to Nicolas's throat.

"No," Kaitlyn said. "Please."

A change came over Aelron's face, like the look a person gets when they've made a decision they can't be talked out of.

Nicolas tensed. If he was going to try something, it would have to be soon.

Kaitlyn gave him a look that was clear; *Not yet.*

Aelron flipped the dagger until he held it by the blade.

"They told me it was impractical to learn how to throw these," Aelron said. He tossed the dagger to his right, where it stuck in a tree next to Kagan, about ten feet away. "The secret's in the weight. I prefer mine handle-heavy. The extra weight takes some getting used to, though."

Aelron retrieved the dagger and tucked it into his cloak. He held the coin up for Kaitlyn to see. The moonlight reflected off it, creating silvery patches of light that danced from the ground to the surrounding trees as he spun it between his fingers.

"Do you have any idea how much *this* weighs?" Aelron asked, brandishing the coin in front of Kaitlyn's face. "Even when it's in another room, I *feel* it. Pressing down on me like the boot of a sadistic father."

Aelron stared down at the coin in his hand.

And I thought I had daddy issues.

"I understand what it's like," Kaitlyn said. She stepped forward, took Aelron's hand in hers, and looked at the coin it held. "The pressure builds and builds until you're certain the world will come crashing down around you if you don't give in. And by the time you finally flip that coin, you don't even care which side it lands on. You just want it over and done with."

Aelron looked up from the coin and into her eyes.

"You're not alone in this," Kaitlyn said.

"You have a *coin* of your own?" Aelron asked.

"I've worked with people who have the same…*weight* bearing down on them constantly. I've watched them get better. You don't have to live like this."

Aelron started to draw his hand back, but Kaitlyn held firm.

"Can I take a closer look?" Kaitlyn asked.

Aelron seemed reluctant at first, but he nodded. Kaitlyn took the coin and closed her hand around it.

"I think I know how this works," Kaitlin said. "A coin only has two sides. Tell me, Aelron, do you think we should camp for the night or keep going?"

Aelron's breathing grew heavy and he reached for Kaitlyn's hand, but she drew away.

"No," she said. "You don't need this. You just need to answer the question. I promise nothing bad will happen. We'll do whatever you suggest. What do you think we should do?"

"You don't understand," Aelron said. "If I don't—"

"Camp or keep going," Kaitlyn repeated as she stepped back.

Aelron turned away from Kaitlyn, and she gave Nicolas the same look. She clearly thought she could talk Aelron down, but Nicolas could see him clenching and unclenching his fists, over and over.

Nearly a minute passed before Aelron looked down and closed his eyes.

"Camp," Aelron said. "We're all tired. We need rest."

Aelron opened his eyes and looked around the small copse of trees, like he was expecting some unseen enemy to attack.

"This doesn't feel right," Aelron said.

Kaitlyn took his hand, placed the coin in his palm, and closed his fingers around it.

"You don't need this," Kaitlyn said.

With a yell, Aelron flung the coin out into the darkness.

"I hope you're right," Aelron said as he walked past Kaitlyn. "I hope I didn't just kill us all."

Contrary to what Nicolas expected, Kaitlyn seemed shocked. Isn't that what she'd planned?

Nicolas stepped away from the dwarf tree as Kagan rose from the ground and took a step toward Aelron.

Nicolas told him to stand down. Aelron had made his decision, and something told Nicolas he wouldn't go back on it. Besides, he could have killed Nicolas the first time he threw that dagger, but he didn't.

"What changed your mind?" Kaitlin asked. "I know it wasn't what I just said. That wouldn't have been enough for you to just throw it away like garbage."

Aelron stared into Nicolas's eyes, expression blank once more.

"It lied to me," Aelron said. "On the side of the road, where we met. It lied. It led me to believe you would be the source of great evil in this world. Well I *know* evil. You're not evil."

"I'm glad we had this little *come to Jesus* meeting and you saw the light and everything," Nicolas said, "but I can't have you traveling with people I love if you're gonna snap."

Aelron looked at Kaitlyn, who nodded in response.

"And what is *this* all about?" Nicolas asked, staring at Kaitlyn. "You've been talking like you know *him* better than you know *me*."

"I can't explain it," Kaitlyn said. "After he drank from my water skin, I started...*knowing* things about him. You need to hear what he has to say."

Kaitlyn *had* shared her water when Aelron's skin ran dry. Could this be what the cichlos were terrified of? Had she somehow *imbued* the water skin with magic?

"Do you remember what you were thinking the last time you held that water skin?" Nicolas asked.

"You were a babe when our father sent me away," Aelron said.

The water skin could wait. Did he hear what he *thought* he heard?

"Are you saying you're...my *brother*?" Nicolas asked.

"Aelron Ardirian," Aelron said. "Your *elder* brother. Kagan's firstborn."

Nicolas rubbed his forehead. If that were true... "That means, *you* should be archmage. Not me."

Aelron smiled, but there was a sadness to his eyes. "Therein lies my particular tale of woe. I don't have magic. A fact our father didn't handle very well. I was five years old when he sent us to live with the Shandarian Rangers because of it. At least, that's what the rangers told me. Our father didn't grant me the luxury of an explanation before sending us away."

"Us?" Nicolas asked. "I was told I was taken directly from the Pinnacle to…" *Maybe best to keep that close to my chest for now.* "To where I'm from."

"I was talking about our mother."

Nicolas's legs stiffened, and for a few moments his heart raced. He'd spent so much time dealing with everything—getting pulled to Erindor against his will, saving a world from a despotic religious leader who turned out to be his father—that he'd spent no time at all wondering about his mother. How could he have gone through all of this and never tried harder to find out? What kind of person was he?

"Where is she?" Nicolas asked. "*Who* is she?"

Aelron turned away. Nicolas must have touched a sore spot.

"I need to know," Nicolas said. "I just…need to know."

Aelron rubbed the back of his neck for a few moments, then faced Nicolas.

"I haven't told this story in…decades," Aelron said. "Our mother was the daughter of a Shandarian ambassador. She wasn't a magus, but she traveled to the Pinnacle with our grandfather once, and that's where she met our father. She joined me at the Elysian Fortress, but we weren't allowed to see each other because of my training. She wasn't supposed to be there at all, actually—women can't be spending time around a bunch of celibate men, you know—but they took her in as a courtesy to Kagan."

"What's the Elysian Fortress?" Kaitlyn asked.

"The mother house of the rangers," Aelron said. "North. In the Great Algidian Peaks. By rights, I should have returned to the Pinnacle twenty years ago, but we were cut off by the yellow dome."

"Is she still there?" Nicolas asked.

Aelron's face contorted. Nicolas knew the answer before he spoke.

"About a year after we arrived, she took ill," Aelron said. "They say they don't know what sickness it was. I'll spare you the details my brother rangers didn't spare me."

The pain was brutal and unexpected. Nicolas's heart ached the way it had when his dad died. His adoptive father. Not this shambling ex-tyrant zombie standing next to him.

The hope that his mother lived disintegrated. He'd never get to know her. More sin to lay at Kagan's feet. He was beginning to think he'd only scratched the surface of that man's depravity.

"What do you have to say for yourself?" Nicolas asked Kagan, who had sauntered up between them. "Is any of this true?"

"Every word," Kagan said. "*Most* every word, at least."

"And which part did he get wrong?"

"I didn't send them away because my son would never be a magus. I sent them away because I knew what I was about to do, and I didn't want them here when I did it. Something my mentor said...well, I inferred it wouldn't be safe. At the very least, the result would be unpredictable. I didn't want them around to reap the suffering I would sow. So I sent them to a place I knew the Barathosians couldn't touch."

"You're saying it was an act of kindness?" Nicolas asked.

"You were supposed to go with them too, Nicolas," Kagan said. "But when I sent for you, it was too late. You were already gone."

It was too much. The sociopath traveling with them turns out to be his brother. Their mother was sent away to be safe only to die alone. He'd never know her.

Kaitlyn put her hand on his arm.

"I'm twenty-one years old and I just learned my mother died thirty-nine years ago," Nicolas said. "Any idea how freaky that feels?"

Toridyn came up from behind Kaitlyn, holding and petting Toby.

"What's all the commotion?" Toridyn asked.

A cold breeze blew through the copse of trees, carrying with it the scent of a distant rain.

"Why would you say you're twenty-one?" Aelron asked. "That's not possible."

Nicolas considered telling the story. But brother or no, he didn't know this person.

"*My* mentor once told me time doesn't always behave," Nicolas said. "Let's leave it at that for now. Until we know each other better. But you don't look any more middle-aged than I do. How do *you* manage it?"

Aelron shook his head. "When I discovered who you are, and I saw that you looked no older than I do, I started hoping *you* would have the answer to that question. It was another reason the rangers cast me out. I was too different for them."

Nicolas nodded.

Wait. Mentor.

What was it Kagan had said? Something about having a mentor around the time the barrier went up? Mujahid never mentioned anything about that!

"Tell me about this mentor of yours." Nicolas said.

"Kindly old man," Kagan said. "He'd come across the ocean with the Barathosians. Once he discovered how *open* to his knowledge I was, he decided to stay. He was surprised I'd discovered so much about vitapotency on my own, so he helped me perfect the rest. His name was Azazel. I knew much, but I had been going about it all wrong. And…"

Nicolas waited for words that never came. "Any day now."

Kagan remained frozen in place. Nicolas turned inward to the necromantic link, but every message he inserted vanished like water down a drain. He nudged Kagan with his elbow and the dead man looked up.

"I was about to tell you," Kagan said, "that you were supposed to go with them. But when I sent for you, it was too late. You were already gone."

Nicolas narrowed his eyes. "You said that already."

"I did?"

Great. My penitent has dementia now.

"You were talking about Azazel one minute, then you froze like Han Solo in carbonite the next."

"You realize he has no idea what you're talking about, right?" Kaitlyn said.

"Azazel?" Kagan said. "That's a name I haven't heard in…"

Kagan froze again.

"Can somebody tell me why my penitent has Alzheimer's?" Nicolas said.

"You were supposed to go with them," Kagan said. "But—"

"When you sent for me, I was already gone," Nicolas said.

"You knew?"

"Oh *hell* no."

What in blazes was going on with Kagan? Confusing images. Freezing at the name of…

Wait a minute.

"Azazel," Nicolas said. "Isn't that a demon's name, Kait?"

"Azazel?" Kagan said. "That's a name I haven't heard in…"

"There he goes again," Aelron said.

"I think it is," Kaitlyn said.

"...kindly old man. He came across the ocean with the Barathosians. Once he discovered..."

"I think you broke dead Kagan," Toridyn said, flicking Kagan's shoulder with his over-sized finger.

"The Old Testament uses the word a couple times," Nicolas said. "But not as a demon, now that I think about it. The usage is a bit confusing there. But when dad made me read the Book of Enoch, it was used as the name of a fallen angel. In fact, if I remember correctly, Enoch says Azazel was responsible for damned near every evil ever committed."

"Charming," Kaitlyn said.

Aelron sniffed. "This Enoch of yours would reevaluate Azazel's contribution to evil if he knew about Kagan."

"I don't like this," Nicolas said. "If I can move between worlds—"

"You do *what*?" Aelron asked.

"Then it stands to reason I'm not the only one," Nicolas said.

"Wait," Kaitlyn said. "You're saying you think a demon flits back and forth between Earth and here?"

"It can't be a coincidence," Nicolas said. "I've seen too many things here that are similar."

"Of course you have," Kaitlyn said. "They're just as human here as we are."

"No, you don't get what I'm saying. How do you explain a baroque cathedral under a mountain in the Shandarian Union?"

Kaitlyn pursed her lips.

"Mujahid's pad," Nicolas said. "Looked like Saint Peter's Basilica. Now how do you explain that? They don't have our religions here, but they build a structure based on Roman mythology? They have to have gotten it from someplace."

"Or *we* did." Kaitlyn said.

Nicolas had once said the same thing to Mujahid. Did Erindor get the symbolism from Earth, or did Earth get it from Erindor?

"Either way," Nicolas said. "If there's a fallen angel involved in this, we have bigger problems than the Barathosians."

Nicolas put his hands on top of his head.

"It's too much, Kait. Just one of these problems is enough to make me lose sleep, and we've got like...twenty-seven now."

"And we'll solve them all," Kaitlyn said. "One at a time."

Nicolas exhaled through pursed lips. "You're right. Let's get back to camp and get these people to Caspardis. The sooner we get there, the sooner we can see about the city's defense. You never told me what you did to that water skin, by the way."

"I don't know what I did," Kaitlyn said. "I can't even tell you what I was thinking the last time I held it."

"I reckon the cichlos were right to give us the boot."

"You *reckon*?" Kaitlyn asked. "Twenty years in Texas and you never *reckoned* anything, now you're all cowboy?"

"I'm bringing culture to the heathen," Nicolas said with a smirk. He faced Aelron. "What about you? You planning on killing anyone else tonight?"

Aelron shrugged. "I usually don't *plan* on it."

"That's good enough for me." Nicolas shook his head. "I have a brother. Go figure. Every time I come to this damned world, I end up with a new family member."

"Let's get our dead father back to the refugees before his demon friend makes him go on another genocidal rampage," Aelron said.

"You see?" Nicolas said. "It's statements like *that* the nuns didn't prepare me for."

Kaitlyn took his hand and they walked back to camp.

CHAPTER SIXTEEN

Of all the edifices known to have been constructed with magic, there is none more mysterious than the Mukhtaar Estate. Ahmed Lord Mukhtaar was said to have been deeply troubled by it, finding something new—a room, an object (unsubstantiated rumors even claim a person)—every time he returned.
  - Coteon of the Steppes, "The Mukhtaar Chronicles: Coteonic Commentaries" (circa 680 BCE)

Mujahid channeled power into his eyes, and the narrow tunnel winding through the underbelly of the Algidian mountains came into sharp focus. The porous stone of the tunnel walls seeped moisture. Coffins that once lined the passage in neat alcoves lay strewn about, spilling bones this way and that. His vision came to an abrupt end a hundred feet ahead, stopping at the limit of the light spell he'd cast on his eyes.

He could sense the portal he sought in the distance, like the nagging presence of another person in a dark room.

Judging by the debris in the tunnel and lack of any tracks, it was doubtful the Barathosians had discovered it yet. There should be time to unseal the estate and relocate the portal.

Mujahid touched the sigil pouch at his waist to comfort himself. Even if the Barathosians detected the portal, they'd have to defeat his sigil magic to access it.

Mujahid stopped when he spotted a smooth, flat stone—about the size of his palm, though much thinner—resting against the tunnel wall. A flood of emotion caught him off guard.

Mordryn had always enjoyed playing games with him when she was here, and this stone was the result of one such game. He'd asked if she'd always love him. She'd responded by tossing a stone over her shoulder, stating if it came to rest leaning against the wall, that would prove her undying love.

And so it did.

There it remained to this day, through decades of quakes. He'd tried to move it himself once, but no strength or power he had in his possession could dislodge it.

Do you love me still, Mordryn, wherever you are? Do you think of me with longing or regret?

Mujahid turned away from the stone and kept walking. After all, she'd turned away from him.

The tunnel widened into a ramp, and he descended into the small settlement of Paradise Minor, which was a massive circular cavern, approximately one hundred yards in diameter. The entrance to the Mukhtaar Estate would be behind a cube of rock, on the other side of the cavern, beyond the ruined merchant stalls, beyond the area they'd once set aside as an infirmary.

When last Mujahid was here, he and Nicolas had been in a great deal of haste. Pinnacle Guard had invaded—with the help of some traitor within the clan whom Mujahid had yet to identify. The destruction of the Orb of Power burned in his memory, and the fumes from the burning vendor stalls still stung his nostrils. But he wasn't prepared for the wave of necropotency that swept over him as he walked into the ruined settlement.

Death was everywhere.

Burned corpses—preserved in the dry, cool atmosphere under the mountain—littered the massive, circular cavern. The Council magi and

Pinnacle Guard had slaughtered hundreds of innocents to retrieve Nicolas for Kagan's nefarious purposes.

A familiar glint of metal drew his attention to the frame of a burned-out merchant stall to his right. It was the merchant stall where little Geoffrey, a boy no more than seven years old, once played while his father worked. Mujahid peered around the side of the frame and had to close his eyes.

Charred remains clutched a tiny ball in arms outstretched in a pugilistic pose.

Gods no.

It had to be Geoffrey. He was the only child in Paradise Minor — another unintended consequence of Kagan's barrier.

Mujahid couldn't leave the boy here like this. It may not be possible to give him a proper burial, but at least he could perform the purification.

He ignited the symbol of ascension and cast the energized skull symbol into the child's corpse.

The symbol rebounded into Mujahid's mind and he smiled. There would be no purification necessary for the child. He was beyond Zubuxo's power now, having moved on to the Plane of Peace.

But how many others awaited a purification he didn't have time to offer? He'd have to return with more priests, once he'd relocated the portal to the estate.

I will give you rest, brethren. I vow it.

He left the burned-out stalls and charred corpses behind and hurried toward the only thing that mattered here anymore; a cube of vitrified rock, ten feet on each side, guarding the passage to the portal. He'd created that cube to make the entrance to the estate impenetrable when he and Nicolas fled the caverns.

Mujahid ignited the symbol of ascension and wove the symbols for water and fire together. This was going to take considerable power, but there was no shortage of necropotency here. He had the Council of Magi to thank for that.

Alone, the symbol of fire was used for cremation of bodies. Alone, the symbol of water was used for...well, what water was always used for, in quantities both great and small. But combined — a feat only a Mukhtaar Lord could accomplish — they could liquefy solid rock and forge it whole once more.

He cast the combined symbols forward into the vitrified rock and became a conduit of power.

The heat struck him long before any visual change occurred. The rock glowed, first a dull red, then a bright orange, until it radiated white hot and flowed like viscous lava.

Mujahid channeled necropotency around the rock to guide it away from the tunnel, until a bright yellow stream formed and flowed along the side of the cavern wall.

When the last of the rock melted and flowed away, Mujahid cast the symbol of water at the cavern floor and stepped back as steam filled the tunnel. He may have guided the molten rock away, but the ground would melt the soles of his boots if he didn't cool it down.

As the steam faded, Mujahid stepped back in surprise and ignited the symbol of ascension.

He wasn't alone.

A small figure stepped out of the dissipating steam from a place no human should have been. A place closed off behind tons of rock.

A diminutive man, no more than four feet tall, in bright, multicolored patchwork robes.

"Lord Mujahid," Digby said as he bowed at the waist. "What a most expected *non*-surprise."

Mujahid gaped. "Where were you? And where's Nuuan?"

Digby waved his hands in a placating gesture.

"Both are interesting questions, no doubt," Digby said. "And both are equally impossible to answer. Other than to say *here* and *there*, though I'm sure that's not a very satisfying answer."

Mujahid liked Digby, but he and Nuuan had been missing for months since vanishing from within a cyclone of death and slaughter outside the walls of Rotham-on-Orm. An explanation was in order.

"Nuuan is missing precisely when I need him most," Mujahid said. "I would know why and how!"

"Time is not on our side, Lord Mukhtaar. Nuuan cannot help both you and the girl simultaneously. Not yet."

"What girl?"

"Kaitlyn, of course."

What? How did Nuuan know about Kaitlyn? What in the festering hells was he up to?

"I must speak with him," Mujahid said.

"In due time. Kaitlyn is his sacred charge. He must attend to her first. All else comes second to that. The goddess cannot intervene directly." Digby shook his head. "Oh dear. I've likely said too much."

Heat rose in Mujahid's face.

"What does that mean?" Mujahid asked. "And how did you get in here? That rock was mystically sealed."

"Yours isn't the only entrance, Lord Mujahid," Digby said.

"Impossible."

Digby spread his arms and bowed. "Behold the impossible."

Mujahid ignored the bow and shoved past Digby, toward the wall that concealed the portal. He channeled power into the sigil pouch at his waist and the wall vanished. What remained was a pitch-black mystical field that filled the space within a door-sized archway. The symbol of ascension—a levitating person in meditative pose emanating rays of light from their eyes—burned at the top of the arch, indicating its destination was the Mukhtaar Estate.

At least he hasn't manipulated the portal. But how in the hells did he get in here?

Mujahid stepped through the portal beneath the archway and rematerialized in front of the estate.

The familiar gold and black scroll work decorating the palatial estate, reflected the light from the multicolored orbs floating within the cavern. He climbed the wide marble steps, past the undead guards in the shadow of Zubuxo's statue, to a small entrance embedded within the middle of three monolithic doors at the top of the steps. A door within a door.

Footfalls behind told him Digby had followed.

"I need to visit the crypt before I relocate the portal," Mujahid said. "You dodged my question adroitly, by the way."

"And which question would that be, Lord Mukhtaar. There were so many."

Mujahid narrowed his eyes.

"What did you mean by *sacred charge*?" Mujahid asked. "What does Nuuan have to do with Kaitlyn, and how is he *helping* her?"

Digby looked up at Mujahid without raising his head.

"Knowledge in the absence of wisdom is a dangerous thing," Digby said. "I understand you're fond of that saying. And well you should be."

"*What...did...you...mean?*" Mujahid said, enunciating every syllable. He wouldn't let the little man wriggle his way out of this again.

"Very well," Digby said. "Nuuan has waited a long time for Kaitlyn's arrival. At Mordryn's request."

Mujahid had to press his hand against the door jam to keep himself standing.

"Did you say *Mordryn*?" Mujahid asked.

Digby walked under Mujahid's arm and made a show of ducking, though he didn't need to. He walked toward the staircase leading up into the higher levels of the Mukhtaar Estate.

"You have a guest in your chambers who can shed light on recent events," Digby said. He climbed the stairs without looking back.

Mujahid's stomach clenched. The crypt could wait.

Not only had Mordryn left without warning or provocation, but she had also conspired with Nuuan in the process.

His pulse, which had been racing with anticipation and urgency earlier, slowed. His breathing became shallow.

How could Mordryn have known anything of Kaitlyn? Even if Mordryn could somehow travel between Erindor and Earth, she disappeared forty years ago—twenty years before Kaitlyn's birth.

In a daze, Mujahid climbed to the fourth level of the estate and approached the two intricately carved wooden doors leading to his chambers.

Digby stopped and gestured for Mujahid to open the door.

"These *are* your private chambers," Digby said. "It would be rude of me to barge in ahead of you."

Mujahid stared at the door, but his eyes were focused beyond it at no definite point.

"Lord Mujahid?" Digby asked.

Mujahid pushed the door open, revealing the large windows on the other side of his chambers that opened out upon the floating lights in the cavern surrounding the estate. He turned toward the bed he hadn't slept in for more than a year and almost didn't notice a person sitting on its edge.

His eyes refused to believe what was right before him.

"Hello, Mujahid," Mordryn said. "It's been a long time."

CHAPTERSEVENTEEN

Orbs of power are among the rarest of rare objects of power in the multiverse. Rarer still are the molds in which they were forged. Oh the divine power they must contain! They are the very archetype of Orb of Power. The final state of perfection the Orb of Power strives to achieve, just as every other object in the multiverse strives toward its own incarnation of perfection.

- Coteon of the Steppes, "The Mukhtaar Chronicles: Coteonic Commentaries" (circa 680 BCE)

Caspardis was the last place on Erindor Nicolas ever wanted to see again, but there it was, looming over him at the end of the road. Armored guards walked among flags of Caspardis—a cat's eye on a red field—that flew at regular intervals along the crenelated, sandstone parapets. Something glinted in the shadow beneath the city's arched sandstone entrance. The portcullis was down!

Why is the city still on lock down?

Kagan, who was pulling a hand-drawn wagon behind the group, had said it meant Caspardis was either keeping something in or keeping something out. Had the Barathosians tried to attack already?

A gust of cold wind brought the smell of the lake to Nicolas's nose, and he suppressed a chill. If the sight of the Caspardis flag didn't bring back bad memories, the smell of dead fish, slaughter houses, and tanneries certainly did.

The brisk wind carried with it the sound of voices.

Robert and Philomena were arguing with the gate guards, but the guards didn't seem interested in opening that portcullis any time soon.

Nicolas would have to do something about that. There was little time to waste.

As he stepped forward, the statuette he'd found on the road poked into his leg, so he pulled it out of his pocket and stared at it. It was a happy little figurine, smiling and clasping its hands.

A lot happier than Caspardis should be.

His mood grew dark, and he forgot why he'd taken a step.

I should level the city. I should summon another penitent, fight my way to the magistrate's court, and slaughter everyone there.

It was less than they deserved. He wanted them to suffer. And the more he stared at the smiling figure the more pain he wanted them to feel.

He needed the gate opened. Wasn't that reason enough to attack? To slaughter? To force them into submission the way they'd forced him? Maybe he should treat them the way the argram once treated humans…pulling their limbs off and—

Someone slapped the figurine from his hand. Aelron. His big brother.

"Hey!" Nicolas said. His mood improved, but he was still shocked by Aelron's reaction.

"You'd have done the same if you were looking in a mirror," Aelron said.

"What do you mean?"

"That look on your face," Aelron said. "You were *snarling*. And it gets worse every time you touch that thing."

Nicolas glanced at the figurine, which was laying in the dirt at his feet. Was it an object of power of some sort? Was he witnessing another case of something being *imbued* by an enchanter?

"The things I was thinking…they weren't like me," Nicolas said. "Whatever that statue is, I don't think anyone should touch it for now."

"It's in the dirt. Maybe that's where it should stay."

"No. If it has the power to change someone's personality, I can't risk some innocent person finding it. Kagan, hand me Robert's pack."

Kagan lowered the wagon, retrieved Robert's large green rucksack and handed it to Nicolas.

After some rummaging, Nicolas emptied the contents of a hide satchel into the pack and knelt over the figurine. With great care, he placed the open end of the satchel around the figurine and picked it up, tightening the satchel around it.

Just like cleaning up after Toby.

"I think this should do it," Nicolas said. "If this was imbued, then maybe it doesn't work unless someone's touching it."

"Let's hope so," Aelron said. "You're the only decent person I know. If *you* change, I might as well just give up on humankind right now."

Nicolas chuckled and started walking toward the gate. Aelron followed.

"There's lots of decent people," Nicolas said. "But decent people aren't immune to doing bad things from time to time."

"You excuse sin with such alacrity?"

Nicolas shrugged. "My dad taught me that things are different when you make an effort to look through someone else's eyes."

"I didn't think he had it in him."

It took Nicolas a moment to realize what Aelron was saying.

"Not Kagan," Nicolas said. "My *adoptive* father. Back home. I'll tell you about him some day."

"Sounds like a decent man," Aelron said.

Nicolas smiled.

His mood returned to normal after the brief exchange with Aelron. It was strange having a brother. Sure, their relationship had a long way to go, but they'd made a start. There was already an unspoken bond between them. He could feel it.

Nicolas looked at the gates of Caspardis again.

What happened to him there no longer mattered. He was the archmage now. If there was anything he could do to help them defend themselves, it was his duty to do so.

Kaitlyn approached with Toridyn, waving her arms as she spoke.

"They're not letting us in," Kaitlyn said. "Something about a hunt for an escaped prisoner."

"They can't open the gate and watch us enter?" Nicolas asked. "I don't care if they search us, but we need to get in. Maybe this will help."

Nicolas pulled his chain of office out of his robes and made sure it was visible.

A guard stood inside the portcullis, watching Robert and Philomena like an old man watching teenagers on his front lawn.

Nicolas marched up to the gate and faced the guard. He was young, not much older than Nicolas.

"We need to get these people into the city," Nicolas said. "Quickly."

"As I told the lady *and* the other two, the city's closed," the guard said. "Trust me, friend, you don't want to enter. The Shandarian Rangers lost track of somebody."

Aelron turned away from the wall.

"You'll be safe if you go around the north side," the guard said. "Marauders won't come this close to the city."

Nicolas held up his chain. "I really need you to open that gate."

The guard glanced at the chain, then back at Nicolas. "That supposed to mean something to me?"

"Kind of what I was hoping," Nicolas said.

"Sorry, mate."

"Don't suppose it would help if I told you I'm the archmage."

"Something we seem to agree on."

Nicolas stepped a few feet away from the gate, and Kaitlyn and Aelron joined him.

"Don't you have other ways of opening that gate?" Aelron asked.

"I'm trying to *save* lives, not take them," Nicolas said.

Nicolas shook his head. Isn't that what Mujahid had tried to teach him right from the beginning? That's why he'd gotten so upset when he'd had to banish his own friend because of Nicolas's incompetence.

Wait! That's it!

"Kait, that trick you pulled on me after you Awakened…Do you think you could repeat it? If the other guards think one of their *own* opened the gate for us, it'll be less likely to turn into a fight."

Kaitlyn shrugged. "Maybe. I'm not entirely sure how I did it the first time. It just sort of came to me."

"When I use my power," Nicolas said, "I sometimes have to make images in my mind that represent what I want. Like metaphors, in a way. When I subdue a penitent, I create an image of a dog on a leash, or a prisoner in shackles, and it just…*works*."

"I don't remember doing anything like that last time. But I suppose I could try."

Kaitlyn faced the guard behind the gate and Nicolas did the same.

The guard shook his head, rubbed his temple, and started *pulling* on the portcullis like a prisoner rattling a jail cell. There was no sensation of power emanating from Kaitlyn. No indication that she'd done anything at all.

"What in the six hells are you doing, Thomas?" a guard yelled from the wall. She disappeared for a moment and emerged next to the portcullis. She grabbed Thomas's arm and started pulling him away from the gate, but he wouldn't budge.

"I don't think that worked," Kaitlyn said.

"What image did you create?" Nicolas asked.

"You're *looking* at it."

Maybe he'd given her bad advice. Was Kaitlyn's magic somehow more *literal* than necromancy?

Thomas stepped away from the portcullis and disappeared behind the wall. The other guard followed, pulling at his arm. Thomas must have won the struggle, however, because the portcullis creaked then began to rise a moment later.

There had been no detectable flow of power. Whatever Kaitlyn was doing, it didn't work like necropotency at *all*. But he could see the concentration on her face.

Nicolas hurried the refugees through the gate. He had no idea how long Kaitlyn could maintain her control over Thomas. Or how long it would take the other guard to stop him.

When the last of the group entered Caspardis, Nicolas followed.

The city's west gate opened into a long, bustling plaza with three stone fountains forming a line down its center. It looked identical to the plaza he'd ridden through with the Rangers a year ago, but *that* plaza was on the other side of the city. Buildings of varying height, each one the same shade of sandstone as the city wall, towered over the fountains. Canvas tents of bright colors circled the center of the plaza, where people browsed merchants' wares. A cacophony of flutes, each one playing a different tune than the last, echoed through the plaza and grated on Nicolas's sense of good melody.

A wide boulevard opened across the plaza. And judging by the ominous circular fortress at the far end, he knew where it led; it was the fortress in which he'd been held prisoner.

"Hey!" The guard who had been struggling with Thomas ran toward them. "Turn around and walk out the way you came in!"

Nicolas stepped forward and she stopped, surprised.

"I'm Archmage Nicolas Murray. I'll answer any questions you have, but these people are under my protection. Whomever you're looking for, it's not them."

The guard glanced at Aelron, who turned away.

When she looked back at Nicolas, her gaze fell on his chain of office with wide eyes. She bowed at the waist and stammered.

"Archmage," she said.

"We can't leave that gate open for long," Nicolas whispered to Kaitlyn.

Kaitlyn nodded. A moment later, Thomas was lowering the portcullis.

When Thomas approached, Aelron pulled his hood up. Why was he acting so oddly?

"Who's in command at the wall?" Nicolas asked.

"I am, Holy One," the guard said. She bowed once more.

"Enough with the Holy..." Nicolas couldn't finish the sentence. It was no use. He didn't have time to correct everyone he spoke to. "And who are you?"

"Corporal Bennet," she said.

"You're in charge? You look my age."

And the closer Nicolas looked, the more he wondered if any of these guards were older than he was. He'd learned enough about combat in the past year to know complacency when he saw it. These guards leaned against the crenelations on the wall, speaking casually with one another. Most of them weren't even looking out at the surrounding countryside.

If Nicolas was able to breach the city's defense with nothing more than Kaitlyn playing mind games with a guard, how much easier would the Barathosians have it?

"Corporal," Nicolas said, "do you know about the Barathosians? Does that name mean anything to you?"

"My mother told me they were the reason the archmage Kagan made the Great Barrier in the sky."

Her mother spoke the truth, Kagan said.

Should I ask if her mother knew how many priests you had executed?

"They're back," Nicolas said. "And if Caspardis doesn't prepare for an attack *right now*, they'll appear outside that wall and tear it down."

The guard furrowed her brow. "That's not possible. That wall is solid Religarian sandstone."

"They have weapons that make yours look like..."

This would never work. He could stand here arguing with a low level city guardswoman—only to have to explain himself all over again to someone of higher rank—or he could talk to the one person who ran this city.

The man he'd hoped never to see again.

The magistrate who'd had him flogged and executed.

An idea started to form. Maybe there was a shortcut.

"Kagan," Nicolas said. "Does Caspardis know you're dead yet?"

Corporal Bennet's eyes widened.

"I would expect all of the Shandarian Union and Kingdom of Tildem to know by now," Kagan said. "It's *possible* Dar Rodon knows, though all formal communication was severed the moment I died. Information has flowed in one direction only—from Religar to the Pinnacle."

Nicolas swore. He'd hoped if the magistrate recognized Kagan, the man would be more likely to follow orders instead of waste time asking questions.

So much for that *idea.*

"Tor, I need you to do something for me," Nicolas said. "Stay here at the gate and keep an eye out for the Barathosians. Aelron, you too."

Aelron winced and looked around the plaza.

Why is he acting so jumpy?

"Where are *you* going?" Toridyn asked.

"That fortress beyond the plaza," Nicolas said. "The guy who runs this city is there. Kait, I'd feel better if you came with me. I don't like the thought of us getting separated in this place."

Kaitlyn shook her head. "I don't think that's a good idea."

Had Nicolas heard her correctly? He thought for certain she'd want to stay close to him.

"If the Barathosians *do* show up while you're away," Kaitlyn said, "Toridyn and I are the only magic users here. I may be new at this, but I can do more than one of those *spear carriers* on the wall."

As much as he didn't want to hear it, she was right. Caspardis needed all the help they could get.

"Keep an eye on him, will you?" Nicolas nodded toward Aelron, who was looking around the plaza like a secret service agent expecting an assassination attempt.

Kaitlyn grabbed his hand. "Stay safe."

"Corporal Bennet," Nicolas said. "I need you or one of your guards to take me to the magistrate. I'd rather not waste time convincing someone to let me into that fortress."

"Yes, Archmage," Corporal Bennet said. "Thomas! You're in charge until I get back."

Nicolas squeezed Kaitlyn's hand, then followed Corporal Bennet into the plaza.

"This isn't a walk, Corporal," Nicolas said. He jogged ahead of her. "Let's go!"

Nicolas cut a path through the crowd, narrowly avoiding the merchant tents. Corporal Bennet overtook him as they exited the plaza onto the main boulevard.

The fortress dominated the street beyond a large open courtyard.

Nicolas remembered that courtyard well.

More importantly, he remembered the two flogging posts at its center. The posts he'd been tied between and scourged, losing consciousness only to be awoken by buckets of water.

He pushed the thought out of his mind. There were larger concerns now. He took a quick inventory of his power and realized he had sufficient necropotency to summon a penitent. The knowledge gave him a boost of courage, but he cursed himself for not obtaining a *siborum* — the small portable sources of power used by cichlos necromancers — before leaving Aquonome.

Something tugged at the periphery of Nicolas's consciousness. Someone was watching him. He was certain of it. He wouldn't have even noticed if he hadn't focused on his necropotency.

But whoever or *whatever* it was, there was little he could do about it now.

They entered the sandy courtyard beneath the circular fortress, and Nicolas tried — and failed — to avoid looking at the two flogging posts. Each post had a metal hoop at the top, to which a guard would secure a prisoner's wrist before scourging him. The ground between the posts, though stained red by the blood of countless torture victims, was dry.

At least there hasn't been another scourging recently.

The fortress, with its crenelated parapet, had been falling into disrepair the last time Nicolas had seen it. Sandstone slabs had split and sections of it had been strewn about the courtyard. But now, those sections were either repaired or stood behind scaffolding, where construction workers smoothed grout and shaped stone, replacing the old larger slabs with sandstone bricks.

"Which way?" Nicolas asked. There was a simple stone door at the base of the fortress, but when the rangers marched him through it a year ago, it led to the dungeons.

"Here," Corporal Bennet said. She jogged toward a small stairway that led to a pair of wooden double doors.

The double doors led to a wide hallway with an arched ceiling. As far as he could tell, there were no guards. It seemed like this was little more than a government building, like every other government building he'd seen. Some facets were different. The walls were sandstone instead of drywall. And the ceilings were high and arched instead of low and flat. Sconces decorated the walls, but natural light flooded through wide doors spaced evenly apart along each side of the hall. Men and women in matching purple robes came and went through the doors, carrying documents and scrolls. Those who weren't dressed in purple sat on stone benches against the walls.

If it weren't for the Renaissance fair clothing and preindustrial architecture, Nicolas would think he was back at the Travis County Tax Assessor's building in Austin.

A guard emerged from one of the rooms ahead, and Corporal Bennet picked up her pace.

"Sergeant!" she called.

The man faced her and furrowed his brow.

"Bennet," he said. "For your sake, you'd better have caught her. That or you've come here to tell me I won the general's lottery."

"No sign of the escaped prisoner yet," Bennet said. "But there's something you need to hear."

"Who is—" the sergeant dropped to his knee. "Archmage."

These chains of office come in handy.

The sergeant glanced at Nicolas without lifting his head.

Oops!

"Rise," Nicolas said.

The sergeant stood.

"Can you take me to the magistrate?" Nicolas asked.

"Court began a few minutes ago," the sergeant said. "I'm not sure what the protocol is here."

"The enemy army my predecessor stopped before they could destroy us is back, and they're about to invade Caspardis," Nicolas said.

"Forget protocol," the sergeant said. "Court room is at the end of the hall."

They ran toward a pair of whitewashed wooden doors, ten feet high beneath a sandstone arch.

Two guards stood post on either side of the door, but they lodged no complaint when the sergeant pushed the doors open by their golden handles and stepped into the courtroom.

Nicolas couldn't say the same for the men sitting along a stone table on the other side of the room, however. One of the men, dressed in purple robes trimmed with gold fringes, stood and stared with wide eyes.

"This is a closed session!" the man said.

Nicolas had been here before. This was the very room he'd been sentenced to death in.

And the old man sitting at the center of the table, reading from a large, hidebound book, was the man who did the sentencing.

The feelings of anger and desire for retribution returned, but Nicolas pushed them aside. It was a good thing Aelron had slapped that figurine out of his hands. There was no telling what he'd have done if he were still under its influence.

As Nicolas walked down the long, downward-sloped center aisle toward the magistrate, the old man looked up from the book and stared at Nicolas.

"It can't be," he said.

"Magistrate," Nicolas said. "Is it safe to assume you recognize me?"

"But...*how*?"

"I'd like to say I don't hold any grudges, but that would be a lie."

"Forgive me, Archmage. I was doing my duty."

Nicolas chuckled. "Do you have any idea how much evil in the multiverse has been justified with those very same words?"

The magistrate blinked rapidly and stood.

Nicolas waved for him to be seated. "I didn't come here for your *hide*. I came here for your *help*."

The magistrate sat with a grunt and gestured toward the hidebound book.

"I'll help in any way the Shandarian Justice Protocols allow," the magistrate said.

"A very powerful enemy is about to ring your western doorbell," Nicolas said. "They destroyed Tur and they're on their way here. They have weapons that can punch through solid stone. They'll turn your city wall into rubble and march right on in. You're in charge of this city, right?"

"To an extent, yes."

"A large enough extent to order every guard you have to the walls? Not *on* the walls, mind you. The walls are as good as gone. In fact, you need to pull the guards *off* the wall as soon as possible. They need to be prepared for the street fighting that's going to happen.

The magistrate smiled and waved at a nearby guard. "Take the prisoner back to the cell. We'll reconvene shortly."

The guard saluted and escorted an elderly woman from the court room. When the door closed behind them, the magistrate spoke once more.

"Archmage, please. While your very presence here is enough to convince me that miracles are possible, I'm not dimwitted. I have scouts traveling all roads coming in and out of Caspardis for more than a hundred miles in each direction. If I needed a list of every man, woman, and child on the road between here and Blackwood, it would be placed in my hand within hours of requesting it. Caspardis is safe because there *is* no army on their way here. Now, if you'll excuse me, I have a city with a particularly high crime rate to govern."

"I'm the archmage," Nicolas said. "Does that mean *nothing* to you?"

"Certainly," the magistrate said. "I have the utmost respect for your position as shepherd of humankind. And when you become the duly elected Chancellor of the Shandarian Union, I'll be more than happy to take orders from you on secular matters. Until then, please confine your concerns to *religion* and leave state matters in the hands of state officials."

Nicolas took a deep breath. Frustration was clouding his thoughts when he needed clear thinking the most.

Kagan, why isn't the magistrate following my orders?

Why should he? He answers to the Chancellor, not you.

And the Chancellor answers to me, right?

Of course not, Kagan said. *You're the archmage.*

Then would you kindly tell me what authority I do have? How did you get everyone to do what you needed them to do?

Forging the words of a god was particularly convincing.

This was getting him nowhere. What good was being the *pope* of a new world if —

That's it! The pope!

Popes throughout history wielded two of the most powerful political weapons of all; interdict and excommunication. If a king refused a pope's request, interdict would prohibit priests from performing the sacraments in that king's country. And if the king remained stubborn, the pope would threaten excommunication.

And no one liked the idea of burning in hell, particularly a bunch of rich men who'd grown accustomed to their lifestyle.

I do control the religious orders and temples, don't I?

You do, Kagan said.

"Magistrate," Nicolas said. When the old man looked up, Nicolas turned and started walking back up the sloped aisle. "You *will* order your men to the walls, and you will do it *within the hour*."

"I've already told you—"

"And if you do not, I will close every temple in the Shandarian Union effective immediately. I will recall the Orders to the Pinnacle and expel the Shandarian ambassador. I'll leave it to you to explain the reasons to your chancellor."

Nicolas left the room and Corporal Bennet caught up to him.

"Are you really going to close the temples?" Corporal Bennet asked.

Nicolas glanced at her. She was staring at him.

"Is the magistrate a religious man?" Nicolas asked.

"Very."

"Then you've got nothing to worry about."

Nicolas walked back out into the courtyard with Corporal Bennet behind him. It was time to head back to the wall.

By the time Nicolas and Corporal Bennet returned to the west wall, three detachments of soldiers stood in the plaza in formations of six columns each.

Fortunately, the magistrate had taken Nicolas's threat seriously. Nicolas had no idea how he would have gone about closing the temples had the magistrate called his bluff, but at the very least it would have involved a quick trip back to the Pinnacle to chat with Tithian.

Thoughts of Tithian reminded him of the topic of their last conversation.

Protoforge fragments. Tithian was supposed to be testing them for use in the war effort. Nicolas offered a silent prayer to Arin that Tithian was correct and the fragments would help.

Realization struck him.

Did I just do that? Did I just pray to Arin?

"Nick!" Kaitlyn called from the wall. Toby followed her on his leash.

Nicolas was grateful for the interruption. He didn't want to deal with that particular theological quandary yet.

She hurried down the stair on the inner side of the wall.

He caught a glimpse of Toridyn on the wall, and the necromantic link told him Kagan was about thirty yards to his left. But where was Aelron?

Nicolas took a look through the portcullis that served as the city's western gate.

Nothing but a dirt road heading toward the horizon.

"Looks like everything went well," Kaitlyn said, nodding toward the soldiers.

"There was some give and take," Nicolas said. He glanced back up at the wall. "Where's Aelron?"

"I don't know. He mumbled something about being watched or followed, then ran off."

Watched?

When Nicolas approached the fortress earlier, he'd felt like someone was watching him too.

"He can take care of himself, I suppose," Nicolas said.

"And I've felt this strange *presence* around me," Kaitlyn said. "It's hard to describe, but it's like someone's following me too. Or *watching* me."

"A *presence?*"

A collective gasp went up among the soldiers on top of the wall.

"Prepare for attack!" a soldier yelled as he ran down the stair.

What?

Nicolas looked back through the portcullis and his face grew cold.

The western horizon was no longer visible. A entire Barathosian military camp—tents, hitching posts, siege weapons, soldiers with wide-brimmed hats, and mounts—had materialized less than one hundred yards beyond the gate.

But the most troubling new arrivals were six cannons, and they were aimed directly at the wall.

"Get everyone away from the wall!" Nicolas yelled as he ran back into the courtyard. "Away from the wall! Now!"

Soldiers scattered back toward the boulevard as the detachments broke apart, but some of the guards presented a more stoic front. Probably veterans.

A blur of white appeared in front of Nicolas. By the time his eyes had a chance to focus on the twelve-inch blade thrusting toward his neck, Kagan had knocked the man to the ground, retrieved the blade, and twisted the man's head until it was facing the wrong direction.

A rush of necropotency entered his well.

Nicolas looked around the plaza and saw the same event playing out at random intervals, but Toridyn was the only other person lucky enough to have a penitent of his own.

Gunfire echoed through the plaza. It was enough to send even the veterans scattering.

The Barathosians were teleporting into the city itself! This defense, whatever it was, wasn't going to work.

Kait!

Kagan pointed to Nicolas's left and Nicolas turned.

Kaitlyn was face-to-face with a Barathosian, who was aiming a pistol at her head.

Nicolas ordered Kagan forward, but before he could act, the Barathosian dropped the pistol, screamed like someone was skinning him alive, and ran head-first into the wall.

Kagan, how strong are you, now that you're dead?

Kagan picked the Barathosian soldier up in one hand and lifted him off the ground.

Send them a message.

Kagan threw the soldier up and over the wall, leapt toward the corpse of the Barathosian he'd killed, and repeated the feat of strength.

Moments later, the Barathosian soldiers in the courtyard vanished.

"I bought us some time," Nicolas said. "Minutes if we're lucky. No more."

He picked up the pistol the Barathosian dropped.

It looked and felt like a solid piece of brass. A metal lever, forward of the trigger guard and slightly above, held a slow-burning cord in a clamp. The cord was lit on both ends, and a small bowl, no larger than a quarter, protruded out from the barrel.

Nicolas's adoptive father, Dr. Murray, had taught him about guns like this. It was a matchlock pistol. When the shooter pulled the trigger, the lit cord would strike the flash pan—the small bowl that held priming powder—and ignite the larger charge inside the barrel through a small hole in the side.

Nicolas released the burning cord from the clamp. The priming powder had already scattered into the dirt, but he still aimed the gun downward. He felt inside the barrel with his small finger.

No rifling.

That meant they'd only be accurate at close range. *Very* close range. Without rifling, the projectile would tumble through the air instead of remaining stable enough to travel in a straight line over a long distance.

Tithian needs to know about this. He'll know who can best use the information.

Tithian.

The protoforge fragments.

That was the answer!

Nicolas tucked the gun into an inner pocket of his robe.

"Kait, we have to go," Nicolas said. "I think Tithian has something that can stop these Barathosians from teleporting wherever they want."

Kaitlyn looked toward Toridyn, who was standing halfway across the plaza. And from the looks of things, he'd summoned another penitent. When Kaitlyn looked back, her face held a somber expression.

"You're not seriously considering staying here, are you?" Nicolas asked. "This is a war zone!"

"I've been thinking a lot," Kaitlyn said. "This has to have happened to me for a reason. And you saw what I was able to do. That soldier couldn't have shot me if he wanted to."

"And what about his friend? The one twenty yards away that you couldn't see because he was hiding behind a merchant tent?"

Kaitlyn shook her head. "There wasn't anyone else."

"There *could* have been."

Kaitlyn took his hands in hers. "I know you worry about me. But I have a gift that I need to use. I don't have any illusions about saving the day. But I can do *something.*"

"Kait, there's no time to talk about this," Nicolas said. "They'll be back. Soon. And they're going to hit us with everything they've got."

"I know. You need to leave."

"Kait."

"We'll talk when you come back."

Kaitlyn handed him Toby's leash and took several steps back.

"He'll be safer at the Pinnacle," Kaitlyn said.

Kagan, you protect her, dammit! Do what she tells you!

"I'll be back as soon as possible," Nicolas said. "I'm going to get one of those protoforge fragments and come straight back."

"I'll be waiting."

Nicolas retrieved the translocation orb from his robe and allowed a small amount of necropotency to flow into it.

Caspardis receded in front of him in a small pinprick of light.

CHAPTER EIGHTEEN

The gods have interacted with the world since the earliest period of recorded history, and they continue to do so during the Rite of Manifestation. But we would be ignorant to think they are somehow constrained by this ritual. It should no more surprise me to learn my walking staff was the god Arin than it would to see the sun rise in the morning.

- Coteon of the Steppes, "The Mukhtaar Chronicles: Coteonic Commentaries" (circa 680 BCE)

"Why?" Mujahid asked. It was the only complete thought he could form.

Forty years without a single message, and now Mordryn sat before him, looking no older than the day she disappeared from this very room. Her flowing red hair rested on her shoulders and draped over her crimson dress. Her skin was the same smooth porcelain he remembered. In some ways he expected it. She had always been more powerful than he, and *he* was coming up on one-hundred and seventy years old. She might not be a Mukhtaar Lord, but she held some secret of longevity.

Her blue eyes bore the look of wisdom. But they also showed a measure of concern.

"Your suspicions are correct," Mordryn said. "It's time to relocate the portal."

Mujahid stepped between the bed and a simple wooden chair next to the dresser.

"You spoke with Nuuan," Mujahid said, "and neither of you had the decency to say anything to me."

Mordryn gazed out through the window. "The Barathosians cannot gain access to the crypt."

"Forty years. Where were you?"

"If their magi get within ten leagues of the mountain, they'll sense it."

"Why didn't you warn me? Why didn't you say something?"

"We may be able to use this to our advantage. If you move the portal to—"

"Bugger the festering portal, woman! You owe me an explanation!"

Mordryn faced him, expressionless.

"I'll tell you everything," she said. "But I need you to assure me that regardless of what I say…regardless of how you *feel* about what I say…you'll relocate the portal immediately."

The thought of her asking for a blanket promise after what she'd put him through made the heat rise in his face.

But he trusted her. After all these years, he trusted her still.

"I'm listening," Mujahid said.

"You were…you *remain* everything to me," Mordryn said. "The work of the gods is mysterious."

"I have *all* of the pastoral platitudes memorized, I assure you."

"I left that day because leaving was the only way to save Kaitlyn."

Mujahid rubbed his temple.

"You left twenty years before the girl's birth," Mujahid said. "Perhaps more. She's not even from Erindor."

"Nuuan was there when I left," Mordryn said.

"I know that now."

"He tried to hand me my dagger. In my haste, I'd left it here. He was concerned I'd need it where I was going."

"And where was that?"

"The portal closed before I could take it," Mordryn said. "Had Nuuan hesitated a moment longer he would have lost his arm. The dagger took the brunt of it. I'm sure you found the other half?"

Mujahid nodded.

"You're wrong about Kaitlyn. She's Erindorian."

Mujahid's eyes widened.

"She would have been a target here," Mordryn said. "She had to be taken to Earth with Nicolas for *both* of their sakes."

"Had to *be taken*?" Mujahid asked. "I don't understand. Did *you* take her or didn't you?"

"Zubuxo took them both."

"As I suspected…"

"Because I asked him to. Before we entered Kagan's vitapotency construct."

Mujahid stammered. "The Great Barrier? Only the gods entered…"

When realization dawned, Mujahid had to grab the chair to steady himself. It all made sense. Her wisdom. Her perpetual youthfulness. Her intuitive knowledge of magic. Her fondness for roses.

And the timing of her disappearance.

"Shealynd," Mujahid said.

Mordryn smiled.

"What does that make of us?" Mujahid asked. "Our past? Our *future*? Did I fall in love with an illusion?"

Mordryn took his hands in hers. "This is *me*, Mujahid. *Mordryn*. A woman. A *real* woman. The woman you grew to love."

"*Still* love."

There was someone else in this relationship, though. And Mujahid was having a difficult time accepting the conclusion his necropotency-enhanced mind had reached.

"Kaitlyn," Mujahid said. "But, it can't be."

"You know it is. You sensed it when you first set eyes upon her."

"She's my daughter."

"*Our* daughter."

Mujahid sat in the chair, and Mordryn did the same on the bed across from him. She never let go of his hands.

"Help me understand," Mujahid said.

"What you think you know of us…of the gods…is flawed. Your knowledge is based on the words of an ancient man with good intentions but poor foresight."

The *Origines Multiversi* formed the beginning of the *Mukhtaar Chronicles*, and was written by the prophet *Habakku*, one of the holiest men in Erindor's history.

"The *Origines* forms the basis of all theological wisdom. If what you're saying is true..." Mujahid couldn't bring himself to finish the thought. "But what does any of this have to do with Kaitlyn?"

"Malvol needs her."

"But why?"

"The God of Hate has accelerated her Awakening," Mordryn said. "Beyond that simple fact, I cannot say why. Cognitomancers are a rare breed."

"The girl is an enchanter?" Mujahid asked.

"She's much more than that. But she's Awakening to her cognitomantic powers now, and Malvol will seek to use her. There is much you don't understand about the nature of *deity*, Mujahid. You're familiar with the concept of *apotheosis*, I'm sure."

"Are you suggesting Malvol wasn't always a god?" Mujahid asked.

"I'm not merely suggesting it. I'm stating it as *fact*. Such is the nature of *all* of the gods. It is my contention Malvol needs her to complete his transformation."

Mujahid's pulse quickened. The fundamentals of everything he had been taught, everything he *believed*, was crumbling around him.

"The *Origines* is a lie?" Mujahid asked. So often had he read the *Origines Multiversi* that he remembered the words as if they'd been imprinted on his mind. "'The Power reached into his being and pulled the gods from within. The first he named Arin, for Arin was his exalted firstborn. The second he named Shealynd, for Shealynd emerged from his Love. The last he named Zubuxo, for Zubuxo was last in all things.'"

Mordryn squeezed his hand. "Please, Mujahid—"

"Shall I continue?" Mujahid asked. "The Power *created* the gods. You suggest some other beginning?"

"Does the Origines reveal *how* The Power created the gods?"

Mujahid sat in silence. If anyone in the multiverse understood the truth of the Origines, it was Mordryn, yet she spoke as if this lunacy were objective truth.

"You stopped your recitation too soon," she said. "What are the first words attributed to my brother Arin in the Origines?"

Could Mordryn be right? All those years of scholarship. All those years of studying the sacred text. How could he have missed something so crucial?

Mujahid closed his eyes and recited the words. "'Why have these great and terrible powers manifest themselves within us?'"

Mordryn chuckled. "That's far more poetic than what he *actually* said. But ask yourself; why would he ask that question if his powers were always innate?"

"I..." Mujahid couldn't fathom it. "Everything I thought I knew..."

"Malvol was once a man," Mordryn said. "In many ways, he still is. He used his considerable influence in life to gather a following of devout worshipers. Their faith fed him until his powers became godlike. But it wasn't long before he discovered that wasn't enough. The final step, deification—*complete* deification—requires the intervention of a god."

"And Malvol intends to use Kaitlyn for that purpose," Mujahid said.

"Kaitlyn is merely a demigod, so she cannot serve in my place," Mordryn said. "But as my daughter, she will eventually have physical access to me."

"Which means she'll be able to compel you with cognitomancy," Mujahid said.

Mordryn stood.

"We call Malvol the *God of Hate*, but that name is incorrect. He thrives on *chaos*, not hatred. He feeds off it. The more chaotic the world becomes, the more people believe in his influence. The more people believe in his influence..."

"The more powerful he grows," Mujahid said. "The more powerful he grows, the more chaotic the world becomes."

"And on and on it goes."

"Who is he? If he was once a man, where did he come from?"

"Your brother seeks that answer at this very moment."

Mujahid stood and squeezed Mordryn's hand.

"You've answered my questions," Mujahid said. "But I...need some time. And there's a portal I need to relocate. I'll return shortly."

"We will see each other again, but it will not be today," Mordryn said. "Multiple threads of reality converge, but I cannot see the outcome. The decisions that would collapse potential reality into objective reality have not yet been made. And *you* have some role to play in this. There are decisions *you* must make. But promise me one thing."

"Name it."

"Promise me you'll keep Kaitlyn safe. Until she takes her rightful place at my side, she's vulnerable."

Mujahid nodded. "Of course."

Mujahid left Mordryn in his chambers. But he didn't need to glance back to know she was no longer there.

CHAPTER NINETEEN

In the year 1180 BCE, Yusef Mukhtaar stepped over the threshold, becoming Yusef Lord Mukhtaar. He ascended during a time of great famine in northern Religar (1181 BCE - 1175 BCE). Clans Catiatum and Zerubula sought to take advantage of him, demanding unreasonable amounts of gold and salt in exchange for grain. Clan Ezeki, however, demanded nothing in return except goodwill. Clan Ezeki rationed itself and its surrounding villages and shared half its grain with Clan Mukhtaar, bringing everyone through the famine.

- Coteon of the Steppes, "The Mukhtaar Chronicles: Coteonic Commentaries" (circa 680 BCE)

The alliance between Clan Mukhtaar and Clan Ezeki spanned more than a thousand years, but Tycon Mukhtaar destroyed that as well. The evil of that man knew no bounds.

- Mujahid Mukhtaar, Private Commentaries, 12 CE

elron pulled his cloak tight as he crouched on the roof of a three-story building. Though the coin that had once sat in a pocket in his cloak had been small, its weight had been

significant. He could feel its absence every bit as much as its presence. He'd had it since he was a child. And now, a lifetime later, he had to find a way to make it through the world without it. Something to replace its incessant draw.

Footsteps echoed up from below, but he wasn't worried about being seen.

People never look up.

Hundreds went about their routines in the plaza below, shopping in tents surrounding the three stone fountains. Those who weren't shopping were strolling along the boulevard between the plaza and the circular fortress at the end of the street.

Whoever had been watching him must be down there somewhere. He didn't know who or what it was, but as soon as he climbed the building, the prickly feeling on the back of his neck went away.

He'd considered asking that cichlos priest Toridyn to lend him the help of a penitent. But he didn't want to alarm the group. Besides, if his suspicions were correct—if Jacobson and the other rangers had decided to pursue him after all—it would be better to not involve the others.

It had to be Jacobson. Who else would want to follow him?

No. Jacobson would never go back on a decision. That's not his way.

So who was it?

The drumming of boots on dirt mingled with the sounds of the crowd and the plaza's cascading fountains. Dozens of soldiers formed ranks and faced the western gate.

Aelron stepped back from the ledge and ran along the roof to the next building, closer to the fortress side of the plaza. If he could reach one of the two buildings that formed the eastern exit from the plaza, he'd have a better view.

The next closest building was one story shorter than the one he was on, but foot-wide clefts in the brick architecture formed ersatz columns that could slow his descent.

Aelron hopped off the roof and spun until he faced the building. He quickly gripped the brick of a partial column with both hands and feet and entered a controlled slide.

When it felt right, he pushed away from the wall, spun, and landed on the roof below with a shoulder roll.

He was still two buildings away, but each were the same height as this one, with a street running between. An easy jog—except for the leaping across urban canyons bit.

Before he could start, a familiar sight passed below him into the plaza. Nicolas and the guard he'd left with. Kaitlyn must have spotted Nicolas too, because she left Toridyn's side and ran down the stairs to greet him.

Aelron needed to focus. If someone was following them, it would be better if he found the follower before anything bad happened. Nicolas might be a powerful priest, but his tactical sense was shite. Kaitlyn didn't understand her own power—whatever it was—and the cichlos priest seemed more interested in sightseeing than anything else.

No, Aelron would have to be the one to make this particular trouble go away.

He scanned the crowd as Nicolas and Kaitlyn struck up a conversation. The last time he felt those eyes on him, he could have sworn it came from this side of the plaza. That would place whoever it was right below him, if they'd stuck around.

But that was unlikely.

Commotion broke out on the western wall. An entire military camp appeared from nowhere, just beyond the gate. Voluminous tents supported by tall beams, soldiers in foreign uniforms, mounts twice the size of adda, siege towers, everything.

They simply *appeared*.

"Prepare for attack!" a soldier yelled.

Screams came from below. Barathosian soldiers appeared, ran Caspardis guards through with curved blades, then vanished. The dying guards never stood a chance.

This was no good. He had to help somehow.

Aelron ran to the ledge of the roof and peered over. A group of six Barathosian soldiers, each with wide-brimmed hats and feathers, were sweeping across the plaza in a line.

Six hells!

Climbing would leave him open to attack. He'd have to drop behind the building instead.

He gripped the side of the building and shimmied down the brick column.

A series of popping sounds echoed toward him from the gate. As he looked, several Barathosians, shrouded in smoke, pointed small objects at the crowd.

He knew what those were. They were the small metallic tubes the Barathosians used when he was hiding in the wagon.

The sensation of being watched returned, but this time the source felt much closer than before.

"You," a woman's voice said. It was confident. Commanding. "It's *Aelron*, isn't it?"

Aelron spun toward the voice.

Sharp, stabbing pain shot across Aelron's side before he could see what happened. He reached down to check the damage and pulled back a crimson hand.

A black blur passed in front of his eyes, and the woman was gone before he could get a good look.

The sound of strangled choking came from behind. When he turned, the woman stood over two Barathosians who were clutching their throats in a futile attempt to staunch the flow of blood.

She'd been unnaturally quick.

And she'd saved his life.

She glanced at his wound. "You'll live."

Another black blur later and she was four paces away, staring. Though she displayed no weapons, Aelron got the impression she was heavily armed. She wore fitted material that looked like leather, but it was silent when she moved. It covered everything except her head, upon which her blond hair was tied in a top knot. Her armor wrapped up and around her neck, though the buttons were open at her collar bone. Her full-length cloak, black as obsidian, had a strange quality he couldn't place; it bore the look of rich tailoring, and its sheen reminded him of Arinwool. But every time he tried to look at the fine details, his eyes wouldn't obey. His glance would slide right off it. All he could see were a series of concentric black rings with an iridescence that moved as his eyes moved. He'd be willing to bet that cloak could help her disappear in a pinch. Even her sleeves, which ended in gloved hands, were exquisitely tailored.

Her back stiffened, and she crossed her arms.

"Are you finished *examining* me?" the woman said.

The Barathosian corpses vanished, and a silence descended on the plaza.

"This isn't over," Aelron said, staring at the dirt where the corpses had left impressions.

"We have, at most, two hours before that wall comes down," she said. "You're going to die if you don't follow me. That false bravado of yours won't save you this time."

"Whatever bravado I have, it isn't false," Aelron said. "The time you have to tell me why I should follow you grows shorter by the second."

She lifted her hands, palms up, and looked to the side. It was as if she were asking the fountains if they believed what they were hearing.

Aelron didn't care for the tone of that gesture.

The woman shook her head and started walking away from the plaza, passing him without another glance.

"If you survive, we'll speak again," she said.

As she walked toward the boulevard, her image faded. No. He could see her on the periphery of his vision, but only if he looked away.

Has to be that festering cloak.

That Barathosian had appeared right behind him. Had it not been for the woman, he'd be dead. And there was no denying her unnatural agility. Maybe humility would be the better part of valor in this instance.

"Wait," Aelron said.

The woman stopped, but she didn't turn around.

"You're right," Aelron said.

She remained still.

"I need to warn my friends," Aelron said.

"Your friends are *exactly* where we need them to be," she said. "Right now, I need someone like *you* with *me*."

"What do you know about my friends?"

The woman started walking again, faster this time, and she was heading farther into the city instead of toward the wall.

Aelron hurried to catch up with her.

"Name's Aelron."

"Good for you."

"You have a name?"

"Yes," she said.

He'd had enough already, and they hadn't made it a hundred yards. He grabbed her by the shoulder and spun her toward him.

"Look," Aelron said. "All I'm trying—"

When the stars faded from Aelron's field of vision, he was lying on his back in the dirt, holding his jaw. The woman was squatting at his side with two daggers crossed over his throat. Her turquoise eyes were fierce. A small part of him wanted to shrink away.

"Touch me again, Elroy, and you'll not live long enough to bleed out. I say this once, as a courtesy. Because I'm curious about you."

"It's *Aelron*."

"Like I said, *good for you*. Now follow or leave. Those are your only two options."

He would have paid good money to watch her and Master Nigel spar.

When she released him, he rose to his feet and dusted himself off. His side stung a little worse than before, but he'd had worse.

She led him out of the plaza and around a corner, then gestured for him to stop.

"You've been following me for hours," Aelron said.

The woman chuckled. "I've been following you far longer than that. We'll discuss it later. Morrigan, by the way."

"What?"

"My name is Morrigan."

"Well met. Now, why are you following me?"

Morrigan ignored the question, ran to the corner of the next building, and peered into a street running parallel to the main boulevard. She waved for him to follow.

The dilapidated buildings across the street bore damage too old to have been caused by the Barathosians. It was a striking contrast to the way it looked years ago.

The last time Aelron had been to Caspardis, it was pristine. He was a child back then. A frightened, nervous child on his first journey away from home, waiting to be introduced to the local Shandarian Ranger recruiter.

He remembered waiting for hours. And when the recruiter—a ranger named Sergeant Saren—had arrived, Aelron cried when he saw the ranger's feline eyes.

"Don't worry, child," Saren had said. "I'm more like a kitten than a big cat. And I promise you, our big cats won't hurt you. They don't hurt good boys. And I can tell you're a good boy. You'll be learning all of our secrets before long."

"Can I ride an adda-ki like you do?" Aelron had said.

Saren smiled and pulled a coin from his pocket. "Which do you like the most, adda or adda-ki?"

"Adda-ki! They're invisible! And nothing can kill them!"

Saren flipped the coin. "Well you're in luck. Adda-ki it is. But here's your first ranger secret." Saren gestured for Aelron to move in closer. In a whisper, he said, "Adda-ki aren't invisible. Rangers *make* them invisible."

Aelron's eyes had widened at the revelation.

Saren placed the coin in Aelron's palm. "Don't you lose this now. It's special. It tells the future."

"No it doesn't!"

Saren lifted Aelron into his arms and placed him on the back of an adda-ki.

"See?" Saren had said. "It told me you'd eventually ride an adda-ki, and here you are."

Aelron had looked at the coin with reverence and tucked it into his pocket.

"I'll protect it always!" he said. "I swear!"

The ringing sound of a large bell brought Aelron's mind back to the present.

He'd broken that oath to Saren, and the missing coin accused him like the phantom of past sins.

"The garrison is preparing for the next attack," Morrigan said. She glanced to her right, where a bunch of boxes and crates stood against a wall. "In here."

Morrigan moved the empty crates and nodded for Aelron to help. When they finished, a narrow metal door stood before them.

Aelron followed her through the door into a dark, dusty warehouse that smelled of mildew and dirt. He had to suppress a sneeze as a cloud of dust billowed up from the floor where he'd kicked a crate by accident.

The warehouse was empty, except for some crates and boxes. A table on the far side of the room had a chair on one side and a door on the other.

But worse than the dust and mildew was the vile stench of death that permeated the room.

"What is this place?" Aelron asked. He brought his fist up to his nose to block the smell.

"A safe house. The Sodality owns it, though we haven't used it in years."

"Sodality?"

Morrigan looked at him as if he'd asked which way was up. "You really *don't* know, do you?"

"I'm not exactly from around here," Aelron said. "Well...I am, and I'm not. It's a long story."

"Give me the King's brief."

"My father sent me away when I was little. He's dead. Now I'm back."

"Turian Exports Company," Morrigan said. "Heard of it?"

"No."

"The Moon Lake Sodality. You've never heard of that *either*?"

Aelron shrugged. "If I have, it wasn't memorable enough to stay with me."

"Well that certainly explains a thing or two."

"Exports. Like what, Shandarian powder?"

"No! Not *that*! Do I look like a powder dealer to you?"

"Whatever you are, you're far more dangerous than a powder dealer."

Morrigan headed toward the door on the other side of the warehouse and nodded for Aelron to follow.

The putrid scent intensified as they approached the door.

Morrigan gestured to the chair and pulled the door handle as Aelron sat.

"Wait here," Morrigan said.

She covered her nose and mouth, then closed the door behind her.

A moment later she emerged with a spool, a needle, and a bottle of whiskey.

"Want to do this yourself, or shall I?" Morrigan asked.

He pulled his cloak open and lifted his shirt. Damned Barathosian got him good. The cut wasn't deep, but it stretched too far back for him to reach it all.

"You'd better," Aelron said. "Just…go easy."

Morrigan knelt beside him and threaded the needle. When she was finished, she uncorked the bottle and poured a small amount of the peaty liquid on the needle and thread.

"Don't pour too much," Aelron said. "Doesn't look like there's enough as it is."

"This isn't for you." Morrigan took a long drink.

"Oh great," Aelron said. "A drunk physician is just what I need."

"You're in good hands, Elrob. Don't worry."

"It's *Aelron*! How many times do I have to—ow!"

Searing hot pain shot up Aelron's right side.

"For Arin's sake, woman, *getting stabbed* didn't hurt that much!"

"Stay still, you big baby. This is going to *really* hurt, if you keep squirming."

"Do you know what you're doing, or are you guessing?"

"I've hunted and cleaned boar that didn't squeal as much as you."

Morrigan poked the needle through his skin again and Aelron winced.

By the time she finished, Aelron was pretty sure he'd rather bleed to death next time. His side was stiff, and every minor twist and turn made him fear he'd rip the stitches out. And the last thing he wanted was her coming at him with a needle again.

The fetid stench from whatever was behind that door wasn't helping his mood either.

Morrigan stood and opened the door.

"You going to tell me what's in the other room?" Aelron asked.

Morrigan handed him the bottle. "You're going to need this."

There was a swig or two left, so Aelron downed it. The spirits warmed his throat and lightened his mood a little.

Morrigan peeked through the door, then looked down at the floor.

"It began with small raid groups," Morrigan said. "Three or four would appear out of thin air, rob a caravan, then disappear. But not just *any* caravan. *Military* caravans."

Aelron thought back to the wagon he'd hidden in, and the strange soldiers that vanished right in front of him. Morrigan was telling the truth so far.

"The Sodality is in danger," Morrigan said. "Kagan's barrier did something. With the birth rate as low as it has been, we need everyone who is capable of surviving the training."

Aelron folded his arms and stifled a wince from the tightness of his stitches.

"It's why I've been tracking you," Morrigan said. "That's how the Sodality works. Someone like *me* finds someone like *you*. You run for your life because you think you've stepped into a nightmare. I catch you. You refuse to listen, and I pretend you're not wasting my time for an hour or two. Eventually, your better judgment forces you to hear me out. But *we don't have* two hours."

"You don't see me running, do you?"

"You don't see the irony in that question?"

Morrigan squatted beside him until they were face to face. She had the same fierce expression as before.

"The Turian Exports Company is a cover for the Sodality," Morrigan said. She paused, as if expecting a response. When no response came, she continued. "And judging from that stupid look on your face, you have no idea what in the six hells I'm talking about."

Aelron remained silent. He wouldn't allow awkwardness to force him into talking. That's how people said things they'd later regret.

Morrigan pursed her lips and nodded as if he'd passed some sort of test. She stood.

"The Sodality is an ancient order of Zubuxo," Morrigan said.

"You're no priest," Aelron said.

"And you're not listening. I never *said* I was a priest. Priests bring people *back* from the dead. What we do is…For the love of Arin, didn't your mother tell you tales to frighten you into obedience? *The Tale of the Cloaked Demon? The Hellwraith and the Adda? Piercing the Veil?*"

"My mother died when I was little."

Morrigan stammered. "Apologies."

Aelron shook his head. "That was a long time ago. But what do you mean *someone like you*? What, exactly, am I *like*?"

"I know a kindred spirit when I see one. I know the *craft* when I see it, regardless of how poorly it's been passed on. And I know you're *long lived*."

"I don't know what you're talking about."

"That's the only reason you still draw breath. That Council magus in Blackwood was my mark. My sacred duty. I wanted him *alive*…for a time. But because of what you did, I couldn't *purge* him properly."

"If you were there, you'd recall he killed *himself*."

"I assume you stole Arinwool from the rangers?"

Aelron's face went cold. Just how much *did* she know?

"Why were you after the magus?" Aelron asked.

Morrigan stared at him. "Not every human who walks this world has a human *soul*."

"Now *you're* the one telling tales."

"You'll have a different opinion when you glimpse beyond the veil. Demons don't always have wings. Forget about the magus for now. I'll teach you the rest later. What's important, is *this*."

She pulled a long black feather from her cloak.

"*This* is where the Barathosian's power comes from," Morrigan said. "*This* is how they travel."

He took the feather from her and examined it. Twelve inches long. White quill with two black stripes. Tapered vane, also black. Narrow leading edge on one side of the vane and a wide trailing edge on the other—a flight feather. Ordinary in every possible way. He handed it back.

"It's just a feather," Aelron said.

"It's much more. And I have proof. If you've seen them, you know the hats they wear, right?"

Aelron nodded.

"Have you ever seen a Barathosian without one?" Morrigan asked.

"They've never invited me to dinner, but I assume they take them off eventually."

"I fought them outside of Tur. It's no small thing when I tell you it was a challenge. But what's important is what happens when they're *not* wearing this feather. For weeks I watched them appear and disappear, often wearing different clothing, even different hats. But always the same black feather. Yesterday, there was another attack. Several appeared in this safe house. But they were scouts, not fighters. I concealed myself. One of them started shouting numbers, always decreasing. Sixty. Then Thirty. Then fifteen, and so on. Just before he reached zero, I knocked the feather from one of their hats. The man who owned it screamed horrifically. The others tried to retrieve it for him, but when the counting man reached zero, they all vanished. All except the one without the feather."

Aelron stood. "The man with the missing feather is in that room, isn't he?"

Morrigan pursed her lips for a moment. "Most of him."

"Show me."

Morrigan stepped through the doorway.

Aelron followed her into a room that was darker than the last and smelled like death itself. A single window, high in the opposite wall, cast a beam of yellow light on the center of the room at a steep angle. Particles of dust drifted through the light. He suppressed another sneeze.

But it wasn't the darkness, the solitary beam of light, or the motes of dust that concerned him. What concerned him was the man on the floor at the other end of that beam of light. Or rather, what was *left* of him.

Half of a man's *torso* lay on the floor. A shell of flesh with internal organs hanging precariously from fascia. The remains of a stomach hung twisted within entrails that wrapped the fleshy mass, binding it together like a macabre sack. A sack resting in a pool of rotten food, feces, and urine.

Aelron suppressed a gag. "Gods."

"When the others disappeared," Morrigan said, "that one ended up exactly like you see him. Their powers of transport *must* have something to do with the feather."

Another bell tolled, this time louder than the first.

"Barathosians?"

Morrigan nodded. "A second bell means an attack is imminent."

"Then we need to get to the wall."

Aelron turned toward the door behind him, but Morrigan was already standing there, blocking his exit. She'd somehow covered fifteen paces without him seeing her move.

And she wasn't out of breath.

"First," Morrigan said, "I need something from you." She took slow steps toward him. "No one who hears the story I told you leaves this building unless they're with the Sodality."

Aelron glanced at the door.

"There's power in you," Morrigan said. "Your friends and family might not see it, but I do. Just like you'll see it in others someday. I'm not making a threat, Aelron. I'm making an offer."

Aelron had suspected it would come to this at some point, with all that talk of training and tracking. Strange as it was, the notion appealed to him. He'd spent decades of his life with a group of people who didn't want him around. What would it have been like to spend decades with people who *did*?

He always wondered why he'd stopped aging. And there was no reason he shouldn't have been able to moor with an adda-ki. Maybe Morrigan had the answers he sought.

But there was another reason to consider her offer; the pull of the phantom coin had diminished since he'd met her.

"Suppose I'm interested," Aelron said. "We hardly have time for some elaborate initiation ritual."

"Do you want me to complete the training the rangers started? Do you want to become a member of the Sodality? A warrior of Zubuxo?"

So she *did* know he was a ranger.

Aelron stared at her. His brain was telling him to say no. He'd traveled here with a brother he'd just met to fight a war against an enemy he didn't know. Nicolas and Kaitlyn were coming to rely upon him, to some degree. They were going to need his skills and expertise, even if they didn't know it yet.

But his heart had different ideas. There'd been a connection with Morrigan. What kind, he couldn't say, but it was there all the same. She had answers to questions he'd been asking for more than twenty years. She made him believe that all the things he hated about himself had some greater meaning. Some greater purpose.

"I can't say I understand why," Aelron said. "Not completely, anyway. But yes. I do. I want to join your order. I want to know why I don't age. I want to learn about this *veil* of yours."

"Then consider the elaborate initiation ritual concluded."

"You have a spare one of those cloaks around here?"

Morrigan huffed. "This is a sacred garment, forged from the veil at the headwaters of the Great Orm River. Zubuxo himself imbued it on the night of the new moons—a night that comes but once every five years."

"Yeah. One of *those*."

"Regarding your *wall* comment earlier," Morrigan said, ignoring him. "We don't want to be anywhere *near* the wall when this attack starts. I saw what they did in Tur. We wait for them to get inside the city, *then* we attack."

"What can we do that the Caspardis militia cannot?"

Morrigan smirked and jogged toward the door. "Time for your first lesson."

He followed her into the street. "And how many lessons are there?"

"As many as it takes."

CHAPTER TWENTY

In the year 1077 BCE, Imran Mukhtaar stepped over the threshold, becoming Imran Lord Mukhtaar. Though lord Mukhtaar entered the Rite of Ascension with his brother Kyran, Kyran was never seen again. The loss of his brother led Lord Mukhtaar to forbid future generations from allowing more than one family member to attempt ascension.
- Coteon of the Steppes, "The Mukhtaar Chronicles: Coteonic Commentaries" (circa 680 BCE)

If Lord Imran's restriction was meant to be perpetual, he did a poor job of promulgating it. There have been numerous occurrences, centuries before our birth, of sons ascending while the father yet reigned. I will have to make some explicit comment about this in the Chronicles. It wouldn't do to let this stand as an impediment to ascension for the worthy.
- Mujahid Mukhtaar, Private Commentaries, 15 CE

Nicolas materialized, and the low hum of the Orb of Arin greeted him. The multi-hued swirls of divine power on its surface emitted an iridescent vapor, obscuring the turquoise sky through the window behind it.

The sanctuary.

Nicolas was thankful the translocation orb had taken him to the heart of the Pinnacle. The Pinnacle was a city-sized structure, built atop an island in the Sea of Arin. The last thing he needed was to have to scour the place for Tithian.

He needed one of those protoforge fragments immediately. Caspardis was in trouble, and he couldn't leave Kaitlyn and the gang there for too long.

Toby pulled at the leash and bayed. But when Nicolas faced the direction Toby was pulling, he saw nothing.

Nicolas rubbed at his right eye. For a moment, he thought he'd seen a shadow jumping up from a dark corner. And he couldn't shake the feeling that he was being watched.

But no one was there.

Toby calmed as a Pinnacle guard opened the sanctuary door and entered.

"Archmage," the guard said.

"The Prime Warlock," Nicolas said. "Where is he?"

"I saw him last in the Great Hall, but that was hours ago."

"Find him. I don't care if it takes the entire Pinnacle Guard. Find him and tell him to come to my chambers without delay."

"Archmage." The guard saluted and ran down the great spiral stairs.

Nicolas's head throbbed.

What I'd give for a couple of smart phones right now.

He walked down the twisted spiral stairs, in the general direction of his chambers. As he rounded the center column—a twenty feet diameter of sandstone—he noticed all of the sconces were in their place. For him, mere *days* had passed since he'd crept up this very passage on the way to confront his birth father, Kagan. The sandstone walls looked much the same, but the sconces that once lay in pieces on the floor now hung in pristine condition.

When he circled the column once more, he emerged onto a landing formed by two hallways running opposite one another. Four guards in Pinnacle livery—billowing material with yellow and red stripes from shoulder to toe—stood at attention along the back wall of the landing, pikes in hand. They saluted as Nicolas looked up and down the hallways, trying to find a familiar door, scratch on the wall, or any other sign that would lead him in the right direction.

Nicolas returned the salute.

"Forgive the presumption, Archmage," one of the guards said. "Frederick mentioned fetching the Prime Warlock to your chambers. You'll find them *that* way, Excellency."

"Thank you," Nicolas said. Word must be spreading about his dislike of being called *Holy One*. But *Excellency* was a new one.

The corridor didn't look familiar, but Nicolas tugged at the leash and led Toby onward.

Again, the strong sensation of being watched returned, and he glanced up and down the hall.

No one.

As he approached a large window that looked out over a vineyard, he recognized the door to his chambers. It rested within an arch of sandstone, and bore two gold mosaics; one resembling the Orb of Arin, and the other in the image of Arin's helm.

Last time, he'd approached from the opposite end of the hall.

No wonder I'm lost. This place is a labyrinth.

Two guards on either side of the door saluted as Nicolas pushed it open.

Nicolas glanced around the room—what he could see of it—before entering. He was a man without a home, and it never occurred to him until this moment. The thought of going back to his life in Austin seemed foolish. A naive longing, at best. Austin held nothing for him anymore. What was he going to do? Go to grad school? Get a job as a field archaeologist? Teach?

He could no sooner put Erindor behind him then he could Kaitlyn.

But as much as he felt a connection to Erindor—by birth, by duty, by divine calling—this wasn't his home *either*. They said he was the master of this place. The Pinnacle. But he couldn't even find his own room without directions from a guard whose armor looked like it was designed by Michelangelo.

He wasn't the master of this place. The Pinnacle was *his* master.

If that giant map on the wall was a map of the Pinnacle, it would be of some use!

The back of his head throbbed, and he massaged it. But the sound of footsteps in the corridor—hurried, judging by how close together the footfalls were—made Nicolas step into his chambers.

Toby spun around and whipped his tail back and forth as the footsteps stopped.

"Archmage," Tithian said.

"Good," Nicolas said. "The proto—"

Nicolas thought better of it and stepped around Tithian to shut the chamber door.

"The protoforge fragments," Nicolas said. "I need one."

Tithian's eyes grew wide, and he stammered. "I haven't had a chance to test them yet."

Nicolas liked Tithian. The man was incredibly helpful. But how could he have dropped the ball like this?

"This was the single most important priority here," Nicolas said. "What could have possibly kept you from testing them? There's a war starting out there!"

Tithian made a placating gesture with his hand. "It still is. And I will begin my tests the moment they arrive. I assure you."

"But you said they were *here*, didn't you?"

Tithian shook his head. "My contacts in Tildem are bringing them here as we speak. But it's a long journey. And I can't translocate them for the reasons I've already mentioned."

How the hell could I have forgotten that?

When Tithian had tried translocating to retrieve the fragments in the first place, something *deflected* him fifty leagues away—one hundred and seventy five miles.

"These contacts," Nicolas said. "Are they trustworthy?"

Tithian looked away for a moment and raised an eyebrow.

"That bad?"

"They can be trusted to do what they're paid to do," Tithian said. "Believe me when I tell you there was no other way. These are the people you go to for a job like this. The Azure Dawn."

"The *Azure Dawn*? Sounds like a made-up terrorist group from an eighties action flick."

"The Azure Dawn can be a touchy subject at the Pinnacle. The governments of the Three Kingdoms look the other way in exchange for service, such as now."

"We're letting a bunch of criminals off the hook because they *do stuff* for us?"

"The Dawn is ostensibly a shipping guild," Tithian said. "And they're highly secretive about their clientele, which is exactly what we need."

"I don't see how it helps them *or* us if everyone knows who they are and what they do."

"The myths surrounding the Azure Dawn are legendary. No one wants to get on their bad side."

Nicolas considered for a moment. He wasn't comfortable with the idea of the Pinnacle—seat of the religious authority on Erindor—climbing into bed with organized crime because it was expedient. Yet, if they didn't do everything they could to stop the Barathosians, there might not *be* a Pinnacle to worry about.

He glanced at the giant map on the wall next to the bed.

"You said the fragments are in *Tildem*?" Nicolas said. He traced a finger north along the line that represented the Great Orm River, running through both Tildem in the south, and the Shandarian Union in the north. "By river or land?"

"River."

Nicolas tapped the map. "Why not put them on a boat here at Arin's watch?"

"That part of the Sea of Arin isn't navigable this time of year. The safest path—"

"Would be *here*." Nicolas slid his finger north and tapped again. "Near the city of *Dyr Agul* off this tributary. *Dyr Agul*...Odd name."

"Religarian. *Dyr* for small villages, *Dar* for large cities. *Agul* for...*Agul*."

Nicolas glanced at Tithian.

Tithian shrugged.

"But that tributary leads back out into the Sea of Arin," Nicolas said.

Tithian nodded. "A much *calmer* portion of sea. The shriller crags are farther south."

"Any idea where they are now?"

"Probably north of Three Banks by now."

Nicolas stepped away from the map and grabbed his chin. "It looks like I'll have to help Caspardis the old fashioned way."

"Caspardis? I don't understand."

"The Barathosians attacked. I bought them some time, but not much. For all I know, they're fighting as we speak."

"The Lady Kaitlyn!"

"Finally noticed she's not here, did you?"

"The Awakening?"

"She's fine now. But I have to go back and help her protect the festering city."

Tithian smiled.

"What?"

"You're swearing like a Shandarian fisherman now."

Nicolas returned the smile and rubbed his head. The throbbing had lessened somewhat, but it was still there, in the background, making him wish there was time to lie down for a while.

"I'm just a little jumpy," Nicolas said. "It's felt like someone has been following me from the moment I arrived."

Tithian looked concerned.

"I'm sure it's nothing," Nicolas said. "Is there a way to make that translocation orb bring me straight back here when I return?" At least he'd have a quick way back to his room.

"Yes...but...I'm not sure you'd *want* to do that. You won't be the only person using it, and..." Tithian gestured at the king-sized bed against the wall.

"On second thought, let's not do that," Nicolas said. He handed Toby's leash to Tithian. "I need someone to look after him for now. Someone you trust. He can't be off the leash unless that door's closed. And if it is, someone should be here with him."

"I'll take care of it."

Nicolas reached into his robe for the translocation orb, and his hand brushed against the Barathosian pistol.

"I almost forgot!" Nicolas said. He retrieved the pistol and handed it to Tithian. "This is what the Barathosians are using for close combat. It's called a gun. In this case, a matchlock. We have these where I'm from, only *much* more advanced.

"What does it do?" Tithian turned the gun over in his hand, held it up to his face, then stared straight into the barrel.

Nicolas snatched the gun back from him. "For the love of Smith and Wesson! Don't do that!"

"Do what?"

"This thing fires small balls of metal at a very high speed. Never point that open end at yourself or anything you don't want to destroy. It's not loaded, but still...best always to treat it like it is."

Nicolas took a few moments to explain gun powder, to the best of his ability, and how a controlled explosion would propel a projectile down the barrel. He couldn't recall exactly how a matchlock was loaded, but he gave Tithian the general idea.

"But what does the burning agent consist of?"

"Charcoal and sulfur, for starters," Nicolas said. "I seem to recall there's a third component, but I can't remember what it is. I'll try to get some from the Barathosians. In the meantime, is there anyone here capable of researching this? Of really studying it?"

"We have chemists that may be of help."

"Then it's time I headed back. Take care of Toby."

"You have nothing to fear."

"We'll see about *that* in Caspardis."

Nicolas channeled necropotency into the translocation orb and the void surrounded him.

elron's anxiety rose as a series of thunderclaps came from the west gate of Caspardis.

But the sound was strange. Short and punctuated, not rolling.

"We need to hurry," Aelron said, picking up his pace. Kaitlyn and Nicolas were at the west wall when he'd last seen them. They could be right in the middle of whatever was happening.

"I told you already," Morrigan said, running several paces in front of him. "There's little we can do until they breach the wall. From the sound of those siege weapons, it won't be long."

"That thunder came from *siege weapons*?"

"It's not thunder," Morrigan said as she came to a stop at the plaza entrance.

There was too much dust in the air to see into the plaza, but screams and shouts said it all—the militia wasn't expecting the attack.

"They use beasts like adda," Morrigan said. "Larger. With horns. They call them *orox*. The orox push the weapons into place, and a soldier ignites a thread. A few moments later, there's a bright flash. Then comes the sound you heard. But by the time you hear it, it's too late. See for yourself."

As the dust in the plaza settled, Aelron could see the countryside west of Caspardis through large holes in the city wall.

"And this was just the first volley," Morrigan said. "If they haven't changed tactics, there'll be at least two more."

Morrigan retrieved a small crossbow from under her cloak.

"You know how to use this?" She asked.

Aelron nodded.

Morrigan handed him a thin quiver of bolts she'd been concealing with the crossbow. She pointed at the roof behind them, just beyond the plaza entrance.

"Take position up there," Morrigan said. "Before they destroy the wall, they'll appear down here. That's their way of evening the odds before entering the city en masse. You'll have fifteen seconds. Thirty at most."

Aelron stared at her.

"What?" she asked.

"How in the hells did you conceal a crossbow and quiver under that cloak? It clings to your back."

"How about you start climbing and save the questions for later? Meet me back at the safe house when this is over, regardless of the outcome. Just get close. I'll find you. There are ruins of a farm not far from the city. We'll retreat to there and use it as a base of operations."

"You're not coming with me?"

"I'll be more useful elsewhere. Take out as many as you can, then head back. Stay alive."

Aelron looked at the side of the building to see if it was scalable. When he turned back, Morrigan was gone.

How in the hells does she move so fast?

Aelron focused on the building once more. He could probably scale it, but it would be a lot quicker to go inside and walk up the stairs.

He ran to the front door and tried to enter, but it was locked.

Of course. Oh well. No time for elegance.

He hooked the small crossbow onto his belt and pulled the quiver over his shoulder. With a firm kick, the frail wooden door flew open.

When he reached the topmost floor, three stories above ground, he ran to a room at the back and crawled onto a windowsill.

The exterior brickwork was identical to the other buildings. Bricks protruded from the outside wall, some forming columns and others forming a checkerboard pattern.

Using the windowsill for leverage, he leapt up and to the side, aiming for the checkerboard. He grabbed one of the protruding bricks and pushed off. His momentum, combined with his upper body strength, was enough to launch him toward the roof's ledge.

With a final heave, he grabbed the ledge and hauled himself onto the roof.

The building was higher than the arched plaza entrance, giving Aelron a decent view of the wall about a hundred yards to the west. Toridyn was easy to pick out of the crowd; the cichlos was two feet taller than any other person in the city. Kaitlyn stood next to him, and the older man by her side was probably Kagan.

Something changed in the periphery of Aelron's vision.

Three Barathosians in white uniforms and black feathered hats appeared at the eastern plaza entrance, less than fifty feet away. It was disorienting, seeing them appear from nowhere.

Bloody hells! Morrigan said I'd have fifteen seconds!

He unhooked the crossbow and laid the quiver on the roof.

Ten seconds.

He placed the stirrup of the crossbow — a metal loop at the head of the bow — onto the ground, knelt, and placed his foot into it for leverage. Taking the string in both hands, he spanned the bow by standing until the string locked on the nut.

Low-pitched *popping* noises were followed by screams in the plaza.

Five seconds.

He placed a bolt in the groove and took aim, using the ledge for stability.

The Barathosians vanished.

Festering hells! I should have spanned the bow sooner!

Morrigan had called it down to the second.

Aelron glanced up the street toward the circular fortress, wondering if more Barathosians were farther into the city.

Thunderclaps resounded from the plaza.

When Aelron turned, a cloud of dust and dirt was rising from a missing section of wall. The portcullis was gone, and the arch that supported it had been reduced to rubble. The gate tower had a hole in it large enough for a person to walk through.

Three Barathosians appeared in the boulevard, but this time the crossbow was loaded and ready.

He took aim and fired.

The bolt punched through a Barathosian's armor.

The soldier clutched the bolt as he fell, and the other two Barathosians looked around frantically.

Aelron stepped back from the ledge and spanned the bow once more.

By the time he stepped forward, the remaining Barathosians were gone.

He swore.

I'm useless here.

He needed to find Nicolas and Kaitlyn. He'd be a lot more effective in melee than hiding on this festering rooftop waiting for targets of opportunity.

Aelron dropped the crossbow next to the quiver and ran toward the rear ledge. Without looking, he hopped off and spun, grabbing the protruding column of brick on the way down.

In moments, Aelron was on the ground and running toward the wall.

Dead Caspardis soldiers lay strewn about the plaza, next to abandoned merchant tents. A few opportunists thought the battle would be a good chance to pilfer some wares, but the Caspardis militia was treating them every bit as hostile as the Barathosians. There were no prisoners, only the living and the dead.

Three Barathosians materialized ten paces away, facing the gate. The rightmost raised his arm, and light glinted off the metal tube in his hand.

Aelron drew his daggers from his cloak. The first he grasped by the blade and threw at the Barathosian with the tube.

The handle struck the back of the Barathosian's head and bounced off.

Aelron swore again. With luck like this, it was amazing he hadn't tied his own boot laces together.

The Barathosian reached for the back of his head, but when he swung his arm around, a boom went off, and the Barathosian in the middle dropped to the ground.

Maybe Aelron's luck was holding after all.

Before the remaining Barathosian could turn, Aelron plunged his other dagger into the base of the man's neck. In a single motion, he withdrew the dagger and flung it toward the Barathosian with the tube.

The man vanished, along with the two corpses, and the dagger passed through empty air.

Toridyn yelled something unintelligible. He was twenty yards away, near the base of the wall, standing next to his three cichlos penitents.

"Thank god," Kaitlyn said. "Where have you been?"

Kagan followed her as she ran toward Aelron.

Toridyn spotted Aelron and yelled something else, but Aelron couldn't make it out.

She pointed at the tower with the missing side.

Aelron shook his head. "Not a good idea. It's unstable. And when they fire those *siege weapons*, you'll be an easy target."

"I must agree with Aelron," Kagan said.

"That's why I need to get up there," Kaitlyn said. "I think I can do something about the cannons."

"Cannons?"

"The *siege weapons* you're talking about."

"Your power can defeat them?" Aelron asked.

"I don't know. But I have a better chance than anyone else here."

"This isn't a good idea," Toridyn said as he drew closer.

"Where's my brother?" Aelron asked

Kaitlyn massaged her temples. "We can catch up later. Can you help me get up there or not?"

"If the ladders are intact, it won't be a problem."

"It's not the climbing I'm worried about. It's the Barathosians. I'd feel better with you *and* Nick's father to help."

"Let's go," Aelron said. "But don't let Nicolas hear you talk like that. About dead Kagan, that is."

"What am I supposed to do?" Toridyn asked.

"Just keep doing what you're doing," Kaitlyn replied.

"What *is* he doing?" Aelron asked.

"Risking his life for a friend," Kaitlyn said as she ran toward the tower.

The hole in the gate tower was so large, they didn't need to bother with the door. But several ladders ran from the ground to the top of the tower, broken only by small platforms every ten feet or so.

"I need to see all of the cannons," Kaitlyn said.

"What are you going to do?" Aelron asked.

"Whatever I can."

"Kagan should stand guard down here," Aelron said. "I'll climb up with you. If anything happens, he can raise an alarm."

They climbed three ladders to a platform just beneath the parapet. Kaitlyn stopped.

"This is good enough," she said, looking through a hole in the wall.

When Aelron joined her, he saw what she was looking at.

Several large, rectangular military tents stood outside what remained of the west wall of Caspardis. Beyond the tents, in a large field farther west, several dozen Barathosians gathered in formation.

But the most ominous part of the scene below were the six large metal tubes, suspended on square, wheeled racks, aimed at the city wall. The racks were constructed of metal, and behind each was an *orox* like Morrigan described. It was like an adda—bulky, six muscular legs ending in cloven hooves. But these beasts had four horns facing forward.

Kaitlyn's brow furrowed in deep concentration as she extended her arm toward the Barathosians.

L ucan saw the woman on the tower with her arm reaching toward him, but he put it out of his mind. He had to prepare his cannon. He was one of six elite Barathosian crewman whose mission was to support the invasion of Caspardis. A single volley would demolish the sandstone wall, allowing the ground force to sweep into the city unopposed.

A violent dizziness came unexpectedly, but he steadied himself against the cannon for support, closing his eyes until the nausea passed. When the dizziness ebbed, the ground shook and Lucan opened his eyes.

Blood drained from his face as he saw the source of the quake.

Across the field to his right stood a reptile nearly four hundred feet tall, upright on hind legs. Stone-like spikes ran down the length of its back and out onto its massive tail. Its feet were larger than any of the command tents they'd brought with them, and it stood amidst a frantic group of Barathosian soldiers.

The creature threw back its head and roared, high-pitched at first, then tapering off into a deep base that rolled across the plain. But when it lowered its head once more, the stone-like spikes began to radiate a bluish-green light.

A beam of energy came forth from the creatures maw and sliced through the Barathosian siege camp, destroying any structures it touched and igniting the rest into columns of flame.

A thought pressed into his mind. *Turn the cannon and fire it!*

Lucan pulled the stoppers from behind the wheels of the cannon and signaled his *orox* to turn the massive barrel of metal.

Aelron watched as the Barathosian on the rightmost of the six tubes pulled a stopper from behind the wheels of the rack it rested upon.

The beast behind it—the orox—stepped forward and inserted its four horns into the back of the rack. With a powerful thrust of its legs, it rotated, turning the entire rack, until the tube faced the other five. When it withdrew its horns, the operator replaced the stopper behind the carriage wheels.

As the operator touched the side of his tube with a torch. The other Barathosians dove away.

A flash and burst of smoke was followed by a resounding boom, and the closest tube to the blast blew apart as it slammed into the next, sending shards of metal and wood in all directions. The third tube split in half as it crashed into the fourth, tearing through its carriage and knocking it into the fifth. When the smoke settled, the tube operators hadn't faired any better than the tubes. Except for the soldier who had fired it, who was running toward the largest command tent.

Only one tube remained intact.

"Did you do that?" Aelron asked.

Kaitlyn slumped to the floor.

"Kaitlyn!"

Aelron knelt at her side. She was breathing but unconscious.

He couldn't leave her here. He scooped her up and placed her over his shoulder.

As he stood, he glanced out through the overlook to see what the Barathosians were doing.

They were gone. The entire fortification, along with the soldiers manning it, had vanished.

"Kagan!" Aelron called. "Something's happened!"

Kagan stepped into view. His expression didn't change when he saw Kaitlyn's limp form draped over Aelron's shoulder.

"Drop her," Kagan said.

Aelron's pulse quickened. "You're more evil than Nicolas gives you credit for, if you're suggesting I leave her here. I'd just as soon take my chances with—"

"Don't be stupid, boy. I'm suggesting no such thing. Drop her. I'll catch."

Kagan extended his arms.

"Does death make you insane, or were you always delusional?"

"My physical abilities are greatly enhanced in this form. Now drop her!"

Aelron stepped down onto the ladder. He wasn't about to trust Kaitlyn in the hands of the man who tried to kill Nicolas to protect his own power.

When Aelron reached the bottom of the tower, guards in the plaza were cheering.

"What did you do to her?" Toridyn yelled.

Aelron set Kaitlyn down. "She did it to herself. One moment she was standing at the overlook getting rid of the Barathosians. The next, she was on the floor. Now you know as much as I do."

Kaitlyn groaned and turned her head toward Toridyn. When she opened her eyes, an expression of fear crossed her face.

"I can't see!" Kaitlyn said. "What happened? I can't see!"

Aelron stammered. "I don't know."

"Tor," Kaitlyn said.

"I'm here," Toridyn said, kneeling beside her. "Maybe I can fix this."

Aelron was torn. He needed to get back to Morrigan at the safe house and tell her what he'd seen. But he couldn't leave his Kaitlyn like this.

"Where's Nicolas?" Aelron asked.

"He should return shortly," Toridyn said. "He went to the Pinnacle in search of something that might end this battle."

"*She* ended this battle. Efficiently, too."

"I saw through his eyes," Kaitlyn said.

"The cannon operator?"

Kaitlyn nodded, tears streaming down the side of her face.

"I watched it all," she said. "But now I can't see anything."

Aelron couldn't stay. Now that the battle was over, he needed to learn more about this Sodality Morrigan had inducted him into. The urge to head back to the safe house was as urgent as reaching for the coin had ever been.

Was that all he'd accomplished? Had he exchanged one obsession for another?

"Kaitlyn," Aelron said, "Can I leave you with Toridyn for a while longer? There's something I must do."

"She'll be fine with me," Toridyn said.

"I won't be long," Aelron said. "I promise."

Aelron ran back through the plaza, past the fountains and abandoned merchant tents, past the corpses of Caspardis soldiers, and retraced his steps to the hidden door Morrigan had led him to.

When he opened it, the stench from earlier had decreased somewhat.

Morrigan stood next to the door across the room. She noticed him, but looked back down at whatever she was doing at the table.

Aelron approached her.

"You need to stop throwing your daggers," Morrigan said. "I could throw a rock with better efficiency, and rocks are easier to come by. That Barathosian would have killed you if not for misfiring his weapon."

"I'm usually good about hitting them with the pointy end."

"And then what? He would have turned and shot you. Your blades aren't heavy enough to strike a killing blow like that."

As Aelron approached the table, he took a closer look at what Morrigan was working on. There was a disturbing array of instruments—an assortment of bloody knives and tools, and a blacksmith's glove.

"If you want to throw something," Morrigan said, "I'll train you with metal stars. You can coat them with fast-acting poisons and throw them by the dozen, if you wish. What I *won't* do is watch you waste a fortune in master-crafted weaponry. Our resources are thin and our supply lines unpredictable."

"I had a good view of what happened out there," Aelron said. He told her the story of the clumsy crossbow, and how he'd decided to take a more active role in the battle. When he got to the part about the cannons and the Barathosian camp vanishing, Morrigan's eyes widened.

A muffled groan came from the closed room, and Morrigan picked up a knife.

"You're interrogating a Barathosian in there, aren't you?" Aelron said.

Morrigan glanced at him, then stepped into the other room.

Gone was the partial corpse responsible for the fetid stench lingering in the air. A furnace—a stone enclosure Aelron hadn't noticed previously—blazed with fire in the corner of the room. It narrowed at the top and vented through a chimney. A man, bound and gagged, sat in a chair next to the furnace. His hair was gray, matted down with blood, and a small section of his beard had been torn away. Burn marks traced a path up his arms and across his chest.

If Morrigan was responsible for this, she'd been brutal.

Before he'd met his brother, Aelron would have hardly noticed the man's wounds, or the look of terror on his face. The broken nose and shattered eye orbit would have been of little interest to him. In fact, he'd have questioned none of it a few days ago. The man's condition would have been nothing more than line items on an inventory. Random facts about the environment for Aelron to keep straight. Potential weaknesses to exploit. Necessary elements in his situational awareness.

But something stirred inside, and a solitary thought ran through his mind.

What would Nicolas think if he saw this?

Would Nicolas help Morrigan torture the man without mercy?

No. He'd help him up and offer to carry him on his shoulders if he couldn't walk. Just like the refugee.

"This isn't right," Aelron said. "You can't just beat him to death for information."

The man moaned and nodded, clearly in full agreement with Aelron.

Aelron walked toward him. Was he going to set him free or not? Odd that he wasn't sure, even while putting one foot in front of the other.

Stranger still was the lack of desire to flip a coin.

"This is *his* fault," Morrigan said. "The entire invasion."

"The invasion is hardly the fault of *this* poor bastard," Aelron said.

"The archmage," Morrigan said. "Him and his barrier. *He* caused this."

"You're talking about *Kagan*. He's dead now, you know. There's a *new* archmage."

"And now the world has *another* Ardirian arse to kiss."

"It's not like that. The new archmage is a decent person—from what I'm *told*."

Why did he want to hide his relationship with Nicolas? He didn't need Morrigan's approval.

Aelron wanted to tell her that Nicolas was a kind man, as different from Kagan as a person could get, but there was a fire in her eyes that burned too hot for reason. And her apparent dislike of all things *Ardirian* didn't put him in a good position either.

"Are you going to help me get information, or not?" Morrigan asked.

"He's not going to talk," Aelron said.

"Of course he will."

"If you were him, would you give us any answers?" Aelron asked. "I've known you less than three hours, yet I'm fairly certain a torturer would be wearing your skin as armor and hair as a wig before you gave him so much as a name. And even then, it would be a fake one, wouldn't it?"

Morrigan smirked.

"I find it hard to believe that *torture* is what this Sodality is all about," Aelron said. "You've told me the Sodality is a sacred order. Is torture now within the purview of Religion?"

"Your question implies there was a time it *wasn't*." Morrigan looked away and took a step back. "What do you propose?"

"Do you still have the feather?"

"Of course."

"Then we should—"

Bells tolled through the street outside the safe house. They were more numerous than before.

"Shealynd's protuberant tits," Morrigan said. "I thought you said the Barathosians were gone."

"I saw them vanish with my own eyes."

"The entire city is on alert now. Let's go. There's someone I need to warn before we leave the city."

Morrigan ran for the door and Aelron followed her into the alley.

"Just use that speed trick of yours," Aelron said. "I can catch up."

"It doesn't work that way. There's a cost. And I may need it later."

Halfway to the plaza, Morrigan turned left into a side street.

"There," Morrigan said, pointing to a three-story sandstone building across the street.

The sign out front read *The Boring Jester*.

Aelron stopped behind her next to a corner building.

"We need to be fighting, not scouting," Aelron said.

Morrigan's expression grew serious. "A dear friend of mine is in danger. And *not* because of Barathosians."

"I have friends in this too, remember? If you think I'm going to abandon them and hide in some ruined farmhouse with you, you need to think again."

Shouts came from the cross street ahead.

Six Shandarian Rangers rode into view, spurring their bright-red adda-ki north at breakneck pace.

Aelron pressed his back flat against the corner building until the last of them rode out of sight.

Morrigan gave him a questioning look. "Afraid of rangers? Weren't you one of them?"

It was clear she hadn't seen how he'd arrived in Blackwood, prior to killing the magus. If he was going to be serious about the Sodality, maybe he should begin with a little trust.

"Forget about them," Morrigan said. "Come."

When Aelron caught up, Morrigan pushed one of the doors open and entered *The Boring Jester.*

"It's important you let me do the talking," Morrigan said.

Aelron nodded and they stepped inside.

The tavern's common room was well lit from natural light pouring through expansive windows on two sides of the building. People huddled under the tables, and several gave a start when the next bell tolled. A portrait—depicting a court jester leaning against a wall and checking his fingernails—hung above a modest fireplace in the back of the room.

The matron, who was comforting one of her frightened customers, eyed Morrigan nervously.

"Something isn't right here," Morrigan said.

Aelron's pulse quickened.

Four paces to the matron. A dozen people in the room. None visibly armed.

Morrigan strode over to the bar and knocked twice on the countertop. When the matron approached, Morrigan spoke. "I've stabled the adda, but it has a problem with one of its hooves."

The matron's eyes widened. "The farrier doesn't live here anymore, miss."

Morrigan looked away from the matron.

"I...I thought you knew," the matron stammered.

Morrigan grabbed Aelron by the shoulder and nudged him toward the door.

"He finally did it," Morrigan whispered. "The new Traveler finally did it."

"The *who* did *what*?" Aelron asked as they stepped into the street.

"We have to leave Caspardis. Now!"

"Whoa! You haven't told me what's going on."

Morrigan clenched her eyes shut for a moment, then opened them. "Come."

"Morrigan—"

"Let's go!"

Morrigan started running toward the west gate and Aelron ran after her.

"What has you so shaken?" Aelron asked. "Who was that traveler you were talking about?"

"*The* Traveler," Morrigan sad. "He's..."

She stopped and faced Aelron as the next bell tolled.

"My handler...the *farrier*...is dead. Not just dead. Assassinated. By the Traveler—the head of the Sodality. If my handler was targeted, I'm next. And now that *you* are with *me*, you're just as much a target as I am."

It was too much for Aelron to process. A few hours ago he didn't know the Sodality existed, and now he was a target by association.

"Why would the Sodality want you dead? You just *recruited* me into this festering organization!"

"Because I'm not one of them anymore!" She turned and started jogging toward the west gate, which came into view less than three hundred yards up the street.

Aelron followed, but he couldn't help thinking about something she'd said earlier. She'd called him a *kindred spirit*, and now he understood why. It was more than the *craft*, or his *training*, or whatever innate ability she'd seen in him.

Like Aelron, she was on the outside of the group she'd most identified with for years. She'd lost her *family*, even if it wasn't blood.

"Only a small group of people know the Traveler's true identity," Morrigan said. "We call them the Watchers."

"They watch the Traveler?"

"They watch the *sky*. Not *literally*. Not anymore. I told you, the Sodality is ancient."

Morrigan looked away for a moment.

"My handler uncovered a coup," she said. "Since only the Watchers knew the Traveler's identity, he went to his handler, knowing *that* handler would go to *his*, and so on, until eventually a Watcher would find out. But before he did, he showed me something. He showed me who was planning the coup. I know the identity of the new Traveler. Not by name, but I'd know him on sight. And *that's* why he wants me dead."

Another bell tolled, and a squad of Caspardis guards ran past.

Aelron picked up his pace toward the west gate, and Morrigan followed. When they entered the plaza with three fountains, Aelron stopped.

The large, circular merchant tent at the center of the plaza had been converted into a military command pavilion. But that wasn't what stopped Aelron.

Looming over the west wall were six towers, each topped with two cannons and a squad of archers.

The wall was no longer defensible.

On the rightmost tower, four flags rested in stands along the rear, and a Barathosian soldier stood next to them. He retrieved a blue flag from its stand and waved it back and forth.

A series of loud *booms* reverberated through the plaza as the first volley of cannon rounds tore through the command tent and surrounding fountains.

Aelron leapt to the side as a piece of marble the size of a wagon wheel flew toward him. As he landed against a wall of a building, he caught a glimpse of Kaitlyn and Toridyn running from the city wall.

Toridyn must have fixed Kaitlyn's sight.

Aelron glanced behind to check on Morrigan. She was leaning against the same building as he.

More cannon fire—dull, as if at a great distance—came from behind Aelron.

The city must be surrounded by these towers. We don't stand a chance.

The flag bearer waved a red flag this time.

A second series of *booms* had Aelron and Morrigan covering their ears.

The west wall collapsed into a cloud of dust and debris.

"This is no good," Morrigan said. "We need to retreat now."

"I can't."

"If your friends were anywhere near this wall, they're gone!"

"They're not just my friends!"

Aelron faced Morrigan. "There's something you need to know about me. And you're not going to like it. The new archmage is my brother. He and his betrothed are in that mess somewhere. And so is Kagan. He's dead, but he's in there. He's my brother's penitent."

Morrigan's face was expressionless, and she glanced over Aelron's shoulder.

Aelron looked back toward the plaza to see what had caught her attention.

The dust was settling, and the field beyond the west gate was a sea of Barathosian soldiers.

Morrigan placed a hand on Aelron's shoulder. "Let's take care of your family. But if there's any chance of getting them out of this alive, I need you to do everything I say. Without question."

Aelron nodded as the first wave of soldiers entered the city.

The battle for Caspardis had begun.

CHAPTER TWENTY ONE

In the year 1018 BCE, Sajid Mukhtaar stepped over the threshold, becoming Sajid Lord Mukhtaar. Lord Mukhtaar added twenty-five covens to Clan Mukhtaar, which is a considerable number given the conflict between Clan Mukhtaar and Clan Davith. When the star fell from the sky, it struck the very desert where Mukhtaar and Davith priests battled one another.
- Coteon of the Steppes, "The Mukhtaar Chronicles: Coteonic Commentaries" (circa 680 BCE)

It took several decades for me to decipher the meaning of that last sentence. I had an encounter in that very desert recently. I am now convinced it is speaking of the formation of the Oasis of Zarush, in the Religarian desert, on the road to Dar Rodon. I don't know how best to pass this knowledge on. Kagan is purging necromancy from the Three Kingdoms, and I have been banished. I am a pariah in my own land, hunted, as are all of my fellow priests.

What am I saying? Did I learn nothing from Father Dominic? There is hope. Shealynd's prophecy will give me strength.I shall begin by writing the story of my journey on the road to Dar Rodon. Perhaps future generations will glean something. I will include it as an appendix to the Mukhtaar Chronicles. I suspect it won't be the last story to tell.
- Mujahid Mukhtaar, Private Commentaries, 105 CE

Nicolas materialized on the shore of Lake Caspar, and the necromantic link he shared with Kagan grew more prominent in his mind.

As he finished materializing, the acrid odor of charred wood and burning pitch made him cough violently.

Waves of necropotency filled his well of power. There had to be an enormous amount of death nearby to pull that off.

As he turned to see the city, he grew cold.

The city of Caspardis was gone. In its place stood a field of ruins that spanned more than a mile to the west and north. The fortress was the only building still standing.

Nicolas dropped to his knees next to a dwarf tree.

Kait! God, no!

Siege towers ringed the burned-out ruins, and Barathosian soldiers came and went in small groups.

He looked toward the harbor. Ships sailed away from the city, but the few remaining in port were on fire and sinking rapidly.

Anger replaced terror, and a stinging pain formed in his palms.

He'd been clenching his fists.

Hours ago, he'd fantasized about leveling the city for the sake of justice or retribution. But the reality of the devastation made him ashamed of himself. There were families in those ruins.

Had anyone survived?

His anger grew as sporadic gunshots echoed through the ruins in the distance.

They're probably executing anyone left.

A group of people bolted from a ruined building and ran toward what was left of the harbor. The Barathosians fired their weapons, but the people were out of range of the primitive pistols.

A small cloud materialized over the city and began to disperse. Tiny specks of dark brown broke away from the cloud and fell toward the running people.

No. The specks weren't falling. They were *diving*.

This isn't a cloud. It's a swarm!

High-pitched screeches emanated from the swarm and echoed through the ruins. Within moments, the swarm tore into the people, ripping them apart and tossing limbs and chunks of flesh this way and that.

When the feeding frenzy was over, the swarm flew back into the air as one and headed deeper into the city. But they vanished moments later, as the Barathosian travel magic returned them to wherever they'd come from.

Nicolas stared at the ruins in a daze.

The thought of Kait being one of those victims brought cold rage to the surface. But it was different this time. This time, she wasn't the only person on his mind. She was one face among many. Aelron, Toridyn, the refugees. And countless others he would never see or know.

Had he delayed too long? Had it been wrong to take Kait to Aquonome when he should have been fighting this war?

He blinked as something changed in front of him.

The siege towers. There were fewer of them now. And as he stared at the ruins of Caspardis, more towers began to vanish, one by one, until none remained.

He wanted—needed—to do something. Summon as many penitents as he could and march into the city. Unleash enough necropotency to strike down every last Barathosian in the city.

Something. *Anything.*

But if the Barathosians were capable of this much destruction, there was no time to help Caspardis. No time to take revenge or seek justice for the victims. Dozens of other cities—some larger than Caspardis— would be destroyed the same way if he didn't stop the Barathosians.

And there was no time to wait for Tithian to receive and test the protoforge fragments at the Pinnacle. That could take weeks. One way or another, Nicolas had to get the fragments to Dar Rodon himself. They'd either help take down the Barathosians or they wouldn't. The only thing he was certain of was that waiting would be the surest way to lose this war.

He stood.

The necromantic link.

Kagan was still alive, such as it was. And judging by the link, he was outside the city. Perhaps a mile or two to the northeast.

"You," a woman's voice said.

Nicolas spun in the direction of the sound, but no one was there. Was he hearing things now?

He shifted his weight to lean against the dwarf tree.

"Watch the hands!" the woman said.

The tree stepped backward.

Nicolas *leapt* backward.

What the hell?

There was movement around the tree. It was subtle at first, but grew more pronounced. The markings on the bark shifted and transformed, in much the same way a flower opens in sunlight, until a single opening appeared in the center.

One hand emerged, followed by another. They gripped the sides of the opening and folded it back into a hooded cloak as black as the Obsidian Throne.

The tree had disappeared entirely.

The hands released the cloak, reached up to the hood and drew it back.

A woman with blond hair tied in a top knot stared back at him.

"Archmage Nicolas, right?" the woman said. "Not what I expected."

Nicolas stepped back once more. "How do you know who I am?"

He prepared to open a channel from his well of power to the skull symbol.

The woman pointed at his chest.

"You're wearing a chain of office," she said.

Nicolas glanced down and saw the chain hanging out of his robe.

"Oh," he said. "Yeah. I guess I am."

"*And*," she said, "your betrothed told me this is where you'd appear."

Kaitlyn *sent* her?

"She and Aelron aren't far from here," the woman said.

"Are they with Kagan?"

The woman's face cycled from expressionless to rage to expressionless in the span of a moment. If Nicolas hadn't been holding necropotency, he would have missed it.

"There's a Turian Exports farm," she said. "It's far enough from the city for the Barathosians to ignore."

"Then let's go…"

"If you're anything like your brother, you won't let me rest until I tell you my name. So, it's Morrigan."

"Nice to meet you."

He followed her to the northeast, skirting around the area where the siege towers once stood. As they crested a hill onto the plateau where Nicolas was once held captive in a military camp, he saw a farm in the distance. But the closer they got, the older the farmhouse looked. Most of the thatch roof had collapsed in on itself, and two of the stone walls had fallen into ruin.

"Nick!" Kaitlyn yelled. She started running out from behind a wall, but Morrigan transformed into a black *smudge* and crossed the distance between her and Kaitlyn—close to one hundred yards—in less than two seconds flat.

Nicolas jogged closer to them.

"What are you doing?" Morrigan said to Kaitlyn. She'd taken Kaitlyn by the shoulders and guided her back into the ruins. "I told you it's not *safe* out here. The Barathosians, or their *pets*, could be anywhere."

When Nicolas got close to the ruins, Aelron and Toridyn stepped out from behind the wall and welcomed him.

Kaitlyn embraced Nicolas.

"Toby?" Kaitlin asked.

"He's fine," Nicolas said. "Thank you for keeping them safe, Morrigan."

"I just led them here," Morrigan said. "They kept *themselves* safe along the way. Toridyn killed five Barathosians by himself. Your brother ran one through, and Kait managed to convince one to kill *himself*. I've never seen that kind of magic before."

Kait? I'm the only who calls her that.

"It was a close one," Kaitlyn said. "If I hadn't seen the look on Aelron's face, I wouldn't have known the Barathosian was behind me."

The thought of it made Nicolas take a deep breath.

"A second more and she would have been a toaster," Toridyn said. "I had to guide her myself after she went blind."

"What's he talking about?" Nicolas asked.

"When I use my power, I can't see for a while afterward. I'm probably just doing something wrong."

"You have my thanks, all the same, Morrigan," Nicolas said.

Morrigan looked away.

Nicolas opened his mouth to speak, but Aelron narrowed his eyes and shook his head *no*. There was more going on here than Nicolas was privy to.

"Kait," Nicolas said. "A word?"

Kaitlyn led him farther into the ruined building, through a half-fallen archway into another room.

"This *Morrigan* person," Nicolas said. "You trust her?"

Kaitlyn shrugged. "Aelron seems to."

Nicolas raised an eyebrow.

"I know," Kaitlyn said. "What can I say? We've been through a lot in the last couple hours. She's been helpful. And really nice. A little *standoffish* since *you* got here, though."

Nicolas tugged at his chain of office. "This seems to have that effect on people. She was a freaking *tree* when I met her."

"You saw the speed trick. I have no idea what kind of magic she uses."

Nicolas smiled. "Listen to you, talking about magic as if it's the most normal thing in the world."

Kaitlyn smirked.

"Plans have changed," Nicolas said. "I'm going to need all the help I can get."

He waved the others into the room, and soon they formed a semicircle around him. Kagan stood at a window, looking toward Caspardis.

"What I'm about to tell you stays among us," Nicolas said. "Aelron, can we trust her?" He looked at Morrigan, whose face was expressionless once more. "No offense, but I don't know you."

"A magus wondering if he can trust *me*," Morrigan said. "Now I've seen it all."

"Morrigan," Aelron said.

"I won't spill your secrets, Archmage," Morrigan said. "When I give my word, I mean what I say. When I take an oath, I fulfill it. When I take a vow, I live by it. That's *far* more than you can say about the magi who surround you at the Pinnacle."

Nicolas chuckled. "You can say *that* again. Nothing but a bunch of asshole politicians."

Shock registered on Morrigan's face for an instant, then disappeared.

"The reason I went back to the Pinnacle was to retrieve a piece of something known as a protoforge."

Kagan turned from the window.

Nicolas spent the next few minutes recounting what Tithian had told him about the protoforges. He recounted how the fragments deflected Tithian away from Hiboran when he tried to translocate there. When he got to the part about the fragments heading for the Pinnacle, he looked each of them in the eyes, one by one.

"But we don't have time to wait," Nicolas said. "Not after what's happened here. We need to intercept the fragments and take them to Dar Rodon. That's where the bulk of the Barathosian force is. That's *probably* where these smaller raiding parties and siege towers are coming from. If we can stop them from translocating, then they can't travel any faster than we can. That should even things up a bit. We have a long trip ahead of us, so—"

"If these *are* protoforge fragments," Kagan said, "then you cannot know *what* they'll do. They are not mere objects of power made by the hands of humankind. They are *divine*. Their power is *mystical*, not *magical*."

"I'm aware of the—"

"They could just as easily strip you of your power and give it to the Barathosians," Kagan said, "because of nothing more than a stray thought you didn't even know you should control. They could send the armada away—"

"I'm *aware*—"

"—and drop them right on the Pinnacle," Kagan said. "You think the *Barrier* was bad? At least it killed *slowly*. Predictably. The protoforges could take this continent and turn it upside down. They are *divine catalysts*. Only the mind of a god can perceive what they're capable of. They could be our undoing."

"Maybe this isn't such a good plan," Kaitlyn said.

"I'm aware of the risks!" Nicolas said. "But remember what I told you about Tithian. It's like he tried to hit Austin but landed in Dallas instead. If there's another way, I just don't see it!" He looked at Kagan. "You're worried we don't know what the fragments will do? So am I! I'm not an idiot! But we have to *try*, don't we? I see two possibilities; if we do nothing, the Barathosians will win. If we try this, the Barathosians will *probably* win. I don't know about you, but I'll take the latter. And the more time we spend *discussing* it, the more people are dying like they died outside that window."

An awkward silence stretched on for several moments, and Nicolas took several calming breaths. No one in this room deserved to be the target of his frustration.

Kaitlyn broke the silence. "If time is a problem, and these things are as unpredictable as Kagan thinks, then I might have a better idea."

"I'm all ears," Nicolas said.

Toridyn looked him up and down.

"*Figuratively* speaking, Tor," Nicolas said. "*Figuratively.*"

"Twice now, I've been able to get into their heads," Kaitlin said.

"She destroyed several of their larger *tube* weapons," Aelron said.

Kaitlyn nodded. "I sort of improvised. I made the cannon guy see the first scary thing I could think of. But the second time was easier. What if I can control one of their leaders? What if I got them to destroy their own armada? What if I could do what the cichlos were *terrified* of in Aquonome, and control one of the Barathosian chimeramancers?"

"Taking on a Barathosian or two is one thing," Nicolas said. "But think about what you're saying. The entire *armada*? It's a long shot at best."

"And the protoforge things aren't?"

"Kait—"

"I'm not saying we should forget about them. I'm saying you don't have to do *everything*."

"I have to fix this," Nicolas said. He pointed out the window. "They destroyed that city...killed *everyone* in it...because of what my birth father did. They rounded up survivors and *shot them*. And the ones that lived...the Barathosians hunted them down with *animals*. Defenseless people! The slaughter has to stop."

Morrigan looked up at him.

"It does," Kaitlyn said. "And you're not alone. You have us."

Nicolas looked around the room at each of them in turn. His adoptive father, Doctor Murray, once told him the best leaders knew when to ask for help. Could Kaitlyn's plan work?

"Aelron," Nicolas said. "If I'm taking Kait closer to the Barathosians, I'm going to need your help getting the fragments to the Pinnacle. Toridyn has to inform the cichlos about what happened here. He won't be able to do it."

"Where are they now?" Aelron asked.

"On a barge on the Orm River somewhere. Tithian said they'd be north of Three Banks by now."

"If their destination is the Pinnacle," Morrigan said, "they'll have to pass through Dyr Agul. On the Religarian tributary."

Nicolas nodded. "That's the conclusion I reached as well."

"Can we make it before the barge sets course for the Sea of Arin?" Aelron asked.

Morrigan gave Aelron an odd look. There was a strange dynamic between the two of them, and Nicolas couldn't figure it out. Eventually, Morrigan nodded, and Aelron looked relieved.

"It will be close, but I think we can," Morrigan said.

"How are they being transported?" Aelron asked.

"Tithian said something about a guild called *Azure Dawn*," Nicolas said.

"The *Dawn*?" Morrigan asked. "No. This won't be possible. We'll have to find another way."

"You're going to back out now because some pirates are involved?" Aelron said.

"You don't understand," Morrigan said through gritted teeth.

"Why are you so afraid of them?" Nicolas asked.

"Who *are* you people?" Morrigan said. Her gaze shifted between Aelron and Nicolas. "Neither of you knows anything about the Moon Lake Sodality, and now you're suggesting you know nothing of the Dawn either? You're the archmage." Her gaze shifted back to Aelron. "And you're a former Shandarian Ranger—who's now my *apprentice*, I might add."

"You're *what*?" Nicolas asked.

"It's a new development," Aelron said and looked away. "And I *am* aware of the Dawn. You think a man can train to be a ranger and not learn about the largest smuggling operation in the Three Kingdoms?"

"There are agreements in place," Morrigan said. "*Ancient* agreements that I cannot break."

"What would you be breaking?" Nicolas said. "The Dawn is transporting *Pinnacle property*. One word from me, and you become an *agent* of the Pinnacle. Problem solved…whatever the *problem* was to begin with."

"I've taken oaths."

"I know the value of oaths," Nicolas said. "I take them seriously. I can't pretend to know your history or understand these *ancient agreements* you're talking about. But I *do* know how much the Barathosians care about the Sodality and the Azure Dawn. Look out that window. That's how much. Look at what's left of Caspardis. Is that a fate you'd wish on every other city in the Three Kingdoms just to protect your *oaths*?"

Morrigan faced the window and leaned on the ruined sill. After a few moments, she brushed the dust off her hands and faced Nicolas.

"The Sodality has survived conquerors before," Morrigan said. "We'll survive this one too."

Nicolas placed a hand on her shoulder, and turned her toward the window once more. He spoke in hushed tones.

"Conquerers don't kill people they want to conquer. They're not here to *conquer*. They're here to *destroy*."

Morrigan looked away.

"As far as I know, we're the only people in the Three Kingdoms who have some idea of how to stop them," Nicolas said. "Help me, Morrigan. Help me stop them from doing this to another city."

Morrigan glanced at Aelron, who nodded at her. A moment later she stared into Nicolas's eyes.

"You're the archmage. Shouldn't be *praying* for a solution from the safety of your palace?"

Nicolas chuckled. "I get it. I really do. There was a time I was every bit as cynical. Then I met a Mukhtaar Lord. A little rough around the edges, but a more devout man you won't meet. He taught me a lot about prayer. The *hard* way. He taught me the gods aren't in the wish-granting business. Praying for people is a great thing to do, if you're of a mind to. But when you finish praying, you *help* them. Because that's how prayer works. You pray. Then you *do*."

Something changed in Morrigan's eyes. Her expression softened.

"A magus I don't want to strangle with his own cincture," Morrigan said. "Wonders never cease."

Kagan placed his arm around Nicolas's shoulders, his cold wrist touching Nicolas's neck.

"It would seem my blood *does* run through your veins," Kagan said.

What Kagan could possibly mean by that was beyond Nicolas, but he wasn't in the mood to get into it.

"I'll do it," Morrigan said.

"All right, then," Nicolas said. "Aelron, Morrigan, you're the backup plan. Find the fragments and get them to Dar Rodon. Hopefully, Kait can find a way to make them unnecessary. But if she can't, at least we'll be able to scout things out for when you get there." He put a hand on Toridyn's shoulder. "Was I correct in assuming you'll need to inform the cichlos elders?"

"I can't promise they'll get involved, this time," Toridyn said. "Now that Kagan's barrier is gone, there is talk about returning to Terilya."

Nicolas nodded. "Can you make it back safely?"

"You see all that water out there? That's my *jam*, bro!"

"I actually think you said that right," Kaitlyn said. She rushed forward and gave him a hug.

"Take care of my puppy," Toridyn said. "He's been through a lot."

"He's not disabled, Tor," Nicolas said.

"Denial is not a quiver in Egis," Toridyn said.

"A *river* in *Egypt*. Never mind." Nicolas wrapped his arms around Toridyn and squeezed. "We'll see each other again."

Nicolas extended his hand to Aelron.

"Brother," Aelron said. As they shook hands, Aelron pulled him close and slapped him on the back.

"Don't get yourself killed," Nicolas said.

Aelron smiled as he stepped back. "I'm hard to kill."

Nicolas placed one arm around Kaitlyn and the other around Kagan.

The ruined farmhouse receded from Nicolas's vision as he channeled power into the translocation orb.

The sanctuary at the Pinnacle rushed toward Nicolas as the translocation orb worked its magic.

When he, Kaitlyn, and Kagan materialized, a gust of cool air embraced them. The sound of a man chanting prayers was the first thing he heard.

He recognized the voice.

Tithian.

"Archmage," Tithian said. He stood from a kneeler in front of the Orb of Power.

"What was the chanting about?" Nicolas asked.

Tithian glanced back at the kneeler. "I must *repeatedly* remind myself you were not raised with our customs. This is a daily devotion you should learn, and it's my fault for your lack of knowledge. You'll be expected to lead prayer, from time to time. I'll teach you as soon as possible."

"Take it easy on yourself," Nicolas said. "Things escalated quickly when I came back."

The feeling of being watched overcame Nicolas, and he looked over his shoulder. No one was there. It was the same sensation as last time, but he'd seen no one then either. He shrugged it off as best he could and tried to focus.

"Lady Kaitlyn," Tithian said. He bowed slightly at the waist. "Nicolas informed me of your success at Aquonome. For that, I am happy."

Kaitlyn grinned, obviously uncomfortable and unsure how to respond.

"The new Shandarian Ambassador arrived earlier," Tithian said. "I was beginning to wonder if the Chancellor would ever get around to appointing one. Emperor Relig will likely appoint one in a month or—"

"We failed. There was nothing we could do. The Barathosians appeared with a column of cannons—"

"A what?"

"Larger, more destructive versions of the gun I showed you. Their soldiers materialized in the city and killed the Caspardis guards. It didn't take long for the cannons to finish the job. The only building left standing is the fortress, and it won't be standing for long."

Tithian's face paled.

"And they're using some kind of flying animal to kill survivors."

"Gods."

"I've had to make some command decisions in the field. I've sent Aelron and a friend to Dyr Agul to intercept the fragments and divert them to Dar Rodon. It sounds like the Barathosians are using the same sort of magic we use to travel. Maybe the fragments will send them back to wherever they came from."

"If the fragments work against them the way they worked against me, the Barathosians will find it difficult to send reinforcements," Tithian said. "I'll spend some time in thought. Perhaps there's some way I can assist. But, were you referring to Aelron *Ardirian* earlier?"

"I was."

If Tithian was shocked by the news of Caspardis, he seemed doubly so at mention of Aelron.

"Aelron Ardirian *lives*?" Tithian asked. "By the gods, how could I have forgotten?"

That's right. I never mentioned him when I came back for the fragment earlier.

"How did he appear?" Tithian asked. "His face, I mean. Did he have the eyes of a Shandarian Ranger?"

"No," Nicolas said. "He's not a ranger. But he looks no older than me. How is *that* possible?"

Tithian looked down.

Aelron's aging mystery aside, this was an opportunity to put his word to the test.

"What do you remember about him?" Nicolas asked.

"The last time I saw Aelron was the day you disappeared. Kagan sent him away to the Elysian Fortress with your mother."

"See?" Kaitlyn said. "Aelron was telling the truth."

"There's another name I'm curious about," Nicolas said. "Azazel."

"Azazel," Kagan said. "Now there's a name I haven't heard in..."

That strange presence returned, and Nicolas fought the urge to look over his shoulder again. The stress of everything must be affecting him more than he realized.

He drew ambient necropotency into his well to enhance his senses.

"I can't say I know the name," Tithian said. "Wait, the old man?"

"You tell *me*."

"By the gods, that was decades ago. He was a pilgrim back before the barrier. A holy man, of sorts, though he professed vows to no particular order. Kagan took a liking to him, but sent him away with the rest of the pilgrims when the barrier went up. Your father knew him well. Why not ask *him*?"

"That's...a problem. Sometimes he refuses to answer me."

Tithian looked incredulous. "He's your penitent. That's not possible."

"Penitent or not, he goes into a loop whenever he says the word *Azazel*. Blacks out, rewinds a few minutes, then repeats himself. And that reminds me...something else is going on. I had a penitent *pulled back* to the Plane of Death. I tried to keep him here by pushing more power into the necromantic link, and it felt like it was going to explode or something."

"I've never heard of anything like that happening. We'll have to ask Lord Mukhtaar about this. If anyone would know what's wrong with your necromantic link, it's a Mukhtaar Lord."

The sensation of being watched became overpowering, and Nicolas turned around. A rush of energy swept past him, and from the look on Tithian's face, he'd felt it too. Wind blew through the room, warm and humid, smelling like jungle and dirt. It whipped Nicolas's hair around until he thought the kneeler would tip over.

A blinding white light appeared near the door and emitted a crackling noise.

A man materialized in the doorway.

But not just any man.

"By Shealynd's rosy arse!" Nuuan said. "*There's* the cross-dressing postulant I've been looking for. Someone call for a Mukhtaar Lord?"

"Mujahid?" Kaitlyn asked. Her eyes were wide.

"Lord Nuuan!" Nicolas said.

Nicolas hadn't seen the Battle for Rotham first hand, but Mujahid had told him about the *death fog* into which Nuuan had disappeared. And Nicolas had personally summoned two penitents outside of Arin's Watch who reported similar events during the Religarian siege. Mujahid had spent months searching for signs of Nuuan throughout the Three Kingdoms. And here he was, standing in the sanctuary.

"Where have you been?" Nicolas asked.

"That question holds no meaning," Nuuan said. "Never mind that. Something is trying to pierce the veil. Something *old*. It's beginning to succeed, and that was enough to pull me back. But the longer I stay on this plane, the more likely this entire business will fail."

"I'm hearing the words, Lord Nuuan, but I have no idea what you're talking about."

"My time here is governed by—" Nuuan glanced at Kaitlyn, then stared at her and smiled.

What is it with these Mukhtaar brothers around Kait?

"This must be the Lady Kaitlyn," Nuuan said. He bowed at the waist.

When Nuuan straightened, it was as if the whole exchange never happened.

"I can't maintain this state for long," Nuuan said. Whatever sweetness his voice held when addressing Kaitlyn was gone. "You're going to Dar Rodon because you think Lady Kaitlyn can do something about the Barathosians. And she *can*. But you'll need the emperor's help."

"How do you know all this?"

"I can *teach*, or I can *do*. There isn't time for both."

Nicolas took a deep breath and nodded.

"There's something you need to do when you get there," Nuuan said. "You'll be tempted to hide what she is from Emperor Relig. Don't."

"But secrecy is the key to the whole plan."

"Cognitomancers are a rare and precious thing," Nuuan said. "The emperor has employed one throughout his reign, but he's yet to find another. And the man he employs in that position has grown old.

Emperor Relig will see Lady Kaitlyn as an opportunity. He'll protect her."

Something wasn't adding up.

"Why would she need protection from the *emperor*?" Nicolas asked. "It's the *Barathosians* we should be worried about."

"Toren Relig is a Barathosian puppet," Nuuan said. "You'll need leverage, if you're going to make him fall in line."

"But Emperor Relig was one of Kagan's most fervent supporters," Tithian said.

"Did you ever hear me say I trusted him?" Kagan asked.

"If this is true, Nicolas could be walking into a trap," Tithian said. "I can't allow him to do this alone. I'll prepare—"

"You *can*, and you *will*," Nuuan said. "You're needed *here*. That pot you've been stirring with the Sodality isn't boiling yet."

Tithian widened his eyes.

"What's he talking about?" Nicolas asked.

"How can you know that?" Tithian whispered.

Kagan chuckled. "Our *Prime Warlock* was always one to have his eyes set on multiple horizons."

"It has nothing to do with either of you, so back on topic," Nuuan said. "Toren Relig is an old emperor accustomed to conquest and crushing young men like you under his heel."

"True," Tithian said. "But Nicolas holds more leverage than Emperor Relig is aware of." He faced Nicolas. "The Book of Life. Kagan's lie made him who he is. Your truth can undo him with a single word."

"How?" Nicolas asked.

"Have you never wondered why this place is called the *Three Kingdoms* when only one nation has a king?" Nuuan asked. "There's a *union*, a *kingdom*, and an *empire*."

"As a matter of fact, I asked your brother that once. He dodged my question."

"The Shandarian Union was a result of democratic process," Kagan said. "But a slip of my pen transformed Toren Relig from *king* to *emperor*. In one of the pages I forged in the Book of Life, I made reference to the Religarian *Empire*. King Relig assumed those words came from the god Arin as a sign of divine favor."

"And ever since, he's called himself *emperor* and believes he has a divine right of conquest and manifest destiny," Nuuan said.

"Strange to hear that here," Kaitlyn said. "It was a term used —
loosely — to justify expanding the borders of a nation back on Earth."

"That is *precisely* what Toren Relig believes, my lady," Nuuan said.
Why is he being so formal with her?

Nuuan faced Nicolas. "Yet now you know otherwise. With a single
decree from *Your Most High Holy Pen of Self-Righteousness*, the Religarian
Empire can become the *Kingdom* of Religar once more."

"I get it," Nicolas said, gesturing for them to stop. "But, I'm no
politician. I have *no idea* how to *actually use* this information."

"The emperor will do anything to protect his dynasty's status,"
Tithian said. "Make it clear to him, in no uncertain terms, that failure to
help will come at a price he's unwilling to pay."

"Exactly," Nuuan said. "Threaten to make him a lowly *king* again and
he'll piss himself trying to assist you. But if you shrink away from the
authority he believes you to have, he'll end your life in the name of
religious purification."

"So," Nicolas said. "If I hear this correctly, what you're telling me —
what you're *both* telling me — is I need to march into the Religarian
Empire and act like the king of all assholes?"

Tithian and Nuuan looked at each other, then back to Nicolas.

"Yes," they said in unison.

"That's what I would do," Kagan said.

"Okay, then," Nicolas said.

Nuuan faced Tithian. "Mujahid will have questions. And I can't go
where he's going — by the hells, I shouldn't even be *here*. But he'll
eventually come here to find me. Take this." He opened his right hand
and a rose of Shealynd materialized, pervading the room with fragrance.
"Tell him to place this at the base of Shealynd's statue."

Whatever magic Nuuan had used to achieve that little trick, it *wasn't*
necromancy.

Tithian nodded and took the rose.

"In your chambers, Tithian," Nuuan said. "I placed a parchment in
your desk. Read it when you're alone."

Nuuan lowered his arm and vanished.

There'd been no warning. No change in Nuuan's tone or demeanor.
Just a disappearance.

"I'll keep this in the vestry for Lord Mujahid's arrival," Tithian said,
staring at the rose. "This day has been...eventful."

"Why does Nuuan seem to think you're involved with the Sodality?"

Tithian looked down. "I was going to discuss this with you in due time."

"Isn't this something I should be aware of?"

"In *general*, yes. But there are realities of running the Pinnacle you haven't been exposed to yet. The less you know of the specifics, the more protected you'll be...should anything go awry."

"That sounds a lot like someone shielding a politician from illegal acts," Kaitlyn said.

Tithian faced Nicolas. "You're the leader of the Arinian Church now. You might not be a politician, but don't fool yourself into thinking your position isn't political. The people hold you in awe because of your relationship to their gods. But your work isn't accomplished through *prayer*. It's accomplished through *influence*. Influence requires knowledge. But knowledge comes at a price. My primary concern is guaranteeing that *price* is not the esteem in which you're held."

"I could be oversimplifying this, but I would think if the act is something that would tarnish *anything*, it's something we should *avoid*."

Tithian grinned. "You're right, of course. But the Pinnacle is a ship built for strategy, not tactics. Come about too quickly, and we risk capsizing."

"So you're saying this has something to do with Kagan's reign?" Kaitlyn asked.

"Among the various things the Sodality does, it acquires knowledge," Tithian said. "It is one of *many* religious organizations in the Three Kingdoms, though it is among the most ancient. Kagan allowed the organization free reign."

Tithian was right. There was much about the politics of the Pinnacle Nicolas knew nothing about. He had no other option than to trust Tithian in this.

"Can we at least get a meal before we leave?" Nicolas asked.

"Of course," Tithian said. "I'll have food brought to your chambers while I'm retrieving the translocation orb...and the *mystery parchment* Lord Nuuan spoke of. The Religarian orb will take you directly inside the palace to an imperial reception room."

Nicolas nodded and took Kaitlyn's hand. It would be nice to have a quiet meal, even if only for a few minutes.

CHAPTER TWENTY TWO

In the year 400 BCE, Tycon Mukhtaar stepped over the threshold after murdering his father, Lord Baladi, who intended to stop him. A tyrant of unmitigated evil, Tycon Mukhtaar believed himself immortal and enslaved the priesthood of Zubuxo for four centuries.

The Cult of Malvol thrived under Tycon's reign, and Clan Mukhtaar made no concerted effort to quell the heresy.

Toward the end of his reign, in the year 20 BCE, a small group of slaves revolted, sparking what later became the Necromancer Wars. An agent of the Pinnacle, with the assistance of a newly emancipated slave, assassinated Tycon in 15 BCE.

Lords Nuuan and Mujahid Mukhtaar eventually exhumed, dismembered, and incinerated his body. His ashes were warded in a hidden place within the Mukhtaar Estate, where Zubuxo commanded he remain, impenitent, for one thousand years.

- The Mukhtaar Chronicles, Second Cycle, 10 CE
Redacted by Mujahid Lord Mukhtaar in 45 CE.

If I could make it two thousand years, I would. But Pelagon Ardirian tells us Zubuxo's decision is final. Perhaps I should consider getting more involved in Pinnacle affairs. Maybe then I'd find some way of communicating directly with

Zubuxo. In the interim, Nuuan and I have stripped Tycon of his title. We can at least take some comfort in knowing Tycon will never again be referred to as Lord.
- *Mujahid Mukhtaar, Private Commentaries, 45 CE*

Pelagon's son Kagan, our new Archmage, has asked me to join him as Prime Warlock. This would grant me access to the sanctuary during the Rite of Manifestation. Perhaps this is the opportunity I've sought for decades? I'll have to give it careful thought. A Mukhtaar Lord sitting as Prime Warlock is unprecedented. There may be unintended consequences I've yet to consider.
- *Mujahid Mukhtaar, Private Commentaries, 86 CE*

Mujahid and Digby emerged from the estate, underneath the statuary and past the undead guards, who stood silent in their golden armor and weapons. The guards weren't Mujahid's or Nuuan's penitents. They weren't anyone's. They were simply here. Always. Thirteen skeletal guards. They didn't communicate. They didn't patrol. Mujahid couldn't command them. They stood there with their chests heaving as invisible lungs drew breath, their glowing white eyes staring ever forward.

When Mujahid and Digby rounded the front corner of the palatial estate, Digby stopped.

"I should show you the second entrance," Digby said.

"Is there any danger of the Barathosians stumbling on it?"

"Doubtful. Shealynd—forgive me...*Mordryn* located the other portal at her shrine at the Pinnacle. On Nuuan's request."

"Leave this side open for me and I'll take care of it when I return. I wonder how I haven't discovered it myself, by now." He strode ahead, toward the Algidian portal.

"Lord Tycon was always one for secrets, was he not?"

Mujahid rounded on Digby. "Never utter that word again so close to Tycon's name."

Tycon. It was a name Mujahid hadn't heard spoken aloud since the end of the *Necromancer Wars* more than a century ago. One of the most evil, tyrannical necromancers in history. And not only was he a Mukhtaar Lord. He also happened to be Mujahid's and Nuuan's thirteenth great-grandfather.

Digby nodded and Mujahid continued walking.

"Tycon Mukhtaar was a demon hardly worthy of the title *Lord*." Mujahid said.

"He ascended every bit as much as you did, did he not?"

"He ascended for his *own* sake, not the Clan's. He oppressed and enslaved necromancers for four centuries, my father included. Is it any wonder people feared us when we ascended? Is it any wonder people were expecting the terror to begin anew?"

"Some fought to keep him alive."

"The people didn't care about Tycon any more than they cared about Kagan," Mujahid said. "They cared about the Clan. Four centuries he ruled and refused to mentor *any* on the path to ascension, because of the misguided belief he was immortal. Of *course* there were priests who fought for his life! They knew the consequences of his death. Nuuan and I *lived* the consequences. Or have you forgotten? A clan without a lord."

"Forgive me, Lord Mujahid. It wasn't my intention to dig in the dirt. He certainly made your job all the more difficult."

Mujahid sniffed. "Can you imagine if the estate had remained hidden? If we hadn't sensed the portal, I don't know how long it would have taken to find it. What if I placed a stone somewhere on the surface of Erindor, and said you must get within ten leagues to sense it? How would you choose where to begin looking? How long might the search take?"

Digby nodded as Mujahid stopped before the Algidian portal.

"Nuuan and I pieced the clues together after we discovered Tycon's writings," Mujahid said. "He had a slave camp in the southern deserts of Religar. The disgusting creature had a *harem*. He forced people to worship him as a god! When we got to within a day's ride, we both sensed it. I relocated the portal to the Algidians, and there it remains."

Mujahid gestured at the black field of nothingness, embedded with an arch under a pictograph of a mountain range.

"I have a leaf from a tree in the great northern forests," Mujahid said. "With it, I can relocate the portal near the Elysian Fortress. It will serve until I can venture farther north and retrieve another attuned object."

"There is something you must know," Digby said. "Malvol is not the only one who seeks deification. Your brother does as well."

If Digby had head-butted Mujahid in the nethers, he wouldn't have been more shocked.

"Who better to fight an elevated human than another elevated human?" Digby said. "The gods may not intervene. Mordryn tells us it is forbidden to interfere with someone on the path."

"No. He couldn't. He *wouldn't.*"

"Lord Nuuan told me you'd feel that way. But time is not on our side. If Malvol achieves deification, his power will rival the other three gods combined. Your brother is helping Kaitlyn come into her power fully. So, he needs *you* to approach his priests on his behalf."

"His *what?*"

How could Nuuan betray everything they held dear like this. His occasional blasphemies were one thing. But starting his own *religion?* Not even Nuuan was capable of something so detestable. He of all people knew the evils of Tycon Mukhtaar.

"Please, hear me out," Digby said. "No matter how *questionable* you find this course of action—"

"Questionable? *Immoral!*"

"—you must make your way to his temple and fulfill his prophecy."

"How is this any different than what Kagan would do? Or *Tycon!* *Both* would say the greater good justifies any means. They only differ in how they define *greater good.*"

Strong emotion was threatening to take over, bubbling up from Mujahid's deep-rooted religious sensibilities. But anger and rage would only serve to delay.

He needed to refocus on the portal. When that was taken care of, he'd seek Nuuan out and get to the bottom this.

"And where is this temple of his?" Mujahid asked.

"In the lion's den itself. Barathosia."

Mujahid stared at Digby.

"I'm merely the messenger, Lord Mukhtaar. But I can tell you this...I trust your brother with my life, as I know you do. He knows things. Things I do not. And *that* is saying something. If he says this is the way...then this is the way."

"It matters little," Mujahid said, "To relocate the portal, I need an object that is attuned in some way to the destination. Either magically or naturally. And whatever it is will be consumed in the process. Where am I going to find something with strong ties to Barathosian soil?"

Digby plunged his hand into his pocket and jostled some items around. After a moment, he pulled out a small object, three or four inches in length by one inch wide, and handed it to Mujahid.

It was like a bone fragment, chitinous with a jagged edge, though Mujahid sensed no necropotency coming from it. It felt like solid rock, but Mujahid *knew* it had to be organic.

"Ancient," Digby said. "In fact, well beyond even *your* notion of ancient. So old, and so well-preserved, any part of it that once contained life has long since been replaced by stone. It was in your crypt."

Mujahid furrowed his brow. He didn't like the idea of anyone going near the crypt without his oversight.

"That crypt is dangerous," Mujahid said. "Even to *me*. There are mystical wards in place that could have done *far worse* than kill you."

Digby smiled and shrugged. "I left them in place for you."

Mujahid looked at the bone fragment for a moment, then at Digby.

"Who are you?" Mujahid asked.

"As I told you when we first met, Lord Mukhtaar," Digby said. "I am Digby, master necromancer."

"Well, Digby...*master* necromancer. It is time to move this portal."

Mujahid held the ancient bone fragment at arm's length and let the ambient necropotency run through him. Moving a mystical portal was unlike other magical endeavors. There were no symbols of power involved, no telekinesis, no sigils. In some ways, the portal moved *itself*, though that was an oversimplification. The intervention of a magus was required, though to what extent, Mujahid wasn't certain. Portal manipulation was a necropotency-assisted act of will, wherein the magus formed a request, solidified by an attuned object, then *asked* for the intended result. It had more in common with *praying* than casting a spell, though magic was involved.

And it required a clear mind.

Mujahid used the necropotency in his well to calm himself and let go of his thoughts. Not an easy task, thinking of *nothing*.

With an uncluttered mind and an attuned bone fragment, Mujahid opened his eyes, tossed the fragment into the air toward the portal, and asked, without words, for the portal to move to the point of attunement—the point most mystically entangled with the object.

The fragment disappeared into the black field without any indication something had happened.

But subtle movements at the top of the arch told Mujahid otherwise.

The pictograph of the mountain range signifying the Algidian Peaks was fading, changing in intensity and shape. It flared with an inner light that danced like living fire until a new pictograph emblazoned itself into the stone arch.

It was shaped like a hive—a cave entrance, or burrow, with honeycombed tunnels extending down into the ground.

"It would appear you were successful," Digby said.

"No," Mujahid said. "It merely appears that I've moved the portal to wherever Nuuan intended. Time will tell if this means success."

"When you reach the place you're going, *remember*," Digby said. "Dominance often unlocks doors that would otherwise remain barred and bolted." Digby shook his head and chuckled. "Amazing how even your brother forgets that on occasion. Oh, and the high priestess should be awaiting you on the other side."

"Dominance," Mujahid said. "I'll keep that in mind. One thing, though. You mentioned Nuuan wishes me to fulfill a prophecy. What prophecy?"

"*When I bring the temple to you, you will rouse the hive and fight.*"

"That's no *prophecy*. That's the feverish rambling of a man deep in his cups."

"Fetch one of his priests and let him see *this*." Digby swept his arm to indicate the Mukhtaar Estate. "The prophecy will be *thoroughly* fulfilled."

Mujahid stepped forward, but something stopped him. He faced Digby.

"Will I see you again?" Mujahid asked.

Digby bowed at the waist, arms spread out to his sides. "Of course, Lord Mukhtaar. Though I cannot say when or where."

"Cannot or will not?"

Digby smiled. "As my lord prefers."

When Mujahid stepped through the portal, a blast of warm humidity struck him. He had to shield his eyes, so bright were the rays of light shining through the canopy of trees. Their oblong, emerald green leaves swayed in a gust of wind that smelled of damp earth and moss. But piercing through the smell of the moss and lichen was a strange perfume Mujahid had never smelled before.

His energy well filled at a trickle. But there was another kind of energy, a type of energy he hadn't experienced before. Try as he might, there was no way to touch it or interact with it.

Enough of that. He needed to find this *temple* of Nuuan's.

The jungle stretched before him and came to an abrupt rise. He glanced around, looking for anything obvious; a path, a village, anything.

Nothing.

He'd just have to head over the hill and see what was beyond it.

The sharp mental probing of the ambient energy came and went several times as he navigated the fallen tree stumps, shallow creek beds, and rolling moss-covered hills. There was nothing to be done about it, though. Whatever form of energy this was, he didn't understand it, and he couldn't manipulate it. It didn't appear to be causing any harm, so he chose to put it out of his mind for the time being.

As he crested another hill, he dropped into a crouch and slid behind a nearby boulder, scraping his hand on the hard granite surface.

The faint outline of a megalithic ziggurat sat upon the horizon, shrouded in haze. At that distance, it must be taller than the Mukhtaar Estate.

Nuuan's temple.

A torrent of emotion bubbled to the surface. He felt *so many* things, it was hard to pinpoint any single one as the strongest.

Anger? Yes.

Confusion? Of course.

Concern? Without a doubt.

But most of all, Mujahid felt betrayed.

Nuuan had started a religion. It violated everything a Mukhtaar Lord was supposed to uphold. And if what Digby had suggested was correct, he did it to achieve deification.

What was Nuuan thinking?

If there was one thing Mujahid was certain about, it was that Nuuan never did much of anything without a plan. He often failed to *share* those plans with anyone else, but that was a separate issue.

Mujahid continued forward, choosing to trust. What else could he do? Wallow in betrayal? What purpose would that serve?

The answers, if any, were in that temple. Not in any emotion he was experiencing.

As he crested another rise, a large settlement came into view between him and the ziggurat.

No. Not a settlement.

Whatever the purpose of the buildings he saw, it wasn't commerce or residence. If anything, they were religious in nature. Ceremonial. All of the structures were carved from the same greenish-blue stone, and the brickwork was masterful. The entire complex was a collection of smaller ziggurats surrounding the mammoth one at the center.

And each of the smaller ziggurats were identical in proportion.

As he walked the wide streets between the small ziggurats, listening to the faint sounds of drums and exotic instruments, he became certain of one thing.

This was a temple complex.

After a left turn and a right turn, Mujahid was staring down the central thoroughfare at the gargantuan ziggurat in the distance. Taller than the Mukhtaar Estate, which itself stood more than five hundred feet tall, it must have required as much stone as every other ziggurat in the city combined. A stairway as wide as the main thoroughfare climbed the structure, and two enormous fires blazed on each side of the stairway at its base. Two concave troughs, stained red, ran down the length of the stairway on each side and ended at the base.

The closer he came to the massive structure, the louder the music became.

A procession of dancers, acrobats, and musicians rounded the corner of the ziggurat as the sun broke over the temple. The group of fifty or more was enveloped in sweet, fragrant incense from a circle of men and women carrying bowls at the end of long, golden chains. The smoke wafted around the procession in miniature vortexes as the dancers spun and the acrobats tumbled.

When the prevailing breeze blew a cloud of it at Mujahid, he recognized the fragrance at once. It was his and Nuuan's favorite incense from the temple rituals they had grown up with—and later performed themselves. But that fragrance was produced in one and only one place; Religar. Mujahid's supplier claimed it required a rare herb that grew only in the darkness of the Mines of Abder Razi, combined with the bile of a Northern Religarian rockhound. Mujahid didn't believe such a sweet fragrance could be produced from those vile ingredients, but he wasn't a fragrance trader. One thing was certain, however; someone had transported that incense across the ocean and traded it to these people.

The procession wound its way in a serpentine pattern along the front of the ziggurat. They stopped in front of several mosaics and swung their hanging incense bowls at them, obscuring them with the fragrant smoke. As the end of the procession rounded the corner, a row of children throwing flower petals on the ground came into view.

Look at them all! Praise the gods Kagan's evil didn't touch this place!

A woman wearing a cape of vibrant feathers — and not much else — followed the children. Behind her were three lines of men and women in scandalously sheer golden robes.

It took several minutes for the procession to spread out in front of Mujahid and come to a stop. The music faded, the tumblers stopped tumbling, and the dancers stopped dancing.

The children with the flower petals emerged from within the crowd and formed a line, several paces away from Mujahid. The gold-robed men and women were next, forming a line closer to him. The woman in the feather cape emerged last and stopped in front of him.

"Greetings, Exalted One," the woman said. "I am High Priestess Thalina, chief priestess of Digby. He told me of your impending arrival. Have you come to join us for the sixty-third Orgy and Ale Festival?"

Mujahid didn't know where to begin. "You've celebrated sixty-three orgies in the name of this *religion*?"

"Oh no, Exalted one! That would be *shameful*."

"At least you have the moral sense the gods gave you —"

"We've celebrated seven-hundred and fifty-five orgies. One for each new moon, as instructed. That is only counting the *formal* ones, of course."

There was going to be a reckoning. When Mujahid saw Nuuan and Digby again, he'd knock *both* of their heads together.

"I came here to speak with the priests of Nuuan," Mujahid said.

Apprehension appeared on Thalina's face.

"Of course, Exalted One," she said. She gestured toward the ziggurat. "The temple is this way. The holy wardrobe lies within. Follow these men and women into the temple. They will present Digby's Rod of Domination and the Great Horned Phallus of Nuuan at the climax of the ritual lovemaking — which you will lead us in, of course."

Mujahid gaped. "I'm old enough to be their grandfather, for the love of Arin! Their *great great* grandfather! There will be no...*lovemaking* happening today!"

One of the women in sheer gold leaned toward Thalina and whispered. "Are you sure he's the God Nuuan's brother, Priestess? Maybe he's not feeling well?"

"I'm feeling *quite* well, young lady, thank you very much! Perhaps we can move along into the temple now? And perhaps you can fetch some proper clothing for them while we're at it."

The young lady shared a chuckle with the similarly clad young man next to her, but if Thalina noticed, she didn't say anything. Instead, she strolled toward the ziggurat, gesturing for Mujahid to follow.

"Come, Exalted One," Thalina said. "I will show you the Temple of Nuuan."

Mujahid exhaled and followed her into the Ziggurat, hoping there'd be no *Rod* or *Horned Phallus* involved.

CHAPTER TWENTY THREE

In the year 917 BCE, Tayyib Nazari stepped over the threshold, becoming Tayyib Lord Mukhtaar Nazari. The reign of Lord Tayyib is remembered mostly for the Nehem/Mose clan wars. Clan Mose, in an attempt to drive Clan Nehem out of the Shandarian foothills, poisoned several of Clan Nehem's water sources. Two of Lord Tayyib's priests discovered a Mosean submerging poultices of Hiboranian Milkweed in Nehemen wells. War erupted between the clans for five years, ending in the capture and execution of the Nehemen clan leader, Hovan Ghazni.

- Coteon of the Steppes, "The Mukhtaar Chronicles: Coteonic Commentaries" (circa 680 BCE)

The world rushed toward Nicolas as if he were strapped to the front of a train emerging from a dark tunnel. It was disorienting, and the vertigo made him want to lie down, but the sensation eventually passed and he regained his balance.

He kept a firm grasp on Kaitlyn as she materialized next to him. *Where are we?* Nicolas said through the necromantic link.

In response, an image of a grand palace overlooking a bay entered his mind.

"I know that," Nicolas said. "I meant where *are* we?"

"This is the translocation room outside the imperial throne room," Kagan said. "The emperor established this site for my convenience more than twenty years ago."

"This place is a little gaudy," Kaitlyn said. "Don't you think?"

Gold filigree accented the whitewashed translocation room, creating an ornate pattern on the ceiling, from which hung a chandelier of solid gold. Gems of all colors rested in sockets where candles should be, and they radiated inner light that created star burst patterns on the walls like some sort of gothic disco ball.

As he lowered his gaze, Nicolas discovered they weren't alone.

Guards in billowing white robes ringed the room. He assumed they were guards, judging by the dual scimitars hanging from their belts. Their robes flowed up from behind and wrapped their heads in disproportionately large turbans. Aside from the size of the turbans, their dress reminded him of the Moroccan desert nomads he'd met in Marrakesh when his dad took him to study the Saadian tombs. But from their serious expressions, they weren't about to offer him mint tea and dates.

The two guards on either side of the arched entryway took three long strides, faced each other, then stomped their feet on the tiled floor. The two guards to either side of them marched along the wall to the entryway, spun toward the entrance, and stomped once more.

An escort? But how did they know we were coming?

A blue-robed man of advanced age and balding head entered the room from the hallway and gave a bow.

"Archmage Kagan," the man said. "I am Saleem Abdul Bishara, attendant to His Imperial Highness."

Wait. They don't know I'm the archmage?

How could this be? According to Tithian, Nicolas had been gone six months. In all that time, word of a new archmage hadn't reached the Emperor of Religar? Even before modern communication on Earth, it wouldn't have taken six *weeks* to get a message from Paris to Rome. And Dar Rodon was half that distance from the Pinnacle. The Council must be in a shambles if basic diplomacy no longer functioned.

Maybe it would be best to play along for now.

Nicolas tapped at his chest. When he was certain his chain of office was concealed, he leaned into Kaitlyn and whispered.

"Just go along with it."

Kagan, you're going to do the talking...but you're going to use my *words.*

When the image of assent came back from the link, Nicolas began sending messages.

"Rise, Saleem," Kagan said.

When Saleem lifted his head, his gaze fell on Kaitlyn and he paused. The pause was nearly imperceptible, and Nicolas wouldn't have noticed a year ago. But there was a pause, he was certain of it.

Saleem reached for Kagan's hand, undoubtedly to kiss the ring of office. But Nicolas ordered Kagan to stop him.

"That ain't necessary," Kagan said. "I won't have people bowing and scraping every damned time I enter a room."

"Pardon me, Archmage?" Saleem asked.

Damn! This ain't easy!

This would be much more efficient if you'd allow me to speak freely, Kagan said.

Okay. But no funny business. You know why we're here.

"Forgive me," Kagan said. "I'm attempting to learn a primitive dialect of the northern bush tribes. They're organized, but lacking in basic education."

Real funny.

"No forgiveness necessary, Holy One," Saleem said. "I'm sure your *travels* can be confusing at times."

"Indeed."

"I'll take you and your retinue to the emperor immediately. I must say I can scarcely believe the haste with which you arrived."

"I do not wish to impose," Kagan said. "It is not my place to take the emperor away from his imperial duties. I would be content to wait upon his convenience."

"The emperor would insist, Holy one."

"Then by all means."

Smooth.

You have much to learn if you presume to step onto the stage of world politics, Kagan said.

No doubt. Did you happen to catch that comment about our haste, *or could you not see it from high up on that stage of yours?*

The sensation of paranoia radiated out from the necromantic link. It was so strong, Nicolas had to resist the urge to look over his shoulder.

Why were they were expecting us?

If Kagan had any ideas, he wasn't elaborating. But he couldn't conceal the distinct sensation of heightened caution emanating from the link.

Saleem bowed and paused again to look at Kaitlyn. A moment later he led the procession out of the translocation room.

"I have a bad feeling about this, Nick," Kaitlyn whispered. "There's something about Saleem I can't explain. It's like there's something radiating out of him, like a glow, but only some of the time."

"Nuuan said we'd be tempted to keep your talent a secret. It's like he knew we'd feel a little skittish."

"I don't know."

They emerged into a massive chamber of whitewashed walls and gold filigree. A voluminous dome rose over the room, and archers, dressed like the guard escort, peered down over a banister circling the inside of the dome. Directly beneath them was a raised platform, on which rested a golden throne with thick, rounded legs and a high, gem-encrusted back.

Two men stood at the top of the platform to the side of the throne. The older of the two wore a robe with a golden, gem-encrusted chain draped across his shoulders. But the most noticeable thing about him was the ridiculously long mustache that covered his upper lip and ran down the sides of his face to the middle of his torso. He seemed upset at the younger man. Angered. And when he glanced down at Kagan, his eyes widened. But something else lingered behind those eyes. Was it concern?

The younger man had no facial hair, and there was something in his bearing that smacked of military training. His hair was closely cropped, and a jacket with intricate lacing was concealed, in part, by a brown overcoat extending to the man's mid thigh. Knee-high boots, polished to a sheen, looked as if they'd never seen dirt.

Saleem sauntered up the stairs and whispered something into the older man's ear. He nodded, and Saleem stepped to the side.

Mr. Mustache must be Emperor Relig.

He is, Kagan said.

Who's the other person?

He's not Religarian, Kagan said. *Beyond that, I do not know, save to say my instincts tell me this is a trap.*

The golden throne was facing a gargantuan pair of golden doors. A cage of some sort stood at the foot of the raised platform, but there was no indication what it might be used for. And Nicolas had seen enough cages in the Three Kingdoms to know it couldn't be anything good.

Work your magic, Kagan, but remember we're on a short timer here. We need to find a way to get Kait close enough to the armada to do some good.

You should bow, Kagan said. *Now.*

Nicolas did as Kagan suggested, and Kaitlyn took his lead.

"Holy one," the emperor said. "Your presence here honors me. Thank you for coming so soon."

Maybe Nicolas had misread the situation. Maybe the emperor wasn't nervous about the younger man, but about meeting the archmage instead. Tithian did say the emperor was a religious fanatic.

"I trust this summons was urgent in nature?" Kagan said.

"Of course, Holy One," the emperor said. "I asked you here—"

Kagan waved his hand. "Before we get to your reasons, I need to see this Barathosian threat with my own eyes. The Pinnacle has been talking. And the Council is using words I never expected to hear uttered in the same breath as *Toren Relig.* A shame, too. The temples operate so efficiently in this country."

The emperor's wide-eyed gaze snapped up toward Kagan for a moment, then became expressionless.

You definitely have the "king of all assholes" part down.

Amusement returned from the link. *I prefer to think of it as "emanating an aura of command."*

Well keep emanating. The gods only know what Aelron is up against. I'd like to end this before we need the fragments.

"Of course," the younger man said. "I can arrange to take you to the harbor personally. Guards, prepare a detail!"

Two guards clicked their heels and approached the platform.

Great job.

It is far too early to celebrate, Kagan said. *Do you not wonder why this young upstart was allowed to give a direct command to the court? Something is very wrong here.*

"Who are *you* to speak for the emperor?" Kagan asked. "Who is this man, Toren?"

What are you doing?

If it wouldn't have given the game away, Nicolas would have winced. Calling the emperor by his first name couldn't be a good idea.

"Please forgive Zorian's lack of decorum," the emperor said. "I am still teaching him proper court etiquette. But he is my most trusted adviser."

Zorian coughed and the emperor's gaze flicked toward him.

"And he speaks with my authority," the emperor said. "Forgive me, Archmage, but I must attend to matters of state. Zorian will discuss the urgent matter you referred to earlier."

Emperor Relig walked down the opposite side of the platform toward a small golden door at the side of the room.

I may be new to this job, but wasn't that pretty poor form?

Something is very wrong here, indeed, Kagan said.

We can't let him leave yet! Remember what Nuuan said!

"I suppose I can save introductions for later," Kagan said. "You'll want to meet this young girl, though. She recently Awakened to cognitomantic power."

Emperor Relig stopped.

Saleem took several steps down the platform, eyes fixed on Kaitlyn.

"I see," Emperor Relig said. He turned. "Zorian, I trust you'll handle this with the import it deserves." He stared at Kaitlyn for several more moments before leaving the throne room through the small golden door.

Zorian stepped down from the platform and extended his hand toward Kagan with a huge smile on his face.

"Zorian Osa," Zorian said. "Primary adviser to His Imperial Highness, as you are now aware."

Kagan ignored the hand. "As you say."

Zorian waited awkwardly for a handshake that never came. He lowered his arm and lost his smile.

"Yes," Zorian said. "Well then. I'm afraid it would be inappropriate to discuss matters here. The guards will escort you to a more *appropriate* location."

Zorian nodded at a guard, and the entire patrol surrounded Nicolas and Kagan.

As the guards led them into a dark passage, Zorian nodded to his left, and three other guards formed up around Kaitlyn.

"Forgive me, Archmage, but the emperor wishes to have a private conversation with the girl," Zorian said.

Absolutely not!

"She's my servant," Kagan said. "I'll allow no such thing."

Nicolas put his arm around Kaitlyn and pulled her toward him. There was no way he was letting anyone take her.

T he picnic had been wonderful. How they'd managed to find Nicolas's favorite beer—from a local Austin brewery, named 512—he'd never know.

"Isn't that Pecan Porter the nectar of the gods themselves, Kagan?" Nicolas asked.

Kagan shifted on the blanket and raised his tankard, tapping it against Kaitlyn's.

Nicolas had been holding her close a moment ago, but he had to pull his arm away so she could fill up her drink.

The grassy meadow they relaxed on overlooked the northern coast of the Pinnacle island, and small waves lapped gently against the crags below them.

Such a beautiful day. Not a cloud in the turquoise sky.

"Nicolas," Mujahid said.

Where had *he* come from.

Nicolas turned and shielded his eyes from the sun.

Mujahid, Nuuan, and Tithian were walking down the hill from the Pinnacle proper and—

A sharp pain exploded in Nicolas's head.

What the hell?

He hadn't had *that* much beer. Besides, Pecan Porter never made him feel sick. But he doubled over as a wave of nausea struck him.

The sky went black.

No, that wasn't it. The sky *changed*. Into a gold-trimmed *ceiling*. Three Religarian guards approached with a blue-robed man, and—

The sky was turquoise once more. The pain and nausea vanished.

Mujahid, Nuuan, and Tithian approached with a Council magus in blue robes. Strange color for Council robes.

Had the magus been there before? Nicolas didn't remember him, but...

Kagan raised his tankard and clanked it against Kaitlyn's.

"A most excellent brew," Kagan said. He filled a tankard for Mujahid, who had just arrived.

Where's Nuuan? Wait, weren't Tithian and a Council magus here too?

"Nicolas," Mujahid said. "I hope you don't mind, but I need to borrow the Lady Kaitlyn for a moment."

Of course he did. That's what Mujahid did here. He borrowed people. But he always brought them back. He was a good man. Just like Dr. Murray, who was clanking a tankard of Pecan Porter against Kagan's, and singing a Maori party song he'd learned in New Zealand.

"Sure," Nicolas said. "Just bring her back."

Mujahid nodded. "That's what I do. I bring people back."

Nicolas smiled and laid against the blanket. He drifted off to sleep, as Dr. Murray and Kagan finished the Maori song.

Saleem smiled as Nicolas returned to consciousness in the hallway outside of Emperor Relig's throne room.

Perhaps *loss of consciousness* wasn't the right way to describe it. The reality of his experience was unquestionable. Right down to the taste of the 512 Pecan Porter. When Mujahid had come to take Kaitlyn away, he—

Kait!

"Where did you take her?" Nicolas asked. His pulse raced, and a sweat broke out on his forehead. He drew on as much ambient necropotency as he could find, but there was little to be had. "Where is she?"

"Calm yourself," Saleem said. "We wouldn't want any unfortunate accidents to happen."

"If you touch her—"

"Guards, take them to the holding room."

"I demand an explanation," Kagan said.

"You demand?" Saleem asked. "You're in no position to demand anything."

Saleem waved his hand and three Religarian guards took Nicolas and Kagan by the arm.

Nicolas cursed not having asked for a *siborum* from the cichlos. Now he was powerless and being led away, something he swore he'd never let happen again.

There was no choice now. He'd have to go along and bide his time.

The guard gave him a shove as he followed Kagan down the hallway.

CHAPTER TWENTY FOUR

In the year 852 BCE, Mustafa Sabbag stepped over the threshold, becoming Mustafa Lord Mukhtaar Sabbag. Born into Clan Ezeki, Lord Mustafa emigrated from the Kingdom of Shandar with a group of miners seeking their fortunes in the foothills of the great Algidians. On his journey, he became friends with a local Mukhtaarian priest, embraced Mukhtaarian theology, and became a full member of Clan Mukhtaar.

- Coteon of the Steppes, "The Mukhtaar Chronicles: Coteonic Commentaries" (circa 680 BCE)

Simply unprecedented. In all the Chronicles, this is the only tale of a priest not only changing clans, but becoming a Mukhtaar Lord as well. My own experience of the Rite of Ascension makes me certain of one thing: his conversion was not false. Were it so, he would not have survived. It also makes me certain that members of other clans can ascend, under the right circumstances. This eases my mind somewhat. Clan unification weighed heavily on my mind. I'd been worried we'd made a horrible mistake.

- Mujahid Mukhtaar, Private Commentaries, 25 CE

Aelron and Morrigan rode east without stopping, so eager were they to reach Egis. Game was scarce, but not as bad as it had been farther west. His hunting skills had kept them fed.

They'd entered a valley running north and south less than an hour ago, and the ridge on the far side was steeper than the one they'd ridden down.

He was getting tired of shielding his eyes from the sun, and the speed they rode made it impossible for his hood to stay in place. If they could stop until midmorning, the sun wouldn't be an issue anymore. But they couldn't afford the delay. They had to get to Egis and find a riverboat bound for the Sea of Arin. The sooner they intercepted the protoforge fragments, the sooner they'd be on the road to Dar Rodon.

"It's not much farther," Morrigan said.

"I just wish I had one of those spheres Nicolas uses," Aelron said. "Would have been nice if we could have just *necromanced* ourselves to the fragments."

"I'm not sure that's actually a word," Morrigan said. Her posture stiffened, though her face was cautious. "How much time did you spend with him?"

Aelron's chest tightened. His brother could be a difficult subject around Morrigan.

"Not very long," Aelron said. "A few days."

"Long enough to know his character?" Morrigan said. She gave him a skeptical look.

"Time doesn't reveal character. *Power* does."

"You're a philosopher now?" Morrigan said.

"I suppose you could say it runs in the family."

Morrigan chuckled and Aelron drew his mount to a stop in front of her.

"I need you to hear this," Aelron said. "In a span of days, I watched Nicolas put himself last, in almost all ways. He had a penitent to do his work, had he chosen. Yet he was planning to carry a crippled man from Blackwood to Caspardis by himself. He saved my life and showed me mercy when I didn't deserve it. He revealed more kindness and strength of character in those few days than the rangers did in my forty years with them. I don't need philosophy to know a good person when I see one."

"I'm not saying I don't believe you," Morrigan said. "I'm just…reserving judgment. My experience with magi hasn't been quite as *positive* as yours."

Aelron nodded. He couldn't ask more of her than that.

They crested the ridge and Aelron relaxed. Their ride would soon be over.

Egis lay before them, across a barren plain half a league to the east. Most of the city was in silhouette from the rising sun, but a single tower beyond the city gate stood out among the buildings. It was narrow. No more than fifteen feet wide. Yet it stood well over fifty feet in height, crowned with a pointed, tile-covered roof. Buildings of lesser height sprawled eastward along city streets that splayed out like a fan. The streets converged at the harbor, which was busy with riverboat traffic. The Great Orm River flowed from the north horizon to the south. Though boats in need of mooring filled the docks, the river outside of Egis was devoid of traffic.

Aelron shifted his gaze back to the wall.

The city gate was guarded, but that was to be expected given Morrigan's tale. She'd told him the Religarians invaded and set fire to Egis some months ago, mostly because of a lie Kagan told. It was hard to tell with her, though. Her blind hatred of the man no doubt had her exaggerating.

Morrigan brought her adda to a halt and cursed.

Aelron saw the problem. Soldiers with tall, black feathers extending from large, wide-brimmed hats manned the wall and gate.

The Barathosians had taken Egis.

When Aelron faced Morrigan again, he blinked to check his vision.

Morrigan sat atop her adda as before, but gone was her cloak and fitted armor. In its place was a yellow dress. Her blond hair was freed from its topknot and swept down onto her shoulders.

"How in the six hells did you do that?" Aelron asked.

Morrigan spurred her adda forward.

"If they're occupying the city," she said, "this won't be easy. We may need to steal a boat if we're going to intercept the fragments."

"I don't have a problem stealing something that needs stealing. But that's not a group of incompetent dockworkers down there. That's a disciplined military."

"There are two Sodality safe houses in the city," Morrigan said. "We can resupply at one of them." She smirked. "Scared?"

"It's all fun and games until I get a crossbow bolt in my arse cheek."

"Yours isn't the only arse on the line."

"Spoken like someone who can just turn into a tree and leave."

Morrigan stifled a laugh for a moment then let it out.

When Aelron realized why, he shook his head. "Sure. Laugh it up."

He wanted to be annoyed, but her infectious smile had him smiling back as she trotted ahead.

The city wall of Egis wasn't as high or elaborate as Caspardis, though it was the same sandstone color and equally dilapidated. The gate was open, which Aelron took as a good sign. If the Barathosians felt secure and comfortable, they wouldn't be as alert as they otherwise could be.

Still, he couldn't help preparing for the worst.

Twenty paces to the first guard. Wall is fifteen feet high. Two guards at the gate and two up top. Probably two on the other side of the gate as well.

If it came to a fight, he would concentrate on the wall guards first. That would give him an elevated position from which to take the others. The wall was too high to vault from the ground, but if he stood on his mount he'd have a fair chance.

But what's my exit strategy? Taking out six guards is one thing. Taking out six guards and disappearing is something else.

The closer he got to the wall, however, the less anxious he became. The Barathosians at the gate didn't appear concerned about who came or went from the city. One of them leaned against the inner wall scratching the back of his neck, while the other faced *into* the city, chatting with someone Aelron couldn't see.

Aelron and Morrigan rode past without either of the guards taking notice.

And *that* shouldn't be possible.

"I don't like this," Aelron whispered as they crossed under the open portcullis.

But the lackadaisical gate guards weren't half as unsettling as what lay *beyond* the gate. He'd been expecting to see many things; burned down buildings, guard patrols enforcing martial law, even bodies in the street.

What he *wasn't* expecting to see were people going about their business as if nothing had happened. In fact, many chatted and laughed with the guards as they passed by homes and businesses. There were burned and gutted buildings, to be sure, but a small group of

Barathosians carried roofing tiles and other construction materials into a nearby street.

On second glance, the burn marks weren't fresh. Could they be the result of the Religarian invasion Morrigan had told him about?

As Aelron looked down one street then the next, one thing became certain; the Barathosians weren't *destroying* Egis.

They were *rebuilding* it.

The sound of a hammer striking iron came from a group of workers hammering a boardwalk into place across the street.

Not only were the Barathosians rebuilding the city, they were *improving* it.

"Does this make any sense to you?" Aelron asked.

"This road leads to the dock," Morrigan said. "Keep your mind on how we're going to grab a boat."

"At this rate, we'll merely have to *ask*."

Morrigan shook her head. "You saw as well as I. There weren't any river boats *leaving* the city. As peaceful as this place looks, you can bet the Barathosians have it locked down."

"The gate was open."

"Do you spring a trap *before* it captures your prey?"

She had a point.

The buildings they passed fell into two categories; those that were burned out, and those that had been rebuilt. From the look of things, not a single building had survived the Religarian invasion untouched.

Was Morrigan's story true? Had his father *caused* the war that nearly destroyed Egis?

Poor people. They survive one war only to be thrust into another.

But the farther they rode, the more he doubted anyone realized there was a war going on at all. Egisians smiled and waved at the Barathosians as if the invaders were old neighbors out for a stroll.

They passed a stable on the main thoroughfare that was busy catering to civilian riders. The Barathosians hadn't bothered to take control of it.

"I can see the dock now," Morrigan said.

Aelron brought his adda to a stop, and Morrigan looked at him twice before turning hers around.

"What are you doing?" Morrigan asked.

"We're missing an opportunity here."

"I know. The dock is *that* way."

"Take a look around. Nobody cares that we're here."

"So?"

"*So*," Aelron said, "we have the advantage. We know who the Barathosians are and what they're doing *outside* these walls. But the people of Egis don't know. And the Barathosians don't know *we* know. You know?"

"I'm not going to like this, am I?"

"We have a chance to get information, and we'd be stupid not to take it."

"It's *stupid* to stay in this country any longer than we have to. You heard your brother. He's counting on us to intercept those fragments. It's taken us a week to get here as it is!"

"You told me back at Caspardis you wanted to know what their weaknesses were. Their objectives. You wanted to know so badly that you tortured a man for information. Well now's our chance. Now we can get some *real* information."

"There's a *but* on the end of that sentence. I can hear it."

"*But*...this time we do it *my* way."

Morrigan turned her adda back toward the dock. "Yep. I don't like it. We agreed to accomplish a mission, and that's what I intend to do."

"Every piece of information we gather now can help Nicolas and Kaitlyn. They're fighting blind. And that's if they haven't been captured already. We can make a difference. Nicolas said so himself...his plan is a long shot at best. We could learn something here that puts the odds in our favor."

Morrigan lowered her head. After a few moments of silence, she turned her adda back around and spurred it forward.

"Where are you going?" Aelron asked.

"We passed a stable back there," Morrigan said. "*Innocent* people who *aren't* trying to subvert a government stable their mounts when they enter a city."

Aelron grinned and followed her.

It didn't take long to stable the adda, and when Aelron finished paying the stable master, he found Morrigan standing behind him with her arms crossed.

"What?" Aelron asked.

"For a man in search of information, you sure don't ask many questions."

"What questions?"

"How about finding out what he knows of the Barathosians? How many visitors enter the city every day? Does anyone ever *leave*? You know…questions people ask when they're up to no good but trying not to *look* like they're up to no good?"

Aelron caught sight of two Barathosian soldiers standing idle across the street.

"I'm not interested in the stable master right now," Aelron said. He walked past her toward the street. "I'm interested in *them*."

Aelron nodded toward the Barathosian soldiers. Both wore the familiar wide-brimmed hat, and both wore the same white tunic and trousers, the latter of which were tucked into their calf-high boots.

"Why not get the information we need straight from the source?"

"You *do* know the difference between bravery and stupidity, right?" Morrigan said.

"Just act normal," Aelron said.

"Normal for *me* or normal for *you*?"

"Don't kill anyone. I'd hate to see you ruin your pretty yellow dress."

The Barathosians had begun walking and turned into a side street.

"Walk beside me," Aelron said. "If anyone asks questions, you're my wife."

Morrigan stopped. "I beg your pardon?"

When Aelron faced her, he'd never seen her eyes as wide as they were in that moment.

"Trust me," Aelron said. "We're newlyweds."

"And you take me to a burned-down city occupied by a foreign military for our honeymoon? Why Aelron…I had no idea you were so *romantic*."

"Real funny. Now start acting…*domestic*."

Morrigan raised an eyebrow. "I'll find a broom to carry, then."

"That's the spirit."

"So I can shove it up your arse and carry you like a child's ice treat."

"When we're finished here, I want a divorce," Aelron said.

Aelron crossed the street, thanking the gods for vows of celibacy.

After a few moments, he and Morrigan settled into a comfortable walk a short distance behind the Barathosians. The soldiers didn't seem to care or even notice them, judging by how they carried on.

"Fourth Expeditionary should have been here by now," a soldier said. His voice had the ring of concern to it. "I told Karen we'd have some time together before the worst of it begins."

The other soldier smacked him gently on the back of the head. "Idiot! You've been deployed *how* many times, and you think you're going to get to play with your new wife?

"A man can hope, can't he?"

"Hope isn't going to get Karen's unit through that blockade any faster."

Blockade. That didn't bode well for the plan to get out of the country. It explained the lack of ships on the river, though. But why blockade a city's port and not impose martial law? Anyone could bring supplies right through the city gate and defeat the blockade.

When Aelron turned away in thought, he spotted a man and a woman hurrying toward the Barathosians. The man was dragging the woman across the street by the wrist. She begged him to stop, but he kept pulling.

As the Barathosians turned toward the street, one of them noticed Aelron and Morrigan.

"Ranthos," he said. "Take care of…whatever *that* is." He nodded toward the man and woman in the street."

The man called Ranthos nodded and turned back toward the street.

"Malcolm," the Barathosian said. He tipped his hat. "Excuse us for a moment."

Morrigan returned the nod.

Aelron expected a lot of reactions from the Barathosian, but *politeness* wasn't one of them.

"Let's keep this short," Malcolm said.

"I'm well aware of the time," Ranthos said.

The man in the street dragged the woman closer. "Long live the Glorious One."

"Long live the Glorious One," the Barathosians said in unison.

"I call on Barathosian justice to do something about this woman," the man said. "Not only is she a thief, she's one of those *insurrectionists*."

Ranthos looked the woman up and down and chuckled. "Okay. Tell me what happened."

The man shoved the woman to the ground in front of Ranthos, and Aelron got his first clear look at her. Her tattered gown was covered in filth, and mud caked on her bare feet. Knotted and matted tawny hair fell to her shoulders. And judging from the smell, she hadn't seen a bath in weeks.

"Touch her like that again, and you'll find yourself in a cell tonight," Ranthos said.

The man raised his hands in a placating gesture.

Malcolm bent and helped the woman to her feet.

"She ran into my shop yelling…." The man stopped as if unable to speak.

"Yelling what?" Ranthos asked.

"I can't bring myself to say it," the man said.

"Try," Ranthos said.

"She was yelling *death to the Glorious One!*"

"I did no such thing!" the woman yelled. She lunged toward the man but Malcolm held her back.

"Then she stole a basket of bread and ran out!"

"Ahh," Ranthos said. "So *that's* what this is about."

The woman glared at the man in the street.

"You're no insurrectionist," Ranthos said. "You're no more interested in who governs this shite hole than you are in training carrier pigeons."

"I don't know anything about pigeons," the woman said. "But I know when I'm starving."

Ranthos pursed his lips. "How much is that basket of bread worth?"

The man opened his mouth to speak, but closed it again. He put a finger on his chin and looked back and forth between the two soldiers.

"Five crowns," the man said.

Ranthos stepped closer until the broad rim of his hat touched the man's forehead.

"I'll ask again," Ranthos said. "How much is that basket of bread *worth?*"

The man glanced up at Ranthos then looked back down.

"Half a crown," the man said.

"That sounds right to me," Ranthos said. He retrieved a coin from his pocket and placed it in the man's hand. "One crown."

"Long live the Glorious one!" the man said. He didn't waste any time bowing and hurrying back across the street.

"As for you," Malcolm said, facing the woman. She gave him a fearful look. "I know you had good reason for the theft, but poverty is against the law. We've posted the official notices. Ignorance is no excuse."

Against the law? How can they do that?

"And how am I supposed to eat?" the woman asked. "*You* killed my family. *You* killed my husband!"

"I assure you, madam, I've killed no one in this city. And neither has Ranthos."

"As good as!" the woman yelled. "We didn't ask for your *Barathosian Justice.*"

"I'm sorry for your loss, madam. I truly am. War is a nasty business, and no one suffers through it as much as the innocents. Perhaps we can help." Malcolm placed his arm around the woman's shoulder and faced her toward the side street. "Barathosian Justice may be harsh at first. But we pay reparations to anyone deserving. Go that way. Three blocks. Turn right, then another three blocks. Can you remember that?"

The woman nodded reluctantly. "Three blocks, right, then three more blocks."

"You'll see the old warehouse. Ask for Len. He'll be wearing a hat like mine. Tell him Malcolm sent you. Tell him I excused you from reporting with the others. He'll take care of you. When next I'm in Egis, I'll check up on you."

The woman reacted as if she couldn't believe what she was hearing.

"Go on," Malcolm said. "There's food and shelter. If you're not suitable for work in the city, we'll hire you. There's always work to be done. If not here, then *elsewhere.*"

The woman smiled and nodded. "Long live the Glorious One!"

Malcolm tipped his hat toward her as she ran off.

Something scratched at the back of Aelron's mind.

Insurrectionists.

He had to be missing something. There would *be* no insurgency if the Barathosians were taking better care of Egis than the Shandarian Union had. Sure, there'd be an initial resistance. But that resistance would crumble at the prospect of employment.

Jobs meant food and security.

Yet there were those among the citizens of Egis that wanted the *old* government back?

Why?

"You look concerned," Malcolm said. "No need to be. She's in good hands now. Off the streets and set to a purpose. And she won't want for food or clothing anymore."

"It's time," Ranthos said. "We need to eat before Dar Rodon. Place is huge. It won't fall as easily as this dump."

"If you'll excuse us," Malcolm said. "Word of advice, though. *Work curfew* begins in less than an hour. Anyone out on the street will be given a job to do."

Aelron bowed slightly at the waist. "Long Live the Glorious One."

As the Barathosians walked away, Morrigan leaned close to Aelron. "Why do I feel like that woman is about as safe as an adda in a charnal house?"

"What do you know of Dar Rodon?" Aelron whispered.

Morrigan shrugged. "Like he said. Big city. Bigger than Shandar. Never been there, though."

"If you ask me, Dar Rodon is *exactly* the sort of information my brother needs. If that's their next target, he needs to know. And I think it's a little strange they're *occupying* Egis and paying *reparations* when they've occupied no other city, don't you?"

Morrigan nodded. "It's time we left."

"How?" Aelron said.

"I told you before. There are two safe houses here. One of them is our way out. Follow me."

Morrigan jogged into the cross street and headed north.

CHAPTER TWENTY FIVE

In the year 841 BCE, Sadiq Qureshi stepped over the threshold, becoming Sadiq Lord Mukhtaar Qureshi. He led Clan Mukhtaar for some seventy years, ultimately giving all authority to his son Aziz, who ascended in 791 BCE. Lord Sadiq lived another forty years after the transfer of power.

The Zerubulan Revolt (845 - 839 BCE) demanded most of his attention in the early part of his reign.

- Coteon of the Steppes, "The Mukhtaar Chronicles: Coteonic Commentaries" (circa 680 BCE)

Coteon was uncharacteristically silent with regard to the Zerubulan Revolt. Perhaps because of how short-lived it was. I've pieced together enough to learn Clan Zerubula brought charges against Clan Mukhtaar in front of what was known as the Necromantic Council. It was a territorial dispute of some sort, alleging Clan Mukhtaar had illegally expanded into southern Religar. Lord Sadiq made the case that the expansion was lawful. The Council agreed and that was the end of the matter. Legally, at least. History shows Clan Zerubula had other plans.

- Mujahid Mukhtaar, Private Commentaries, 22 CE

The ziggurat pulled Mujahid toward it, so massive was its scale. The sensation was an illusion, a trick his mind would play when perceiving something so large, but the effect was unbalancing. Sweat ran into his eyes and down the sides of his face. And if that wasn't annoying enough, flies had begun to pester him as well.

High Priestess Thalina led him toward a squared entryway cut into the center of the main stairs. As they drew closer to the steps, Mujahid's gazed traveled up to the summit. It would take him hours to climb that high, and he'd have to stop a few times along the way.

"How often do you climb to the top?" Mujahid asked.

Thalina smiled. It was neither humorous nor sarcastic. It was the amused smile a parent gives when a child asks if they'll ever grow a tail.

"Only Digby travels to the top, Exalted One," Thalina said. "That is his sacred place."

Mujahid needed no reminder of Digby's telekinetic skills. He'd managed to leap off the wall surrounding Rotham to save Mujahid, then leap back to the top. The little man could probably reach the ziggurat's summit without his feet ever touching ground.

"Tell me," Mujahid said. "You refer to me as *Exalted One*, and my brother as *The God Nuuan*. Yet you call Digby…*Digby*. Why? What is Digby to you?"

Thalina appeared surprised at the question. "Digby is Digby. Nothing more. Nothing less."

At least her logic was unassailable.

The entrance to the temple was pristine, as if it had been swept shortly before their arrival. And it bore none of the telltale musty odors he'd expected. The tunnel, constructed of masterful brickwork with mortar that shone like liquid gold, came to an end across from a curious mosaic between two torches.

It was a depiction of Digby engaged in various acts of lewd conduct on the platform at the top of the ziggurat. Wine flowed up from the center of the platform into a fountain of red jewels that cascaded into Digby's cup and all over the men and women he was engaged with. Digby, smiling, held a rod in one hand, and his eyes glowed as if he were a Mukhtaar Lord. He pointed the rod at the sky, which depicted the smiling face of Nuuan looking down on the temple. Amber-colored gems surrounded Nuuan's face like a halo. A giant right arm swept out from behind a cloud and ended with a hand pointing straight down at the temple.

Thalina bowed before a placard that read *The Queen's Retreat*.

Leave it to Nuuan to commission such an affront to good taste.

Tunnels leading left and right continued for a dozen yards or more, then turned inward toward the temple's depths. Thalina chose the left tunnel and led Mujahid farther into the temple.

Torches lined the inner wall, casting an orange glow where natural light couldn't reach. Phallic statues sat upon pedestals in niches along the walls. Images of grapes, wine chalices, and scenes of revelry were carved into the stone between the niches.

While the imagery was distasteful, it also made sense. If Nuuan's purpose here was to achieve deific ascendance with haste, and such ascendancy required worshipers, it would be at cross purposes to create a religion requiring heroic sacrifice and prudish morals.

Preach the sanctity of wine, sex, and revelry, however, and the religion would sell itself.

As they continued down the hall, the images grew more gruesome. Each image, of which there were a dozen or more, was similar to the others in one disturbing way; they depicted a person reaching for the rod Digby held, then burning until their features melted into nothingness. They writhed and screamed as their liquefied skin dripped to the paver stones beneath their feet.

Mujahid and Thalina rounded a corner in the passage and came to a square entrance as wide as the hallway. A gossamer curtain stretched across the entryway, and pinpoints of light shone through from beyond. The scent of Nuuan's favorite ritual incense was strong here.

"The Temple of Nuuan lies beyond," Thalina said.

Thalina drew the curtain aside and motioned for Mujahid to step through.

What Mujahid saw next made him turn around and check the stone over the entryway for a pictograph.

How can this be?

He gazed at the floating green lights in the distance, trying to absorb the significance of what he saw. Standing before him, contained completely within the gargantuan ziggurat, was an exact replica of the Mukhtaar Estate. But where a statue of Zubuxo stood over the entrance at the true estate, a giant statue of Nuuan stood instead.

Heresy. My own brother is a heretic.

Familiar gold and black scroll work wound its way around the massive structure and up the wide stone stairs that spanned the width of the building. Three monolithic ceremonial doors stood at the head of the stairs. All that was missing was the contingent of undead guarding the entrance.

The walls of the ziggurat sloped upward and inward as if Mujahid were underneath a grand staircase. But the steps vanished into the darkness above. Not even the floating green orbs illuminated the top.

Thalina walked ahead of him, then indicated they should stop.

"Where are the priests?" Mujahid asked. "I must speak with them."

"What you ask is not possible."

"Have they no ears or mouths?"

Thalina looked dumbfounded. "Of *course* they have mouths. I *believe* they have ears as well. That is to say, I believe they *hear*."

Mujahid cocked his head to the side. Was she truly uncertain whether the priests had ears? Or was she being sarcastic?

"Regardless," Thalina said. "No one enters the hive except for the God Nuuan."

Hive? When I relocated the portal, a pictograph of a hive appeared above it. This was growing stranger by the minute.

"You mean the priests are not in that large structure ahead?" Mujahid asked.

"Yes. They are."

Mujahid walked forward and Thalina grabbed his arm.

"No, my lord!" Thalina said. "This is not right!"

Mujahid shook her arm off and took another step.

He wished he hadn't.

It was as if he'd walked into a solid wall of power, but one which contracted then slammed into his chest when he touched it. The release of energy sent him reeling backward until he stumbled and landed on his bottom.

Thalina shook her head. "The God Nuuan disapproves."

"The festering *god Nuuan* can eat a..." He needed to get control of himself. "Never mind."

Mujahid ignited the symbol of ascension and tried to probe the invisible wall, but the power wouldn't leave him. The ambient probing energy he felt outside entered his mind and absorbed the power. No matter where he went or how much power he drew, the ambient probe dominated him, rendering him powerless.

Dominated.

What was it Digby had said? *Dominance often unlocks doors that would otherwise remain barred and bolted.*

Mujahid called to mind the image of *The Queen's Retreat*. Digby had been pointing a rod at Nuuan, who in turn pointed at the temple.

Mujahid wasn't certain, but it was worth trying.

"Thalina," Mujahid said. "I need you to bring me something. *Two* somethings, in fact. Bring me the Rod of Domination and the Great Horned Phallus of Nuuan."

"I can bring you the phallus," Thalina said. "But not the Rod. It is not possible. I will show you."

Thalina touched the wall, and it made a grinding noise. A section eight feet tall by six feet wide swung open, revealing two small niches containing the items Mujahid sought.

On one pedestal rested the phallus. It measured a half-meter in length, and multiple curved horns protruded from the surface in no identifiable pattern.

The second pedestal was different, however. Hovering an inch or two above the surface was a translucent cube of energy, within which floated a rod bearing remarkable resemblance to the rod in *The Queen's Retreat*. Above the cube was another mosaic, smaller than *The Queen's Retreat*, but recognizable as the face of Digby.

Mujahid retrieved the phallus and knew he was in the presence of magic.

Just like Nuuan to turn a phallus into an object of power.

It was possible the phallus alone would get him beyond the energy field. But first, he'd rather not be wrong and get tossed across the room again. And second, the more he thought about things, the more he realized how necessary the Rod of Domination would be.

Mujahid reached for the rod, but Thalina grabbed his arm, pulling it away from the hovering cube of energy.

"The God Nuuan will disapprove of this as well, my lord," Thalina said. "I've seen men try to take the Rod of Domination before. So have you."

"I have?"

"The burning people."

Mujahid remembered the horrific images in the mosaics leading into the temple.

If these objects were the key to getting through the energy field, then perhaps the symbol of ascension was the key to getting into the hovering cube. What other reason would Digby have to depict his eyes as glowing in *The Queen's Retreat*?

Mujahid ignited the symbol of ascension and extended his arm.

Again Thalina tried to stop him.

He faced her and she shrank away.

As his hand passed into the energy cube, a surge of heat engulfed the horned phallus. Images of the burning men in the mosaics flooded through his mind, and for a moment he thought he'd made a horrible mistake. But the heat that likely would have burned him alive diverted from his hand into the phallus. When the last of the heat subsided, Mujahid retrieved the Rod of Domination.

Thalina looked at him as if he would burst into flame at any moment.

The rod was an object of power. Mujahid could sense the energy within. But there was something else. The moment he grasped the Rod of Domination, the ambient field of probing energy evaporated. And he was convinced it would no longer restrict him from using necropotency.

Mujahid walked toward the invisible energy field. He glanced at Thalina. "Are you coming along?"

"Only one may pass," Thalina said.

Mujahid stepped past the threshold where the energy field had stopped him. But there was no difference between that step and the last.

As he walked farther, lights flickered into existence in the darkened alcoves at the top of the stone steps.

A rush of wind blew past him and up the stairs as the center door swung open with a creak.

An ominous sign. The estate's central door was known as the Mourning Door. And the Mourning Door only opened upon the death of a Mukhtaar Lord.

He climbed the steps in the shadow of the statue of Nuuan, offering a silent prayer to Zubuxo for protection and safe passage. Only Nuuan and Digby knew, with any certainty, what was inside the temple. And they were keeping quiet on the subject.

His mind worked quickly now that he was capable of using necropotency again. Events whose significance had gone unnoticed earlier were revealing their true weight with every step he took.

At the *true* estate, when he'd moved the portal from the Algidian Peaks to this place, the symbol had changed to a hive. Nuuan's prophecy mentioned a *hive*. But there was more to the prophecy than that. If he recalled the words, they were "when I bring the temple to you, rouse the hive and fight."

When I bring the temple to you.

This could be no coincidence. The temple was an exact replica of the Mukhtaar Estate. From a certain point of view, moving the portal could be interpreted as bringing the temple to them.

And then there was Thalina's confusing comments about the priests of Nuuan.

Whoever he found inside this temple, he no longer believed they would be human.

Any similarities that existed between the outside of the temple and the outside of the Mukhtaar Estate vanished when Mujahid reached the top of the stairs.

The Mourning Door looked in upon a long, wide tunnel, which was illuminated by an inner light source that cast striated shades of amber along the walls. The tunnel wall was coated in a slippery substance that gave Mujahid the impression of stepping inside a living being. It cambered downward to the left, until anything farther was out of sight.

Mujahid glanced back at Thalina, who had prostrated herself on the ground.

Stone slab gave way to dirt and pebbles as Mujahid stepped into the tunnel.

But the sound that returned from deep within made him stop.

Dozens of feet walking—no, *clicking*—came from the corridor ahead. Mujahid considered going forward, but the creature emerging from the lower tunnel filled him with a terror he'd not known in decades. Perhaps ever.

It landed in front of him with the grace of an adda-ki and held six tarsal swords extended straight out to the sides. The nightmarish insectoid figure towered over him. More than a dozen eyes filled an ant-like skull, and four independent pincers opened and closed around its elongated mouth. The overlapping scales covering its body would make it impervious to steel, and the muscular legs, bent backward at the knee joint, would make escape impossible. This creature could reach the top of the ziggurat in two jumps.

Argram!

What Mujahid was seeing couldn't be real. Argram were predators that once hunted humans to near extinction. But they themselves had been extinct since before recorded time.

Not even the battle with the ancient cyclops had paralyzed him with as much terror as he felt in this moment.

But he had to fight. He had to survive.

He ignited the symbol of ascension and opened a channel to the skull symbol.

The probing energy returned and entered his mind. This time it didn't stop him from casting.

Be at ease, Mukhtaar Lord, a voice said in his mind. The voice was like a thousand people speaking in perfect unison. But it was calming. Hypnotic. *We are the Emissary. We are the Speaker. We are peace.*

The argram folded its tarsal swords and bent its knees until it was the same height as Mujahid.

The presence of this creature defied everything Mujahid knew of natural philosophy.

Yet here was an argram, folding its deadly tarsal swords—swords that were natural extensions of its chitinous exoskeleton. And it spoke of peace.

Mujahid released his grasp on the necropotency and extinguished the symbol of ascension. It had been a foolish move born of fear anyway. Had he chosen to fight, it would have been the shortest battle of his life.

"This can't be," Mujahid said.

The argram cocked its head to the side and walked around Mujahid, viewing him from all angles. Its pincers clicked and clacked as it circled.

Mujahid swallowed.

"You are exactly who we know you to be," the argram said.

"I may not be who you *think* I am," Mujahid said.

"You are the *other*," the argram said. "Your nestling told us you would come."

Nuuan.

"Come," the argram said. "We have much to discuss. But we cannot do so here."

The argram nodded toward the temple's entrance, and Mujahid saw Thalina out of the corner of his eye.

"There are those who would not understand what we are about to tell you," the argram said.

"I have questions," Mujahid said.

"Questions only the queen can answer."

The argram strode farther into the tunnel.

Mujahid swallowed again.

In his most feverish imagination, marching into a hive of curiously *non-extinct* argram was a thought Mujahid never entertained as possible.

He took a deep breath and followed. His life was in the argram's hands now, for better or worse.

CHAPTER TWENTY SIX

In the year 791 BCE, Aziz Qureshi stepped over the threshold, becoming Aziz Lord Mukhtaar Qureshi. By the time I had become a man, Lord Aziz had already passed into the Plane of Peace. While Clan Zerubula considers Lord Aziz a tyrant, it is of interesting note that Aziz's most staunch supporter, Jagur Babayev, was a Zerubulan priest. Babayev writes that Zerubulan claims of tyranny began with a failed assassination attempt. Clan Zerubula found Lord Aziz to be a most uncooperative target.

In the final decade of his life, Lord Aziz sealed the Mukhtaar Estate to Catiatum and Zerubulan priests and ordered the suspension of all ritual in Catiatum and Zerubulan territories.

- Coteon of the Steppes, "The Mukhtaar Chronicles: Coteonic Commentaries" (circa 680 BCE)

Coteon was close, but he didn't have the entire story. The true origin of Clan Zerubula's claim was after the Necromantic Council ruled in favor of Lord Aziz's father, ending the Zerubulan Revolt, an event that took place several years before Lord Aziz was born.

- Mujahid Mukhtaar, Private Commentaries, 22 CE

A elron brought his fist to his nose as the stench grew overpowering.

He and Morrigan stood on a stone landing, several stories under the city of Egis. They'd carried torches down from the safe house above, but the underground chamber was so large that the light didn't reach beyond a few feet into the murk.

The house was nothing more than a concealed stairwell leading to the city sewers.

"Don't touch the water unless you absolutely have to," Morrigan said. She tugged at a mooring line until a boat came into view.

Boat was overstating it. It was a raft with thick boards nailed into place to form side rails.

"Where's it go?" Aelron asked.

"This is a river of shite and brown water. Where do you *think* it goes?"

The boat slid up along the platform and rocked from side to side in the water that *wasn't* water.

"The Sodality uses these sewers for clandestine meetings," Morrigan said. "Usually with the Azure Dawn. If there are any Dawn down here, they might agree to smuggle us out of the city."

"And if not?"

"Then nothing changes. Hop in." She nodded toward the boat.

Aelron glanced back toward the stairs.

"Have you forgotten something?" Morrigan said. "I'm not exactly in the best standing with the Sodality right now. If they find me they'll kill me. Then they'll kill *you* for seeing them kill *me*. Do you think staying beneath one of their safe houses for long is a good idea?"

Aelron rubbed his temples, then climbed into the wobbly vessel. It nearly toppled when Morrigan climbed in after him. He tried to steady it by placing his hand on the platform, but the boat had drifted farther from the landing than he'd thought, and his hand wound up in the fetid water.

When he pulled his hand back, he had to spend a few minutes scraping it on the corner of the platform to get the sludge off.

"Brilliant," Aelron said.

"I wouldn't pick my nose with that hand, if I were you."

"I wasn't planning on picking your nose."

Morrigan groaned a fake laugh and steered the craft away from the platform with a beam of tapered wood that served as a makeshift rudder. She aimed it toward a darkened tunnel entryway.

The stench was no better in the tunnel, and Aelron was sorry they'd left the torch behind. If the Azure Dawn was down here somewhere, they could float right by without Aelron or Morrigan being any wiser.

Stories of the Dawn's ability to blend in were as close to myth as he'd ever heard at the Elysian Fortress. The elder rangers made it sound as if a person's own mother could be Azure Dawn, and they wouldn't know until she traded them for a shipment of Shandarian Powder—the Dawn's primary source of income. Aelron saw an adda-ki throw its ranger once while out on patrol. The rider accused it of being a Dawnmaster in disguise. And two others believed him until Jacobson told them all to bugger off and learn how to ride.

Some years later, Aelron learned the Dawn always wore a sapphire tattoo of a sun. It had something to do with their initiation ritual, or their religion, or an oath no one fully understood.

They passed several more landings. He couldn't see them well, but the splashing of the water would change whenever they emerged from the tunnel into a chamber. The noise would fade rather than echo.

A shaft of light broke the darkness up ahead, and before long they were drifting into a tunnel that made them shield their eyes.

"Get ready," Morrigan said. "There's a landing up ahead, just before the tunnel opens. We'll leave the boat there and head out under the pier."

Aelron closed his eyes and imagined what might be beyond the tunnel.

"You've been here before," he said. "What does the pier look like?"

"Narrow steps to the right, probably for sewer workers. Large crossbeam supports to the left."

"Then we should go left and climb," Aelron said. "Oh, and you're not my wife anymore."

"You bastard. You broke my heart."

"If we're seen, we're fishermen. I went to check our nets and stumbled. You came down after me. We're young and agile. We'd do something stupid like climb the pier with a twisted ankle instead of walking across the harbor to use a perfectly safe stairway."

"You're half right," Morrigan said. "*I'm* young and agile. You just age well, *grandpa*."

Morrigan guided the craft to a small ledge on the side of the tunnel. When they climbed out of the boat, she stretched.

"Your fishermen idea is shite, by the way," Morrigan said. "We shouldn't be talking to *anyone* for *any reason.*"

"We can't stop them from talking to *us.*"

Morrigan held up her hand and silvery light glinted off the blade of her dagger.

"Yes we can," she said. "We don't have time for conversations. Anything that slows us down brings us closer to Zubuxo's throne than I care to be."

"Then what do you suggest?" Aelron asked.

"You're right about climbing the pier. The beams will give us some concealment. But once we're on the platform, we make our way to a boat as quickly as possible. No matter how many Barathosians we have to cut through to get there. Understood? No hesitation. We cast off and let the river do the hard work."

"And what about the blockade?"

"The blockade isn't what's going to kill us on the platform. Focus on the present. We'll worry about the blockade when we know what we're up against. Having a strategy is well and good, but no strategy we could devise right now will survive contact with the Barathosians."

"Are you *training* me?"

Morrigan smirked. "Follow my lead. When it's time to attack you'll know, because you'll see me fighting."

She ran to the end of the tunnel and leaned around the corner. After a moment, she glanced at Aelron, waved him on, and leapt across the narrow tunnel to the walkway on the opposite side.

Aelron made a similar leap and glanced toward the crossbeams supporting the pier.

The beach formed a small hill under the pier. The climb would be much shorter there.

Ten feet from the sand to the deck. Not too bad.

Morrigan must have had the same idea, because she placed her dagger in her mouth and ran toward the small hill. When she reached the safest spot to climb, she gestured for Aelron to move quietly.

She pointed to top of the pier and held up a single finger.

One guard up top.

When he looked back at Morrigan to nod his confirmation, he blinked. Gone was her yellow dress. Once again she wore the enigmatic black cloak, and her hair was pulled into a top-knot.

Aelron climbed up onto the beam next to her. When he steadied himself, Morrigan nudged him and crossed her eyes downward. It took him a moment to realize she was referring to the dagger between her teeth.

He retrieved the smaller of the two blades in his cloak and did the same. As Master Nigel used to tell him, "It's better to have it and not need it, than to need it and not have it."

Sand and pebbles struck Aelron in the forehead as they climbed. Someone was walking on the platform above them.

Morrigan climbed over the last beam and up onto the platform without a sound. Aelron doubted he could have done it better.

For that matter, he doubted he could do it *as well.*

When Aelron pulled himself up to the topmost beam of the support structure, he scanned the platform.

The platform was a large u-shaped boardwalk that was open to the river. Three wide streets emptied onto the platform, each across from one of the harbor's three piers, and a mixture of stone and wooden buildings lined the innermost side of the boardwalk. Mostly businesses, judging by the signs and shingles hanging from their entrances. There was everything from government offices to taverns and inns. Even a chocolatier had set up shop next to the harbormaster's office, though it was boarded up.

Two riverboats, one upstream and one down, docked against the southernmost pier, and the downstream boat had a landing craft joined to its side by a system of ropes and pulleys.

If they were going to make their way through a blockade, that would be the boat to take.

Movement caught Aelron's eye.

Three guards patrolled along the platform, two abreast and one following. But there were few people at the docks for a city of this size. Cleaning tools—brooms, buckets, rags, and brushes—lay abandoned next to ropes, hooks, and other implements used in managing river traffic.

Aside from the guards, the entire pier was deserted.

Morrigan was crouched behind the rearmost Barathosian guard, and her dagger was no longer in her mouth. She held it up beside her at the level of her head, point facing the Barathosian, and she prowled toward him.

Morrigan straightened, wrapped a hand around the rearmost guard's mouth, and plunged the dagger through the back of his neck. As the guard fell in a pool of his own blood, Morrigan became a black blur on the periphery of Aelron's vision. The other two guards turned, but Morrigan was too fast. The blur resolved into Morrigan long enough for her to slice her blade across the next guard's throat. Once more she *blurred* to the next, thrusting her blade into the guard's chest. The blur flashed over to Aelron, then resolved into Morrigan once more, no more than two paces away.

She panted and doubled over.

"I shouldn't have..." she said.

As Aelron opened his mouth to speak, Morrigan's eyes rolled back. Her face drained of color and she began to collapse.

Aelron lunged forward and caught her before she struck the wooden pier.

"Morrigan," Aelron whispered. He tapped her cheeks lightly as she lay across his lap.

After a few seconds of unconsciousness, Morrigan groaned. The color returned to her cheeks.

Aelron's tension drained away when he saw her coming around.

"You have to teach me how to do that," Aelron said.

"How to almost kill yourself?" Morrigan said, her eyes half closed. "We'll start tomorrow."

"I need to get you off the pier before they spot us."

Morrigan shook her head and tried to sit up. She failed and landed in Aelron's lap once more.

"I just need a minute. Festering hells, I shouldn't have. Now it will be *hours* before I can *shadow step* again. Maybe a day."

She sat, this time managing to push herself up into a crouch.

When she stood, Aelron brushed some stray dirt off her cloak.

"Are you going to tell me what *shadow stepping* is?" Aelron asked.

Morrigan nodded at a group of people emerging onto the platform from a wide street between two buildings.

The people huddled together and kept looking over their shoulders.

"The short version," Morrigan said. "Hunting escaped demons often requires stepping into the land of the dead. *Piercing the veil*. We call it *shadow stepping*. I enter in one place and emerge at another. And every time I do, it takes something from me. That's how the *veil* repairs itself…with the life force of the hunter."

"It *kills* you?"

"It can. But I'm not *that* reckless. I'll recover in time. But until I do, I'll be weaker than usual."

Morrigan grabbed Aelron and pulled him behind one of the tool racks.

Aelron glanced toward the cause of her reaction.

The lady whom Malcolm had sent away for food and shelter was among the crowd of ten people huddled together.

Three Barathosians followed the group. They each wore the same wide-brimmed hats with black feathers, but one of them was shirtless and carrying a whip. Every time the group slowed, the Barathosian cracked the whip in the air behind them.

When the group reached the central pier, they seemed uncertain what to do. Aelron was frightened for them, worried the Barathosians would execute the innocent townsfolk by marching them off the platform.

The Barathosian with the whip walked around the group until his back was facing Aelron and Morrigan.

"Say goodbye to Egis," the Barathosian said. "You're all property of the Glorious One now. The empress will make you useful yet."

Aelron hadn't taken his eyes off them, but one moment they were huddled together, afraid for their lives, and the next…*gone.*

We've got it wrong!

The Barathosians wore their black feathers, but the people of Egis had none. They disappeared right along with that Barathosian slaver and the two guards that had followed him onto the platform.

"There's more to this than we know," Aelron said. "I don't think that feather has anything to do with what's making them appear and disappear. Or, if it does, it's not in the way we think."

"What else can it be?" Morrigan asked. She glanced around the dock and put her dagger back in her cloak.

"I don't know. But the sooner we get this information to my brother, the better off we'll be."

"Then let's get to the landing boat," Morrigan said.

"My thoughts precisely," Aelron said.

They ran to the end of the pier, not stopping to look back or even check the side streets that emptied into the harbor.

Morrigan dove and Aelron followed.

It didn't take long to unpin the landing boat once they'd climbed into it, but as the boat drifted away from the larger ship, the city alarm went up. At least two bells tolled, and Aelron could hear boots and shouts coming toward the harbor.

The current of the Orm River was swift, so Aelron and Morrigan didn't need to row. There'd be no way for the soldiers in Egis to catch them now. It would take longer for the Barathosians to launch a boat than for he and Morrigan to be south of Egis.

But from the looks of the two ships in the river ahead, the soldiers wouldn't have to catch up.

"It may be time to start worrying about the blockade," Morrigan said.

Two riverboats anchored at angles to one another and spanned from one shore of the Orm to the other, leaving only a small gap between them. But judging by the smaller craft surrounding them, the big ships weren't the problem.

Six boats, three times the size of the landing boat he and Morrigan shared, floated on this side of the riverboats. There was no way to navigate past the larger riverboats without coming within grappling range of the smaller ones.

That, however, wasn't the most troubling thing. Aelron was prepared to fight.

What he wasn't prepared for were the Barathosians doing *nothing* while he and Morrigan drifted past. And the expressions on their faces were ones of...*amusement*?

"Why are they just staring at us?" Morrigan asked.

Aelron's mind worked double time as he tried to figure out what they were up to. Then it hit him.

"They're not *watching* us," Aelron said. "They're *herding* us."

It made sense. The angle of the riverboats, which created a small opening at the river's center. The position of the smaller ships, which made sure he and Morrigan couldn't deviate to one side or the other.

What was on the other side of those riverboats that made the Barathosians willing to let him and Morrigan sail straight for it?

As the landing craft passed between the riverboats, someone yelled "Make ready!"

When they cleared the other side, there was nothing waiting for them except open river.

Every yard they drifted, Aelron expected an attack. There was no way the Barathosians were letting them escape.

They made one-hundred yards. Then two-hundred.

At three-hundred yards, a distinct blast of smoke and fire erupted from the side of a riverboat. A moment later, a deafening boom had Aelron covering his ears as something tore through the bow of the landing craft. The force toppled the boat, and Aelron plunged into the swift water.

Something shot past him, followed by another boom, and boards from the sinking boat struck the water's surface above him.

Whatever the Barathosians had done, it had destroyed the landing craft entirely.

Morrigan!

He searched the wreckage, trying to find some sign of her, but there was nothing except broken boards and an oar.

His lungs burned. He hadn't been prepared for the dive, and he'd submerged before catching his breath.

A small group of wooden planks floated by. He swam up toward them hoping to hide in their midst so the Barathosians would think him dead.

As he broke the surface, he filled his burning lungs with air.

He stole a glance up river at the Barathosian ships. They weren't pursuing.

He moved as little as possible—he couldn't risk being detected yet— but Morrigan was nowhere in his field of view.

He dove.

She had to be here somewhere!

Aelron swam among bits of wreckage that had sunk, looking for any sign of her.

Nothing.

He swam back toward the drifting boards and broke the surface again, but this time he faced downriver.

A patch of brown material drifted close to the eastern bank.

There!

Aelron dove once more. He could swim faster under water than at the surface.

Sharp rocks along the eastern bank combined with the swift current, making it impossible to drift toward the shore.

"Morrigan!" he said.

She waved and pointed toward the drifting wreckage.

Good idea. Some of those boards are still seaworthy.

The Orm had banked to the west, and the Barathosian riverboats were out of sight. He lifted her out of the water and placed her on a piece of wreckage three boards wide. It would have to do for now.

Voices downriver drifted up on the wind, and it took Aelron a few moments to realize he wasn't alone.

"There!" Morrigan said.

A riverboat with a covered deck, smaller than the two blockading the Egis port, traveled up from the south, its great wheel spinning fast against the raging current.

That's why the bastards didn't pursue us. They knew there was another one coming.

What should he do? Should he look for help or take his chances? The shock of the explosion was clouding his mind.

Morrigan began shouting and waving.

"What are you doing? They're Religarians!"

"No. It's a cargo vessel!"

A brown-turbaned Religarian with thick muttonchops pointed at Aelron and was shouting to someone else on the ship.

"Grab the lines!" the man yelled. He never took his eyes off Morrigan.

Two thick ropes landed in the water next to Aelron and Morrigan.

"Hurry!" the man yelled. "They have spotters!"

Aelron nodded and fastened a rope around his waist while Morrigan did the same with hers.

As the strangers lifted them out of the water, the turbaned man approached the side of the boat and pulled the right side of his shirt open.

On his chest was a sapphire tattoo of a radiant sun.

"Dear gods," Morrigan said. "What have I done?"

CHAPTER TWENTY SEVEN

Coteon's death in 669 BCE was a great loss to the scholarly community, and a great loss to Clan Mukhtaar. I say this because Nuuan and I found the Mukhtaar Chronicles to be largely neglected in his absence. I can only hope one of the countless sealed chambers within the Mukhtaar Estate contain additional works and commentaries of his.

I've removed the insane ramblings of Tycon Mukhtaar and placed them into a separate volume. The writings are little more than "pure blood" propaganda, legitimizing genocide in the name of keeping the Mukhtaar Lordship "sacred". I'll make them public one day so that the priesthood can judge for itself.

I shall endeavor to fill in the gaps where Coteon left off. Following his example, I will not continue the system of numbering verses. The chronicles of the lords is not intended to be a collection of sacred writings as was the Origines, and I do not wish to lend any more weight to my words than they deserve.

- Mujahid Mukhtaar, Private Commentaries, 12 CE

Nicolas paced between a gold-trimmed buffet and a door with a golden handle.

One minute, he'd been escorted from the throne room, and the next he was having some crazy acid trip about a picnic at the Pinnacle, complete with a healthy dose of *512 Pecan Porter* and Kagan singing Maori party songs.

Saleem must have had something to do with it. Was he the aging cognitomancer Nuuan had warned him about?

And speaking of Nuuan, how could he betray them like this? Had Nicolas followed his gut, he would *never* have told the emperor about Kaitlyn.

There has to be something I can do!

Nicolas leaned his head back and looked up.

He stood under a ceiling trimmed with gold crown molding. A spiderweb pattern of gold filigree led from the molding to the center of the ceiling, where a gold-trimmed chandelier hung. The room was well appointed. Not in a "this place has tasteful furniture" sense. It was more like a "let's cover everything in gold to let people know we're rich" sense.

But it wasn't the waiting or boastful display of wealth that was upsetting Nicolas. He had no idea where Kaitlyn was or what they were doing to her.

The imperial guard had brought them there to wait on Zorian, according to Saleem. And while it wasn't a proper jail cell, the guards posted outside made it clear he wasn't welcome to roam.

"You're smart enough to know you're in danger, I presume?" Kagan asked.

The sudden sound of Kagan's voice was startling.

"What do you mean *I'm* in danger?" Nicolas said. "You think you're making it out of here alive if they turn on us?"

"If I make it out of here *alive*, it will be a miracle for the chroniclers."

"Semantics. You need to find a way to tie them up in conversation so I can slip out and find Kait."

"That's not a good idea."

"I *know* it's not a good idea!"

The golden door handle turned, and the door swung open.

Zorian Osa and a man in simple tunic and trousers entered. Zorian swept his gaze around the room and settled on the gold-trimmed buffet. He made a clicking noise with his tongue and looked at the other man.

"Tullias," Zorian said.

The man in simple clothing stepped forward and bowed.

"The emperor's manners are lacking," Zorian said. He flashed a fake smile at Kagan. "Have refreshments brought from the kitchens."

"At once, Zhuma."

Tullias bowed and left.

Start doing what you do best, Nicolas said through the necromantic link.

What I do, as you put it, doesn't simply happen, Kagan said. *It requires weeks…months of meticulous planning. Politics isn't magic. Zorian has all the advantages here.*

"Zhuma," Kagan said. "Correct me if I'm wrong, but that is a Barathosian word, is it not?"

Zorian lost the fake smile and stepped closer to Kagan.

"I serve the Diamond Throne," Zorian said. "I am here to bring you to justice for the death of Yotto. The Glorious One demands it."

Kagan chuckled.

"You find this amusing?" Zorian said.

"Your empress's son breached protocol and failed to identify himself," Kagan said. "Do you think I'd be foolish enough to kill the heir of a foreign nation while trying to establish diplomatic ties? Summon the emperor. At *once!*"

Zorian casually went to a gold-painted chair next to the buffet and sat facing Kagan.

"I'm afraid there's been a change of puppet masters, Archmage," Zorian said. "I hold Toren Relig's strings now. And you'll find I have a firm grip. He may fear losing his soul to you, but I assure you he fears losing his empire to me much more."

Kagan sat in the chair facing Zorian, adjusted his clothes and leaned back.

"Then we are at an impasse," Kagan said.

Zorian clicked his tongue. "An impasse is only possible when power is in balance. Your power was forfeit the moment you arrived."

Every word he spoke is correct, Kagan said. *He holds the power here. You bumbled into his trap like a fool, and now we will pay the price.*

"Need I remind you I'm a magus and you are not?" Kagan said.

"You disappoint me, Archmage. I was told you dealt with such matters with grace and finesse. Yet here you are threatening me like a cutpurse with a blunt object. Come now. It's beneath you."

"Then you tell me," Kagan said. "This is your show. How does it play out?"

"*Show* is a wonderful choice of words, for reasons I'll come to. Suffice it to say I'll not arrest you. You're free to go."

What's his angle?

I have no idea, Kagan said. "Setting me free is an odd way to bring me to justice."

"I have a great deal of respect for you," Zorian said. "I'm told you are—or were, forty years ago—an eminently reasonable man. I intend to appeal to that sense of reason. We will have two conversations. Consider it a play in two acts, to use your earlier metaphor. I have every confidence that by the end of our second conversation, you will come with me to Barathosia of your own free will."

Is he insane?

You can bet your life he is in full control of his faculties, Kagan said. *This is a very dangerous man.*

"If you decide to do *otherwise,*" Zorian said, "there is a *very* angry admiral sitting off the coast who would love nothing more than to take vengeance on you in the name of the Diamond Throne."

"*Now* who's threatening with a dull object?" Kagan said.

"Some dull objects are sharper than others."

Tullias entered the room carrying a tray, which he set on the buffet.

"I'll return soon for our first conversation," Zorian said. "I won't keep you waiting long."

Zorian and Tullias left, closing the door behind them.

"I am at a complete loss," Kagan said. "He could have had me killed or arrested, yet he leaves me here to wait on a *conversation.*"

"There's something bigger at play here," Nicolas said. "If he represents the Diamond Throne, and that Admiral does as well, then why do they seem to be at odds with one another? The *angry admiral* wants you dead, but Zorian wants you to go with him?"

"Whatever this is, it will not end well. Perhaps you should take his offer and leave."

"I know you're not that ignorant."

"Ignorance would have you remain in danger when you should flee to safety, *Archmage,*" Kagan said.

"You don't see how trapped we are because you don't care a whit about what happens to Kaitlyn."

"There are many females in this world, boy, and many of them will want to spend time with a man of your status."

Heat rose in Nicolas's face.

"Was that how you saw my mother?" Nicolas said. "Just another *female* in the world?"

Kagan stood, toppling the chair behind him. "No! And don't you ever suggest it!"

That was...unexpected.

"So you *did* have feelings for her?" Nicolas asked.

"Of course I did! I loved Allyson!"

Kagan sat once more.

"This existence is a strange one," Kagan said. "I don't know how much of what I do is my own volition and how much is compelled. I don't know where I stop and you begin."

Nicolas sat in the chair Zorian had left behind.

"I've never heard a penitent speak like you," Nicolas said.

"You commanded me to be myself. I suspect that has something to do with it."

"One thing is certain," Nicolas said. "There's no way I'm slipping out of this room with those guards outside."

"Then all we can do is wait."

Nicolas nodded. But he couldn't help wanting to fight his way through that door.

Hold on, Kait. I'll be coming for you.

True to his word, Zorian didn't keep Nicolas and Kagan waiting long. He returned to their well-appointed, gold-encrusted, wealth-exuding room about an hour later. His servant Tullias followed with a full dinner tray, which he placed on the buffet.

A small part of Nicolas was surprised the food wasn't gold plated too.

"I'll begin our first conversation with a very simple question," Zorian said. "Will you accept that what you did was wrong, a crime against the Diamond Throne, and turn yourself over to me?"

Zorian held up a finger to forestall a reply.

"Before you answer, there's a story you must hear," Zorian said. He stood from his chair and paced.

"Sixty-seven years ago, the Glorious One gave birth to a child," Zorian said. "Yotto. Her first of what would be fifteen children. On his twenty-sixth   birthday, his mother, our empress, presented him with a duty given her by the gods themselves during the Incarnation Ceremony."

What is he talking about?

That's what the Barathosians call the Rite of Manifestation, Kagan said.

"'Go to the new land in the west,' she said. 'Tell them of our ways. Show them how to harness vitapotency. For they have discovered it, but know not how to use it properly.' And so Yotto's diplomatic training intensified. As is our custom, only a member of the Imperial family may forge a diplomatic relationship on behalf of the throne. But we had an archmage already, and Arin's instructions said nothing of what to do about the archmage across the ocean."

Zorian faced Kagan.

"So the Glorious One, in her benevolence, made a decision that shook the foundation of our society," Zorian said. "She commanded a *second* Temple of the Gods be constructed in Barathos, but this one for the westerners. For *you*. She ignored Tradition, saying our understanding of the world had been incorrect."

A sense of confusion seeped from the necromantic link into Nicolas's consciousness. Kagan had never been told of this.

"For the first time in the history of our ancient empire, there would be two archmages," Zorian said. "They would share power and duties. The west would be welcomed like a lost brother. But this would put a strain on resources the Treasury couldn't sustain. It would have not only emptied the Imperial vault, but also the combined treasuries of the three largest great families."

"Nonsense," Kagan said. "Your empress had no such intentions. She would have replaced me at the order of her own archmage."

"At first, the people didn't respond well to this," Zorian said. He continued as if from memory. "Many rose up in rebellion and sought to depose the Glorious One. So the Glorious One gathered the five weakest great families and convinced them to come together as one. Their combined might quashed the rebellion."

"What does any of this have to do with Yotto?" Kagan asked.

Zorian stepped forward. "Together, they gathered the resources required and built the Temple of the Gods. The Glorious One called the people to gather below the Bridge of Diamond. She promised open trade between East and West would refill the drained treasuries."

Zorian took another step forward and leaned over Kagan.

"She swore this on the life of her youngest son," Zorian said. "So you see, Archmage, you didn't only kill *one* of the Glorious One's children."

"What right did she have to swear that oath without speaking to me first?" Kagan said.

"But she did. Through Yotto. The year he spent with you was productive, was it not? You learned much about us and we about you."

Is that true?

A sense of resignation returned from the link.

It is, Kagan said. *I was quite fond of the boy, actually, even without knowing his true identity. But when he spoke of another archmage across the ocean...I brought this to Azazel's attention, and...*

No! Don't think about Azazel!

"What right did she have to swear that oath without speaking to me first?" Kagan repeated.

Aww shit.

Zorian gave Kagan a look of confusion that turned to anger.

"You expected the Glorious One to travel here *herself* to speak to you?" Zorian asked. "You're more foolish than I thought you'd be."

Nicolas wasn't sure how much longer they could keep this up. If the mere passing thought of Azazel could send Kagan into a loop, it would give the entire ruse away. The only thing keeping Nicolas out of the hot seat was dead Kagan, and he intended to keep it that way.

Nicolas had to end this himself.

Under no circumstances are you to tell Zorian about me. As far as he's concerned, you're the archmage and I'm your servant.

I wish to have clarity on your command, Kagan said. *Are you instructing me to lie as a means of purifying my soul? Are you instructing me to deny the Barathosians the justice they rightly deserve to save your life and the life of your paramour?*

There's a greater good to consider here.

Precisely what I told Yotto when I killed him. When I pondered the consequences of creating the Great Barrier, I told myself there was a greater good to consider. Those words rang in my mind once more when I sought to govern an ungovernable Council of Magi by distracting them with chaos in their homelands.

It's not even remotely the same thing.

It was a greater good that forced my hand in Tildem, and again when I would have struck you down in the Sanctuary. So remember those words when a priest calls you from the grave. Remember to tell him you did everything for a greater good.

Enough! Surrender to Zorian.

Nicolas sent the command through the necromantic link in such a way Kagan couldn't refuse. This was an order from priest to penitent with no recourse. No appeal.

"Your words have moved me this day," Kagan said. "I see now how deeply I hurt the Glorious One and her family. Not to mention her honor. I surrender willingly."

Zorian straightened his back. "Rumors of your sense of reason and logic were not exaggerated, Archmage. Your decision here will speak greatly in your defense when you stand before the Glorious One. But first, I must prepare for your transfer to the fleet. I'm afraid my Admiral didn't have the forethought to consider you'd actually surrender. At least not so soon. I will need your traveling device, of course."

Crap! Didn't think of that! Ask him to reconsider that!

"Would you consider leaving the device in the hands of my servant?" Kagan asked. "The Council of Magi will need to be informed of my surrender so they can move forward with the succession."

Zorian looked at Nicolas.

Come on! Say yes!

"No," Zorian said. "I'm afraid I can't allow that. The emperor will have word sent to the Pinnacle on your behalf once you're both in a holding cell. But I need the device."

"I'll give you the device, of course," Kagan said. "But may I ask one more thing?"

"Go on," Zorian said.

What are you doing?

Saving your life, boy.

"Look at the youthfulness of my servant," Kagan said. "It should be obvious he wasn't yet born when these events transpired. You have my peaceful surrender. You'll have my translocation orb. Let my servant go. He merely attends to my mundane needs, nothing more."

If Nicolas hadn't heard it with his own ears, he'd never believe Kagan capable of it.

Zorian folded his hands and tapped his lips with his index fingers. After several moments, he spoke.

"You're free to go," Zorian said.

Nicolas offered a slight bow.

"The device," Zorian said.

Nicolas retrieved the orb from his robes and handed it to Zorian.

"And how does this work?" Zorian asked.

"I don't know how one would accomplish it with life magic," Kagan said. "But you channel a small amount of necropotency and it transports you to the Pinnacle."

Zorian pursed his lips. "Clever. Right, then. The guard will remain outside, but I'll inform them your servant may leave."

Something in Zorian's demeanor changed when Kagan surrendered. It was more than a reaction to a simple victory. He all but danced out of the room.

"I'll do what I can," Nicolas said. "I'll sever the link if it comes to it."

"And you'd be a fool to do so."

"Why?"

"Questions like that make me doubt your paternity. *And* your training. I've been dead for months."

Kagan was right. If Nicolas severed the link and Kagan collapsed, his decomposition would accelerate to match his true state. It would be obvious to the Barathosians Kagan had been a corpse all along.

They'd come back. And they'd keep coming back until they got what they wanted.

"Perhaps in a year," Kagan said. "Maybe two. They'll have exacted their punishment by then and cast me into whatever grave they intend to dig. You'll know when because I'll tell you."

"You've gained some purification today."

"Spare me the platitudes," Kagan said. "Go save that young woman who's leading you into insanity and an early grave."

Nicolas didn't know what else to say. He didn't exactly *like* Kagan. But he didn't exactly *hate* him anymore either. He hadn't expected it to be difficult to leave him behind.

He walked to the door, nodded his head at Kagan, and closed the door behind him.

CHAPTER TWENTY EIGHT

In the year 711 BCE, Fahad Morcos stepped over the threshold, becoming Fahad Lord Mukhtaar Morcos. A contemporary of Coteon of the Steppes, Lord Fahad and Coteon worked tirelessly to illuminate the Mukhtaar Chronicles. Lord Fahad was said to be an invaluable source of knowledge of applied theology for Coteon, and he was instrumental in deciphering the Origines Multiversi.

When Coteon died of an unknown lung illness in 669 BCE, Lord Fahad agreed to serve as chief celebrant at the funerary rite. Coteon thanked Lord Fahad, informed him of the location of unpublished commentaries, then passed into the Plane of Peace before a single hour had elapsed.

- The Mukhtaar Chronicles, Second Cycle, 10 CE

T he guards ignored Nicolas as he left the holding room. He double-checked his chain of office to make sure it was concealed. He had to keep his identity hidden, if he wanted to stay alive long enough to find Kaitlyn and get out of here.

The gold-filigreed walls stretched out before him on both sides of a narrow hallway, which wound through the guest wing of the imperial palace. The floor sloped down toward an intersection that would pose the first problem for Nicolas.

He had tried to memorize the twists and turns when they'd escorted him to the holding room. But the palace was so large, and each hallway so similar, it didn't take long to lose track. The wide hallways near the throne room had grown narrower when they took him to the guest quarters. Maybe he could backtrack by focusing on the width of the hallway.

Several guards stood alert along the way, arms concealed within their voluminous desert robes. But none of them so much as blinked as he walked past.

As he reached the next intersection his pulse raced. The intersecting hallway was at least twice the width of the one he emerged from. The only question was whether to go left or right.

Left it is.

The hallway curved right and narrowed.

Necropotency trickled into Nicolas's well of power. The relative size of his well made it seem like a small amount of power, but he was certain it would have filled any other necromancer's well.

Someone died. Nearby.

And whoever it was, it came from farther into the narrow hall. An odd place for a random death. This wasn't a residence wing, as far as he could tell, and there were no signs of an infirmary nearby.

Just focus on finding the throne room.

Another trickle of necropotency entered his well.

Dammit! Two?

Nicolas turned inward and allowed a small amount of necropotency to touch the *guide* symbol—the one that looked like an arrow with a broadhead tip and feather fletchings. The guide would tell him where the nearest source of energy was. Whatever had just died should be that source.

The guide came to life in the form of an ethereal arrow hanging within his peripheral vision. It pointed farther into the hallway.

Necro GPS. Gotta love it.

The hallway grew darker the farther he walked. There was very little natural light in this part of the palace, and widely spaced torches created large swathes of shadow.

Nicolas crept along the wall. If there had been a murder, whoever did the murdering wouldn't take kindly to being watched.

The necropotency grew stronger as two doors on opposite sides of the wall came into view. The source had to be in one of those two rooms.

As he crept along the wall, the guide turned toward the door across the hall.

There it is.

The door cracked open and Nicolas jumped back into the shadow.

Tullias—Zorian's servant—emerged from the room and ran farther into the darkened hallway.

A high-pitched screech came from the room beyond the open door. There was something familiar about the sound, but he couldn't place it.

Nicolas released the necropotency, and the guide disappeared from his field of vision. At least two people had been killed in that room. And from the look of it, Tullias had done the killing.

The presence of necropotency grew stronger as Nicolas stepped toward the door.

"There now," Zorian said.

Nicolas startled until he realized Zorian's voice had come from within the room.

"Now you know them," Zorian said. "Tell your sisters. Their hunger will soon be over."

The screech came again, this time louder, and an image of a cloud materializing over the ruins of Caspardis formed in Nicolas's mind.

Nicolas peered through the gap in the door. When the source of the screech came into view, he stepped back and flattened himself against the wall.

A small shriller, no more than three feet tall and ten feet long, wings the length of a minivan, had been feeding off the dead corpses of two palace guards. It had the same concentric rings of scalpel-sharp teeth. But where a full-sized shriller was turquoise and had a feathery mane around its neck, this smaller version looked leathery, like a tiny dinosaur.

Could these be the creatures the Barathosians had used to hunt survivors in Caspardis? Zorian had been stroking its head like a cherished pet. Had they been domesticated somehow?

A third screech came from the room, and it was the loudest of all. A great gust of wind swept over Nicolas as the shriller flew out through the doorway and up the hall toward Tullias.

Nicolas began to suspect he had the whole situation wrong.

Zorian is going to use those shrillers here just like in Caspardis. I can't let that happen again. I can't just take Kait and leave.

Nicolas pulled all of the ambient necropotency he could gather into his well, and mental clarity washed through his mind. His thought processes sped up. Pieces of information he once thought dissimilar grew connected. Patterns formed where previously none existed.

His suspicion became a certainty. The emperor was hiding something.

When Saleem greeted them on arrival, he'd reacted as if it were normal when Kagan spoke with Nicolas's dialect. He'd said Kagan's *travels* were probably causing the confusion. But he'd emphasized the word *travels* as if he didn't really believe it was *traveling* that made Kagan odd.

Saleem had commented on the haste with which Kagan arrived, as if the emperor had sent for them.

And the patterns didn't end there.

When they'd entered the throne room, the emperor was angry with Zorian. He'd given Kagan a strange look that Nicolas had interpreted as concern. But to a necropotency-filled mind, it was obvious there had been more to it than that. There'd been an ever-so-brief instant of shock, disgust, and caution.

Nicolas had seen that look many times in the last year. It was the look of an average person gazing upon a penitent.

The emperor had known Kagan was dead.

And *that* must mean the emperor had been playing along with the charade.

But Emperor Relig didn't even glance in my direction. He doesn't know about me.

He'd called Zorian his most trusted adviser. The emperor must be working with the Barathosians. Zorian all but confirmed it when he'd made the *puppet master* comment.

Nicolas knew what he had to do now.

The only way he and Kaitlyn would get to safety would be to confront the emperor himself. Toren Relig was the only person in Dar Rodon with enough power to make it possible.

But he'd have to cut Zorian's *puppet strings*, somehow.

I could kill Zorian right here and end it all. I have enough power.

The words of Siek Lamil rang like bell in his mind. "When life finally leaves your body, you will make the journey to the Plane of Death with the blood of many men on your hands. It's the horrible certainty of our vocation."

No.

I can't just start killing people when it's convenient. That's how Kagan got us into this mess in the first place!

It was time he acted like a man who could make kings tremble. It was time to flex some muscle.

Nicolas ran.

He passed the intersection leading back toward the guest wing and continued forward, past more whitewashed walls and golden doors.

When he reached the next intersection, the gargantuan gold doors of the throne room stood down the hall to his right.

He smoothed his robes and walked across the hall, toward two guards in Religarian livery. They guarded the throne room doors with six foot tall pikes, leaning inward to form an ersatz archway.

When he got within ten feet of the door, the guards crossed their pikes.

Nicolas retrieved his chain of office and allowed it to dangle freely in the open.

The guards noticed, but they didn't step aside.

"This won't do," Nicolas said. He extended two ropes of necropotency, wrapped them around the guards' pikes, and pulled them aside.

Nicolas stepped between them. And as they struggled against the necropotency in a futile attempt to free their weapons, he pushed the throne room doors open.

A dozen or more people spoke in private conversations around the periphery of the room.

"I sent for no one," Emperor Relig said when Nicolas entered the throne room.

The private conversations came to an abrupt halt.

Saleem and Kaitlyn stood next to the emperor on the dais.

Kait?

She seemed fine. In fact, she seemed pleased to be there.

Kaitlyn smiled and moved to greet Nicolas, but he gave her a look. He had to play this carefully.

As Nicolas drew closer, the emperor saw the chain of office and stepped off the main platform.

"Holy One," Emperor Relig said. He sounded like a man who was greatly relieved about something. "My sincerest apologies for our misunderstanding. The Lady Kaitlyn recently informed us of your true identity."

She what? *What if I was still working Kagan as the archmage?*

"Had I known *you* were our new archmage," Emperor Relig said, "proper introductions would have been made. I certainly wouldn't have allowed Zorian to arrest and detain you. I would have flogged him myself for merely suggesting it. I'll understand if you must exact punishment for my sacrilege. I throw myself on your mercy, which I know reflects the abundance of Arin's holiness—may he be praised."

Emperor Relig bowed his head and raised his hands in a gesture of prayer.

Nicolas wasn't quite sure how to react. He'd been expecting many things, but apologies and obeisance wasn't among them.

"No punishment necessary, Emperor Relig," Nicolas said. "There's no way for you to have known. No one questions your devotion and faithfulness. But, like I tell everyone else, ease up on the *Holy One* title. I'm no holier than anyone else. The way I see it, it's my job to serve the people, not the other way around."

The emperor looked up, and when their eyes met, his expression spoke volumes.

Nicolas had lost respect. Awe. Authority. Emperor Relig had been expecting—*wanting*—hellfire and brimstone. But Nicolas had given him Kumbaya and a campfire.

"I'll consider it," Emperor Relig said. His tone had changed. He was speaking to a *subordinate*. "Now, if you'll excuse me, *Archmage*, I must discuss this with Zorian. He's under the *mistaken* impression that *Kagan* still reigns. He'll no doubt be as disappointed as I."

Remember what Tithian and Nuuan told you, idiot! King of all assholes, remember? You're a pope. A medieval pope. So act like one.

Emperor Relig started to turn away.

"You turn away from Arin so easily?" Nicolas said. It was the best he could come up with.

The emperor stopped and faced Nicolas once more, a look of defiance on his face.

Nicolas was going to have to do *much* better than *that*. He stepped close and whispered.

"I'm generally a nice person, *Toren Relig*. But if you *ever* disrespect me like this again, I'll command the religious orders to leave this place and end the pilgrimages. I'll close every temple in Religar, excommunicate you, and see you tried for heresy and sacrilege. How long before your subjects depose you to quell my anger and restore their sacraments?"

Shock entered the emperor's eyes.

But Nicolas wanted *awe*.

He took hold of one of the golden chains hanging across Emperor Relig's chest and pulled him closer.

"Or perhaps I'll simply call you *King* from now on. I'm sure Arin will agree to nullify my predecessor's proclamations."

Emperor Relig stepped back, dropped to one knee, and lowered his gaze.

Awe had returned.

Time to drive it home.

Nicolas stood over him and looked down. He raised his voice for the entire court to hear.

"And when the day comes that someone *does* manage to stick a blade in your disloyal heart," Nicolas said, "I'll make certain your corpse rots in a place no one can find it. No priest will raise you for purification. The Plane of Death will be your home for eternity."

Emperor Relig lowered his gaze farther.

"Forgive me, Archmage," Emperor Relig stammered. "I will spend the rest of my days atoning for the treatment you've faced in your short stay under my roof. Say the word and I'll order myself flogged in public. But please...I'm *begging* you...*please* don't abandon Religar! We will not survive without Arin's grace!"

The weight of what Nicolas had done pressed down on him. He was no better than Kagan. He may not have killed anyone, but he'd threatened the eternal salvation of a nation.

Was that what it took to rule the Pinnacle? Did Nicolas have to be like Kagan, granting spiritual favors to some and withholding them from others, all to achieve a political goal? Start a pilgrimage here, close a temple there. Hell, maybe throw in a free, guaranteed purification to boot! The popes may have sold indulgences during the dark ages, but they had *nothing* on Nicolas. Oh no they didn't! He could actually raise their decrepit asses from the grave and declare them pure or impure, all with a god in his back pocket to carry out the sentence.

Why would the gods allow any human being to have that kind of authority?

He couldn't. He *wouldn't* be that sort of archmage.

Kaitlyn's face looked like she was struggling with something. At first, Nicolas thought she was disgusted by what he'd done here. She had every right to be.

But Saleem stood next to her, grasping the sides of his head like it would explode if he took his hands away.

He's been trying to attack, and she's keeping him at bay. I have to speed this up!

"Rise, Emperor," Nicolas said. "You're no good to me strapped to a flogging post. I have a better use for you."

Emperor Relig stood, but his gaze remained lowered. "Anything."

"If that's your man," Nicolas said, pointing at Saleem, "then I expect you to control him. If Lady Kaitlyn is harmed, not only will I follow through on every threat I made here today, I'll invent a few new ones."

"Saleem," Emperor Relig said. "You *will* do as the archmage commands."

Nicolas nodded at Kaitlyn, and the struggle left her face.

Saleem lowered his hands and faced Kaitlyn. "That's not possible. How did you do it?"

"I need you to get Lady Kaitlyn and I out of the palace," Nicolas said. "Out of Dar Rodon, if possible. Before Zorian discovers Kagan's true state."

"But your translocation orb?" Emperor Relig said.

"Zorian has it. And I assume he *outranks* you here."

Emperor Relig glanced away.

"I can't pretend to understand all you've been through, Emperor. And I'm not so naive anymore as to believe the situation is black and white. But whatever your reasons for giving them what they want, don't you think it's time you started making amends to those who have suffered because of it?"

"Zorian monitors every entrance to the palace," Emperor Relig said. "But there is at least one he knows nothing about. My personal chambers have a hidden door that will lead you to a tunnel beneath the palace. It served my great-grandfather well when the northern tribes sacked the city."

"Good enough," Nicolas said.

"But it doesn't lead *out* of the city. It leads into the city's *heart*."

"What kind of escape strategy is that?"

"When you're presumably the world's greatest naval power, you prefer escaping by ship to trekking more than three hundred miles across a barren desert."

"Point taken."

"You won't have long," Emperor Relig said. "When Zorian discovers your identity, he'll use my own army against you."

"What does he have on you?"

Emperor Relig stared at Nicolas, but his expression wasn't one of contempt or disrespect this time. It was of a man searching for words that wouldn't come.

"I'm no saint, Archmage. But this isn't about *me*. When my Church…my *gods*…failed me, I did what I *had* to do to guarantee the freedom of the Religarian people. And it's a choice I'd make again. But now I may fail them anyway, because I'm refusing to do the one thing the Barathosians asked of me; sacrifice your life for the lives of my people."

Nicolas wasn't sure how to respond. If he said what he *wanted* to say—that he understood, and that part of him thought the emperor had done the *right* thing—would Emperor Relig take that as another sign of weakness? There was no way to know. So he did the only thing he knew the emperor would understand. He extended his hand forward, palm out, and held it over Emperor Relig's head.

"May Arin, Shealynd, and Zubuxo, bless you and preserve your people," Nicolas said.

Emperor Relig crossed his arms over his chest and bowed his head. When he looked up at Nicolas once more, there was something new in his eyes.

Gratitude.

The emperor hurried toward the small golden door next to the raised platform, and Nicolas and Kaitlyn followed.

With any luck, Nicolas would be able to leave the city with Kaitlyn before Zorian found out.

Arin, if you are *watching from somewhere, I hope you're seeing this right now.*

CHAPTER TWENTY NINE

*In the year 450 BCE, Abd Al-Hakim Shadid stepped over the threshold,
becoming Abd Al-Hakim Lord Mukhtaar Shadid. Lord Abd Al-Hakim died
without children. But he was a great mentor to several blood Mukhtaar priests,
one of whom (Baladi) eventually ascended.*
  - The Mukhtaar Chronicles, Second Cycle, 10 CE

*Though the reign of Lords Abd Al-Hakim Shadid and Sayyid Cham
overlapped by several years, there are no writings hinting at the strange cloud of
energy that formed around our wells of power when Nuuan and I ascended.
After more than forty years, I still have no idea what it might mean. And if the
God of Death knows, he remains curiously silent on the subject.*
  - Mujahid Mukhtaar, Private Commentaries, 45 CE

Mujahid watched as Tithian opened the vestry's ornate
mahogany cabinet.
  "Your timing is impeccable," Tithian said. "I'm leaving for
the Shandarian Union within the hour."
  "To what end?" Mujahid asked.

The strongest, most beautiful rose sent wafted out of the cabinet and permeated the room. It could be only one thing; a rose of Shealynd.

"It was a request from your brother," Tithian said.

Tithian retrieved the rose and handed it to Mujahid, who cradled it in his hands as if it would disintegrate on touch.

"What was the nature of this request?" Mujahid asked.

Tithian shook his head. "He told me to retrieve a parchment. I did. The parchment vanished, along with my memory of reading it. But I know I *must* travel to the Shandarian Union, and *your brother* is the reason."

Nuuan and his secrets will be the death of me.

Mujahid hefted the rose. "Nuuan gave you *this*?"

"He told me you should place it at the base of Shealynd's statue. He said that—"

Mujahid bolted from the room. Tithian yelled something from behind, but he didn't hear or care what it was. All that mattered was getting to the shrine. He half-jumped, half-ran down the great spiral staircase, brushing past several council magi, then sprinted across the gallery—much to the chagrin of the serving staff, who guarded their trays of food and delicate glassware as if the wind from Mujahid's robe would topple them.

A small, neglected entrance to the Pinnacle gardens sat within an alcove on one side of a wide passageway. The shrine wasn't far.

He jogged the rest of the way, sweating and out of breath, and placed the rose on the ground next to Shealynd's statue.

"It's about festering time," Nuuan said. "I did everything but draw you a map."

Mujahid turned at the sound of Nuuan's voice, which had come from behind him.

"Brother!" Mujahid said. "By the gods. Part of me thought you dead. Another part thought you beyond reach forever."

"It's a little early for a celebration."

Mujahid stepped toward Nuuan, arms open to embrace his twin.

"Hold," Nuuan said. "Don't touch me, I'm bi-locating."

"Where's your *better* half?"

"Observing events in Dar Rodon. Physical contact might snap me back here fully."

"You knew all this time and said nothing."

"I could fill an adda's gaping arse with all the things I'm not saying."

"If you fancy yourself a god, I suppose it's no surprise you act like one."

"*Elevated human*," Nuuan said. "Get it right. And I don't fancy myself *anything* except a man with a job. The whole *god* business is a means to an end."

"You started a religion! Are you insane? And how could you involve the argram?"

"I see you found my magical cock," Nuuan said.

"Nuuan—"

"Yes, I started a religion. Because I knew you wouldn't. Just like when we unified the festering clans."

"What are you talking about? There was never so much as a hint of what you were up to."

Nuuan turned away. "Do you remember that day outside Father's tomb, Muj?"

Had Nuuan confessed to being a woman, Mujahid wouldn't have been more surprised. In all their considerable years, Nuuan had never *once* brought this painful subject up, regardless of how much Mujahid wanted to discuss it.

"It wasn't your fault," Mujahid said. "I shoved you at the wrong time. It could have happened to anyone."

"But it didn't, did it? It happened to *me*. *I* was the one to summon our father from his festering grave. Him and all his sins and secrets."

"It changed you," Mujahid said. "You became...a *darker* person."

"Is that your new word for *womanizing alcoholic*?"

"Brother—"

Nuuan held up his hand. "Peace. I'll spare you the details I drown with women and wine. But there are some things you *should* know."

"It's not right. There are reasons it's forbidden."

"And I've lived each of them. But it's not about our father. Not entirely. It's about Malvol."

Mujahid narrowed his eyes. "What does our father have to do with the god of hate?"

"It took decades to put some of the pieces together," Nuuan said. "Until recently I still wasn't sure I'd done the right thing. But Digby discovered something after the Battle of Rotham. Something that vindicated *every last one* of my choices going back some seventy years. Apotheosis was the only answer. The super-spatial universal consciousness transcends what you may think of as *person*."

"You're losing me, brother."

Nuuan folded his hands and tapped his thumbs against his bearded chin.

"This is difficult," Nuuan said. "I'm not yet a god, but my mind is greatly expanded. I forget what it was like to be…"

"Mortal?"

"Come now, brother. You're far from mortal yourself."

"Parlor tricks keep me alive. You're something else entirely now."

Nuuan smiled. "There are events taking place…cosmic events that you should be aware of. It involves Malvol."

"I already know. He's an elevated human seeking deification."

"It's *far* worse than that. He's a Mukhtaar Lord. An *ancient* one."

"Nonsense," Mujahid said. "You know the Chronicles as well as I. Shall I recite the names forward or backward?"

"Malvol is a *false* name."

"Then which one is he?"

"I don't know. But does it matter?"

"Of course it bloody matters! We control the Chronicles now! We can leave a legacy of truth! But how do you know this? How did Digby discover it?"

Nuuan shook his head. "You are one of the smartest men I've ever known. Perhaps among the wisest throughout all of Erindor. So understand this is no slight when I say you're *incapable* of comprehending my explanation. It requires hyper-dimensional reasoning and super-spatial awareness. Some of it requires *more than one mind* operating in tandem under the direction of a controlling entity. A collective with a mental focal point. Think of it like—"

"The argram."

Nuuan smiled. "Like I said. Among the wisest men of Erindor. You do our family proud, brother. Malvol seeks deification. *True* deification. And if he succeeds, he'll be powerful enough to challenge the other gods. Perhaps even annihilate them. But he's *still* just a man. He still *thinks* like one, regardless of his expanded consciousness. Think, brother. Go back to the formation of the Barrier."

Mujahid drew ambient necropotency into his well. He needed the clarity of power if he was going to wade through this mental swamp.

What do I know with certainty?

First, Yotto traveled to the Pinnacle to open a diplomatic relationship. But Kagan, in his irrational fear, murdered Yotto, sparking the war with Barathosia and the formation of the Great Barrier.

There has to be more.

Kagan went on to become a tyrant, ruling the Three Kingdoms in all but name. He managed to go so far as to forge entries in the Book of Life—the sacrosanct journal of the god Arin—without anyone being any wiser. In so doing, he elevated a king to the status of emperor with the slip of a pen. And he orchestrated the failure of a decades-old treaty that kept war in check within the Three Kingdoms.

Yes, but how is it all related?

Mujahid drew more power into his well, allowing it to flow through his mind and coalesce his thoughts. In moments, it all snapped into focus.

I'm not finding a pattern because no pattern exists. It's chaos. Chaos in its purest form.

"Correct," Nuuan said.

So Nuuan could read minds as well.

"Sometimes," Nuuan said. "But to your point, Kagan was able to achieve what he did by shifting all eyes away from himself. He pitted the Shandarian Union against Tildem, and Religar against them both. Anything to draw attention away from the Obsidian Throne."

"Malvol brings chaos to the world to draw attention away from his *true* plan. To use Kaitlyn to compel Shealynd to grant him full deification."

"I've done everything possible to point you in the right direction without violating mystical laws older than the multiverse itself. There may be repercussions for what I'm about to say. Unless another Mukhtaar Lord ascends, Malvol will become a god. He will consume the power of the other gods and give birth to chaos of a magnitude you cannot comprehend without a non-elevated human mind."

There wasn't a member of the clan who would survive the ascension process, as far as Mujahid was concerned. To become a Mukhtaar Lord required near-perfect self-knowledge and a mastery of necromancy few possessed. It required intuitive understanding and acceptance of Mukhtaarian philosophy. But more, it required the anointing of a god.

"*We* did it," Nuuan said.

"*We* were *ready*."

Nuuan sniffed. "You have a selective memory."

Nuuan's body flickered, disappeared, then pulsated back into existence.

"This is taking more power than I can afford to expend," Nuuan said. "I'll make this quick. That *fog* you're always wondering about...the one surrounding our well of power? It changed when you ascended."

"What do you mean?"

"When I emerged from the Rite of Testing, it appeared around my well. But it was dormant. When you stepped out of the Rite, it crackled to life. It's a weapon. And I believe it takes three to wield it."

Mujahid might have suspected the same thing, had he been the first to ascend. Being the second, he only knew the fog in one state—energized.

"Then we have work to do," Mujahid said.

"What's your plan?"

"We must prepare Nicolas for the Rite."

Nuuan's eyes narrowed. "The cross-dressing postulant? His bollocks haven't even dropped yet. He has, what, three symbols of power?"

"Two, last I checked."

"Two? Why don't you just toss him into the lake of fire yourself and save Zubuxo the effort? How in the hells will he survive the Rite with two symbols of power?"

"You've always underestimated him. He's accomplished in a year what you and I took more than a decade to achieve. Lamil himself presented him for ordination. Sabba agreed. Arin asked him to be the archmage. *Arin!*"

"Zubuxo save us from philosopher fishmen," Nuuan said. "Are you sure about this?"

"Of course not."

"Well...that's good enough for me."

"I know your mind in this, even if I can't read it," Mujahid said. "Believe me when I tell you our Nicolas is the only person in the clan who stands a chance."

Nuuan's image flickered once more, and his eyes widened. "Oh no."

"What is it?"

"Six hells! This is my fault! The festering time streams aren't synchronized!"

"What are you—"

"Brother, we need to hurry. Meet me in the sanctuary. It'll be easier to explain when *both* of me are in one body. Now, go!"

He had no idea what Nuuan saw, but whatever it was had scared him.

Nuuan said he was observing Dar Rodon. Six hells indeed! Have the Barathosians begun their invasion?

Mujahid turned and ran, grateful that Nicolas and Kaitlyn were safe in Aquonome.

CHAPTER THIRTY

In the year 637 BCE, Diya Al-Din Kassab stepped over the threshold, becoming Diya Al-Din Lord Mukhtaar Kassab. Lord Diya Al-Din was the son of a nomadic tribesman from the Zarush region of Religar. Upon his ascension, he suspended all ritual associated with the sacred light. His effort to lead a simplistic reign backfired, however. A group of Catiatum priests mistook his humility for weakness and attempted to assassinate him, thinking a weakened Clan Mukhtaar could be subsumed. They failed magnificently. The skins of the Catiatum priests hang in the great hall of the Mukhtaar Estate as a reminder.
- The Mukhtaar Chronicles, Second Cycle, 10 CE

Not anymore. I refuse to look at those disgusting trophies while I eat. I won't destroy them, though. They are a part of Clan Mukhtaar's history and will be afforded the proper respect. But that doesn't mean they need to decorate my dining room.
- Mujahid Mukhtaar, Private Commentaries, 15 CE

The wooden deck of the riverboat glistened from the sprinkling rain. But compared to the river, it was dry and empty of Barathosians. As far as Aelron was concerned, that was the best he could hope for.

Morrigan wasn't happy to be in the turbaned man's presence. Especially after discovering he was a Dawnmaster. Whenever he came near, she watched him as if he was a feral dog.

As the turbaned man approached from the passenger galley, Morrigan's posture stiffened.

"I"m Vanni Yarwen," the man said. "Dawnmaster of this vessel."

"Forgive us, Dawnmaster Yarwen," Morrigan said. "Had I known, I would not have violated the *concord* by signaling to you. I did not come here to attempt harm, and the Sodality is *not* transporting goods along the Orm. This was a terrible misunderstanding. We'll jump and swim to shore if you like."

"Nonsense," Vanni said. "You've violated no concord. I pulled *you* out of the water."

"Your benevolence is appreciated."

"Hold your thanks. You may reconsider in a few moments."

Vanni turned toward the passenger galley and waved. The door opened.

A man in the midnight blue robes of a master necromancer came toward them. His wavy black hair fell to his shoulders, but his mustache and goatee were trimmed close. Around his neck was a chain of office, but Aelron didn't recognize it.

What he did recognize, however, was the terror on Morrigan's face.

"Gods no," Morrigan said. She backed away into the ship's railing.

A *whooshing* sound swept around Aelron, and a skeleton appeared behind Morrigan. For a moment, it looked as if the penitent was going to jump overboard, but it climbed back down from the rail and stood beside her.

"However fast you are, I assure you this penitent is faster," the man said.

"What's going on here?" Aelron said. "Morrigan, what is it?"

"It's him," Morrigan said. Her lip was quivering. "It's the *Traveler*."

Aelron's stomach did a somersault. This was the man who had killed the previous Traveler of the Sodality and was hunting Morrigan.

"Tithian Bel-Enrog," the man said. "Prime Warlock…among other things. Fear not, Aelron. Your brother ordered me to treat you like family, and I have every intention of obeying."

"And what of my friend?" Aelron asked. "I won't let you kill her. I may not be able to stop you, but by Malvol's festering flatulence I'll die trying."

Tithian's gaze went back and forth between Aelron and Morrigan several times before settling back on Aelron with an amused expression.

"It would seem Shealynd hasn't only been busy at the Pinnacle," Tithian said. "Nevertheless, Morrigan doesn't understand what she *thinks* she does."

"Don't trust him," Morrigan said.

Aelron had never seen her paralyzed with fear before. It was unsettling.

"I saw what he did," Morrigan said. "And he wants me dead because of it."

Tithian rubbed his temples. After a moment, he lowered his hands and faced Morrigan.

"I'm not trying to *kill* you, girl," Tithian said. "I'm trying to *promote* you."

Morrigan stammered. "Why should I believe you?"

"You won't," Tithian said. "You never believe *anyone*. That's why I need you. You think for yourself. You're immune to the fancy words of powerful men. You're the best demon hunter I've ever seen. And it took the intervention of a deity to find you—well, near enough to deity. I need someone like you."

"You killed the last Traveler," Morrigan said.

"Of course I did," Tithian said. "Now, you can leave here in the Pinnacle's employ, or…"

"Or what?" Aelron asked.

"Or she leaves as a *permanent guest* of the Pinnacle," Tithian said. He faced Morrigan again. "I'll not *kill* you, girl. But it would jeopardize the archmage's position within the Council if my identity was revealed. I won't allow that."

"You're saying you killed the last Traveler to protect my brother?" Aelron asked.

"As surely as I stand here, *everything* I do is to protect your brother," Tithian said. "In my forty years of life in that dungeon of politics, your brother is the only man to wear the Qiyaaht who is worthy of it. If he spoke of me at all, then you know my part in your father's downfall."

"What's a *key-yacht*?" Aelron asked.

"By the hells," Tithian said. "You're just like him. In more ways than one."

"What does that mean?"

"Surely you must have questioned your agelessness before. You think your failure to moor with an adda-ki is because of lack of ability? Lack of fervor? It's because your vocation lies not with the rangers. But Morrigan has told you this already, no?"

"How can you know any of this?"

"My boy, I wouldn't be much of a Prime Warlock if I didn't. We share the same goal. The same enemies. And a *smattering* of the same natural ability."

"If you wish to protect my brother, then help us now," Aelron said. "The Barathosians are going to destroy Dar Rodon."

A look of sudden comprehension crossed Tithian's face. But it was quickly replaced by something akin to sadness.

"Did they teach you of the Mukhtaar Lords at the Elysian Fortress?" Tithian asked.

Aelron nodded.

"A Mukhtaar Lord sent me here."

"Then the Mukhtaar Lord agrees. We need to get there. And *quickly* if we're to help Nicolas."

"No," Tithian said.

"We have to *help* him!"

"I know about your plan to bring *certain items* to Dar Rodon. The items you seek are on this very vessel."

"Then we can still succeed! Nicolas's plan might work!"

"Nicolas walks a different path from you," Tithian said. "But you *will* go to Dar Rodon. You *and* Morrigan. Dawnmaster Yarwen will see to your safe passage. When the Barathosians take the city, I'll need someone on the inside."

"What?" Morrigan said.

"You may not trust me, girl, but I trust you. I *know* you. Perhaps better than you know yourself. If you reveal my identity, it isn't me who will suffer the consequences. It's a good man who is trying to change this world for the better."

"But you just said it's too late for him."

"I said he walks a *different path*," Tithian said. "Even if you double your pace, you'll never get the items he needs to Dar Rodon in time. You have days more to travel by ship, and more than a week across land. Nicolas is there *now*, dealing with the problem."

"What about magic?" Morrigan asked.

"I can't teleport them. They disrupt magic. I was lucky to summon that penitent. And after I did, I nearly couldn't control him."

Morrigan fidgeted with the end of her cloak and looked down. Morrigan *never* fidgeted.

"This ship will take you to a coastal village in the Religarian Empire," Tithian said. "Dar Rodon is a ten-day ride from there. You'll pass a caravansary that is more than what it appears. I'll need you to do something there, Morrigan. That is...if you'll be one of my *Skywatchers*."

Morrigan lifted her head. "Are you joking?"

Aelron remembered the term from what Morrigan had taught him. The *Skywatchers* were the Traveler's inner circle.

"You'll need to complete Aelron's training, of course," Tithian said. "The rangers may be stealthy, but they're no Sodality. Not on their best day."

"What of the Sodality who *hunt* me?" Morrigan asked.

"They'll answer to you now," Tithian said. "Not directly, of course. You'll have to establish your own network. I'll assist where I can."

Morrigan looked away for several moments.

Tithian opened his mouth to speak, but Morrigan interrupted.

"If I do this, I won't kill someone just because you order me to," Morrigan said.

"I'd never ask it of you."

"Well?" Morrigan said. She stared at Aelron. "This involves you too. I'll not speak for you."

"I'm no prophet," Tithian said. "But as long as I've lived, the Mukhtaar Lords have had the best interests of this world in their hearts. I trust them without question. Had I trusted them years ago, the world would be a better place because of it."

Aelron nodded. "That will have to be good enough for me."

Tithian glanced at Vanni. "If you'll leave me in Dyr Agul, Dawnmaster. I cannot risk translocating this close to the fragments."

"Of course," Vanni said.

"What of the caravansary?" Morrigan asked. "What are we to do there?"

"You'll be contacted when you arrive. Two weeks from today. Begin Aelron's training with haste."

Tithian spun and marched back into the passenger galley.

"Are there quarters we can use, Dawnmaster?" Morrigan asked.

"Within the galley."

She shook her head. "I'd love to know how the Traveler of the Sodality is in a position to give orders to a Dawnmaster."

Vanni smiled. "Perhaps someday you'll learn the answer."

Morrigan faced Aelron. "Let's go. I have two weeks to pass on knowledge that took me ten years to acquire."

"Where do we begin?"

"In the land of the dead."

"Land of the…" Aelron stared after her as Morrigan left for the galley.

When she closed the door behind her, he struggled to absorb everything that had happened. A couple of weeks ago, all he wanted was to return home to his family and start some semblance of a life. Now, he was…*what*? What was Morrigan and this Tithian fellow going to turn him into? A *demon hunter*? The main character in a story mothers would tell their children to scare them into obedience?

He'd be lying if he said the thought didn't intrigue him.

As he opened the galley door, he offered a silent prayer that his brother would be safe, regardless of what may happen in Dar Rodon.

CHAPTER THIRTY ONE

In the year 600 BCE, Sayyid Cham stepped over the threshold, becoming Sayyid Lord Mukhtaar Cham. Lord Cham was in his fiftieth year when he ascended. In the year 565 BCE he took Abd Al-Hakim Shadid as his postulate and taught him the secrets of ascension. He remains the only Mukhtaar Lord known to have taken a postulate.
 - The Mukhtaar Chronicles, Second Cycle, 10 CE

Not anymore.
 - Mujahid Mukhtaar, Private Commentaries, 139 CE

Nicolas and Kaitlyn emerged from a sewage grate in a narrow street.

Where the palace grounds had been grand, with walls akin to alabaster, the adobe buildings of the city of Dar Rodon were haphazard in their construction. Some buildings had a pronounced lean, most likely the result of all the earthquakes. Ropes with drying linens stretched from windows high across the desolate marketplace. Abandoned tents of diaphanous fabric stood along both sides of the street, where merchants herded unsold livestock that looked like something out of a fever-induced dream—mammalian animals with beaks and feathers, insectoid creatures that barked like dogs, and birds with feline eyes and claws.

The marketplace sprawled on for several blocks, spilling into the various cross streets that intersected at odd intervals and angles.

They may have escaped the palace. But how the hell were they going to get out of the *city*?

"Zorian has the translocation orb," Nicolas said. "And we can't exactly get a boat out of here with the armada in the bay."

"You've got this all wrong, Nick," Kaitlyn said. "I didn't ask you to bring me here just to *leave* when things got a little dangerous. The armada is exactly why I came, remember?"

"Things have changed since we made that plan. Zorian has miniature shrillers he's using to kill guards. And then there's Saleem."

"You don't have to worry about Saleem. The reason he took me away was to train me. But he discovered pretty quick that I'm more powerful. And then he started acting like he was afraid of me. Some nonsense about my magic being unnatural. He freaked out when I entered his mind from across the room. Apparently I'm not supposed to be able to do that without physical contact."

Nicolas stopped and leaned against the corner of a sandstone building.

"What about Aelron and Morrigan?" Kaitlyn asked. "They're on the way here with the protoforge fragments."

"Not so loud." Nicolas glanced around furtively, but the only people around were two men in brown robes and white cinctures. Arinian priests. Nicolas recognized the Arinian robes he used to sneak into the Pinnacle and confront Kagan.

Mujahid had mentioned the Arinians on a few occasions. An idea began to form.

"The Arinian priests are sworn to serve the archmage," Nicolas said. "They'll do anything they can to help. Maybe paying a visit to their mother house is in order?"

But where was their temple? Perhaps someone in the marketplace could help.

An old woman passed them in an obvious hurry. She pulled an animal on a leash that was doing its best to *not* be a goat. Six legs—an Erindorian phenomenon Nicolas was still getting used to—lithe body, short hair and tail, tiny horns, hooves, and the same bleating noise. But that's where the similarities ended. The creature's mouth was a set of interlocking pincers, and it had four coal-black eyes—two widely spaced in the center of its face, and two close together on top of its forehead.

It was too disturbing to look at for any length of time, so Nicolas did his best to ignore it as he approached the woman. Hopefully it wouldn't bite. Or slice. Or rip. Or whatever the hell those pincers did.

Nicolas touched her on the shoulder.

"Excuse me," he said.

The woman's eyes narrowed. She yelled something in a language Nicolas didn't understand and dragged the poor *non*-goat away bleating behind her.

Well that was helpful.

He wasn't going to get far if he couldn't understand their language.

And why was that anyway? He understood people in Tildem and the Shandarian Union, who spoke something Mujahid called *the common tongue*. He even understood the Cichlos. But he couldn't understand some Religarian woman pulling a *goatbug* behind her?

"Seriously, Nick?" Kaitlyn asked. "*That's* how you come up on someone in a strange city?"

Bells began to toll. Their deep harmonies intertwined and reverberated from towers along the palace walls.

Nicolas and Kaitlyn crossed the street to the nearest merchant tent.

A tall person with his or her back to them was packing up something that looked like snake skins at the back of the tent.

"Excuse me," Nicolas said.

The merchant turned, and Nicolas jumped.

The merchant—he, she, whatever—was many things, but *human* wasn't one of them.

"Rude," the creature said. "Even for a Council magus."

Nicolas stared, his heart racing.

Its voice was masculine—human-like in its normality, though it hissed like a snake when he said *Council magus*. His eyes were reptilian, and his overlapping, iridescent scales were the color of jade. His snout ended in two tiny holes, and a forked tongue flitted in and out of his narrow mouth.

The merchant drew its—his—shoulders back.

"I appreciate your patronage, sir, but I will not tolerate rudeness. Even if you're the only person stupid enough to be *shopping* when there's an impending invasion."

Nicolas blinked.

"We're very sorry," Kaitlyn said. "We're not from around here, so we don't know the customs."

Nicolas nodded. "And we've never seen a..."

"A *what*?"

Time to change the subject.

"Can you tell us how to find the Arinian temple?" Nicolas asked.

"Gladly," the merchant said. "Their sermons on diversity will serve you well."

The merchant leaned out of the tent.

"Three blocks to the north you'll find the *Sharea Ar-Ra'isi*."

"The *what*?"

The merchant blinked the transparent inner lids of his reptilian eyes. "The *main street*. If you're going to wander around a Religarian city, particularly one that will be a war zone soon, you'd better learn a little Religarian. *Sharea Ar-Ra'isi*. Main street."

"Gotcha," Nicolas said. "Where do I go once I get there?"

"Left. You'll see the temple, don't worry. But stay on the right side of the road until you reach the Shar—the *main street*. There are some who aren't as welcoming to strangers as I am."

"You said this place was going to turn into a war zone soon. I'm aware of the armada, but you sounded as if you meant something more specific than that."

The merchant *harrumphed*. "Barathosian soldiers have been appearing in the streets."

"Have they attacked?" Nicolas asked.

"No," the merchant said. "They appear, draw sketches for a couple of minutes, then vanish."

"I'm sorry," Nicolas said. "Did you say *sketches*?"

"Always in pairs. One soldier in leather armor, with a wide-brimmed hat. The other in a gray robe. It's always the gray robe doing the sketching."

In Caspardis, Barathosians appeared and *attacked*. Now they were *drawing pictures*?

"The bells we're hearing aren't a good thing, are they?" Nicolas said.

"Palace alarm. The guards are after someone."

"Thanks again..."

"Komoden," the merchant said. "You should travel more."

Nicolas nodded. "Thanks, Komoden."

"Komoden is *what* I am, not *who* I am. Now repeat after me. *May you always find the sun.*"

Nicolas was confused, but he did as asked.

"Good," the merchant said. "Now you know how to part ways with a Komoden without sounding like an ignorant human."

"Uh...thank you?"

"May you always find the sun."

Nicolas and Kaitlyn slipped back into the street and crossed to the right side, as the Komoden had advised.

"Sketching," Nicolas said. "Bizarre."

"Not as bizarre as it sounds," Kaitlyn said. "The cichlos said chimeramancers turn dream into reality. If I were going to create a new dream, but I wanted it to be as close to reality as possible, it might be more effective if I knew the area in advance. What could be better than a drawing?"

They came to an avenue at least four times the width of the other streets. This had to be the Sharea Ar-Ra'isi the Komoden mentioned.

The adobe-like buildings were a single story tall, with few exceptions. But one building stood out among the rest, several blocks away. Its whitewashed walls towered over the other buildings by several stories. Unlike the palace walls, however, this building had no gold filigree.

"That has to be the temple," Nicolas said, as the palace bells tolled once more.

A patrol of palace guards marched into the street from an alley near the temple. Nicolas needed to act fast.

Tents lining the main street stood several feet from the buildings, creating a walkway of sorts. Nicolas guided Kaitlyn into the walkway and ducked behind the nearest tent. When the patrol passed, they ran toward the temple.

A booming thunderclap didn't only startle Nicolas and Kaitlyn. It also spooked a strange feline creature with too many legs, which jumped from behind a tent and skittered across the street in front of them.

As they approached the next intersection, another patrol of guards emptied onto the main street. Kaitlyn jumped sideways into an alcove between two tents, and Nicolas followed her lead.

He peeked around the corner and spotted an alley down the nearest side street.

"This way," he said.

The narrow alley was a canyon between two steep walls, blocking what little sunlight shone through the storm clouds. Debris, mostly garbage, littered the alley, creating one obstacle after another.

Several large crates and barrels stood against the wall up ahead.

A popping sound made Nicolas stop as he reached the first barrel. He signaled to Kaitlyn to move back behind the nearest crate, and they squatted as far down as possible.

Two Barathosians appeared in the alley ahead, and one of them—the older one—wore a gray robe. The younger wore the leather uniform of a Barathosian soldier, complete with holster and bandolier across the shoulder.

"You should stay here, Mester Vincen," the soldier said. "I'll scout the alley first."

"Do what you must, but don't slow me down," Mester Vincen said. "And maintain the count. I want this area complete before Gabril nullifies the chimera."

"Forgive me," the soldier said. "Shall we call it ninety? Should be close enough."

"Eighty. Be conservative. Fewer surprises that way."

Mester Vincen retrieved a narrow cylinder the color of graphite from his robe. In his other hand, he held a tablet with a piece of parchment clipped to the surface.

"Seventy five," the soldier said.

Mester Vincen looked up and down the alley, finally settling his gaze in the direction Nicolas and Kaitlyn had been running.

"The harbor is there," Mester Vincen said. "That means the temple is back that way."

The soldier glanced around the alley. "Fifty."

"I need more time," Mester Vincen said.

"Not my area of expertise, I'm afraid," the soldier said. He walked several paces away from the crate Nicolas and Kaitlyn hid behind. "Perhaps you should train Gabril a little better?"

Mester Vincen took measured steps across the alley, then wrote something on the parchment.

"Thirty five." The soldier turned and walked back.

"This will take *hours* at this rate!"

"Why doesn't Gabril *chimeraport* you to one of the mapped locations?"

"And what shall I do then, *walk* back to the harbor?" Mester Vincen scribbled furiously on the parchment. "I can't very well chimeraport *myself*. Focus on soldiering and leave the chimeramancy to us."

"Fifteen," the soldier said. "Yes, but he could at least *transmigrate* us to the same location. Wouldn't that speed this tedious process up?"

Mester Vincen placed the parchment and pencil in his robes. "Gabril does not have that level of control, and I do not have the time or desire to teach you the principles of chimera—"

The Barathosians vanished with a *pop*.

"Did you hear any of that?" Nicolas asked.

"The sketches they're making have something to do with the way they travel," Kaitlyn said.

"But we were wrong. They have two different ways to do it."

"How do we get to the harbor from here?"

"What? I'm *not* walking you into Barathosian central!"

"I came here to do something, and I'm not leaving until I've at least *tried*. You heard that *Mester Vincen* person. They're at the harbor. Lamil told us a chimeramancer made the city of Meculor *implode*. What if I can do something like that to this armada by taking control of one of their chimeramancers?"

Nicolas glanced down and shook his head.

"Two weeks ago—*your* time, at least—you cried because you accidentally killed a baby lizard in my apartment," Nicolas said. "Now you're going to destroy a fleet carrying thousands of *people*?"

Kaitlyn looked away.

"I've killed, Kait. In self-defense. I was *justified*. But It *still* changed me. And not for the better. The more you kill the easier it gets. There comes a point you don't even stop to *think* about it anymore. You just do it. After a while, you don't even *feel* anything. The ones you kill are just obstacles in your way. Not even *people* anymore. Just problems to be solved on your way to the next problem."

Kaitlyn stood. "I'm not going to pretend I know what you went through. But *you* use your skills to help these people. I'm going to use *mine*."

"Kait, I—"

"Are you helping me get to the harbor, or am I going by myself?"

Nicolas stood. "This wasn't what I had planned for us. We were supposed to walk together for graduation. Get married. Start a family. Have a life."

Kaitlyn took his hand and smiled. "No shit, Nick. If I thought *this* was your grand plan for our lives, I wouldn't be looking for the harbor. I'd be looking for the *exit*."

Nicolas squeezed her hand and took off down the alley.

They crossed several intersections unhindered, but with each toll of the palace bells, the patrols increased in frequency. If they didn't get to the harbor quickly, and if Kaitlyn didn't figure something out once they were there, it will have all been for nothing. Zorian would *never* let Nicolas go once he learned who the *true* archmage was.

They waited behind an old wagon as three patrols of six Religarian soldiers passed each other on the cross street.

Nicolas waved Kaitlyn to follow, and he bolted across the street.

"There!" a solder yelled.

Crap!

"Stay close!" Nicolas said. "We'll try to lose them at the next cross street."

They ran through the labyrinthine streets and alleys, making as many turns as they could, but always heading toward the harbor.

Nicolas looked over his shoulder to check on Kaitlyn.

Six Religarian soldiers entered the alley behind them at a full run.

He darted into the cross street and turned right, making sure Kaitlyn saw him.

Another alley ahead on the left looked promising, so he crossed the street and entered it. Kaitlyn was close behind, judging by the footsteps.

An open door in the side of a building rocked open and shut on its hinges.

The soldiers hadn't turned into the alley yet, but the pounding of their boots told Nicolas they were getting closer.

Nicolas bolted into the building and Kaitlyn followed. When she was inside, he pulled the door closed and latched it shut.

Within moments, the sound of boots striking the ground ran past the door and out into the next cross street.

Natural light spilled in from a window on the front of the building. The sweet smells of yeast and honey had Nicolas's stomach growling. They'd managed to run into a bakery.

"Don't touch that!" a corpulent man yelled. He walked out from behind the counter and unlatched the door. "What do you think you're doing? Farouk! Stop them!"

A burly, sweating, shirtless man in torn trousers ran up a short stair case from a basement and locked eyes with Nicolas. He pulled a spiked club from a shelf on the wall.

"Shit," Nicolas said.

He grabbed Kaitlyn's hand and ran toward the front of the building.

As they reached the door, Nicolas released a web of necropotency that wrapped around Farouk and pinned him to the stairs.

Nicolas opened the door and dashed outside. The guard patrol was gone, but another was entering the street a hundred yards to their left.

Nicolas aimed for another alley and kept running.

They crossed three more intersections until the alley opened onto a board walk littered with wooden shipping crates.

No soldiers had followed, but the palace bells were tolling nonstop now.

The sun broke through the clouds over the harbor, and Nicolas shielded his eyes from the light.

When Nicolas got his first glimpse of the Bay of Relig, he understood how the most powerful nation in the Three Kingdoms had been brought to the verge of surrender.

More than a thousand four-masted, multi-deck warships sat off the cost of Dar Rodon. Each of the ships had three rows of portholes above the water, and five ships sat broadside to the city. Subtle motion indicated they were sailing a circular pattern around a tall island in the middle of the bay. A golden beacon shone from the top of the island — a lighthouse of some sort, oddly bright at this time of day.

Nicolas couldn't help calling to mind Mujahid's description of the Barathosian Armada. "There were so many ships you could walk the breadth of the Bay of Relig without stepping in water," Mujahid had told him. At the time, Nicolas thought he'd been exaggerating.

Mujahid wasn't exaggerating.

As clouds obscured the sun, and the beacon on the island stopped shining, Nicolas brought his hand away from his eyes and took a closer look at the bay.

That was no island with a lighthouse. It was the largest ship Nicolas had ever seen. A gigantic catamaran. And the two supporting hulls — wide at the top and narrowing at the bottom — were several times the length of the massive, four-masted warships sailing around it. Its deck must have been a half mile in length at least, and it was ringed by six towers that rose to a dizzying height and bent inward toward a shorter—but much wider—central tower.

The central tower was open at the top, a platform with four columns holding up a roof. Several men stood on its perimeter carrying multicolor flags—emblazoned with symbols Nicolas didn't recognize. The tower grew wider as it descended to the main deck, giving the colossal ship the appearance of a floating ziggurat. But where the warships circling it had three rows of portholes, the big ship had horizontally elongated doors, which were many times the size of the smaller portholes.

As Nicolas refocused on one of the warships, deckhands rolled cannons into place within the portholes.

My god. We don't stand a chance.

"Nick," Kaitlyn said, as she nudged him with her elbow.

Nicolas faced the direction she was looking.

Mester Vincen, no more than twenty feet away, stood before a long table, which was surrounded on three sides by thick white fabric. He was examining rows of parchment on the table, while another chimeramancer—a younger one in a similar gray robe—sat next to a raised sleeping pallet under a canvas tarp.

Nicolas ducked behind the nearest shipping crate with Kaitlyn and peered around the corner.

"At least a third of the city remains incomplete in the *guiding dream*," Mester Vincen said.

"Forgive me, Mester, but I don't understand the urgency," the other chimeramancer said. "We've taken five of their largest cities in a matter of days."

"Your skills with chimeramancy are growing, Gabril, but you have much to learn about war," Mester Vincen said. "We may be able to *take* a city by transmigrating soldiers and cannons at intervals. But we cannot *hold* the city that way. If we cannot complete the guiding dream, Unega will order the landing boats to take the beach. The Religarians will fight back. Whom do you think the Diamond Throne will hold accountable for the failure when thousands of Barathosian lives are lost?"

The palace bells tolled, and the sound of running boots grew closer. Another patrol would be on them soon.

Kaitlyn glanced over her shoulder. "I have an idea. We should split up."

"You're kidding right? Name *one* horror movie where splitting up was a good idea."

"Zorian cares a *lot* more about you than he does me. If you can keep him focused on *you*, I can deal with these chimeramancers."

Nicolas shook his head. "I don't like it."

The boots grew louder.

"We have to *try*," Kaitlyn said.

"This isn't Texas, Kait. I can't just text you if I can't find you again!"

"Us being together isn't going to help anyone when they arrest us."

She was right.

Dammit all!

Nicolas took her hands in his and pulled her close until his forehead rested against hers.

"Don't do anything stupid," Nicolas said.

Kaitlyn chuckled. "*Stupid* is all we're left with at this point."

Nicolas squeezed her hands.

As he turned away, she pulled him back and kissed him.

When Nicolas pulled away, he gave her hands one last squeeze, then ran back out into the cross street, yelling as loudly as his voice would allow.

Shouts went up behind him. His diversion had worked.

The patrol ran past the entrance of the alley that led to Kaitlyn and followed Nicolas instead.

Nicolas passed a sandwich-board sign with a picture of an Arinian monk hoisting a tankard of ale and turned onto a street leading away from the harbor.

If the patrol was still following, he didn't see them.

But as he looked up and down the side streets, he *did* see patrols converging toward him.

When he emerged onto the Sharea Ar-Ra'isi, he wanted to head north. But every time he did, another patrol would converge toward him. He had one option—keep moving south and stay out of sight.

His path led to a hill on the southernmost end of Dar Rodon. Switchbacks crisscrossed their way up the side toward a tower on top of the hill.

If he ran any direction other than forward, the guard patrols would spot him again. The tower might be a good idea. He'd evade the patrols, for starters. But more than that, higher ground was easier to defend. The countless warrior penitents he'd summoned over the past year had taught him that.

Thunder pealed from the clouds overhead, and torrential rain followed.

The dirt switchbacks were wide and covered in old wagon tracks, mostly worn away. Large boulders rested on precarious perches above him, a fact he was grateful for—he could use them for cover as he made his way up the hill.

It wasn't long before the dirt became mud, making the run even more difficult.

When he reached the top, he doubled over to catch his breath. Rain poured over his head and off onto the rocky ground in narrow rivulets, where it collected in pools between the stones and small boulders.

He straightened and chanced a peek over the cliff into the city below.

No patrols followed him up the hill. But something odd was happening.

The patrols that were once converging on him were scattering back into the city, and they didn't appear to be in any hurry.

Something tickled at the back of his consciousness.

He wasn't alone.

He spun toward the tower, but no one was there. It was a fortification of some sort. Three stories tall, with crenelations at its top. Maybe it was part of the city's defense at one time. Whatever it was, it hadn't been used for a while. The whitewashing was reduced to white flecks, and the facade was crumbling.

There door at the tower's base swung open, revealing a familiar figure staring out from a torch-lit room.

"Hello, Archmage," Zorian said. "A pleasure to finally meet you."

Realization dawned on Nicolas. He hadn't been leading the guards anywhere. They'd been herding him here the entire way!

Why didn't I see it?

"Please," Zorian said. He gestured into the tower. "Step in from the rain, and we can proceed where I left off with your predecessor."

Zorian was alone. If he knew Nicolas was the archmage—knew what Nicolas was capable of—why would he come alone?

Nicolas could attack. Maybe even finish this right here.

But why was he *alone*?

If Nicolas attacked now, before he discovered what made Zorian so confident, he likely wouldn't get another chance.

He left Kaitlyn at the harbor to keep Zorian occupied. Perhaps it was time he started *occupying*.

"Hello, Zorian," Nicolas said. "We have a lot to discuss."

Nicolas stepped around Zorian and entered the tower

CHAPTER THIRTY TWO

In the year 661 BCE, Hussein Bata stepped over the threshold, becoming Hussein Lord Mukhtaar Bata. In the first three years of his short twenty-one year reign, Lord Hussein survived fourteen assassination attempts at the hands of Catiatum assassins. He became a recluse, closing the Mukhtaar Estate to all but his own penitents. The circumstances of his death are unknown. His skeletal remains were discovered three years after his last known public appearance.
  - The Mukhtaar Chronicles, Second Cycle, 10 CE

The few remaining writings of Lord Hussein implicate Clan Zerubula for the assassination attempts. For what it's worth, they tried the same with Nuuan some forty years ago. The clan all but disintegrated after the failed attempt. Nuuan claims no knowledge of why this might be the case, though he did seem amused when I asked.
  - Mujahid Mukhtaar, Private Commentaries, 45 CE

N icolas faced Zorian in the close confines of the tower's base. A torch cast long shadows of the sparse furniture and filled the room with the acrid scent of pitch. Kaitlyn needed time to take control of the Barathosian chimeramancers. He'd have to do whatever he could to delay Zorian.

Tullias, Zorian's servant, stood at the base of the stone staircase that wound its way up the outer wall of the tower.

"Saleem told you, I take it," Nicolas said.

"I found it odd when Kagan didn't bleed during his flogging," Zorian said.

"I'm sure it was a dead giveaway."

Another thunderclap, this one louder than the last, thumped Nicolas's chest and vibrated his teeth.

"This will be over soon," Zorian said. "The weather, that is. *You* are a different matter entirely."

As if following Zorian's command, the pace of the rain subsided to a slow drizzle.

"So, what happens now?" Nicolas asked.

"I told Kagan we would have two conversations. As far as I'm concerned, you and I have already had the first."

"Hardly fair," Nicolas said. "What if my answers are different?"

"A necromancer who disagrees with his penitent? You don't take me for that much a fool, do you?"

"You don't know as much about necromancy as you think you do."

Zorian nodded at Tullias, who ran up the stairs and disappeared through a trap door in the ceiling.

"I'll concede that," Zorian said. "I make no claims about my knowledge of the arcane. Come. Let's take in some fresh air, you and I."

The rain had stopped by the time Nicolas left the tower, though the rolling black clouds remained. He breathed in the smell of the thirsty desert as it drank in the remains of the downpour.

Dar Rodon gleamed below them where rays of sunlight broke through gaps in the clouds. It looked pristine from up here. On any other day it would have been quite beautiful. But not today. Not when thousands of enemy ships anchored in the bay.

Zorian walked past him, stepping over basketball-sized boulders and mud puddles as he strode toward the cliff overlooking the city. When he stopped in front of a short, foot-high retaining wall, he folded his arms and gazed down at Dar Rodon.

"I spent months on the command ship," Zorian said. "Every day, I'd step out onto the deck and stare at this city. Just stare and admire it. The palace, with its whitewashed walls. The Temple of Arin, rising into the sky like a spire. Thousands of pilgrims making their way through the city — most of whom are in that very temple as we speak."

Zorian faced Nicolas, his back to the city below.

"It's not that different from our capital city *Barathos*," Zorian said. "It *looks* much different, of course. We have no deserts in Barathosia, for one. Our buildings are magnificent. People walk among them on raised walkways of poured stone, illuminated by Builders' gems. Some say the Builders themselves were Barathosian, given how many of our structures they created."

"I'm sure it makes a beautiful post card," Nicolas said.

"Our Temple of the Gods dwarfs your Temple of Arin. When the archmage — that is to say, *our* archmage — enters the sanctuary for the Incarnation Ceremony, *fifty thousand* people await the words of Arin in the temple proper."

Nicolas looked down at the city, toward the Temple of Arin. The temple's whitewashed walls were all the more brilliant in the overcast atmosphere. Its entrance reminded Nicolas of the basilica of Saint Mary Major in Rome. Five alcoves set within the walls on the ground floor bore the weight of three cavernous arches on the floor above. But unlike Saint Mary Major, there were no statues on the top of the temple. And where the basilica had a tower, a dome rested instead, inlaid with gemstones that glistened whenever a stray shaft of sunlight would hit it.

"Beautiful, isn't it?" Zorian asked. "Fifteen hundred years old, I'm told. And no doubt filled with pilgrims. A throng of people — at least a thousand — arrived today from your *Oasis of Zarush*. Families praying together. Peaceful, devout people, who have no desire to engage in war. People who care nothing for the politics of this world or the machinations of thrones and archmages. All seeking shelter in that magnificent temple."

"I know how they feel. I don't care much for politics either."

Zorian smiled and looked back at the temple.

"Many criticize men like you for possessing property of such value when there are poor to be fed," Zorian said.

"I'll hang a *for sale* sign on it next chance I get."

Zorian waved his hand. "I'm not a critic, Archmage. We have many buildings such as that in Barathosia. And many far older. Buildings with impressive histories, for a person who has a mind to learn."

"Are you selling me a time share or kidnapping me? You brought me here for a reason. How about we get to the point?"

"You murdered the heir to our empire, yet our vivamancers helped you still. They worked tirelessly to make sure your women still bore children, though there were few."

"I know you're not an idiot. You must know I had nothing to do with Yotto's death."

"Someone must pay the price."

"If it weren't for me, Kagan would still be the archmage. That barrier would still be up. I'd *like* to make this a better place. But I haven't had much of a chance, with your plans for conquest, that is."

"Not all of us come to conquer," Zorian said. "I came to collect a debt of honor. Nothing more. When that debt has been paid, I will convince the others to leave the Three Kingdoms in peace. More than that, I'll see to reopening diplomatic channels. We'll establish trade agreements. Treaties. The Three Kingdoms will thrive like never before. Hunger, disease, homelessness, war…these evils will be a thing of the past for your people."

Sure, once you enslave everyone. Emperor Relig had your number, that's why he chose to bide his time.

"Who are you to make these promises?" Nicolas asked. "You told Kagan only a member of the Barathosian imperial family could speak on behalf of the empress."

"Any authority I need will be granted when I return with you alive and well. You need not fear that."

"So, you're making deals based on power you *might* have in the future? Let's knock off the crap for a minute. You and that admiral down there aren't on the same side, are you?"

Zorian clenched a fist and released it. "There's a greater conflict of which you're unaware."

"Then enlighten me. Because if we're friends in this thing, you're doing a *horrible* job of getting the point across."

Something changed in the distance, just over Zorian's right shoulder.

"Two powers collide in Barathosia," Zorian said. "Chaos and order."

Nicolas took a furtive glance at the harbor. Several of the warships vanished.

Keep at it, Kait!

"Your intuition serves you well," Zorian said. "If Admiral Unega comes to power, he will destroy the Three Kingdoms. And no one will be able to stop him."

"What do you mean, *come to power*?" Nicolas asked. "He already controls that armada, doesn't he?"

"It's not that simple. If I fail here, it will be left to the admiral to finish the task. And let there be no doubt that his victory will be swift and decisive. Every living person in that city behind me will suffer the same fate as those in your *Caspardis*."

Caspardis. Nicolas remembered the shriller swarm that butchered the survivors. He'd never be able to unsee it.

He looked past Zorian to the city below.

Kaitlyn was down there. All because of Nicolas. After Arin and the other gods returned, he thought the worst was over. It was *his* idea to bring her back with him. The thought of her being torn apart by a shriller made him shut his eyes.

"The fate of Erindor will be determined by what happens here, in the Three Kingdoms," Zorian said. "I offer you a chance to save not only *your* people, but countless others as well. Come with me."

There was sincerity in Zorian's voice.

But of *course* he'd sound sincere. He would say anything to outwit that admiral down there.

Nicolas opened his eyes and looked at the city once more.

"You said you weren't going to force me to go with you," Nicolas said. "So how does this play out when I say *no*?"

"You'll leave me with no choice," Zorian said. "I'll hand Admiral Unega the very power I seek to withhold. And with it, the Three Kingdoms—and perhaps much of Barathosia—will cease to be."

Several other ships vanished from view, but there were thousands in the armada.

Perhaps he should give Zorian a glimmer of hope. That might draw this out long enough for Kaitlyn to control the chimeramancers.

"And what if I say *yes*?" Nicolas asked.

Zorian offered a reluctant smile. "The situation here is much different from what I expected to find. I came here for Kagan, and instead I found his *son* in power. Given your role in the downfall of my nation's most notorious enemy, I have no doubt the Glorious One will be merciful. I have been empowered to negotiate, should you return with me. Let's discuss terms, shall we?"

Nicolas nodded. "I'm listening."

Come on, Kait. I can't stall him forever.

Kaitlyn turned her attention back to Mester Vincen, as Gabril slept on the mat next to the map table. She pressed her back against the corner of the building.

Manipulating Gabril had been easy, but Kaitlyn had no idea why. Chimeramancers had a natural tendency to sleep frequently, true. But without a teacher, her powers were mostly guesswork.

And her head buzzed every time she touched another person's mind, regardless of whether she succeeded or failed.

Being able to sense the boundaries of her own mind—an amorphous cloud that surrounded her body—was disturbing. Every time her thoughts wandered, the cloud would shift and rotate—sometimes elongating, other times compressing—and a different portion of it would enter her head. Somehow, the memories or faculties she needed to complete a thought were stored outside her body.

That day she and Nicolas went to the Austin Zoo and rode the train? To the left, down near her feet. How she felt when Nicolas disappeared from his apartment? Behind her, near her right shoulder blade. Adding and subtracting numbers? A small patch of fog directly above her.

But the creep factor of sensing her *own* mind paled next to sensing someone *else's*.

Whenever her mind would bump up against another's, it was like trying to force the wrong side of two magnets together.

As far as she could tell, enchanting required overcoming that natural resistance and extending a portion of her mind into the other person's mind, blending them together. Once inside, placing a thought into another person's mind was a simple matter of forming an image in the regions that overlapped.

Saleem had told her this would only be possible if she *touched* the person whose mind she wished to enter. That might be true about *his* magic, but it wasn't true about *hers*.

When her mind entered Gabril's—from more than a dozen yards away—she'd formed the *intent* of going to sleep, and Gabril carried it out.

But now it was time to try something new; controlling a chimeramancer's magic.

Kaitlyn pushed against the boundary of her mind, extending it out ahead of her, until more of it overlapped Gabril's. The more of her mind she could force into his, the easier it might be to control him.

When his mind resisted, her natural instinct was to push harder. But she'd discovered in Caspardis that was the wrong approach. *Pushing* made the person unpredictable, as had happened with the cannon operator. All she'd wanted was for him and the others to step away from the cannons. But when the resistance in his mind grew, she forced it, picturing the strongest thing she could imagine—Godzilla. It was embarrassing when she thought of it, but she'd just been watching a marathon of seventies monster movies with Nicolas. Her imagination had been so powerful, however, that the poor canon operator thought he'd *actually seen* Godzilla! He destroyed the entire column of cannons as a result.

No, overcoming the resistance wasn't about *pushing* or *struggling*. It was about *transformation*. It was about making the portion of her mind inside the other person more *tangible*. More *real*. More...*other*. The more different the *substance* of her mind from the other person's, the more easily she could overcome the resistance. The more easily she overcame the resistance, the more complete her control.

Kaitlyn changed the boundary of her mind that touched Gabril's, making it more dense. It entered his without further effort.

When the absorption was complete, she reversed the process, allowing her mind to return to normal.

The two minds locked together, and Gabril was hers.

But she wasn't sure if any of this would actually work. And her head was buzzing like she'd stuck her head in a beehive.

Let's start small and go from there.

She looked out into the harbor and focused on a single warship. If she could somehow convince Gabril to move *this* ship, she ought to be able to repeat the process with the others.

Kaitlyn imagined the ship vanishing.

Nothing happened.

Not *exactly* nothing. Nothing had happened with the *ship*. But Gabril's mind was firing with activity, increasing the intensity of both the buzzing and the headache that followed.

It was *rejecting* her image, like a nightmare recognized for what it was and shoved aside for happier dreams.

Maybe her image needed more *intent*. More *details*.

Those boats had to come from somewhere.

Kaitlyn focused on the same ship. But this time, instead of simply imagining it disappearing, she imagined it was *necessary* for the ship to return to wherever it had come from.

The warship faded from view, leaving a gap in the pattern of ships sailing around the larger one.

Though she was excited for the success, celebrating it seemed too perverse.

I hope I haven't killed those people.

But wherever they went, she needed to repeat that process with the rest of the ships. This time she'd focus on moving more than one at a time, though.

She picked four ships and repeated the pattern.

All four vanished.

Her vision faded, but returned quickly. As long as she didn't push too hard, she wouldn't be temporarily blinded like the other times.

Her heart raced. It was going better than she'd hoped.

Let's see how many more we can take care of!

Kaitlyn focused on another group of ships, praying her luck would hold out.

CHAPTER THIRTY THREE

In the year 450 BCE, Baladi Mukhtaar stepped over the threshold, becoming Baladi Lord Mukhtaar. Though he reigned in a time of peace, that peace was the result of compromise. Serving the greater good required the sacrifice of a few. The peace of his reign, however, is overshadowed by the rise of the Cult of Malvol in the years following his ascension.
  - The Mukhtaar Chronicles, Second Cycle, 10 CE

Nicolas held out his arm as Zorian stepped over a large rock and started toward the tower. Part of him wanted to launch a bolt of necropotency at Zorian and be done with it. But Kaitlyn still hadn't succeeded in getting rid of the armada. She needed more time. And as long he kept Zorian talking, that armada would stay put.

"If you don't mind," Nicolas said, "I'd prefer to do this out here."

At least here I can keep my eye on those ships. Come on, Kait!

Zorian shrugged. "If you prefer."

"First, I want to know what you meant when you said the *fate of Erindor* is at stake. What does the rest of the world have to do with this?"

Zorian looked away and rested his foot on a basketball-sized boulder.

Another ship disappeared from the bay in the distance over Zorian's shoulder. After a few moments of silence, he faced Nicolas.

"My archmage is a woman of singular wisdom," Zorian said. "I've served her for years, and will hopefully do so for many more. Surely, you've sensed the growing darkness as much as she has. Surely, you've concluded the world cannot continue as it has."

"Imprisoning the gods in a barrier for forty years probably had something to do with it."

Zorian shook his head. "I thought so at first, myself. But my archmage is convinced this started long before your father did what he did."

"You seriously believe this *darkness* of yours will go away if I surrender?"

"Of course not. But it will grant me the power I need to ensure others do what is *right* instead of what is *convenient*. And *that* will allow the archmage to do what she must."

Zorian glanced over his shoulder toward the bay. If he noticed the missing ships, he didn't react to them.

"I was once a naval officer," Zorian said. "I resigned my commission when my admiral ordered me to sink a diplomatic vessel. A vessel that not only housed the diplomat, but his wife and children as well. So understand the depth of my anger, when I see two thousand *predator-class* warships, under the command of that *very same admiral*, poised to annihilate a city of more than a million non-combatants."

"Then this should end peacefully."

"Don't mistake my peaceful nature for a lack of patriotism, Archmage." Zorian pointed at the tower. "There's a signal fire on the parapet of that tower. If I give the order, or if Tullias sees me fall,he will light it. The admiral will proceed with a *military* solution to this standoff. So, again I ask, will you do the right thing and come with me of your own free will?"

Nicolas couldn't strike Zorian down if he wanted to. The bastard had planned for that outcome.

"You'd do that?" Nicolas asked. "You'd pull the trigger on a gun that kills a million people, out of a sense of *patriotism*?"

Several ships vanished from the harbor, and Zorian began to face the cliff.

"Wait," Nicolas said.

Zorian stopped, mid-turn.

I can't let this escalate. I have to distract him a little while longer for Kait.

"This archmage of yours," Nicolas said. "Tell me about her."

As Zorian responded, Nicolas chanced another glance at the harbor. Those ships weren't vanishing fast enough. There'd be no way he could keep Zorian occupied for as long as it would take to get rid of the entire fleet. Not at the rate it was going.

"Is it done the same way at your *Pinnacle*?" Zorian asked.

Nicolas glanced back at Zorian twice before realizing the man had asked him a question.

Zorian spun toward the harbor.

"Clever," Zorian said. "I can't say I'm surprised. But I *am* disappointed. Tullias! Light the signal!"

Nicolas sent a web of necropotency toward the parapet, hoping to stop Tullias before he lit the fire, but he only managed a glancing blow. It was enough to knock the man down and send the torch flying. Nicolas would have to—

Pain erupted on the back of Nicolas's head.

Zorian had backhanded him. But because of the uneven ground, he too had only managed a glancing blow.

Nicolas formed a sharpened cylinder of necropotency and prepared to fire it at Zorian's throat, but he stopped. There was something about this man. Something sincere. He'd left the military to avoid the unnecessary deaths of a handful of people. He implored Nicolas to come with him to avoid the destruction.

Nicolas transformed the cylinder of necropotency into another web, and shot it toward Zorian. It wrapped around him and pressed his arms to his sides.

And then dissipated into the center of his chest.

Zorian clutched at something inside his tunic.

"None of you would survive a day in Barathos," Zorian said. His chest sagged as moisture pooled in his eyes. "What a fool I was to hope you would serve the greater good. Know this, Archmage. What happens here today happens because of *you*. *You* have destroyed Dar Rodon this day. *You* are the man who *pulls the trigger*, as you call it."

Nicolas had to think fast.

Zorian might have protection from necropotency, but it was doubtful he had protection from rocks.

Nicolas wrapped a rope of necropotency around a small boulder. With a mental heave, he yanked it sideways and struck Zorian on the side of the head.

As Zorian fell to the ground, a wave of heat rose behind Nicolas.

Nicolas spun to see an enormous fire blazing on the roof of the tower.

A flag waved on the giant command ship in the distance, and activity erupted on the decks of the warships below. Portholes opened, and cannons the color of brass emerged from each of them.

Clouds of smoke burst from the portholes as the first of the cannons fired into the city.

The explosions reached his ears within moments of the cannons firing. Several buildings collapsed in the distance, and dust billowed up and out toward the harbor.

I have to get to Kait!

Nicolas bounded over the cliff and slid down the sharply angled hill until he reached the switchback. But rather than follow the path, he slid down the side of the hill once again, until finally he reached the road and bolted into the city.

The dome and walls of the Arinian temple seemed to collapse in slow motion. Yet the destruction happened so quickly, so completely, no one could have escaped.

Zorian said there were thousands of people in there!

Nicolas ran along the ever widening street, ignoring the pooled water on the cobblestones. Kaitlyn would be at the harbor, which was to his right.

People flooded into the streets and stared in the direction of the collapsing Arinian temple. But they soon regretted it.

Two buildings on Nicolas's left exploded, sending stone and wood fragments flying. The force was so strong, it knocked him across the street. He hadn't even heard the cannons fire that time.

The few people who remained alive ran screaming farther into the city.

"No!" Nicolas yelled. "You need to *leave* the city!"

Nicolas stood, but pain in his left foot made him collapse once more.

Nothing was broken, but he must have sprained his ankle badly.

He forced himself up and jogged toward the harbor as quickly as his limp would allow.

The bombardment was nonstop. A hundred Barathosian warships sailed a slow circle around the gigantic command vessel, with five ships always broadside to the city. As the lead ship would steer out of the firing line, another would steer into it from behind. By the time the first ship came around again, having sailed around the command vessel, all sixty of its visible cannons—twenty on each of its three gun decks—were reloaded and ready to fire. The result was continuous cannon fire.

A tavern collapsed at Nicolas's right, filling the street with a cloud of dust that started him choking. The tavern's sign—a brown-robed Arinian with a mug of ale—fell to the cobblestone street and shattered.

He remembered that tavern from when he left Kaitlyn at the harbor. She must be close.

Terror-filled cries came from the collapsed tavern.

"Help us!" the voices yelled. "Please!"

Nicolas ran several more steps before stopping.

I can't just leave them.

But it likely wouldn't be long before the armada started firing on the harbor as well.

No, I can do it. I can get these people out of the building, then make my way to Kait.

He ran toward the collapsed tavern as another volley of cannon fire shredded the four-story building across the street.

Stone and glass rained down, and Nicolas pulled his robe over his head.

A massive stone wall had collapsed on top of a young man and woman. The parts of the tavern still standing were rocked precariously. They'd never survive something else collapsing on top of them.

The woman had managed to free all except her legs, one of which was bent at an unnatural angle. But the man was buried up to his shoulders, his face and hair white with dust from the crumbling stone. Both bled freely through torn, white desert robes.

"I'm here!" Nicolas yelled. He tried to lift the side of the fallen wall. If he could budge it just an inch, the woman might be able to crawl free. But it was too much weight.

"I think my leg is broken," the woman said.

"How many are trapped inside?" Nicolas asked.

"The tavern was full," the woman said.

The man spit dust from his mouth. "I should never have brought you here. Now we're going to die."

"No one's going to die," Nicolas said.

Unless I can't get that wall off of them…

Nicolas drew necropotency into his well and opened a channel to the skull symbol. He wasn't certain if this would work, but he had to try *something*.

I need someone strong. Hercules strong. There's no way a normal penitent will be able to lift that stone wall and roof.

When the necropotency embraced the skull symbol, he cast the power outward in no particular direction. The only dead bodies he knew of were too far away for him to reach. There might be some here, but he couldn't see them to direct the power. No, this would be a *pure* summoning—raising the dead without the assistance of a corpse.

But as the power left him, it diverted downward, deep into the ground. The last time that happened, he'd summoned an argram warrior.

What the hell am I summoning this time?

The familiar stream of images raced toward Nicolas's consciousness, and he lived more than forty years in the span of a moment.

The ground rumbled violently as the *namocea* stopped and Nicolas returned to the present. After all his training, it was still disorienting.

The building behind Nicolas began to crumble, but not from cannon fire.

A massive skeletal arm, thirty feet in length, and ending in a ten-foot long hand, burst from under the street next to the collapsing building. Its counterpart erupted from the other side. As the structure collapsed, it parted around a giant skull with a single eye socket in the center of its forehead.

When the gargantuan skeleton tore free of its desert grave, it stood sixty feet tall—twice as tall as the tallest building on the street. Its conical skull had but a single eye socket.

Seriously? A cyclops?

Nicolas took a moment to take control of the necromantic link, and the cyclops—*Tewgar*—stared down at him.

Cannon fire shredded two buildings a block away, sending clouds of dust up and over the collapsed tavern.

I have to finish this and get to Kaitlyn!

"Get that wall off of those people," Nicolas said. "Hurry!"

Tewgar leaned forward, grasped the edge of the stone wall between two fingers and lifted it off the trapped couple.

Nicolas dragged the young woman clear of the wall and went back for her boyfriend.

Muffled screams came from farther inside the collapsed tavern.

Nicolas hurried to pull the man free, then ran farther into the building, uncertain of what he'd find.

I hope the rest of that roof holds.

A man, a woman, and two children huddled in the corner, next to a stove.

"There!" Nicolas yelled over the din of the cannon fire. "Head to the street! Quickly!"

"What *is* that thing?" the man asked, staring at Tewgar.

"It won't hurt you," Nicolas said. "Just go."

The man snapped out of whatever shock he was in, gathered his family, and ran for the street.

The muffled screams grew louder. There were more people in the back room.

This was taking too long! The more time he spent here, the more of a chance Kaitlyn wouldn't survive the bombardment.

He had a choice to make.

The roof creaked once more. It wouldn't be long before the entire thing came down.

Kaitlyn's words from their first night together on Erindor played through his mind. *"You can't save all of your pieces all of the time."*

Is that what he was doing? Was he trying to save everyone and risking the outcome of the entire battle in the process?

She was right. He was trying to save a handful of people here when helping Kaitlyn could save hundreds of thousands in Dar Rodon.

He had to get to her. It was that simple.

As he turned his back on the cries from within the partially collapsed tavern, the ceiling crashed down.

A wave of necropotency poured over him like liquid guilt.

I'm sorry. I'm so sorry.

Nicolas glanced up at Tewgar, who stood with a section of wall in his right hand.

"Can you do some damage with that thing?" Nicolas asked.

Tewgar looked toward the bay and roared. He reared back and threw the section of wall. The sweeping motion of his arm created a wind so great, it drove the dust clouds from the collapsed buildings toward the harbor.

The wall arced over the bay and slammed into one of the gunships edge-first, piercing all three cannon decks and toppling two of its four masts. When the fore and aft decks separated from the blow, the fore deck capsized and the aft drifted into the neighboring ship, forcing its captain to adjust course.

Nicolas ran for the harbor, which was less than two blocks away.

Tewgar stop angry dwarves on boats? Tewgar asked through the necromantic link.

Yes! Take out as many of those ships as you can!

Tewgar picked up another wall section and bounded forward. In four giant steps, he plunged into the Bay of Relig, submerged up to his thigh bones.

Tewgar stop more dwarves, Tewgar said.

You're doing great!

Nicolas rounded the corner of a partially demolished building, and the harbor came into view once more. Tewgar was submerged up to his waist now, waving a warship in the air above his head.

But something had changed in the bay.

The ships that weren't part of the circular firing pattern had come about until they were broadside to Tewgar.

Two ships fired their three decks of cannons, and Tewgar's massive ribcage came apart, raining bone fragments into the bay. In moments, Tewgar collapsed into the water, and his necromantic link winked out of Nicolas's mind.

When Tewgar's massive hands struck the water, the ship they had been carrying fractured apart from the force.

I'll summon you again someday, Tewgar. I promise.

Nicolas ran faster. He could see the chimeramancer's tent and table from here. Just a few hundred more yards.

Saltwater spray washed over him, adding to the strong smell of damp wood.

Kaitlyn sat on the boardwalk, several feet away from them, no longer hiding around the corner. She pressed a hand against the side of her head, as if in pain. One of the chimeramancers was on the ground, but the older one approached Kaitlyn with an arm extended in front of him.

Hold on Kait! I'm almost there!

K aitlyn smiled as more ships vanished, unable to believe her crazy idea had worked.

She pressed her back against a ladder fixed to the side of the building next to her. Mester Vincen and Gabril were no more than twenty feet away, closer to the water on the edge of the boardwalk.

Mester Vincen straightened as he looked out into the bay.

"What are those fools doing?" Mester Vincen said. "This isn't part of—Gabril, look at this. This is what can happen when the *ancillary dreams* collapse. I knew I shouldn't have left this in their hands. Transmigrate me to the chimera chamber." When nothing happened, Mester Vincen shouted. "Gabril!"

Kaitlyn felt a push against her mind. The pushing became shoving, and soon a sharp pain rippled through her head in waves.

Her mind no longer overlapped Gabril's.

All five ships reappeared, precisely where they were before they'd vanished.

"Cognitomancer!" Gabril yelled.

Mester Vincen leapt backward, nearly stumbling over the rope railing into the bay. "Don't let her touch you!"

A concussive blast from the bay made Kaitlyn cover her ears. The returning boats fired their cannons into the city.

She gripped the ladder to steady herself. As she squeezed, the ground beneath her feet vanished and she dangled twenty feet above the roiling water.

Gabril!

If Gabril could create anything he imagined, how could she fight back?

Sulfurous smoke rolled in from the bay, and Kaitlyn started choking.

Her arms grew weaker with every passing moment.

She pulled herself up and started climbing the ladder. If she could hide before the smoke cleared, Gabril wouldn't know where to attack. The cannons were firing farther into the city, probably because the chimeramancers were still on the boardwalk, so she'd be safe on the roof as long as they stayed there.

When she hoisted herself over the ledge, she stood and looked back toward the palace.

The Temple of Arin exploded from the cannon fire. Fragments from its crushed walls and shattered dome so pulverized they were indistinguishable.

Everywhere she looked, buildings collapsed or were already destroyed.

And the cannons kept firing.

She had to get those ships out of the bay. But how could she do it in such a way that they *stayed* gone this time?

She pushed her mind outward once more until it recoiled at Gabril's touch.

Something was different. Gabril was prepared for her attack. Every time she tried to fuse her mind to his, his mind would retract or become impenetrable.

Think, Kait!

Searing flame shot up from the street where she'd been minutes ago. Had she not climbed the ladder, she would have been incinerated.

But Gabril's dream magic had an unintended consequence; the ladder was ablaze.

Great. How am I going to get down now?

Kaitlyn glanced around the roof, hoping the ladder wasn't the only way up. A small shrine at the center of the roof was the only thing of note. It consisted of a stone altar, some kind of helmet painted to look gold, and an offering bowl, filled with something she couldn't see from her vantage point.

Beyond the shrine, however, was a small wooden trapdoor. She almost didn't see it, so well concealed was it under two sacks.

The building rumbled.

She ran for the trapdoor, opened it, and climbed down a short ladder into a well-kept sitting room.

Narrow beams of golden light illuminated dust particles through slats in the large, shuttered window on the opposite side of the room.

The rumbling started again, but it no longer felt like it was coming from the building. She ran to the window and opened the shutters.

A giant skeleton, towering over the surrounding buildings, had climbed out of the ground and was holding what looked like the wall of a building.

Nick!

He *had* to be responsible for this.

The giant hurled the wall into the bay, where it slammed into a Barathosian warship, splitting it in two and sinking it. Moments later, it picked something else up and ran toward the bay.

As the skeletal giant plunged into the water, the resistance Kaitlyn had felt coming from Gabril's mind changed. Maybe it was the distraction of the giant, or maybe Gabril had just grown tired. But whatever it was, Kaitlyn was able to expand her mind into his.

If you can transport other people, then you can transport me too.

She imagined herself standing on the boardwalk, on the opposite side of the fire.

There was no disorientation, or *fading*, as there was when Nicolas used the translocation orb. Her reality simply changed, and the change was immediate. In less than a moment, she'd gone from standing on top of a burning building, to standing on the boardwalk below it.

But she hadn't been specific enough. Gabril had transported her within fifteen feet of him and Mester Vincen.

Mester Vincen turned on her, and before she could react, the world became muffled.

Something slammed into her back.

Kaitlyn reached forward and scraped her hands on something hard mere inches in front of her.

She was inside some sort of box or crate, and she was on her back.

This isn't real. This is just one of his dreams.

She wasn't sure how he had done it. She was told chimeramancers needed to be asleep to work their magic, but Mester Vincen had been wide awake, and Gabril was under her control.

Gabril!

Kaitlyn focused on the region of her mind that overlapped Gabril's. She formed an image of the box vanishing and wrapping around Mester Vincen instead.

Once again, gray clouds hung above her, and the sound of the cannons grew loud.

A wooden crate, about the size of a tall refrigerator, had taken Mester Vincen's place in front of the map table. Wrapped *around* him, to be precise.

"Gabril, no!" Mester Vincen yelled. His voice was muffled. "Control this, or I will!"

The fear emanating from Gabril's mind was tangible.

As another cannon volley exploded, the ships Kaitlyn had transported away reappeared.

The giant skeleton in the bay, holding two ships over his head, collapsed into the water in fragments of bone. The ships he held didn't fare much better.

"Gabril!" Mester Vincen yelled. "The swarm is coming!"

A portion of Kaitlyn's mind was still fused with Gabril's, but something was pushing against it. Stretching it. And the more it stretched, the thinner its structure became.

Gabril's mind tore, and the portion fused with Kaitlyn's faded away.

The standing crate vanished, and Mester Vincen faced Gabril, intense concentration on his face.

If Kaitlyn could touch Mester Vincen's robe with her hand, she could *imbue* it with an alternate reality. One in which those Barathosian warships *had* to return home. Mester Vincen would do all the work for her, and she'd be free to find Nicolas and get out of here.

Now was her chance, while he was preoccupied with Gabril.

Kaitlyn projected her mind forward, toward Mester Vincen.

The boundary of his mind was defenseless, so focused was he on Gabril.

When Kaitlyn's mind entered Mester Vincen's, it struck something solid. Painful. It was like driving head first into oncoming traffic and slamming into a truck.

He hadn't been defenseless at all. He'd been luring her in, and she'd fallen for it.

Mester Vincen pushed back, and excruciating pain exploded in her mind.

She grabbed her head as her vision swam.

I have to fight this! I have to find a way to…

Realization struck.

I'm so stupid! It doesn't matter if my mind enters his, or his enters mine. I just need them to overlap!

Kaitlyn relaxed and let go of her control. She allowed her mind to become pliable, welcoming, accepting.

When Mester Vincen pushed back once more, the outer barrier of his mind crossed hers, and she fused the two together.

Mester Vincen was hers.

She dug through his thoughts and memories until she found images of the one person Mester Vincen cared most about.

Mester Vincen's eyes widened, and he smiled. He reached out toward her and stepped forward.

"Father," Mester Vincen said. "I've missed you."

"Come closer, my son," Kaitlyn said.

The bay grew silent as the cannon fire ceased. But something was changing around the command ship. A black cloud rose from openings at its base. At first, the cloud drifted straight up and spread out. But in a span of moments, it condensed into a column, turned, and began stretching toward the shore.

Kaitlyn had seen this once before. It was a swarm of the creatures the Barathosians sent into Caspardis to slaughter the survivors.

Kaitlyn wove a new reality to imbue Mester Vincen's robes. An urgent call. The entire fleet must return to Barathosia at once. An unknown invader. Massive casualties in their capital city.

He was close now. No more than three steps away. But she was way too dizzy to stand. She couldn't afford losing control of him now.

The flock of creatures was three hundred yards off shore and closing quickly.

Mester Vincen and Gabril vanished from the boardwalk, along with the tent and table.

The recoil from Mester Vincen's mind being pulled that far away that quickly was like the wrong side of a stretched rubber band being released; the boundary of her mind slammed into her, knocking her backward. Her vision went black.

She covered her ears as the horrible sound of tearing metal vibrated the boardwalk.

The screeching of the flying creatures grew louder. As the ravenous creatures drew closer, she imagined Nicolas finding her body shredded and bloody, face no longer recognizable, and she trembled from the anticipated pain.

The only thing she saw, as the sounds around her grew muffled and distant, was Nicolas's face. She held on to that image as long as she could, through the terror, through the trembling, remembering all they'd dreamed of. All they'd wished for. All their plans and aspirations.

A marriage that would never be. A family that would never be.

And when silence came, Kaitlyn let go.

CHAPTER THIRTY FOUR

In the year 957 BCE, Ahmed Mukhtaar stepped over the threshold, becoming Ahmed Lord Mukhtaar. Lord Ahmed's reign began in tragedy. A group of unknown men abducted his only child, a daughter named Sadira. Sadira was never found, though Lord Mukhtaar searched the length and breadth of the Three Kingdoms tirelessly. His travels resulted in the largest growth of Clan Mukhtaar in recorded history, with more than one hundred covens attributed to his name.

Burdened by sorrow and guilt over the loss of Sadira, Lord Mukhtaar never allowed his grief to come before others.

- Coteon of the Steppes, "The Mukhtaar Chronicles: Coteonic Commentaries" (circa 680 BCE)

Lord Ahmed isn't mentioned often, but he should be. Clan Mukhtaar may never have risen to prominence were it not for his indefatigable quest to find Sadira Mukhtaar. What became of her is a mystery I would give much to solve someday. If for no other reason than to help him rest more peacefully than he already does.

- Mujahid Mukhtaar, Private Commentaries, 35 CE

Mujahid entered the sanctuary at a full run, only stopping when he saw Nuuan, who was standing between the panoramic window and the Great Orb of Arin.

"Dar Rodon is under attack," Nuuan said. "I'm sorry, brother. I thought I was viewing the future, but it was the *present*!"

"I agree this is bad news, but I don't understand your urgency," Mujahid said.

"Nicolas and Kaitlyn are in Dar Rodon."

Mujahid's face went cold. "How bad is it?"

Nuuan shook his head.

"Do they live?" Mujahid yelled.

"They were alive when I merged my consciousness. But they won't stay that way for long."

"I'll open an Abaddonian portal," Mujahid said. "I used one to travel to Caspardis. I can grab both Kaitlyn and Nicolas before it's too late."

Mujahid hated that place, with its soot-filled clouds and...buildings constructed from the souls of the damned. But it was the only way.

Nuuan shook his head once more, but this time it was different.

"Won't work," Nuuan said.

"Why not? I can take two people to the sixth hell with ease."

"Yes, but only a Mukhtaar Lord or hellwraith can *leave* again."

The hells were unlike what most envisioned. They were places, true, and Mujahid had visited each. The sixth hell, however, was something else as well. It was a *substrate*, winding its way through all of reality. An underpinning that a Mukhtaar Lord could use to travel, if he knew the destination well enough.

But the sixth hell had its own master. A jealous master.

"You take Kaitlyn and Nicolas to the sixth hell without an *arrangement*, and you'll seal their eternity," Nuuan said.

"I can still travel to Dar Rodon and help them escape the city."

"No. I like your *first* idea better."

"You just told me it wouldn't work!"

"I told you we needed an *arrangement*. Go to Dar Rodon. I'll go to the sixth hell and have a chat with *His Unholy Arseholeness* myself. When you have them in hand, bring them there."

"He's going to *want* something, brother. Something he knows you consider too valuable to give."

"You let *me* worry about that," Nuuan said.

"You'll never get into the Iblisian palace."

"Lilith owes me a favor."

Mujahid scowled. That demon woman was dangerous beyond reckoning. The last time he'd dealt with her, she'd managed to release a plague in the city of Hiboran. Two thousand people died before Mujahid had convinced her father to put a stop to it. There was a reason she was confined to the sixth hell.

Nuuan spread his hands. "Well? *Time* is not on our side."

"Be careful," Mujahid said.

Mujahid reached out to the shadows in the sanctuary, calling them from the tiniest corners and crevasses. When they cloaked him, his body contorted as he took his spectral form—the form of a Lord of Hell.

A tear in the atmosphere opened before him.

"Be careful, brother," Mujahid repeated as he flung himself into the Abaddonian portal.

Nicolas ran.

Kaitlyn was less than two hundred yards away, and Mester Vincen was walking toward her.

As the cannon fire ceased, a chilling sound swept in from the bay.

Screeching mini-shrillers. The same kind the Barathosians had used in Caspardis.

If he could get Kaitlyn into one of those buildings, the shrillers would have a hard time reaching them.

Beneath the cloud of mini-shrillers, Barathosian warships began to reappear. Whatever magic Kaitlyn had been working was failing. The armada was coming back.

A patch of air, fifty yards ahead, shimmered like a heat mirage in the desert. A tear formed in the shimmer, creaking and groaning like two great sheets of metal being ripped in half. A wave of heat engulfed Nicolas, but the nauseating stench of decay, human waste, and burning flesh was far worse. Two writhing tongues of flame shot through the rip in the atmosphere as it widened into a swirling, black vortex, twice the height of a man.

A shrouded being emerged from the portal, its bony hands pushing against the rim of the vortex. It had flames for eyes, a cloak of shadow, and no lower body. A crown of flame ringed its head, dripping liquid fire down the sides and back of the cloak. And when it had freed itself from the portal, two giant, skeletal wings spread open to its sides. The wings arced high above the being's head, and swept down to the ground, well below its floating, shadowy torso.

Nicolas stepped back.

A hellwraith? Here?

He'd seen these creatures before, when he'd accidentally transported himself to the Plane of Death. He'd watched as the hellwraiths came and dragged souls away from the Field of Judgment, to a place even Nicolas's spirit guide had been afraid of.

The Seven Hells.

It shouldn't be possible for one to be *here*.

But there was something different about this hellwraith.

The crown of fire. The others had no crown on their heads. They had no wings, either.

As the tips of the creature's wings struck the boardwalk, they folded back upon themselves. The living shadow that had served as the creature's cloak began to slough off smaller shadows, which struck the boardwalk and fled to the dark places along the harbor. The flaming crown flared out, and the fiery eyes changed from reddish-yellow to brilliant white.

When the transformation was complete, Mujahid stood before him, no more than fifty yards away.

But something was wrong.

Mujahid looked like someone had died.

Or was *about* to.

Mujahid emerged from the portal and spread his skeletal wings.

Nicolas stood before him, disbelief in his eyes.

That's right. He's never seen me like this. I should return to my proper form. It will make this conversation easier.

Loud screeching came from the bay. Mujahid focused his spectral vision. Thousands of small shrillers dove for the harbor from a couple hundred yards out.

Mujahid turned toward the sound of a woman crying out in pain.

Kaitlyn.

She held her head as a Barathosian chimeramancer approached her.

Mujahid glanced at the shrillers.

They would swarm Nicolas and Kaitlyn in a matter of moments.

Kaitlyn stood more than a hundred yards away. But Nicolas stood only fifty.

My daughter!

All his instincts told him to fly toward Kaitlyn as quickly as possible and drag her to the relative safety of hell. But as he turned to do just that, Nuuan's words rang in his mind.

Unless another Mukhtaar Lord ascends, Malvol will become a god. He will consume the power of the other gods and give birth to chaos of a magnitude you cannot comprehend.

If he saved Kaitlyn, Nicolas would die, and with him any chance of defeating Malvol.

If he saved Nicolas, Kaitlyn would die. He'd be responsible for his own daughter's death. And Nicolas might never forgive him.

Mordryn might never forgive him.

Though he had no tears, nor eyes to cry them from, Mujahid wept. The silent, tearless, impotent weeping of a man weary of loss. A man who had known too much suffering in his life.

A man who had to make a choice he hoped the world would someday understand.

In order to communicate with Nicolas, Mujahid transformed as quickly as he could, scattering the shadow to the corners of the harbor.

"Nicolas!" he yelled. "Come! Through the portal with me!"

Nicolas darted toward Mujahid. "Get Kaitlyn! Behind you!"

The screeching shrillers drew closer.

Mujahid ran toward Nicolas.

"What are you doing?" Nicolas yelled. "Take *her*, not me!"

Mujahid extended his arms, and once again the shadows flew toward him, cloaking him in night. His skeletal wings extended, and the crown of flames ignited.

When the transformation was complete, Mujahid shot toward Nicolas.

"No!" Nicolas yelled.

When they collided, Mujahid grabbed Nicolas by the arm and flew toward the black vortex.

"Damn you!" Nicolas yelled.

Mujahid accelerated toward the portal, keeping his eyes off Kaitlyn. He couldn't look at her. He didn't dare.

The boardwalk passed beneath them. As they reached the portal, the shrillers swept over Kaitlyn and the chimeramancer.

Kaitlyn never stood a chance.

Dar Rodon never stood a chance.

Mujahid dragged Nicolas into the vortex, and viscous filth flowed around them, slimy and fetid.

When the portal closed behind him, and rotting limbs grasped at him from within the walls of the vortex, Mujahid closed his eyes and saw Kaitlyn's face.

I'm so sorry.

CHAPTER THIRTY FIVE

In the year 1 (BCE), Nuuan Mukhtaar stepped over the threshold, followed by his twin brother Mujahid, becoming Nuuan Lord Mukhtaar and Mujahid Lord Mukhtaar, respectively. The early part of their reign was fraught with conflict.

- The Mukhtaar Chronicles, Second Cycle, 35 CE
Incomplete Entry, written by Mujahid Lord Mukhtaar

Brother, I'm not certain what else to include for now. Excepting, of course, my work as Prime Warlock under Kagan and your overseeing the Catiatum coven. What would you have me write?
- M

Start with the truth. Fraught with conflict? Rubbish. If you want to reduce the Necromancer Wars and the unification of the clans to "was fraught with conflict", I'll not stop you. But is this a historical record or not? What of your prophecy? What of our acquisition of the Mukhtaar orb of power? What of my ale ranking system? On second thought, scratch the prophecy and the orb. Having a decent way to judge ale is a far greater contribution to Erindor than that other shite.
- Nuuan

Nicolas fell from the vortex and landed on a rust-colored, cobblestone path, surrounded by a fiery wasteland that stretched for miles in every direction.

The cobblestone howled when he stepped forward, so he jumped back.

Two more howls caused him to jump again, but the cries of pain never ceased. Every time he stepped or moved, something else would wail in torment.

He looked upward, hoping the portal was still open. He had to get back to the boardwalk! It wasn't too late for Kaitlyn if he could just get back!

Sooty clouds soared overhead, raining ash and filth around him. But none of it touched him. The rain would strike a point several feet above the pathway, then slide down the surface of an invisible dome.

A deafening roar turned Nicolas's spine to ice.

In the distance, thirteen massive, four-legged beasts, standing more than a hundred feet tall at the shoulder, guarded a white, stone wall twice their height. Flames blazed where eyes should be, and great leathery wings stretched out from their backs. Every step they took shook the ground, igniting more wails of agony. Two colossal chains extended from metal harnesses around each of the winged creatures' necks, rising to unseen points in the dark, smoke-filled sky.

The cobblestone path wound its way forward, past the winged creatures, and ended at a gargantuan gate of iron bars. Beyond the bars, a monumental cube, obsidian black, rose into the ashen sky.

"Better just stand still for now," a demonic voice said. It sounded like five people sharing the same mouth. "Everything in this place is made of...*someone.*"

Nicolas turned in time to see liquid shadow pouring off Nuuan's robes. When the shadows hit the ground, they stood on ghostly legs of their own and ran away, cackling in high-pitched voices and bounding over the fiery landscape.

"Where the hell's Mujahid?" Nicolas said. "He has to take me back."

"I'm here," Mujahid said, walking up from behind. "Is it done?"

"The bargain is struck," Nuuan said. "But we should be quick about it. *Hasat'Tan* isn't known for his benevolence. And...I'm sorry. For what it's worth."

Mujahid looked down and nodded.

"Did you hear me?" Nicolas said. "I said *take me back*!"

"The wards?" Mujahid asked.

"In place," Nuuan said. "Though, probably unnecessary, given you brought only one."

"May Arin grant we haven't made a terrible mistake."

"I just made a deal with the devil, brother. Of *course* it was a mistake. You may as well tell the cross-dressing postulant where he is. If your plan is going to work, you're going to have to tell him a *lot* of things."

"I don't give a *damn* about any plans! You brought me here. You take me back. Now!"

Mujahid glanced at Nicolas and lowered his gaze.

"Welcome to the sixth plane of hell," Mujahid said.

His voice nauseated Nicolas. The image of the mini-shrillers swarming Kaitlyn on the boardwalk returned. It was an image Nicolas would never forget.

"You left her," Nicolas said.

"You're the key to this," Mujahid said.

"How could you? She's defenseless! You could have taken her first while I fended them off!"

"The risk was too great."

"You heartless bastard!"

Nicolas drew his arm back and leapt at Mujahid, but a rope of necropotency caught him mid-air and set him back down on the ground.

"That'll be enough of that," Nuuan said.

"You think I wanted to leave her there?" Mujahid said. "There was *no choice*."

"There was *every* choice. But you left her behind. Why? What made her expendable? Was it because she's not a *priest* like me? Because she's not a member of the precious *clan*? She was everything! My past. My *future*!"

"She was my *daughter*."

Nicolas gaped. He looked to Nuuan, expecting the twin to say it wasn't true. But Nuuan nodded.

"We grew up together," Nicolas said. "I talked about her all the time. I *introduced* you to her, and you said *nothing*."

"I didn't know," Mujahid said. Tears welled in his eyes, and he looked away. Nuuan placed a hand on Mujahid's shoulder and squeezed. "I felt the connection the moment I first laid eyes upon her.

Later, when I was told the truth, it was as if all those years of absence meant nothing. If there was any way to save you both, I would have. But every path except one ended in your death. We can't afford to lose you now."

The winged creatures roared in the distance and stomped their massive feet, sending the stones under their claws into fits of wailing.

"Something ancient stirs in hell," Mujahid said.

"Stranger, and more evil, than any of us considered possible," Nuuan said.

"And it's already reached out into the world, casting its influence far and wide. Tithian tells me you've encountered this already, Nicolas. In the form of a statuette."

Mujahid and Nuuan recounted the story of the ancient Mukhtaar Lord rising from hell as *Malvol*, the god of hate. They told Nicolas about the strange *fog* around their symbols of power, and how Nuuan believed a *third* Mukhtaar Lord was the key to unlocking their full potential and defeating Malvol.

"That's why I had to save *you*," Mujahid said. "That's why I had to sacrifice my own flesh and blood and risk our friendship as well."

Nicolas ran a hand through his hair, squeezing his scalp along the way. He'd lost Kaitlyn twice in the last year, but at least the first time he'd had hope. The first time there had been a chance he'd find his way back to her.

This couldn't be real. How could there be a world without Kaitlyn in it?

Maybe it didn't have to be like that.

"Maybe I could—"

"Don't say it," Mujahid said. "Don't even *think* it."

"We raise penitents for *their* sake, boy, not our own," Nuuan said.

Nicolas's head felt heavy, and he squatted on the ground, resting his head in his hands. "How did you know what I was going to say?"

"You think there's a necromancer alive who hasn't thought about raising a loved one to ease their grief?" Nuuan asked.

"But she needs purification too, doesn't she?" Nicolas asked. "I'm sure it won't be long!"

Nuuan and Mujahid shared a look, and some silent communication passed between them.

Nuuan squatted next to him.

"There's nothing I can say that will make you feel better about this," Nuuan said. "So I'm not going to try. I know you loved her. But don't let your grief paralyze you. There's a Nicolas that doesn't drown when he's bound in chains and dumped in a lake. A Nicolas who brings down a tyrant when Mukhtaar Lords have failed to do so for decades. That's the Nicolas we need here now. As cruel as I know this sounds, your grief must wait. Hell isn't a place one should tarry."

As if punctuating his sentence, the massive winged creatures roared once more.

"Hell," Nicolas said. Didn't they understand? Hell might be a *place* to them. But it was a gaping wound in his soul that would follow him wherever he went now.

Everything—Nuuan, Mujahid, the path, the winged creatures—took on a surreal quality. It wasn't that they'd become less real; the path was solid under his boots, and the oppressive heat had him sweating like a summer day in Zilker Park. It just didn't matter.

He was detached from it.

Separate from.

Nicolas stood. "Yeah, I've seen a statuette like the one you mentioned."

"It's made from a substance called *hellstone*," Mujahid said. "From this very plane."

"And you think Hasat'Tan is involved?"

"No," Nuuan said. "But whoever is responsible knows there way around down here. And they're getting more powerful every day. We need you to ascend to give the rest of us a fighting chance."

"And how the hell am I supposed to do that?" The only thing Nicolas knew about ascending was you either succeeded or died trying. No one failed and lived.

"That's not something we can simply *tell* you," Mujahid said. "I can take you to the threshold of the Rite of Ascension, but it's for *you* to discover *how* to ascend."

A figure emerged from the sulfurous mists, in the direction of the winged creatures. A tall, thin woman, dressed all in white, from the look of it. But she was too far away to see any details, other than her long, straight white hair.

Nicolas shifted his weight, and one of the stones beneath his foot howled.

"And will somebody tell me what in the name of Zubuxo's shadowy anus I'm stepping on?" Nicolas said.

Nuuan grinned. "Maybe he *does* have it in him."

"Compressed soul," Mujahid said. "Hasat'Tan has a singularly cruel sense of retribution."

The woman drew closer much more quickly than Nicolas was expecting. She wasn't wearing white at all. It was her skin, brilliant white, like the white-washed walls of the imperial palace in Dar Rodon. But her eyes were solid black...all *three* of them. Her legs, purely human above the knee, became less and less human the lower they went, ultimately ending in hooves.

"Your *welcome* is wearing thin," the woman said. Her voice was hypnotic. "My father told you to leave. Why do you linger?"

"Lilith," Nuuan said. "I'd say it was a pleasure...if it were a pleasure."

Lilith continued, one slow, silent step at a time, placing one hoof directly in front of the other as if she were walking a catwalk. For whatever reason, the *compressed soul* cobblestones didn't react to her.

"Your father will have what he requires," Mujahid said.

Lilith glanced at Nicolas and smiled.

It wasn't the smile of a person who was content, or happy to make an acquaintance. It was the smile of a person who'd been savagely hurt and saw their vengeance within reach. Her solid black eyes made it impossible to judge her real intent. It was one of the most chilling things Nicolas had ever seen.

"Who is *this*?" Lilith asked. She changed direction slightly until she was walking straight at Nicolas.

As she stepped forward, Lilith struck an invisible barrier and hissed as her skin sizzled.

"What is this?" she said.

Green light, dim, but growing in intensity, spread out along the ground from where she'd collided with the barrier, until it formed a circle around Mujahid and Nuuan, twenty feet in diameter.

"How *dare* you erect a ward in my father's domain?"

"The deal is done," Nuuan said. "Once every Erindorian decade, a Mukhtaar Lord will escort your father into the seventh plane. There he will be permitted to remain a single Erindorian day."

"Then take your charge and leave before I have his soul extracted and compressed."

An oval, the height of a man, opened within the green circle. Nicolas had felt no power released.

Mujahid placed a hand on Nicolas's shoulder and guided him toward the newly formed portal.

"I'll attend to the bargain," Nuuan said. "If I'm right, we should know the moment Nicolas succeeds."

Nuuan stepped out of the circle and followed Lilith back toward the winged creatures.

"I don't know if I can do this," Nicolas said.

Mujahid faced Nicolas, both hands planted on Nicolas's shoulders.

"We can't stop fighting now," Mujahid said. "Please, make Kaitlyn's death mean something."

Nicolas had no intention of stopping now. He stepped through the portal, and hell vanished behind him.

The room they stepped into was cavernous. Polished black marble walls towered above a dais that supported a gem-encrusted shrine at its center. The dais—also carved from black marble—was at least eighty feet square, surrounded on three sides by stone walls, upon which hung portraits of men Nicolas couldn't identify. Four twisting, obsidian columns—they reminded Nicolas of Bernini's Baldachin, which surrounded the main altar at Saint Peter's Basilica—each held a torch of flameless golden light at the platform's corners. Multicolored wisps rose from the central shrine through an opening in the second floor, which was ringed by golden bars that caught the flameless light and cast a warm glow across the black marble. Two winding black staircases, one on each side of the dais, rose to the second level and met at a podium, upon which rested an open book, three feet long by four feet wide.

But the strangest thing of all was an unsupported marble staircase that floated in mid air, ascending back from the podium, toward an elongated oval frame. The ornate golden frame was twice the height of a person, and rippling water formed a mirror-like surface from one side of the frame to the other.

Nicolas didn't recognize the room, but he recognized the ambient scent of the place. He was certain they were somewhere in the Mukhtaar Estate.

"Do not deviate from the path I take," Mujahid said. "This is the Room of Ascension. There is magic here even *I* do not understand."

Mujahid led Nicolas onto the platform and stopped in front of the shrine. He glanced at Nicolas and gestured to remain silent.

"In the days of the prophet Habakku," Mujahid said, "the god Zubuxo anointed the Mukhtaars to ascend above all other priests. Today we seek the anointing of the goddess Shealynd."

"Why Shealynd?" Nicolas whispered.

"Never mind *why*—"

"Because your love for my daughter leads Mujahid to conclude I'd be open to the idea," a woman said.

The cavernous room filled with the scent of fresh-cut roses.

The goddess Shealynd emerged from behind one of the pillars. Her brown hair curled down to her shoulders, and her piercing blue eyes glowed with an inner light, matching the hue of her dress.

"And he's absolutely right," she said.

Nicolas was gobsmacked. First, Mujahid reveals he's Kaitlyn's father, and now *the goddess Shealynd* claims to be her *mother*?

As Shealynd approached, she transformed. Her sky blue dress turned crimson red, and her brown curls brightened until they matched. Gone was the inner glow to her eyes, but they remained piercing blue.

"Shealynd," Nicolas said.

"Call me *Mordryn* in this form."

Mordryn held out her palm, and a small box materialized in a flash of blue light. She opened the box and retrieved a narrow vial of viscous liquid that looked like olive oil.

The box vanished.

"Come," she said, as she walked toward one of the great marble stairs.

"Tell me what you see, Mordryn," Mujahid said. He and Nicolas followed her up the stairs.

"You asked me the same thing the day *you* stepped over the threshold."

"And your words brought me comfort. I seek the same comfort now."

When Mordryn reached the top of the platform, she turned.

"People call us *gods*," Mordryn said. "Perhaps we are, relative to humankind. But we're not omniscient. I said the words you needed to hear that day. Words that gave you the best chance of success. And I will do the same for Nicolas today."

Mordryn placed her arm in Nicolas's and guided him toward the floating stairs that ascended to the golden oval frame. She stopped at the foot of the stairs next to a short marble post, removed the stopper from the vial, then placed the stopper on the post.

"Though my anointing will allow you to survive the journey to the Plane of Magic, it will not guarantee your success. You will face many tests. Each one will require something different. Something only *you* possess."

Nicolas closed his eyes.

Despair threatened to paralyze him as thoughts of Kaitlyn returned, but he couldn't let it in. If he gave into it for even a minute, he'd be finished.

He took a deep breath and opened his eyes.

"But I don't even know what to expect," Nicolas said. "Not even a little. No one has told me *anything* about this. I knew more about the Halls of Power before the Awakening than I know about Ascension."

"The best thing you can do to guarantee your success," Mordryn said, "is to be *yourself*. Be true to who *you* are. Let nothing tempt you to be any different. It's said that to ascend, one must embody the ideals of Mukhtaarian philosophy. You wouldn't be standing here if you didn't. All you have to do is be yourself."

"How long will it take?" Nicolas asked.

"For us, perhaps days," Mordryn said. "For you? Days. Years. Decades…there's no way for me to know for certain. Like the namocea, though you may be gone for an age, you'll remember who you are when you return."

"*If* I return."

"Don't say that," Mujahid said. "You *will* succeed. You *must*."

Mordryn turned the bottle over onto her fingers, set the vial on a post, and massaged the liquid into her hands. She pressed her thumb against Nicolas's forehead and drew a symbol, though he couldn't see what it was.

A low, pulsating hum emanated from the top of the stairs. The rippling liquid in the oval frame vanished, leaving only a patch of *nothingness*. Above the frame, a golden plaque appeared. And on the plaque, the Mukhtaar symbol—a figure in a meditative pose, arms outstretched, with light radiating from its eyes—flared into existence.

"It's time," Mujahid said.

"Remember," Mordryn said. "Be true to who you are."

Nicolas climbed the marble steps. He let the tears well in his eyes as he embraced his pain. Gods knew, he'd had so much of it this past year. With every step he climbed, he absorbed more of it. Welcomed it. Basked in the torment. He couldn't be true to who he was and push the pain away. He couldn't be himself and deny how much he'd lost in such a short time.

Pain was part of what defined him now. Not the pain of the flogging posts that once made him pray for death. It was the pain of the soul...the kind that made him pray for oblivion. His suffering would make him strong.

The tears flowed freely as he climbed the final step and stared into the *nothingness*.

Kaitlyn's face stared back at him, smiling. It was the way he'd always remember her. There'd never come a day he wouldn't carry her with him. She was his *cet*. His inner peace. She was his strength.

And into the Rite of Ascension he'd carry her.

In the year 141 (CE), Nicolas Murray stepped over the threshold.

ABOUT THE AUTHOR

Nat Russo was born in New York, raised in Arizona, and has lived just about everywhere in-between. He's gone from pizza maker, to radio DJ, to Catholic seminarian (in a Benedictine monastery, of all places), to police officer, to software engineer. His career has taken him from central Texas to central Germany, where he worked as a defense contractor for Northrop Grumman. He's spent most of his adult life developing software, playing video games, running a Cub Scout den, gaining/losing/gaining/losing weight, and listening to every kind of music under the sun.

Along the way he managed to earn a degree in Philosophy and a black belt in Tang Soo Do.

He currently makes his home in central Texas with his wife, teenage son, mischievous beagle, and newly rescued Shepherd mix.

Official Website: http://www.erindorpress.com
Wikipedia: https://en.wikipedia.org/wiki/Nat_Russo
Facebook: http://www.facebook.com/NatRussoAuthor
Twitter: @NatRusso
Newsletter: http://madmimi.com/signups/95405/join

A HUMBLE REQUEST

Life seems to get busier every year, and the thought that you've invested some time in my scribblings is a humbling one. Thank you, sincerely, for spending your invaluable time in the world of Erindor.

If you enjoyed your journey with the Mukhtaar Lords, the cichlos, even the Barathosians...I'd like to ask you to take one more moment to leave a review on Amazon, or any other venue of your choice. And please tell your friends! I will owe you a most sincere debt of gratitude.

Many thanks,
Nat
Pflugerville, Texas
May 2016.

ALSO BY NAT RUSSO

Necromancer Awakening: Book One of The Mukhtaar Chronicles
The #1 Fantasy Bestseller that started it all!

The Road To Dar Rodon